The Seed of Yggdrasil

Book One

TILL MYTH DO US PART

DARIUS EBRAHIMI

MYTHICAL BANDIT BOOKS

ISBN: 979-8-9864801-2-1 paperback
ISBN: 979-8-9864801-0-7 ebook

First paperback edition 2022

Edited by Sandra Young
Cover Art by SeventhStar Art

The text of this book is set in Garamond.

Published under
Mythical Bandit Books
San Francisco, California

Visit dariusebrahimi.com

For Riley,
who showed me the power of imagination

Special thanks to my mom,
Who always believed in me,
Love you to infinity and beyond

ONE

DIVIDED

K AI DREAMT OF MORE than heaven. He was already there. Elysium's glorious spires glinted in drought-light, rusting orange as morning dust roused, and the only darkness in the day was the wrought iron fence below that divided Kai from the one he loved.

From atop an under-construction temple spire, Kai felt he could've flown over the small barrier. Yet, rickety bamboo scaffolding and his task kept him grounded.

Maybe the cat had disintegrated the spire's golden dragon head decoration and left for a nap. The one time Kai wanted a myth to be real, it was nowhere to be seen. Leaning on a smooth bamboo railing, the slight sway sent shivers down his spine as he tried to steady himself, and looking out was more comforting than looking down.

With Elysium behind, Kai peered over the fence to the city of Asphodel. A tumult of people and buildings and businesses. Wheels rolled over sidewalks and into streets and back again. A river of rooftops tumbled up and down in cascading size. Disparity. Chaos. Struggle. That was life there. Copper-green spires were hollow shells of the past, and no new ones sprouted. The city was too cramped to waste space.

Yet, Asphodel retreated from an unused quarter of the city. There, the streets were wide and vacant. There, pale shingles fell into undisturbed dust. There, it was better to let things lie.

Kai didn't dare think of the myths lurking there.

However, one did think of him.

A creature of snow and ice padded behind him—a stalking snow leopard. Unperturbed by heat, it walked cool. Fur ruffled, bending under a gust like stalks of white-blue wheat. Eyes glared, oceans of terror, not because of violence within, but by the depth. Still staring at Kai, the leopard arched its back into a stretch, and drifting on the breeze behind, fanned scarlet phoenix feathers shivered on the tail-tip, each bristle brandished like sunbeams. The leopard's whiskers bent forward, inspecting the intruder on its roost.

Kai glanced over his shoulder. "You're what I expected."

He wiped heat-soaked hair off his forehead along with the thought of the black fence below. Despite nonchalance, Kai listened for movement. Even such a silent hunter must make noise.

The leopard unfurled dry lips with a subdued rasping, displaying fangs. It took a breath. Quiet. Calm. Then, the air built and escaped in what should've been a growl, but it was not a growl that Kai heard.

"I'd expect more respect, then," the leopard said.

"My expectations were high." Kai smiled. "Are you surprised to find someone that understands you?"

"Should I be?" The cat yawned; no matter the size, cats seemed to expect all meows, mews, and tail flicks to be understood.

"Most myths are used to swords instead of words."

The cat hissed. "If you call me a myth again, I'll devour you."

"Go ahead, myth." Kai faced the cat and opened his arms as if expecting an embrace. "I'm bitter and stringy as they come, and you'd be saving me from a lot of trouble."

Dark lips tilted, glistening with a tinge of saliva. "With this heat, you're already cooked."

"And what would you know about heat?" Kai crossed unheroic arms. If he was to survive this encounter, strength would do him no good—he would need calm in the face of fear.

"I've seen more droughts than you've seen sunrises," the leopard said.

"Were you created with a backstory, or are you making it up as you go?"

The creature growled. Even Kai heard it; it had no translation. "I am not one of those new creations."

Kai frowned. If he was wrong, the goading would end up with a goring. "Look, I made a deal to rid Elysium of new myths. In this case, one born by those who want snow instead of drought. I've seen snow and wasn't impressed, but if I had to choose between this drought and a blizzard, I'd choose the cold until I was freezing in it. But you say you're not a new myth, so I guess I have no business with you."

"I still have business with you." The leopard tensed the hairs above its icy blue eyes like a raised brow.

The nerves made him laugh. "And what could that possibly be? In need of a translator?"

"Exactly. You know what I am, and I know what you are."

"What's that?" Kai asked.

"My maker."

Triumphant, Kai began to think of how a small success might reverse a smothering tide of failures. "See, you are what I expected—a new myth—one I made. But what could I possibly translate from something I created?"

"You didn't create me. You only remade me. And as you brought me back, I'm here to bring the world back—to fix what's broken. It's time people had something to believe in."

Although Kai did not look behind to the divide between cities, he fell upon a recent feeling, a constant feeling, which inhabited the uncleaned corners of his mind, infecting all other thoughts. "Like love?"

"A different love than you intended."

With that, the leopard grinned. *Pop.* The big cat burst into a flash of golden ash. Dust floated on a slow wind, landing in a neat pile on the sun-bleached wood planks. A sunset-red feather floated down on the pile, stuck upright, waiting to be plucked.

Kai obliged, taking the feather as proof that he had dealt with the myth.

"What a waste of words. But I suppose *you* are not a waste." He twirled the feather between forefinger and thumb, a tightening grip keeping it from slipping to the city below.

Kai headed around the spire to the ladder down. Yet, he waited on the platform, not wanting to descend towards paperwork, family, and his so-called wife, all of which were less routine than dealing with miscreant myths.

Here at the highest point of what others called heaven, Kai could've felt like a god. Elysium's rooftops, shingles, and streets splotched themselves under him on the city's canvas, a tapestry of civility. Spires dominated. Some ornate. Some tall. Some still under construction like this one. Each tower called attention to itself, trying to outdo and outshine the last with precious metals, artwork, and height. But each taller and taller tower seemed smaller and smaller.

His personal life loomed larger.

Somewhere among the white-walled houses and black shadows, his family was out enjoying the day and trying to fit in. Possibly, they were home, and he looked out further towards the well-adorned homes on the hill, but he felt no draw for the smooth stucco and Mediterranean-orange rooftops.

However, as he lingered a little longer, no matter where he looked and what he thought, he kept returning to the iron fence below. In the cause of his misery, he might also find a brief window of happiness.

Kai sped down a ladder and the scaffolding built aside the temple, descending like an archeologist inspecting the architectural record of Elysium's patchwork past. Each level built on the last, reaching for the sky as if to see whether the gods were still there.

There were three main levels. The upper tower was decorative, desperate, and propped up by cracked bamboo scaffolding that looked more likely to fall than the construction it held. Steady grey brick composed the middle layer, the times of which Kai could only imagine but would never dream of. Finally, at the base of the temple were Corinthian columns painted clay-red, which besides color, also matched the construction grounds around in the amount of cracks, dirt by drought and foundation by burden.

Fighting anticipation, Kai stopped between the middle and lower floors. The foreman still might be waiting for him, and that would destroy his opportunity.

Kai waited, and as with every time he saw this temple, the artwork that separated these two sections depicting Hercules's twelve labors captivated him. The band of heroism ranged from lions and boars, triumphs and trickery, legend and godhood, but it lacked the misdeed that mirrored Kai's like the glint of the gold figures—why Hercules chose to undertake the tasks.

Guilt.

Without motive, myth was emotionless recounting. Without reason, without failure, without flaw, Hercules was only what he ended up as—a god, a perfect, shining figure to be worshiped, not the fallible hero worth striving for. And Kai, more than anything, felt less like the gold and more like the cracked bamboo holding him.

Unable to wait any longer, he brushed the gold art with a finger as he passed, smudging the fine film of dust. No one saw him do it, but he'd rather be caught touching the gold than the iron fence across the yard.

Down the final ramp and timing it to perfection, Kai stepped onto dry dirt as the foreman left the construction yard for lunch.

With no one in sight, the wrought iron awaited. Crossing the dusty, dead yard, he grasped black bars and the metal's sear in sunlight was nothing to the pain of separation. Like most fences, it was only a barrier to overcome; yet, it was the consequences of crossing that made even the most determined hesitate.

His youthful face wrinkled, his eyes shining like broken brown diamonds, cracks in crystalline irises cooling and carved by another heartbreak, but despite pain, a stubborn glisten betrayed the hope that survived.

A rustle on the other side of the dead ivy blocking his view. "Sophia?"

Her voice snuck through. "Is it safe?"

"The foreman got tired of waiting," Kai said. "Must've thought the leopard ate me and he didn't want to be the only one still hungry."

"Did the foreman take a good look at you? A leopard would still be hungry."

"That explains why he didn't go up and check." Kai wished the buoyancy of his mood could lift him over the barrier. Failing this, the ballooning cheer met the pinprick of reality, and like that, he wanted more than a sample of true happiness. "I can't see you."

"Imagination is better than reality."

She might've been right. In his head, Sophia was perfect and vague, except for a memory of a single-dimpled smile and mocking eyes, blue as robin eggs. The image radiated the glorious glow of distance. Although he knew breaking beyond the bushes would destroy the perfect picture dancing in his head, his memory of Sophia shifted like sand dunes, and he sought only to renew, rather than maintain, a perfectly false memory.

Yearning for a glimpse, he cracked the sun-bleached ivy, dust raining down like dew, but he only broke through thickets to brown bushes behind. "How is it only the wildest dreams become real, while the simplest remain out of reach?"

"I'm not your wildest dream?" A smile hummed through her words, but sarcasm settled serious. "Are you sure this is a good idea?"

Kai's knuckles whitened around black bars. "If they catch me here, they might sentence me to a better fate than Elysium."

"And what would Elysium do without their hero?"

He let go of the fence, happiness gone with the grip. "I'm no hero. I'm just a janitor putting a bucket under a leak rather than plugging the hole."

"Is it so hard to be satisfied with what you do and what you have?"

"It is until you're here."

A pause lingered, painful. "I know."

The gap between them seemed greater as the words dissipated in the distance between them.

"I've got to get back," Sophia said. "Say hi to your wife."

"Ex-wife." Kai suppressed the annoyance that came with a reality he didn't agree with.

"I'm your ex-wife."

"You're my wife."

"According to the gods, I'm neither." Truth ended the argument. "Going to the temple later?"

Kai nodded, even if she couldn't see him. "My mom insists. I might be an adult and the gods might be gone, but she always had more power over us than any god. Can I see you at the garden?"

"I don't like that spot. Anyone could see us talking. Besides, the council said it would only be a few weeks."

"Until they make it a few more weeks."

Silence, then Sophia said, "Alright, I'll see you then. But I better go before my lunch is over and my stew goes to waste."

Kai's hands clenched as if it would hold onto the moment, too. "Eating stew in this heat?"

"It's cold stew now."

"I'd say that's an improvement."

"Just like this was an improvement on my day," Sophia said. "See you soon."

Her footsteps drifted away on loose dirt, and Kai was left lonely again, but this time, with a hopeful smile that would last him through the unpleasantness that awaited him in heaven.

TWO

BEYOND THE VEIL

ANGEL DUST FILTERED PAST sunrays beaming through a temple's stained-glass window. The glass depicted a leafless tree, roots and branches the same size and extending to a perfectly encompassing circle, tinged red like the sunset outside. While drought made sun fierce and feared, within these walls, heat was taken and imaginative light remained. Reverence, the result. People flocked to pews chosen by light, squinting and smiling, as if their seat was holier. Chosen by chance. By time of day. By being on time.

Kai headed down the aisle to an empty pew with most of his family—mother, father, and his two siblings, Cara and Li. To Kai's annoyance, the ceremony was running later than he was.

"Did you get dressed in the dark?" Cara asked her twin brother sarcastically.

Li wore a starched white collared shirt and brushed the seat before he sat. "There was plenty light."

It was impossible to tell whether Li understood the joke. He was cruel to the air about him. A pristine coldness. Black hair trimmed short at his temples. Darkness slumbered in him, coming closer to the surface of two ice-white eyes when focusing on any one thing. Except, that is, when Li turned his gaze to his twin and his eyes thawed the slightest bit. Yet, that seemed to risk whatever lay beneath escaping.

Cara smiled and shook her head at her twin's lack of humor. In the light of stained-glass windows, her dark hair was sleek black magic, resting over a white dress and sharp collarbones. Her summer-bright eyes turned to Kai.

Kai knew that playful look and he struck first. "You're twins; if you insult him about how he looks, you're insulting yourself, too."

"Nothing wrong with that," Cara said.

"We don't look anything alike," Li said, stern and upright in the pew.

"I suppose—I smile," Cara said, demonstrating before she sat next to her twin. "And I wouldn't cast stones, Kai, you're so weak you'd probably only toss them on your own foot."

"I could at least drop it an arm's length away." Kai returned the smile. While Kai felt ill-at-ease with most of his family, it was his younger sister he found friendship with. To him, family was blood—sticky and something he didn't want too much or too little of—while friendship was more like honey, which while sticky, was also sweet.

As Kai's mother and father shuffled between them, Cara brightened with a new retort, but she was interrupted before she could reply.

An oppressive hush. People around scowled at the late-comers who disturbed the tranquility of their holy place.

Kai's joy became penitent.

As if with recognition, eyes softened, realizing who Kai was. Judgment dropped into reverence. Then, people whispered.

Kai did not blush at attention. He did his best not to frown, either. Instead, he offered a few nods to those who greeted him and kept a remnant smile from the back-and-forth with his sister. When people lost interest and went back to waiting, Kai's smile vanished and he sunk into a seat.

A tall woman with a statuesque expression strode down the aisle and sat next to Kai. "You're late."

"I didn't see you on the way in, Helene." Kai scooted away.

Her cold hands grabbed his, and Helene whispered, "I don't want to be here either, but we have to pretend. At one point, there was love between us. If I can fake it, why can't you?"

"Because you find it so easy to fake."

"Lying was never your strong suit. Don't think of it as lying, think of it as smudging the truth. We were married once." A guarded glance. "How's Sophia?"

"She's fine."

"Good. I like her."

"Why is it that when you tell the truth it still sounds like a lie?"

Kai's mother fidgeted on his other side. She stopped her prayer and glared at him with disciplining eyes for their whispers, before returning to a downward stance, mourning-veil hair covering noiseless words at her lips. Wary of his wife, Kai's taciturn father sat on her other side with martial discipline.

As with many in Elysium, Kai's parents were converts, adopting new names and gods with the fervor and wonder of those who find new horizons instead of being born in them.

A priest arrived, standing stern behind a lectern. Kai wasn't sure which gods this priest wanted them to worship today. There were many temples, more priests, and too many gods. Even when people worshiped the same gods, they believed differently.

The ceremony began. The temple filled with silent rituals and prayers, hopes and fears, all so the gods might take pity on those who flocked these hallowed halls. Golden candles danced, a foot-worn carpet ran down the aisle, and the icons of Greek gods were smiling. The priest expressed the crowd's silent feelings and the audience followed ascendant words. Necks craned in hope of finding the godly above and were awestruck by enormity. As Kai looked up at whale-rib archways and towering columns, he wanted to hear from the gods; yet, he knew all he heard here were echoes.

The chorus began, growing and building in the warbling throats of worshipers, a similar sound came from Kai's taut throat, which fought against the hollowness inside, wanting to scream instead of hum.

Others, too, must've felt the void. In such a situation, it was impossible not to ask for hope. But from who? Kai knew as well as anyone—the gods had gone silent. There were only mortals and myths. The gods surely withdrew for a reason. And their reason must be good. The gods were good. Even now, stories were told of sun gods bringing sunshine to nurture crops, animals, and humanity, while no one here damned the drought that was destroying the world.

As the echoes of worship faded into dusty corners and the cracks of old stone, people began the oldest ritual—gossip.

"I heard they found it in the sewers," someone whispered.

"Imagine if you heard a myth through your toilet."

"You might think it was the gods speaking to you," Kai whispered under his breath.

His mother slapped his shoulder, silencing him. Cara's laugh drifted across.

"Settle down," Kai's father said.

As the priest went to the backroom, the crowd became uneasy, fidgeting in seats with subtle squeaks. A common sacrifice was about to be made in the name of the gods—a goat.

Except this sacrifice was only part goat.

The priest led in a baby chimera: three heads, a lion head leading, a goat head erupting from its back, and a snake replacing a tail. The yellow-brown lion fur was patchy and knotted, the goat's tiny horns were stumps, and the snake dragged, hissing softly with discomfort. A rope leash was buried in the budding mane of the lion, but it was slack. Hooves and paws dragged themselves along as it followed the priest to its doom. Whether it had been sedated or beaten to such a point, the creature seemed already dead.

Surely, others must've been sickened by the state of the piteous creature, but if they were, they didn't show it; instead, they cheered when the creature was led towards a prepared white altar.

Kai's exclamation of disgust and horror melded with the sound. Long had his movements and sounds been synchronized with the crowd, and long had they meant something different. Others could not understand myths and did not have to hear how the chimera suffered. Kai's own voice tried to drown it out—he could not bear to hear last words.

A fight bubbled and built within, struggling against a coming end. Every instinct called for Kai to leap forth and stop the ceremony. Yet, the creature found the fight first.

Feigning weakness, the beast awoke. Sinewy animal legs leapt, yanking the rope out of the priest's hands. The young chimera ducked and dodged the attempts of the priest to restrain it.

And Kai was glad.

As the mythical creature leapt from the stage, Kai was the only one in his seat, calm among calamity.

Limping and lunging down the aisle, the chimera's lion head spat little flashes of fire. With each spurt of flame, it spoke like it had too much saliva. "Where? How? Pardon." A few brave souls tried to block it, and in desperation, the snake-tail perked up. "No! I'm not going back."

Venomous teeth missed a man that ducked behind a pew. A knife slashed, and there was blood on white fur. The priest faced the creature, crimson knife in hand. Although the man looked a frail figure, devotion could be dangerous.

The chimera was frail too, but fire and venom spat in pain. A wad of fiery acid flew over Kai's family and hit the stained-glass, burning into hot sunrays from outside.

If it was just the priest in danger, Kai might've let it play out.

But he had to do something. Clambering over the pews, Kai opposed the torrent of fleeing panic. He waited a moment for the creature's rage to follow the priest, and practiced and patient, Kai leapt onto the creature. Despite mythical magic, the creature was bones and not much more.

"Stop!" Kai yelled, twisting on the ground like a crocodile. "Get off!"

"I will," Kai said, stopping his roll and whispering to the goat head, "I'm Kai. I want to help. Fake strike, I roll, then run straight out. A garden, over the fence. Then, find a forest and lay low. You'll be safe."

The struggle lessened. Then, the creature bucked to try and break his grip. Kai was unsure whether the creature didn't believe him or was a good actor.

It didn't matter.

The snake-tail hissed and Kai rolled to avoid the strike. But another man grabbed the tail before it would've hit him.

Kai looked up—it was his brother, Li. With the snake in his hands, Li grinned. There was a snap that synchronized with a horrible yelp.

The scene calmed, and a third dead already, the creature knew there was no escape and retreated into silence.

Maybe, if it wasn't it for his brother, the creature could've made it away. Broken, though, others were infected by bravery and restrained the beast. In the aftermath, the priest tightened the rope around the creature's neck and a few burly men stood around the creature. Kai was helped to his feet.

Again, the ceremony repeated, and people settled down, having gone from calm to action and back again. Although Kai was back sitting in the same seat, the inaction had a different feeling than before. Kai couldn't blame his brother's attempt to save him; yet, the smile at violence did.

His blame fell upon the present, though. Kai hated how his haunted past had been rewarded, while noble actions—like trying to save this myth—would be punished. He had tried his best.

No. He supposed he hadn't.

There was more he could do. He could still try and free the creature. It would not come without sacrificing more—more than he was willing to give. He was mortified and confused, ashamed that he thought this myth was not worth dying for.

Action would only get him and his family killed alongside the chimera. He felt powerless, except to close his eyes and shut out the violence. In the drowning noise of cheers, there was solemn peace.

A short knife, drawn. A brief whisper, a brief blade. And the creature stilled, no fight left. But as if on delay, the goat bleated. No words. Just pain.

Kai opened his eyes. The white altar turned the color of clouds at sunset. A rain of blood dripped and the priest dipped his fingers in the warm liquid. Robes had been spoiled as a life had.

There was relief and applause. They thought the myth would not grow into a monster, but to Kai, it had made more monsters.

With a pinch of forefinger and thumb, priestly fingers still wet with blood extinguished the flames of the candles around the altar.

Silver-blue smoke coiled upwards, blowing outwards into the rafters and past windows, where light filtered through colored glass. There, it seemed as though the soul of the dead myth mixed with the light of the heavens and the smoke of the underworld, drifting across the twilight temple.

A myth had been snuffed out, but with the thoughts and dreams it created, the death of one might create many more like pine trees sprouting from ash after a forest fire.

Before smoke reached the ceiling, burgundy curtains were drawn around the foreground like a theater performance, leaving people to linger in the smell of smoke and the ruminations of their own thoughts.

People exited the temple, heading into the falling darkness of a starless night. Black lanterns swayed on poles. Dried leaves went by the whims of wind and followed the spotlights, helpless. Through an arched gate was a small park. Flowers and foliage lay bare. No one except Kai thought of the desolate park, not wanting to think of what was lost, and everyone headed home, heads filled with wonder and security.

Kai was not filled with such feelings. He tried to bury the atrocity under the cooling air, and yet, he couldn't forget the myth being slaughtered like an unfeeling beast. Good or bad, monster or not, the creature did not deserve that. No matter how many people and myths Kai saved, he would not forget his failures; he wanted to, but he felt better for being unable to. Loss created feeling. Pity. Sadness. Anger. Kai felt all of these, walloping in lumps of tremendous emotion, struggling against the shackles of a contained face, unable to hold it much longer.

But in a moment, he could channel the strength of feeling into a different release—a creation. One emotion to another. Strong feeling to strong feeling. Weak to weak. Channeled, moving, and directed as a river. This energy would become love.

He waved his family off, saying he wanted to ponder for a while.

Under the halo of a lantern, Kai and Helene stood together. Her cedar hair was braided and the uncontained strands that rested over her front rustled in the breeze. Her amber eyes glittered under lantern flame, reflecting it brighter to Kai than it was otherwise. As his so-called wife, they looked right together, both good-natured and friendly to those who passed, with a smile that was entirely believable and also, entirely fake.

Finally left alone, Helene let go of his hand. "I heard you dealt with a different myth today."

"A leopard with tail feathers. But I didn't deal with it, it dealt with itself. *Pop.*" Hands demonstrated. "If only everything was that easy. It's only getting worse. Last week, something stole all that bread. And of course, the fires. The drought is hard enough by itself."

A thin grin. "We had that sprinkle earlier."

"It's not enough. I wish there was something I could do."

"Can you make it rain?"

Kai frowned.

Helene laid a hand on his shoulder, it was a tender motion, but vaguely stiff. "They may call you a hero, but I think you're something different."

"What's that?

"Noble."

"Thanks, I guess. I'm trying to be."

"That's not a compliment." Her fingers ran over his shoulder and away. "You're trying to be something that doesn't exist. Ideals don't exist. Perfection doesn't, either."

"You taught me that." A bitter, reminiscent night-wind raised goosebumps on his neck.

"See? Your intentions don't matter."

"That's all that matters." Kai looked to the grey park, calming the irritation that attempted to seduce him.

"Then you are a hero?" She had a cold smile, entangling him. "That's what you intend to be."

"You're wrong."

"And you're a terrible liar. You believe in wrong and right. Good and evil. You may lie to yourself, but you believe actions matter as much as intentions."

An echo of guilt broke free. "It's only…I wish they didn't."

"Why?" Helene asked. "So people with good intentions can all laugh and dance in Elysium?"

"Because I've done things there's no coming back from."

"And yet you try so hard to." She brightened. "Maybe you are getting better at lying to people besides yourself."

"I hope not."

"We can't agree on anything."

"Very little," Kai said. "We agreed we weren't right for each other."

"That we did. And then I ended up downstream." She said it jokingly, but it brought a cruel chill down Kai's spine.

"I'm sorry."

"You shouldn't apologize. It's only attractive when something was your fault, otherwise, it makes you look weak. Very unheroic." Helene nudged him playfully. "Besides, now I'm the one holding you back because of it."

Kai squirmed.

"Say hi to Sophia and be careful." Helene wandered off, not one for lengthy goodbyes and leaving Kai alone.

Kai couldn't help but feel something for Helene. He wasn't sure if it was hatred or love, anger or admiration, but he buried it. He was wary of her intentions. Dropping the skepticism to the back of his mind, he grinned. The highlight of his life awaited.

Sophia.

THREE

SO CLOSE YET SO FAR

UNDER THE TANGLED DEAD ivy that twisted and twined in a black archway, Kai passed into a sparse park, a dirt path seemingly spread as the drought dried the garden. Rose bushes rained wilted petals and kept thorns. Trees lacked leaves and bark cracked. At the end, there was a rusted bench and another fence. This time, no ivy—one of the few places to see between the gaps.

As night deepened, heat flash-froze, metal chilling Kai's fingers. Wind blew. Leaves rustled. Ears perked at the sound of footsteps.

When he saw Sophia between ivy, memory rushed back. The image of her in his head faded away, for if it remained, it would've outshone reality like the sun's fire to the moon's pale glow—the same source, different beauties.

In some ways, Sophia was not beautiful. In others, quite so. But to Kai, she was perfect imperfection.

Her radiance came more from Kai's heart than eyes. The effect of her presence made him brighter, too. Neither looked

so good alone as with each other. A genuine smile cracked
Kai's serious face. He looked rather handsome because of the
effect of a feeling that intensified life—love.

Describing his love was to describe life—ineffable,
incomparable, incredible. Words paled in the fires of feeling,
burning through mortal sinews. His heart raged, wishing to
create something larger than itself, something that lasted, as if
such moments could go on long after pulse slowed and the
fire extinguished, leaving a lingering warmth.

"Sophia," Kai said, letting the syllables roll over his tongue.
But the words that came next were not so accustomed to him
and tightness twisted his tongue. "I wanted—well, I thought
you might not—I'm glad to see you."

"Did anyone follow you?"

He shook his head. "You look stunning."

She blushed, one reddened cheek dimpled and the other
not. "Thanks."

But it was at this point that black bars refocused into Kai's
view. Iron kept them separated. Pillars of darkness divided
Sophia's face into two, a single bit of fence keeping them from
getting closer, mere feet from each other.

Kai reached his hand through the gap, grasping long
fingers within his own. Cold. Smooth. Under chilled skin, a
warm heartbeat went from his hand to hers, responding back
and forth so softly it was violent.

"I wanted to say this to you face to face." Sophia grasped
his hand harder. She took a step back with their hands still
conjoined, raising like a rope drawn tighter. "We have to stop
meeting like this."

"What?"

"We're risking everything. You made a deal."

"I wouldn't be the first to break it." The light in Kai's eyes faded, brought down by reality. "I can't give this up. The sight of you makes everything bearable."

Sophia sighed. "In the end, the fence will divide us. Elysium and Asphodel. What happened didn't separate you and Helene, but it did separate us. The gods decided our fates, and the council told us that if you're a hero in Elysium, you can earn me a spot."

"If they even speak for the gods." Kai's smile flickered, hope bursting off and on between an elated and pained heart. "But I had to try. If only I knew earlier, I would've never have converted. I would've avoided heroism like the plague. I would've…I would've done things differently."

"*We* would've done things differently." Sophia's tone tried to be light and joking, but as with many lighthearted jokes, there was truth as the foundation, and that truth was heavy, even when it wasn't intended to be. "But you always wanted to be a hero, even before."

Kai withdrew his hand. "I'm sorry it turned out this way."

"Don't. I wouldn't change anything about what we had."

Kai crossed his arms to save a bit of the heat cut out by the deepening night air and the words spoken in them. "I promised—I still promise—I'll do anything for us to be together. We'll have days like we had before. Like the days at the lake. Do you remember? Even when night fell and it rained, we stayed out together. Of course, you caught a cold, but you were so cute with your red nose and sniffles."

"It was more than some sniffles. I sneezed, too. I'll never forgive you for that."

"Obviously," Kai said with a grin. "For the next few days, you tried to avoid me so I wouldn't get sick, but I brought that big pot of soup and ended up staying."

"It was easier to get rid of the soup than you."

"And when I got sick, you cooked me a pot of soup, too."

Sophia reached through the fence and nudged him. "Because you were pathetic."

Off-balance, Kai stepped back and recomposed, looking up to the empty sky. "There's so much we didn't know. There's still so much we don't." A shake of the head. "We expected the afterlife to be so bland. Elysium was supposed to be some fields, golden gates, a river, a boatman. But it's not anything like what I thought. The world sprouts and grows and changes all the time. Maybe we can find our place through those transitions." The sadness left, and there was hope in his eyes, taking the place of the stars in a starless night. "What if it became a place that wasn't all good nor bad, not heaven nor hell, just a place? What if the lines that divide us, the judgments that cast me here and you there, get smudged, crossed, and erased? The gods are gone. Their word still carries weight, but I have to hope the council can fulfill the deal and the only reason they don't is because they need me to save Elysium. We waited for eternity, and now we just have to wait a little longer. Then, the world will be perfect."

"I love you, but, sometimes, I think you're a little too stuck in the future you imagine in your head." She followed his gaze upwards. "As you said, it'll be unimaginable. Even for an active imagination like yours."

"Unimaginable? Good. Then it can surpass my expectations."

Kai held his beloved's hand through the fence, and they stood there, face to face, feeling each other's breath, which came out in faint plumes of cold air and wrapped them in clouds.

Sophia grew cold. Shivering, but also sterner.

"What's the matter?" he asked.

"What happens when we're reunited?"

"We live the life we would've. A happy life."

"Will we? I mean—will you be happy?"

"It's all I dream about. It's all I want."

Sophia's voice quick-froze. "Until you get it and start to dream of more."

"No," he said, but he nodded, conflicted between body and word, as he was with feeling and logic. "Not in the same way." He tried to explain, but duality was difficult. "Being with you is not the end, it's the beginning. When we're together, they'll always be something to strive for to make us better, to make the world better."

"You always want more."

"Is that so wrong?" A slight annoyance of his pride bit in his words, and there was both a loving, confused, and frustrated look in his eyes.

"No. But life can't live up to your imagination and neither can I. I'm not perfect. I can't be. Look what happened with you and Helene."

"She is not perfect." Kai shuddered from cold memories. "She couldn't be further from it. I don't love her. I did, at one point…or at least I convinced myself I did."

"You made her an ideal and even she couldn't match up. How am I supposed to? I'm not as beautiful or smart or strong."

He bit his lip. "Helene, well, she's Helene. And it took me too long to realize who she is—what she is. Once, I thought she was flawless. But I don't think you are."

Sophia shoved his hand away.

When his words rang back to his ears, Kai almost swallowed his tongue, except that he needed it to explain his idiocy. "And neither am I. Far from it. If I was, I'd realize when to keep my mouth shut." He looked at her full of apology and tenderness. "The way I feel with you is perfection, even if we're not. All I want is someone who makes me believe I can be better."

She remained distant. "Even imperfection is an attempt to distance yourself from Helene. Imperfection is part of your perfection. I don't want to be Helene's opposite. I just want to be me."

"I see you. I chose you. I still choose you." He grasped at the iron. "This is about you and me. That's all. You may not see it, but I see the good in you."

"Then see the bad, too." Her loving eyes challenged him. "I'm in Asphodel for a reason and you're in Elysium for a reason. Dragging me there won't change me. It won't make me deserve it."

"I don't deserve it, either." He sighed. "I'm trying to."

"You have this grand unselfish vision—to be a hero and save the world. And it's admirable and it's flawed. It's why I love you, but that's not how reality works. While you worry about your mistakes and imaginary blood on your hands, there's real blood here. Elysium has you and Asphodel has no one."

"All the more reason to get you out of there. I'll be the first to admit it my reasoning is selfish. I want you to be here because it would make you happy, and that makes me happy. The rest is not my problem.”

“The Kai I know is not selfish.”

“That Kai is dead, just like this world. We can try and delay the inevitable, but it’s useless.”

She snarled. “You’re wrong—I don’t think I’m good for you. You’re risking everything, for yourself, your family, and everyone just to see me. You lived without me before, you can live a little longer.”

“I didn’t live well without you.” A reverberation of past heartache pulsed through him. “But I get it now.” Sadness passed, and he smiled. “You’re trying to upset me. This is *your* version of heroism, trying to protect me, thinking we’ll get caught.”

“It’s not about you. I don’t want people to suffer because of me. If we get caught, there’ll be one less hero.”

“And you think you can get rid of me that easy? Just like when you were sick, it won’t work. Being with you is worth anything.”

“Is it worth other people’s lives?”

Kai hesitated. “We’re all dead anyway.”

“You know that’s not what I mean. Their souls will be lost. Is that really what you want?”

“No,” he said. “You’re right. I’m sorry. No more meetings until the council makes good on the deal. But we’re already here. Can we not argue anymore? Can we just enjoy a few moments before we go our separate ways, until we can be together for good?”

Her smile of forgiveness buried the conflict in Kai’s heart. He felt the dim discord settle down deep within him, and after it rested, peaceful, leaving pride and anger with it, devotion remained. Love resealed their schism.

"I'm sorry, too," Sophia said. "I don't want to destroy what we have. I just care about you, is all. You're not the same Kai I knew, but you're still the Kai I love. And somewhere, I think that old Kai isn't dead."

"Maybe not." Their hands connected through the fence, and Kai was whole again. "I love you."

"I love you, too."

Footsteps fell into their words. Harmony and love were lost as quickly as they had been found.

With an unceremonious entrance came a ceremonious man—the priest. His robe was still bloodied, spray cast uncaringly over white fabric. His eyes dug out the weeds of any garden, especially this one. But without any plant life, the priest dug for what didn't belong—Kai. Especially his demeanor. Normal people did not smile in dead gardens.

And so, the priest looked for what Kai was doing wrong. It didn't take him long to see it—a woman on the other side of the fence.

Sophia squeezed Kai's hand lovingly and longingly, followed by a sad smile and her pulling away. It happened in a second, and that awful moment would run on a loop in Kai's mind forever.

He stayed there, frozen with arm outstretched, reaching and feeling the warmth go cold. Shock and shame numbed.

He had not imagined this in his darkest nightmares.

Finally, Kai stirred himself, and not knowing what to do, he nodded at the priest and strode by, out of the courtyard, past the temple, and into the streets of the city. While his feet moved, his mind lay still, frightened into nothingness at what might come of such innocent coincidence.

At home, he wept.

FOUR

FAMILY, YOU CAN'T LIVE WITH THEM, YOU CAN'T LIVE...

TIME DRIED TEARS, and Kai resolved himself, knowing what would come. Still, it was quiet. A lurking-dread quiet.

Night slept. Shadows crept down a dark river and black banks. Grey grass, stiff from drought, did not waver with the wind. Unheard by sleeping nature, bluster increased, perturbed by the peace and emptiness in its presence. Nightly wind broke the unmoved evening and found a way inside, where people defied darkness, letting the cool night air filter through a hot room.

Kai was home. Or, rather, he was in his house. Within these four walls, there was no safety or security left.

"The clouds are coming down the mountain," Kai's cousin, Marcus, said. He was at the window, trying to stand with the same military manner as Kai's father usually did, exaggerating as to look down on those around. "Zeus is preparing a storm. A good omen."

"It'll be like the others," Kai said. Dreary as the fog, his mood spread through the room, because if it concentrated totally in him, tears would condense and spill. He slunk onto an ottoman, the least comfortable seat in the wide, well-adorned room.

Standing at attention for too long seemed to hurt Marcus' back, and he sat on the cashmere couch with the twins, Cara and Li, ebony armrests trapping tense relations together. When Marcus scowled at the twins, they scowled back. Kai's father sat straight in a leather recliner and kept an eye on them, while Kai's mother sat in a mahogany rocker and brushed a formal dress clean of stubborn dust.

Kai directed his shame towards the colorful floor, where a silk Persian rug's patterns seemed to dance with the candlelight. Unable to think anymore, Kai sat back, quieted his mind, and bathed in the chandelier's lights like those in a shimmering sea.

There was a joyful emptiness in not thinking.

The crystal and candle chandelier danced to the music of wind—golden flames spun and flickered, glittering off brass and prismatic glass. Ember-instilled droplets and spinning beads swirled—a prism of radiance, twirling above, on, and between the family, who were quiet and reminiscent, full from dinner. Smooth sweet-spice of saffron rice wafted with a taste of caramelized onions already eaten, but lingering in stomach and smell. The room churned with the drifting aromas, kaleidoscopic crystals, and the sudden chill of a night breeze.

The draft chilled the mood.

Marcus took up all-too-much space. Wanting to distance herself, Cara pushed into Li. However, Li was like stone in movement and expression.

Everyone, except for Kai's mother, knew what was coming and would've preferred to escape to their own part of the house. Yet, here they were.

Familial silence waited for a fight. Surely, it would come. The argument was easy to predict, rising from bad blood that couldn't be cleansed any easier than blood ties. To an outsider, one argument would've been indicative of them all, but with family, each one felt new.

Kai's father tried to break the tense silence. "I heard you charmed another myth, Kai."

Broken from his musings, Kai returned to the present. "A leopard that thought itself a phoenix." Without meaning to, he reached into his pocket and felt for the leopard's feather. A sharp end of a quill poked him and the shock managed to give him a flash of hope. "It had quite the going-away party, bursting into confetti. Maybe I can convince you to join me, if it gets to a fight, I could use your experience."

His father frowned. "I'd rather forget those experiences."

Across the room, there was a sudden snore from Kai's grandfather. His own noise woke him, and he distancing himself from his wife in the frosty loveseat before drifting back to sleep.

While it was easy to imagine Kai's grandparents as old, having fallen asleep at an early hour, they looked near the same age as Kai, and in many ways, could've passed as his cousins, with grandfather sharing Kai's sweet smile and grandmother sharing hopeful eyes. They slept for a simple reason, though—habit.

Once they settled, Kai's father continued, "I'll stick with my work at the newspaper."

"Because that's so exciting," Kai's mother said, her bubbly features surprisingly grim. "I'll tell you the news. The gods are absent, creatures run wild, oh, and in weather, heaven will be hot as hell."

Kai's father roused in his lounger. "Do you always have to be so pessimistic?"

"I think that's called being realistic," Li said, squirming at the edge of the couch. Fed up, he launched an elbow into Cara's ribs.

Cara elbowed him back, unphased.

"The two of you are disgraceful," Marcus said from the other side of the couch. "Good for nothing."

Cara grinned, sardonic. "When you see yourself in a mirror, I wonder what you see."

"A productive member of society. I have an important job at the newspaper, unlike you."

"And I thought you were clinging to Kai's coattails like the rest of us?" Cara snarled at him; a rarity for her, but Marcus made everyone a bit more extreme. He just had a face, and more importantly, personality, that was akin to a mourning dove—obnoxious and confused into thinking himself an owl when he was only a plumped-up pigeon.

Marcus growled, his hair casting a shadow over his face. However, it lacked the edge to strike fear in anyone, especially Cara. This only upset him more, and Marcus rose to his feet, standing over her.

"You're worthless. I should toss you into the street."

"You'll do no such thing," Li said, his face a violent stoicism. No wrinkles dug themselves in forehead or face.

What he lacked in creases seemed to be hollowed out of his cheeks. No one would call Li handsome. No one would dare call him anything. Expression was merely there. Unmovable. Unalterable. Unmistakable.

Marcus stepped back. Not wanting to display how unsettled he was by Li, how Li sometimes unsettled them all, Marcus pushed back. "I didn't realize you cared for your sister."

"Twin," Li said. "You insult her, you insult me. Isn't that right, Kai?"

Kai was careful with a smile and non-committedly nodded.

"You're going to take his side?" Marcus asked, voice raised.

"I can fight my own battles, Li." Cara stood and confronted Marcus. She was shorter, but her presence stood taller. "If anyone should leave, it's you."

"We're all family here," Kai's mother said, faithfully dusting the dress.

"Marcus is barely family," Cara said. "He just happened to be brought here with us."

Red anger rose, Marcus' lips twitching. "You're a dirty witch. You and your soulless twin. Both of you are so odd, so unnatural."

Li stood by his twin. He provoked Marcus with eyes.

"That's enough," Kai's father said, standing, too. "All of you, head to your room, cool off. Tomorrow, you can apologize, both to your family and the gods for the dishonor you're doing."

The first cracks of anger rose in Li's otherwise emotionless eyes. "I've had enough of him."

Outside, nature roused, too. Spritzes of rain sprinkled down into gravel and dirt and dust. And with this reprieve, ill-thought washed away. Drops bounced off the sill and onto the wood floor, leaving minuscule droplets splattered in an arc below the open window.

"Would you look at that?" Kai's father said.

Even Li cooled with the rain. Desperation created such qualms, and at the first sign of deliverance, elation averted a fight.

The rain pattered down on hard ground in a dark flurry.

The darkness broke briefly. A bolt of lightning struck into the dark river Lethe, sparking across black liquid in a zigzagging spider web.

BOOM.

The house rattled. Pots and pans clattered. The roll and roar of the strike went on, building, fading, only to build again, growling. When the vibration stopped and the foundation came to rest, there was a hush.

The rain stopped, too.

"See what you've done now?" Kai's mother said. "You've angered Zeus. You'll be lucky if the three of you are not cast out of Elysium."

Broken loose by the shaking of the storm, Kai found what he wanted to say, what he had always wanted to say, as if that rumble finally opened the earth and unleashed hell. "You don't have to worry about them, I'm the one leaving."

Stunned and unsure, there was silence. Even Kai's grandparents were roused by nature's wrath and examined him with judgmental eyes.

The first voice of calm was Cara, "What do you mean? You can't leave."

A knock. The family looked at each other, and no one went towards the door.

A letter slipped under the crack and a few drops of rain stained the white envelope, which was the result of the brief drizzle outside that was now a lost moment of reprieve.

Dread realized. Kai saw the messenger flash by the window and knew what the letter said already. "I don't think I have a choice."

All that went through his mind was how he had let his family down and how Helene was going to kill him for getting caught.

Kai's mother ballooned in red suspicion, supporting herself with the wall. "What is that?"

"It's a letter," Li said.

Cara rolled her eyes. "A letter from the council."

"What did you do?" Kai's father asked with a disciplining tone.

Kai had the letter in his hands and returned to the ottoman, not answering. His face, pained. And although his expression was sour, he felt nothing. There was no sadness, no fear, no anger. Kai, merely, was.

Pulling apart the envelope at the corner and dragging a finger across, paper bit and drew a droplet of blood. Just the start of pain to come.

"At least now we'll get what we deserved," Kai said and sucked the cut.

Marcus snatched the letter. "You'll get yourself in trouble, not us. If they take you, they won't take me. They can't."

At the sight of the council's seal, purple wax with a lightning bolt and olive branch, Marcus threw the letter back to Kai as if it burned him.

"Sit down and shut up," Cara said to Marcus. "The only reason we're here is because of Kai. If he goes, we all go."

Kai's grandfather sat up in the loveseat, trying to cast the familial equivalent of high judgment with a solid, somber voice. "Maybe it's better we do. We never belonged here."

"And where do we belong?" Kai's grandmother asked, a small-boned woman with a large bite in her words. "We were travelers, nomads, and now, we've renounced our ways."

Kai's mother tutted. "Both of you never believed, count yourself lucky to be here."

"Respect your elders," Kai's grandfather said, turning to his son on the lounger. "Will you just sit there? Is all reverence for your ancestors gone? Will we spit on every tradition, not just the ones we were raised with, but the ones we were born with too?"

Caught between wife and parents, Kai's father did the sensible thing and remained silent, biting his tongue and hoping someone would save him.

Luckily, Li did. "From where I'm sitting, no one looks like an elder. Just read the letter." Li withdrew into his seat, uninterested like life was merely theater and he was backstage witnessing it until he had to play his part.

No one dared contradict Li, feeling him retreat into a dark aura. The only one who did not seem bothered was Cara.

"Go on," she said to Kai.

Leather squeaked in anticipation.

Kai unfolded the paper, bent in three places to fit the envelope. After a bit of smoothing, which was only to delay further, Kai read, "Caius Vatinius, the gods have witnessed wrongdoing." He thought this strange; a godly man had uncovered the meeting, not the gods. "You were warned. The vow you took cannot be easily nulled, and your meeting with

Sophia of Asphodel tarnishes the oath you swore before the gods. Therefore—" Kai stopped, struck mute.

Li said, "You would think the gods could learn to speak with less pomp and circumstance."

"Don't question the gods, they will…" Kai's mother trailed off, silenced by Li's paralyzing eyes that stared through her, piercing her like a beast hunting prey.

Li grinned as if the power to pacify pleased him. "Kai?"

A gust. The sweeping hand of nature waved out a few of the chandelier's candles. Flecks of red dust clung to white walls like freckles on a pale face, but as the draft receded, the bits fell, spiraling and floating down like blood-tainted snow. Finally, the wind steadied into a hum over a wavering letter, hesitant face, and uncertain family.

"Sophia has been sent to Irkalla," Kai said, focusing on syllables and detached from meaning. "Should you want a good fate, we suggest you repent. However, given your service and deeds in the name of the gods, your punishment is a warning. One and only."

A collective sigh seemed to pass through the room. Maybe it was the wind or selfish concerns being released, but it was peaceful.

"Praise Zeus' mercy," Kai's mother said.

Marcus relaxed. "As things should be."

"You wouldn't know anything about it." Kai's clenched fist crumpled the paper, but he did not lash out beyond the words.

Li remained unmoved, as if any outcome could be dealt with. And although there was no love in his eyes for Kai, he had something more important at that moment—respect. Li said nothing, letting silence be a testament to Kai's pain.

As Kai unrumpled the paper and swallowed the words again, his mouth moving but making no sound, in his head, the words were louder than the boom of thunder.

He couldn't lose Sophia again.

The ground Kai built his life upon cracked, crumbled, and shattered. Sadness burned like venom in veins, overwhelming into numbness. And in the throes of despair, the darkness and brokenness grew quieter, while the fervor of a fiery heart burst. Desolation became anger. And anger wanted action—vengeance, justice, deliverance. Where sadness whispered, rage shouted. Kai's soul felt so much, too much, that he could do and say nothing.

Sand blew into the room like rain and finally, Cara closed the window. With it, the silence was torturous, leaving Kai alone with his thoughts.

"You should be more careful," Kai's father said before retreating to a dutiful silence.

"He's just a boy. A pretty girl destroys judgment." Kai's grandmother looked from father to mother with a raised brow.

Kai's mother scowled. "Remember, tomorrow you two have to go check on your status."

Kai's grandfather asked, "What if we only have an hour left and I waste it in line? That's not where I want to spend my afterlife."

"That's not up to you, it's up to the gods," Kai's mother said. "And I'd watch your tongue or they'll reincarnate you as an ant. Then you'll spend your whole life in lines."

"We all have to do things we don't want to," Marcus said. "I'll go with you tomorrow. I want to register to vote. At work, they were talking about the council's election…."

The family continued chatting, of the next day, of their work, of the lesser and lower things in their life, which was a speck to Kai's sandstorm. They talked of normality, as if this would distract Kai.

He nodded and swiveled between them, pretending everything was better than expected, when it was worse. Despite the occasional 'mhm' and 'no', he didn't hear a word they said.

When most of his family faded to bed, Kai remained; where his mind barred the external world, Kai saw with singular focus.

Sophia.

The beautiful image escaped him. His thought was tainted by what it would become.

In the underworld of Irkalla—no, he couldn't imagine it— her fate elicited anguish Kai could not contain.

A soft hand on his shoulder broke him from the terrible nightmare. It was Cara.

She smiled at him, not a joyous smile, not an ironic smile, but a smile of sympathy. Of belief. Of hope. That everything might still be okay. Even if it wasn't now.

She remained for a minute of solace before heading to bed, knowing he wanted her to go. Finally, Kai remained in the room, alone.

The door opened on oiled hinges, cautiously and quietly. Helene tip-toed in.

"What's wrong?" she asked, dropping caution at seeing him still up. "I haven't seen you so…." She trailed off, noticing the letter in his lap. "The council sent you a letter?"

Kai held out the letter and she grabbed it, taking away the physical representation of his pain but not reading it.

"They sent Sophia to Irkalla," he said.

Helene bit her lip. "And you're upset that they didn't send you there, too?"

"Yes." He exhaled guilt and his eyes burned forge-hot. "And I'd send the council there, too. I'd send the gods there. She doesn't deserve that. I do. They do. It's all wrong." A flush ran through him and cooled to stern steel. "No…I knew the rules and my impatience got the best of me. I'm the one who's wrong."

"Don't give me that. Following unjust rules is an injustice to yourself."

"How're you not mad?" he asked.

Shaking her head was simple, but Helene's eyes stared at him. It wasn't anger, though. "I don't need to punish you. And you shouldn't punish yourself either. They've done that already. What are you going to do to make it right?"

"I can't do anything." Frustration paralyzed him. "The gods may not be walking the street, but the people who work for them are. I'm one of them. I've got responsibilities. To my job, family, and you. This can't be happening. It's a mistake. It has to be. I'll go plead her case tomorrow."

"You know as well as I do, it'll be too late."

"It can't be," he hissed.

"They've already taken her beyond the wall. But that doesn't mean you can't do anything." For a moment, Helene lingered by the window, staring out at the dark night and pondering. When she turned back to Kai, she seemed to have brought some of the darkness with her, and her face was covered with shadows. "That shouldn't be what stops you. Your family has depended on you long enough; they have to learn how to live without you. I can take care of myself. Always have."

"You want me to go after her? All of you would be kicked out of Elysium."

"You could ask the council for permission."

Kai shook his head. "They'd laugh me out the room. A hero asking to leave heaven? I've already tried."

"Of course you wouldn't ask again."

He shrugged the words off. "It won't matter. No one comes back from Irkalla."

"Then how does anyone know what it's like?"

Kai tried his hardest to come up with an answer. "The gods."

"The gods have left us," Helene said. "The council tries to speak for them, but maybe it's time to be our own gods. Take it into our own hands. Besides, if things keep going as they are, not even Elysium will be safe from the drought."

"If I leave, people will suffer. What will happen with the myths? Innocents will die."

Helene laid a hand on his shoulder. "You sound like you've been talking to Sophia too much."

At the mention of her name, Kai went hollow. "I have to do what she would want. Other people shouldn't suffer for my selfishness."

"And I thought you cared about Sophia more than anything," Helene said. "Why won't you go after her?"

Anger reared reflexively. "It's not because I don't care, it's because I care too much." Sadness smothered him again. "Failure would destroy me."

"You'll destroy yourself if you do nothing."

Kai looked down at the rug, wanting the moment of thoughtlessness back.

Helene sat next to him. "What if you taught me how to deal with myths?"

"You hate myths."

"They have their uses. That leopard you dealt with earlier sounded interesting."

Kai was cold and blunt. "You'd kill myths. Abuse them. Treat them like monsters. No, you'd be terrible because you're too good at it. We don't need more heroes like that."

Helene grinned, slender and sly. "Then let Cara and Li do it."

"I don't know how I feel about Li," Kai said.

"Teach Cara. She's got a heart for people and animals. If she gets it, then you could go, conscience-free."

"I can't put her in that kind of danger."

"She can make up her own mind," Helene said.

"I know." Kai breathed deep. "Maybe you're right."

Helene went to the window, this time, looking with over-the-top emphasis.

"What're you doing?" he asked.

"Checking for flying pigs. It's been a while since we've had them. About as long since you thought I was right."

"I said I'd think about it."

"You just don't want to admit it's a good idea. You think I have another motive." Helene turned back to him. "Maybe I just don't want to deal with you being sad all the time. You leaving would cause me more trouble, but it's the right thing to do. This whole thing is unfair, and if anyone can fix it, it's you."

Kai met her enigmatic eyes. He took it to mean that Sophia's situation was unfair, but he also had the suspicion Helene was speaking about something else. "I guess my family will survive without me."

"Does that mean you're going?" Helene asked.

"No. Maybe. Yes."

"Those are the options."

Kai sighed. "If I do, don't tell anyone till I'm out of the city."

"I can't. I'll go with you."

"Why would you do that?" he asked.

"Because I care about you."

"No, really?" He realized she wouldn't give him a straight answer. She never did. "Never mind. Thanks."

Under the charming lighting, Helene's smile beamed at him. She never smiled at him anymore. For Kai, it brought back pleasant feelings and sentimentality. However, Kai knew better. Nostalgia was only the past with a bit of blush.

Once Kai brushed the blush away, he saw the enchantment for what it was. Attracting. Alluring. Absorbing. But not to be trusted. She had some other motive.

"I'll wake you up when it's time to leave," he lied.

Helene nodded and headed down the hallway, leaving Kai alone with his thoughts again.

Like picking up broken glass, Kai grabbed onto bits of his shattered life. Although there was pain, he couldn't let go of love. He had to follow Sophia to Irkalla, and to get to a myth, he would need a myth. However, for now, he couldn't conjure hope, much less a myth. He laid on the couch and a shattered life sliced through his dreams.

FIVE

WITHOUT

KAI'S PREVIOUS LIFE ENDED and the sun rose regardless. An end was not the end, and as he snuck onto familiar streets, it was with unbendable purpose. The new morn's rays rose over the houses of Elysium, and hope rose within him.

Changed by catastrophe, he grasped onto what was left. He chose life when faced with loss. He chose hope when faced with the impossible. He chose love because it was impossible to live otherwise.

Passing near the garden and fence, he diverted; the pain was too recent and brought back too much guilt.

Such guilt compiled. He had left home without leaving a note for his family. It was easier to rip off all connections and feel the pain completely and at once.

But there was less pain than expected—grief did not come on command, heartbreak could not be forced, and he did not believe this was goodbye.

How could it be? He was still in Elysium. The market was opening. The first shop owners smiled at him and he smiled back. The spotless windows and white-brick sidewalks were pristine. The drought's dust hadn't kicked up, still slumbering. Fruit sellers cut watermelons and peaches and pomegranates, placing them on stands outside shops and letting plump juices drip into the street. Sure, lost juices washing down drains was wasteful, but the aroma would linger as fantastic-smelling advertising.

Sweet scents mixed with the scintillating smell of spice. Ceramic pots of cinnamon and cardamom. Porcelain bowls of sugar and salt with ivory serving spoons. Cooked foods smoked from backrooms and teased with the tickle of taste. Kai savored Elysium's food market, reminiscing at how he went there with Cara to experience the flavor of such a place. This time, though, it seemed bittersweet.

He was leaving such memories behind. First, the fence to Asphodel. Then, past the wall and to the lands beyond. And finally, Irkalla.

Kai knew three things about Irkalla, or rather, he had heard two and knew one. First, the underworld's entrance was east near the city of Duat. Second, that during the god wars, the Egyptian gods had dug deeper. Too deep. Last, and the only thing he knew for sure, was that he knew nothing.

Uncertainty presented itself in the territory directly before the gate between Elysium and Asphodel. Despite unease, Kai went forth with a sure step, awakening a dutiful morning.

Brick buildings watched on either side of the street. These houses were for soldiers who guarded, protected, or policed the rest, depending on who was asked. From wall to wall, it was as if the whole neighborhood was in a phalanx, tight in formation. The framework was forceful. Kai was channeled to tighter streets. Crossbars covered closed windows. Through thick glass, watchful eyes stared at him. Columns dominated façades and men stood with similar severity.

Kai approached a grand stone archway, feeling quite unlike how he always thought he'd feel on the way to Asphodel. Two soldiers guarded the border. Luckily, Kai recognized one of them.

However, just because Kai recognized the man didn't mean he remembered his name. The soldier wore traditional garb—red, to mask blood stains—and the way Kai recognized the man was not the indistinguishable stern face under a helmet; instead, it was the man's arm. Leaning on a spear, the man had a robust scar running a serpentine path down the length of forearm to shoulder. The scar tinged red like the blood that had run over it.

"Hey," Kai said. "It's good to see you again."

"No offense, but however good it is to see you again, I'm not glad to," the soldier said. "Means there's serious trouble in Asphodel."

"More and more."

"What's it this time?"

Kai yawned, taking a second to think. "Chimera."

The lie crossed his lips easily. A peculiar grin spread easily, too. There was no going back now. Elysium would endure without him; there were other heroes and others who could become one.

"Nasty things, chimera," the soldier said.

"Kai, wait up," said another voice.

The soldier looked past him. "Company?"

Kai glanced over his shoulder and couldn't help a worried frown. "My little sister."

"Did you forget me?" Cara laid a hand on his shoulder and leaned on him. More than leaning, she seemed to be hanging onto him. "You were supposed to teach me today."

The soldier laughed. "You're teaching your sister how to charm beasts? I'm sure she's charming, but your business is dangerous."

"Don't underestimate her," Kai said. With his eyes, he asked Cara how she knew.

Her bright eyes said how obvious it was and that she wanted to help.

"She's smarter than she looks," Kai teased Cara, and then said, sterner, "Don't judge how she looks, she might do well at myth control."

"Will…" she said. "I will do well."

Kai's tone warned. "As long as she's careful."

The soldier addressed Cara. "Kai's the best teacher you could have. Actually, he helped me out of a tight spot with a manticore." A reminiscent laugh. "If he showed up a minute earlier, though, I wouldn't have this scar, but one minute later, and I wouldn't be here today."

Kai lit up. "Oh, that's right, Albus. I jumped on the beast's scorpion tail and it stung itself."

"Scorpion venom doesn't affect itself," Cara said. "That's a myth."

Kai winked at her. "Myths are not that simple. You'll have to learn quick."

"I'll do my best," she said seriously and followed with sarcasm. "I won't do anything overly risky, just like my teacher."

Kai reddened. "Yeah. We'd better get a move on."

After saying "we", Kai regretted it.

With Cara's presence, the second soldier decided to engage, eyeing her and snarling, threatening as a military-trimmed wolf. "We'll have to check with the commander."

Cara tried to defuse the situation with the less pleasant soldier with a smile that was wide and almost defiant. "Every moment we waste the chimera could eat someone else."

Both soldiers looked at each other.

"The commander cleared it," Kai said with a calmness he did not feel. "I know it's early, so maybe he didn't tell you or didn't think it worth telling. He is a bit stuck in his own head."

The nicer soldier, Albus, went to say something, but closed his mouth and thought better of it, simply giving an unconscious nod.

His unpleasant companion was less moved. "We heard about…you know. You can see why we might take extra care."

"Heard about what?" Cara asked, approaching the ferocious-looking soldier. "Kai got distracted by a girl?" She gave him big, innocent eyes, along with a calm that was more striking than a fist. "Do you really think he'd take his little sister on an escape mission? Kai was in love, people do stupid things for love, but he wouldn't drag his little sister into his problems."

Kai scowled at the wolf-like soldier, who was looking at Cara a little too intently. "I couldn't drag her anywhere."

Cara's long hair swung as she twirled around and walked back to Kai. "He's a good brother."

"She's got a point," Albus said to his compatriot. "The commander probably forgot to tell us. Once something's in *his* head, it tends to get stuck. They say sound can't travel through empty space."

The unfriendly soldier couldn't help a smile. "Fine. Head on through."

"See you later," Kai said, walking between them with Cara.

"You better be more vigilant about your words, Albus," whispered the sour soldier.

"And you should be more vigilant with your eyes," Albus said. "The way she distracted you, maybe she can charm a few beasts."

Protective, Kai glared over his shoulder and made a mental note.

"Wow," Cara said as they passed through the archway. "What a view."

From their raised position, Asphodel expanded in a morning stretch. Stores and stalls yawned in the valley, tarps and metal storefronts opening wide with the beginnings of a new day. People bustled in multicolored hordes. Goods and wares flowed—flamingo and peacock feathers slung over shoulders, buckets of magenta and indigo dye balanced on heads, and burgundy and maroon rugs carried like logs. Most citizens wore chestnut, hare, and fawn brown wools, but some wore white silk with accents dyed Roman red and Byzantine purple; although money could not buy Elysium, it did buy nicer clothes.

Regardless of wealth, people melded, channeled from the large pastures of markets into smaller side streets, where the flow was ever more chaotic. Asphodel was a great quilt-like city that stitched itself together by these smaller streets, connecting large patches. It was a vibrant hub of color and texture and life under a dust-red filter.

Down the hill and unto the throng, Kai and Cara looked up instead of down. Above, eastern-styled rugs draped between mismatched houses on the narrow streets. People stuck sticks out of windows and beat the dust off the fabrics, revealing ore-like patterns.

Cara reveled in the liveliness. That was, until she got a storm of dust rained on her.

But that did not diminish her wonder, and as soon as she brushed it off, she was looking up again.

Kai was glad for her company and the distraction. Turning a corner, his foot caught and he stumbled, but he did not fall. He played it off and kept going, only to wobble again.

Ankle-twisting cobblestone was the cause of his distress, mismatched in size and shape. Forced into caution, he saw that the cracks between uneven stone were filled with debris—dead straw, bits and pieces, and unrelenting amounts of dust. The dried earth powdered grey stone maroon in the morning. The plague of dryness afflicted people around him, too. As Cara had, people swept dust away. Off clothes. Off arms. Off wares. And as the city filled with activity in the cooler morning hours, it clouded with dust.

People set up dirty tapestry stalls in the middle of the street, while clean brick and mortar stores surrounded on either side. The smiling faces stared out of glass storefronts as an advertisement, content with success and desiring more. Meanwhile, those who constructed tapestry stalls were too busy to smile and their wares wallowed in the sand that swept everything under a smell of dryness.

Carrots cracked white, blackberries ran with rivers of grit, and raspberries filled with dust until they appeared more like withered strawberries. The smell was faint with souring fruit.

Everything dehydrated and came with a crunch. Here, water was too precious to waste on washing.

Kai pulled Cara away from curiosity, as she was busy guessing what fruit had withered into browning orbs at one of the stalls. Apples, maybe. But when Kai finally brought her out of the produce, they entered a new street that broke the brick-brown haze with every shade of green—a street of jade. It was carved into rings and bracelets and earrings and figures of exotic animals like lions, elephants, and gods. Some jade was emerald brilliant, while some stayed darker like the depths of foreign forests.

A man struggled to put up his stall. Kai stopped, helping him drape the tapestry over a pole. The man nodded with appreciation, "Do you want to look?"

Unable to refuse, Kai nodded. The tent was shady, but still hot. A few tables were set up, and as the sun rose, it filtered through the morn and followed them in.

"Do you have a plan?" Cara whispered, focused on him rather than the jade.

"We're making a myth."

"Now?"

"No. We have to find a place to plant a story." He bit his lip. "That's all I should say."

"You don't trust me?"

"I do. But I wish I didn't know what little I do, and you shouldn't want to know, either." He stopped pretending to look at the jade and caught her unfaltering eyes. "You should know, though...." Kai checked over his shoulder to make sure the stall-owner was still fiddling with the ties on the tent. "With the reputation of myth control, our words can be dangerous. I think if no one believed in myths, they wouldn't exist."

"Belief makes them real?"

"Depends on the myth. Depends on the person believing. Just trust me, this will work."

"Okay." Cara's eye caught a jade dagger that sparkled sharply. "I do."

Kai watched her eyes light up, glinting with the jade's green reflection. "Do you want a dagger?"

She shook her head. "What use do I have for a blade?"

"If you're going to be part of myth control, you might need it."

"I don't see why. You don't."

Kai frowned. "Not usually. But that's different."

"Why?"

"I can speak to myths. And even then, myths can be dangerous if you don't know what you're doing."

Cara whispered, "Then why are we making a myth?"

"Because I know what I'm doing…or, at least I know that's what we have to do to get past Asphodel's wall and to Irkalla."

They went quiet as the stall-owner came over. He put on a wide smile and motioned towards the blade. "Can I help?"

"We're just looking," Cara said.

The owner flickered towards a frown, his happy mask faltering for a moment. "How about some of these pieces?" He ushered them towards a table of little figurines.

Kai shook his head. "We're actually a bit lost, and we're wondering if you could help us?"

"I've only been in Asphodel a little while," said the stall-owner.

Kai examined the man like the jade, and where stone was pure and clean, the man was dirtied and desperate. Underneath a matted bed of black hair, his skin was well-baked by the sun. Kai wanted to save this man from the plague of drought and destitution, and yet, his desire to go after Sophia conflicted with that and prudent words had to come first. "Is there a place around here where people gather and talk? And also a place to get supplies—food, water, and such?"

"The Central Pub down the street," the stall-owner suggested. "That's where people gather. The market will have the rest, except water. That'll be hard. Expensive. By this time, most wells except the one by the ruins will be dry. People buy out the quota early and sell it later when people are desperate. But maybe you'll get lucky."

"I appreciate the info." He pulled out a bag of coins and drew out a few gold coins—Aureus. The coins were not perfectly circular, like how cookies melted unevenly. "Here, for the advice."

"No. I couldn't." The man pushed his hand away.

Kai insisted. "For the information."

"You didn't buy anything."

All that remained unalterable in the man was strength and a little sliver of dignity and pride. Kai understood this, but it frustrated him; he wanted to help. So, instead, he found a different solution—reverse negotiation.

"What do you think, Cara?" Kai picked up a small figurine of jade, forest green, depicting an owl.

"It's pretty."

"We'll take it," Kai said. "How about—"

Cara interrupted, "But I'd prefer the lion."

Kai rolled his eyes and picked up a lion that fit in the palm of his hand. "How about three Aureus for this?"

The man's eyes widened. "It's not worth that. It's not even worth one."

"I don't have any silver coins," Kai said. "What if I buy something else and we round up?"

"I have change."

"I don't want change."

The stall-owner grinned, as if the fight between them was restoring a bit of life.

Kai held out the coins. "That and the owl, then."

"No."

"That must almost be the price."

"But it's not the price."

"Just take it." Being rebutted again and again battered Kai's calmness like a crumbling wall. Underneath, pride was stung by the refusal of his offer of aid. Kai grabbed the merchant's wrist and handed the gold over.

Coins clattered to the cobblestone.

Kai's voice raised. "What's wrong with you? I'm trying to help."

"I don't need charity." The man averted his gaze from the coins.

Kai vented his frustration in an undignified grunt. "How can you be so stubborn?"

"How can you be?" Cara asked, picking up the coins. "I'm sorry. He's having a hard day. Did you start in Asphodel?"

"No, my wife and I came in a caravan from Duat. My wife is feisty. Wouldn't have made it without her. I thought success was easy, but I didn't know…." He stared outside, where the few customers that walked the street did not glance at any of the stalls. With the wealth of choice, the easiest choice was to choose nothing.

Cara dragged the man's attention back. "Kai's wife was just sent to Irkalla." Cara laid a comforting hand on Kai's shoulder. "Usually, he's a bit less cross. Not much. But he really does mean the best."

Kai smiled at his sister with warmth and sincerity, but there was a nostalgic sadness to it, as the words both affirmed and reminded him. It was a sweet melancholy—reminiscent, pleasant, and utterly sad. "I just wanted to help. I didn't mean to offend you."

The man nodded. "I'm sorry about your wife."

"How about one Aureus for the lion figure?" Kai asked.

"No," the man said simply.

"You won't give me change?"

"If you accept the fair price."

"Of course."

The stall-owner shrugged and smiled. "How am I supposed to argue?"

"Cara, I don't think we're going to make it to the temple today."

Cara gave Kai a trademarked sarcastic look, saying that they wouldn't have gone anyway.

Kai continued looking disappointed. "We won't be able to make a donation." He turned to the shop owner and brightened. "Are you going to a temple today?"

The man nodded.

"Then maybe you take the change and donate it to those in need?" Kai drew out a couple more coins. "And these other coins, too? The gods might smile on us both then."

The man regarded him with suspicion but eventually nodded. "I'll do that."

Kai hoped that a good deed would feed as a stream tricked into river and ocean, and as Kai handed over the coins, he smiled true.

Cara gave Kai a one-handed hug and joined in the smile with a lion figurine in her other hand. As she had stared at the market before, she gazed with interest at the jade, turning it over in her hands and seeing that light did not make it translucent, but, instead, glittered with stars like a green nebula.

Kai and Cara left the stall-owner with a gentle wave, and the man went back to setting up the rest of his stall with a newfound exuberance.

"You did well," Cara said.

"You handled it better than me." A different pride rose within him. "Maybe I should try to be good like you."

"I always thought you were pretty good."

Kai didn't know what to say, but he couldn't help the pleasant flush in his cheeks. "Are you telling the truth or just trying to flatter me so I'll buy you a drink?"

"Can't it be both?" She said. "Now where do you think that pub is?"

Cara distracted Kai with chatter long enough for them to find what they were looking for.

Above the wood door was a sign: 'Central Pub. All welcome.'

Inside, it was one of those places with their first dollar framed on the wall, but for two dollars, they'd sell it. Homely and commercial, the air was cool, but the mood was hot with raucous laughter. For a morning, the pub was busy. Friendly faces gathered in trenched booths, hollowed into the floor like firepits. There, smiles and voices crackled. The pub was not-too-serious, and as Kai walked in, he wished to sit around, here or there, cheered by the smiles that would've been extinguished by circumstance in the outside world and seemed so insolated and cozy within four simple walls.

Bright candles cast away shadows and the sweet smell of incense wafted. With hazel-dry wood and open flames, it seemed rather dangerous. The roof was dangerous, too. Hundreds of spears thatched the ceiling, intertwined like a pile of castaway twigs. As the initial glow dissipated, Kai was beset by a spear-prick of reality. Everyone judged him as he walked in.

Here, he was no hero, only an outsider. He had stared down monsters and myths, and yet, this room full of people seemed a million times more frightful. However, he was here for a reason, and where that did not give him bravery, Cara did.

She was small, but she made up for it with a confidence and nonchalance befitting a strong soul. She melded noiselessly across to the bar and with a smile of resonating warmth, breathed belonging. Judgmental eyes lulled back to their own business. Although Kai could speak with monsters, Cara spoke a universal language—charisma.

"I'll have some mead," Cara said to the bartender, a man with the face of a battering ram, wiping down the wood with a dirty cloth.

"Glass or mug?"

"Cask."

The bartender stopped cleaning. "Excuse me?"

"A round for everyone on us."

Kai whispered, "You mean 'on me', don't you?" He patted his pocket to make sure he had plenty of coins; a promised drink was not something to renege on.

Cara pulled Kai closer. "You wanted to do a good deed, here's a chance to do one that'll pay you back."

"How much?" Kai asked.

The bartender appraised him. "You new here?"

Kai stifled an objection, but he did not deny the truth. "I thought all were welcome? How about a new customer discount?" He smiled, trying to show it was a joke.

The man remained uncracked, stern as the stable counter he leaned on. "No discounts."

Cara broke away from the discerning bartender to the looser audience. "Who wants a drink?"

No one moved, reluctant to trust. A few mumbles. Some eager eyes, but tied tongues.

"What do you want?" asked someone.

"Just some information about a myth, if you have any," Cara said. "We're part of myth control."

Whispers skirted across tabletops, bouncing back with rebuttals. A few words spouted clear through the discordant crowd.

"Elysium…Myth…Deserted…Hero…Forgotten."

"So what? They're here now," said a man, breaking rank. "Whoever doesn't want their drink, I'll take it. What's a minute of our time anyway?" This burly man heaved himself from a tiny booth and lumbered over. "Give me a drink, Horace."

"They're from Elysium. You're going to trust them?" the bartender asked.

"Until they give me reason not to. Besides, you're the one pouring my drink."

The bartender nodded and filled a large wooden mug from one of the casks.

This one defection spread through the crowd ever-so-slowly, and eventually, arguments quieted, people approached the bar, asked for a drink, got a mug, and Kai paid. Before Kai knew it, the pouch of money lightened and all he had to show for it was a splintery old mug and golden nectar within.

"Come sit with us," said the original defector with a half-hearted smile and genuine gentleness in his eyes.

Kai scooted into a booth, sitting across from the semi-friendly man and his companion. It was a bit tight, as if they were in a trench together. And despite that, the built-in tables were quaint and produced a closeness for those within, enveloped from the world.

"I'm Rock and this is my friend, Pebble." Rock was a hulking man with long locks of dark hair and burnt skin, while the smaller man at his side was like a remora to a great white shark.

"Cheers," Kai said and clinked glasses with them, gulping down the liquid in hopes of easing the tension writhing inside. "I'm assuming those aren't your given names."

Pebble left his drink on the wood table and ignored the question. "I thought Elysium left Asphodel to fend for ourselves—in other words, to be the buffer meal for any hungry myths."

Kai set down his drink with a heavy *clunk*. "Myths aren't Asphodel's only problem." He sucked in his lips, trying to recapture the words for twofold reason: it antagonized and he didn't know the depths of their problems. He continued, "But we are part of myth control, here to deal with a myth."

Rather than argument, Pebble was concerned. "Is it about the disappearances?"

"Or the ruins?" Rock followed up.

Kai was relieved by the lack of confrontation, but he still grimaced; he wanted to give them hope, and yet, he couldn't. "Not the ruins. It's only two of us, and this is my sister's first day as myth control."

"We'll try to help where we can," Cara said.

"That's what Elysium keeps promising." Pebble gulped down the rest of drink in a single draft, wiping his lips with disgust. "And here we are, as always."

"I'm sorry," Kai said, trailing his finger on the condensation of the glass, collecting the liquid on his skin until it pooled and fell faster. "I'd say I want to help, but you've heard that before. So, I'll just ask, what do you want me to do?"

"Change the weather," Pebble said.

Rock smirked. "Be fair. He's not a god."

"The gods can't seem to change it either," Pebble said. "Or worse...."

Rock's smirk died on his lips. "Be careful."

"...they don't care." Pebble took Rock's drink, who did nothing to stop him. "All the gods do is watch us suffer like Elysium."

Rock crossed burly arms. "Pessimism doesn't accomplish anything. Optimism won't either, but it's a lot more fun."

"Definitely," Kai said. "Hope is a thread leading us from the present to the future."

Pebble drank more. "Hope is a rope tangled around us, keeping us from actually acting."

"Maybe you should get untangled," Cara said.

"You wouldn't understand, would you?" Pebble said. "You have it easy in Elysium. There's jobs and water. When things go wrong, you decide eight of the nine councilmembers, voted by a ninth of the people."

Cara said, "You're right, I don't understand. But I want to. Then, maybe I can help."

"Elysium is not so much a heaven as you'd expect," Kai said. "If anything, I think Asphodel and Elysium can be the same and better for it one day."

Rock smiled with gentle eyes. "I hope you mean that, hero."

"He does," Cara said. "His wife lived in Asphodel. The council sent her to Irkalla."

Rock's smile became a shadow. "Sorry to hear that."

Kai set down his drink; instead of lifting his mood, he seemed to be sipping reality. "Maybe you could help us? I wasn't expecting that having people listen would be so difficult."

"Trust is hard," Rock said. "For most people, it can't be bought."

"He bought yours," Pebble said.

"No, I just trust that most people are good." He chuckled. "The drink was extra. And now, it's time to pay that back."

Observing the room, Rock waited for a lull. There was tiredness, rumor, and sadness, which lay ready to swing either into raucous or joyous riot, bubbling by the pace of drink and wavering temperament.

Rock banged his drink on the wood, breaking noise into silence. "A hero from Elysium finally wants to help us. I'm no fan of Elysium, you all know that. But there's a difference between a group and an individual. Does it hurt to listen a moment when he offers to help?"

The room softened, and there were murmurs of ascent, spurred by drink, curiosity, and the words of someone they knew. Rock urged Kai up and gave him a reassuring smile.

Kai realized the selfishness of his goal, and as Rock gave him this opportunity, so did Kai hope that one day, he could help these people. "It's a hard time to have faith in anything. I know I'm someone you don't trust, a stranger from Elysium. And although droughts and myths may not affect us all the same, it is something we must face together. The only way we will survive is if we help each other. I'm trying to get rid of a myth, but I need your help to find it."

"Cheers," Rock said, adding a bit of good-nature, sending the room tipping from skepticism to belief. Glasses raised and drinks drunk, lowering the final few barriers.

"Tell us," one person said. "What kind of myth?"

Kai thought of the jade lion but realized it was too dangerous. Instead, he thought of the first figure he picked up. "A bird." He made an expansive motion with his arms. "A really big bird." He paused, not having thought the specifics through, but knowing they were vitally important. Details were important; people clung to details, imagining until they became real and filled in the general. "It's an owl with two green claws sticking out its expansive wings. It's a big beast, large enough to carry two people. But despite size, it's not violent, it's good-natured. Wise, too. You know, like an owl."

"If it's that big, how come it's so difficult to find?"

Kai sipped his drink, stalling. "It burrows. Probably dug its way under an abandoned building."

"I knew it," said a rather loud man, peeking out his booth at the story. "There's that big mound over on Third Street. I've been tellin' ya'."

"Maybe he's right," said another onlooker, latching on to the idea. "There is a big construction site with suspicious marks. Could be a spot for you to start."

"Thank you," Kai said. "I'll make sure it doesn't bother anyone and take it out of the city."

As he sat, the crowd sipped at their drinks with greater cheer, and a happier mood prevailed. Rumbling resounded and grew with momentum, rolling into further rumor, which waved across the room, undulating and splashing side to side. And the more Kai heard, the more Kai smiled.

Kai's myth had escaped into the crowd. His job was done. There were certain people, places, and times where myths could take form. Kai hoped this concoction worked. More than hope, he directed his loss and pain towards this one purpose.

Yet, he didn't dwell, recoiling from grief like fire. Unsure how long it would take, Kai enjoyed the simple moment of being welcomed into Asphodel, this pub, and this booth. Rumors incubated, fueled by imagination and drinks, while Kai and Cara talked and drank with Rock and Pebble for a while, which distracted them from painful past and danger ahead. It remained on Kai's mind, but he disallowed it from affecting their mood. Such small moments were the shine before looming darkness.

As Kai laughed, though, he couldn't help realizing how different this was from what he imagined. It was not the glorious repeated dream of joining Sophia in Asphodel, but it was certainly better than he expected when he embarked. Things had gone so well, he decided to finish his drink—he needed the courage. If the jade-seller was right, to get water, he would need to go near the ruins. But as the golden atmosphere affected him, he was optimistic that would not be the case.

SIX

THEM

OPTIMISM MET REALISM, and they didn't get along. Each water-well Kai visited was closed, the daily quota, already taken. Desperation rose with the day's heat until Kai had no other choice.

While Cara went for food and supplies, Kai braved the area closest to the ruins.

Others avoided it, fearing, or maybe, feeling, what lay nearby. As ruins grew, people fled until a literal line in the sand was drawn. Undisturbed dust covered a bridge. No one crossed. No one's gaze did, either. People pretended the ruins didn't exist, and that repression compressed imagination into reality.

Kai had often seen the ruins from a distance and wondered what might hide there, and now that he was standing by the bridge, it didn't feel the same. From afar, imagination created a fearful place. In the daylight, it was nothing more than dusty ruins. Yet, complacency was naivety.

Almost disappointed that he did not see more, Kai left the bridge for now and turned down a side street to the final watering hole in Asphodel.

A stone, circular well centered a small square. This area did not bustle like the rest of the city, and Kai disturbed the peace. A few eyes peered at him from the houses around. When he looked back, people hid.

A woman with cardinal-red lips smiled at Kai, a friendly face—the well-operator. Her pale skin contrasted lips, and she was cleaner than most, skin barely freckled by a few flecks of dust. Despite glaring sun, she didn't wince at light. Sharp features cut through sunshine like glass.

"Do you have any water left?" Kai asked.

"Of course," she said. "They buy the quota elsewhere."

"Who?"

"First day in Asphodel? Just come from outside?" She crossed her arms. "No, you're too clean. Not one of *them*, are you?"

"Can I get as much water as I can carry?" Between the sun's glare and the destitution around, a frown buried itself on Kai's face.

"You are one of them."

"Who?"

"You'll be an owl if you keep saying that."

"I don't think I'll be an owl." Kai's thoughts turned to the task ahead. He spared a second to imagine a silvery owl again and hoped it would work—not only hoped, but believed. That was key. "Seriously, who do you mean?"

"Water-hawkers." She swept away stray black strands to get a better look at Kai. "They buy out the quota and resell it at exorbitant prices."

"How does the council let them get away with that?"

"They pay taxes. Everyone profits: the well-owners sell their stock, the hawkers make a margin, and the well-workers get bribed." Her red lips firmed violently. "Everyone profits except normal people."

Kai seethed; although he was angry at a situation, his words were directed at the woman. "How can you let that happen? Exchanging your benefit for people's suffering? Skimming their hard-earned money? It's immoral, deplorable, awful."

She smiled at his anger. "I don't sell to them, but I'll sell to you."

Rage defused. "Thank you, I guess."

A clinking, clanging echo bounced off the alleyway behind him. Through the thin space and under the lines of laundry dangling between windows that obscured the view, a couple of men approached. Kai recognized them by their voices and ducked behind the well.

The woman peered over the well at him. "What're you doing?"

"I think they're looking for me."

"What, did you escape from Elysium?" she asked.

"Yes," he said, hushed. "They want me back at my job."

"That sounds like forced labor, not a job."

"The semantics are lost on me at the moment." Kai searched for an escape and decided on another alleyway, but another man came from that direction.

The woman shrugged. "Most of the time, employers don't look for you when you quit, they just replace you. What do you do?"

"I work at myth control—those are my co-workers."

"Heroes?" She raised a brow. "Get in the well."

Not needing any more invitation, Kai vaulted the lip of the rough, hot stone. He reached for the rope and descended. The well was a tepid, humid sauna, and Kai shimmied down with less care than he might've otherwise. A wood lid covered the hole and Kai was left in filtered darkness. Slits between planks projected three slicing beams of light on the damp stone near him.

In the cooler air, Kai found relief from the torturous heat above while his muscles burned. He kicked at the rope and tried to loop it around his foot, but it was impossible. With the heavy bucket submerged in water below, the rope kept taut. His hands started to slip and Kai struggled. A dark fall gaped underneath. Swaying and swinging, he clung harder. His feet found a protruding brick and he leaned over to it like a mountain climber, resting and relieved. There, he listened and hoped.

"I'm sorry gentleman," said the well-operator. "We're out of water for the day."

"Have you seen a man, about this tall, skinny, and looking quite out of place? Like he might belong in Elysium?"

"If only, then I might've gotten more money out of today's quota."

"Well, if you see anything suspicious, let the authorities know."

"Anything suspicious besides three heroes in Asphodel?"

The disdain was evident. "Go crawl back into your hovel and keep your comments there."

"Sorry ma'am," said a different hero. "He doesn't mean to be so rude. The heat gets to his head. We've been searching and the family is very worried. It's a shame you don't have any water for us. Maybe you can go over the quota and we'll pay extra?"

"I just work the well. I don't own it. It's not my job to make those decisions, you'd have to ask my boss about that."

"Bill us later," said the disdainful voice. The lid peeked open, flooding light over Kai.

The lid slammed. "It's my job to defend the well and make sure nobody steals. And when I say nobody, I mean nobody."

"It's not worth it," said the nicer voice.

"Fine, there are other wells that'll take our money."

"Apologies again, ma'am. Remember, if you see anything, let us know."

"Of course."

Angry footsteps rattled the wood lid. When they were gone, the woman removed the lid and turned a wheel, dragging the bucket and Kai out the well with startling strength.

There was cold resolve in the woman's warm, brown eyes. "Your co-workers look more like heroes than you do, but they certainly don't act it."

Kai dusted himself off. "Their job doesn't change who they are, like anyone, even heroes can be jerks. It's possible they're more prone to it than others."

"I hope you're doing something worthwhile if you're leaving heroism to them."

"I'm trying to be a real hero—I mean I tried before, but I'm trying to fix things rather than just…." He stumbled into silence.

"The most dangerous people are those who think they're a hero. Then, everything they do is heroic."

"I'm just trying to save my wife."

She pursed her lips and nodded. "Let's get you some water, then."

"Thanks," Kai said with a smile. "And thanks for saving me. I don't know how to repay you."

"You could pay me extra."

"Really?"

"No," she said, her ruby-lined lips sarcastic. "I don't want money for doing the right thing. Just remember it next time somebody needs your help."

She filled waterskins, careful not to let a drop spill to the devouring dust. A price was agreed and paid. The transaction past, Kai had to get a move on to meet Cara. He had taken too long and she would be waiting for him; he could already hear the jab he would take for being late.

Kai shook the woman's hand, wanting to thank her again. "I won't forget this and I won't forget you…"

"Grace."

"Kai."

Grace heaved the wood lid onto the well with a *thud*. "I've heard of you before."

"You have?"

"You're a famous hero, aren't you?" She padlocked the lid down.

"Not anymore."

"Just another person in Asphodel." She winked and walked away. "Not suspicious at all."

"Where're you going?"

"I sold the quota and more for the day," Grace said. "Time to go to my other job."

She left down an alley and Kai went a different way, heading towards the agreed meeting point with Cara. Quite opposed to the affliction of heat, the warm feeling within Kai was pleasant and infectious. He thought himself too happy for the loss he had experienced; he should've been sad, lost, or angry without Sophia. Yet, here he was, unable to do anything but share a thankful smile with everyone he came across. After expecting to fail so soon, he was hopeful because of the goodness of a stranger. He wanted to pass that on. Was that so wrong? It couldn't be, but it still felt like it was—grief rattled at his good mood.

The bustle of the city distracted Kai and he maneuvered swinging tent poles, carts, and the hordes of people. Immersed in an instinctual rhythm, Kai reached the meeting place with smile intact.

At the construction site, heat haze rippled above soft dirt. As he walked, feet sunk and slipped in the loose terrain. Around him, metal poles were strewn about half-buried, reflecting like powder-dusted mirrors.

The construction was unlike what Kai encountered in Elysium. No tall spire ascended to the clouds, brick and gold were absent, and the walls were dust-stained. The building was a simple thing. Utilitarian. No complex scaffolding held it up; instead, it was merely there, placed with hope that it would hold and tied together by dried grass until a more permanent solution could be found.

Sweat beaded down Cara's brows and cheeks. She looked rather cross at the heat, and it killed her humor. "You're late."

"Almost ran into some co-workers."

Kai gave her some water, and she cooled. "Outwitted them?"

"Got lucky and met a good person." Kai gulped. He saw what he expected, but it still made him apprehensive. "I think it worked."

At the base of the building was a hole dug for plumbing. Shovel marks scarred the earth. Then, more recently, dirt had been dug by something else—claws. On one side of the hole, oblong scratch marks buried in the earth like a bear's scratches on a tree.

Cara nodded. "Not regretting it now, are you?"

"Do you have the meat?"

She brought out a piece of beef, wrapped in banana leaf. The wrapping crinkled as it changed hands. Under the yellow sun, the meat was one of the few things untainted. Red-brown, through and through.

Cara handed him a short rope. "You got water, I got everything else we need."

"Maybe you should be in charge." Kai wrapped the rope around the meat and tied the sinews tight. "I just hope the meat's attractive enough to lead the owl out."

Cara handed him a stick. "Do owls eat cows?"

"No, but only because they're not big enough." The meat dangled from the stick, swaying slightly as Kai moved.

"This one might be."

A voice yelled over the desolate yard. "What're you doing here?"

Panic. Kai's heart leapt and he did, too. It was too soon to fail. Too soon to be caught. He couldn't fight his co-workers.

"Li?" Cara bounded across dirt, feet cratering and sliding in sand. She wrapped arms around her twin. "You scared me."

Li squirmed out the hug. "Sorry, I guess."

Helene followed, quiet and graceful as a cat after its prey. In the daylight, her usual dark hair turned two shades lighter.

"What're you doing here?" Kai asked.

Li's tone was flat. "I asked first."

"We're here to deal with a myth." Kai was vaguely suspicious of even his own brother. It wasn't intentional, but Li had a manner that was off-putting at the best of times and was especially so now. "How did you find us?"

"I followed the rumors." In the heat of the day, Li's words were cold. "You left. I decided to follow."

"*We* decided to follow," Helene said with annoyance. "Or I did, and he insisted on coming too."

"But how did you get into Asphodel?" Cara asked with a slight frown, as if afraid of the answer. "You didn't…?"

Li shook his head. "I told the truth."

Cara shaded her eyes from the brilliant sun with her hand, and still, her eyebrow raised.

Mischief made Li grin. "You went missing. You were after a dangerous myth and we were oh-so-worried. We had to come look for you. People will believe anything if you tell it the right way."

Kai disapproved. By trying to find him, Li and Helene had almost caused him to be caught—that must've been why the heroes were here. Kai, however, couldn't say anything. Not with the way Cara looked at her twin. Kai mellowed. He might've been uneasy with his brother, but regardless of their differences, Cara and Li were twins, and Kai supposed that had to count for something. They were sun and shade—light and lack of. Even if Kai could not understand Li, he still cared for his brother.

"I'm glad you're here," Kai said, half-lying.

Li brushed his shoulders off. "Cara is glad I'm here and you're not. That's okay."

Cara said, "Kai is happy to have you here. He's just not as enthusiastic as I am."

Li grunted non-committedly.

"I hope there's enough room," Cara said. "Our escape is only big enough for two people and now we have four."

"What escape?" Helene asked. "An escape from me?"

Kai shrugged, not nearly apologetic. "A myth that'll carry us over the wall."

"And what was it supposed to be?"

"An owl with jade claws."

"I heard something different." Helene pointed. "I think it did, too."

A head peeked out of the hole, and it was certainly not an owl. A fowl, maybe. A rooster, exactly. Or maybe, not so exactly.

The creature's chicken head was bigger than Kai. The crest on its head was a royal purple and plumage reflected the color of the sun—a blazing, blaring yellow. Beady eyes darted out the hole, a black eclipse on a background of burnt orange. The creature struggled, barely fitting through the hole, and to break free, it scrabbled and twisted. Dust clouded in plumes.

The bottom half escaped even stranger. Where colors had been different, appendages were another matter. It had long, long legs like the chicken had been placed on pinkish scaled stilts—ostrich legs.

As the creature emerged, the stilts were muscular and the beast towered to the second floor of the construction. Besides the daunting task of getting on the uplifted chicken, it was also a dangerous one. Instead of tailfeathers, this myth had arching talons like elephant tusks. The tail-feather-claws were speckled with dust and dirt from where they had dug up the earth, rending and tearing ground. As the creature flecked up its tail like a peacock, the points glinted in sunlight.

Bony backside talons crashed down and pierced earth. With the redness of the dirt and the ivory claws, it was almost surgical—not exact and clean as one might imagine, but bloody and breaking.

"Why is it like that?" Kai asked. "This isn't how it's supposed to work."

"Try telling it that," Cara said.

"That's not an owl, that's a fowl," Li said. "Don't you love it? Myths are supposed to be something fantastic and this one turned out mundane."

Cara glared at him. "This is your version of mundane?"

"It's two animals mixed together, what's so inventive about that?" Li asked.

Kai dangled the meat, swinging with nervous shakes. Unlike the snow leopard, this myth had not gone to plan. Now, only a stick separated him from the bait and the unknown.

Helene smiled. "That's not long enough."

"It'll be fine," he lied.

"We can only hope it's as dumb as you look right now." Helene backed away. "This is going to be quite the show."

Kai addressed the creature. "Roostrich? How about some food? Maybe we can come to some agreement."

A sharp beak swiveled towards Kai and the ostrich legs gouged the ground, exploding dirt like a sandstorm.

HOOT.

Unlike the snow leopard, Kai did not understand this myth.

"Of course that's the only thing like an owl," he murmured. Unwilling to give up, he was convinced that the sound must've been like the snow leopard's threatening growl—untranslatable. "Can you understand me?"

HOOT.

"What're you expecting?" Li asked. "Chickens don't talk."

"They don't make owl noises, either," Cara said.

"It should be able to reason with me," Kai said. "That's how I deal with myths."

Li chuckled. "I know that look, it's about to attack."

Apprehension turned to worry—this myth was not civilized enough to speak. Kai's overconfidence burst. He had assumed his family's safety, thinking he could protect them as he had protected others.

Kai waved the lure, and the roostrich remained focused on him. "Get into the construction above its reach."

"And if it can fly?" Cara asked.

Kai frowned. "I'm more worried it can't."

The roostrich ruffled its feathers, picking at the plumage of the yellow belly with a stiff neck. Satisfied, it snapped its beak.

The sound clenched Kai's heart with adrenaline. The fear at facing death became an undercurrent as calm and clarity surfaced with Kai's practice at meeting monstrosities.

As the others snuck away, the bird swiveled, debating between Kai and his family. Worried, Kai forgot about looking ridiculous; that was only a concern if he managed to survive. He kicked up dust and whipped the stick around, dancing to make him seem like appealing prey. He even squawked and hooted; if the creature would not speak his language, he would speak the creature's.

The monster solely focused on the stupid easy prey—Kai. The others made it to a ramp unimpeded, heading up the construction site.

The roostrich's beak seemed to grin at the prospect of food. Tailfeather-claws rattled against each other. Black, empty pupils stared into Kai's soul and his inclination was to avoid the soulless eyes, but he stared back anyway. His wavering legs wanted to go weak. However, he took a deep breath and exhaled ferocity. There was no going back, no backing down. Failure to escape—whether from this bird or from Asphodel—was death to him.

The roostrich stepped with backward-bending knees, slow and steady as if it could creep on petrified prey. The second step, more substantial. Dinosaur-like feet imprinted in the dirt deep.

Kai sprinted.

But his feet sunk in soft sand, too. The bird followed. Chaos was quiet. Bird and man struggled and stumbled in the terrain. Dirt plagued them both. Without traction, they accelerated by will alone, a struggle against muscles, gravity, and each other, a classic chase of prey and predator— inherited, innate instinct—blank besides images. The goal, a ramp.

The shadow loomed. Funneling to a blur, the distinction between chaser and chased narrowed.

Doubt cramped Kai; he knew he'd never make it. The ramp was too far. Each second made it further, not closer. Meanwhile, the thoughtless bird reeled him in, inevitable as a sunset of his life.

Kai slipped.

Knees cratered. Elbows skidded. Scraped. A shadow fell over him, as the sun was eclipsed by the oncoming bird. For once, shade was not appreciated.

Kai scrabbled and expected a beak to lift him.

HOOT.

The sound was devastating.

A scramble. Kai made it to his feet and ran. Somehow, he made it up the ramp unscathed. Thankful for luck, he looked over his shoulder and found that was not what saved him; rather, he was lucky to have someone on his side—Cara.

Clinging to the roostrich's back, Cara had big fistfuls of plumage in her hand. The creature twisted, but was unable to reach Cara as it bucked and flapped its stubby wings.

"If it hurts her, I'll strangle it," Li said, leaning on a railing above the bird with a relaxed pose and eager eyes.

"She's crazy," Kai said, joining Li and Helene on the construction. "We have to help her."

"Let's join her, then," Li said.

The roostrich was running around like—bar the pun—a chicken with its head cut off, circling the construction with crazed energy and following its own footsteps around and around at dizzying pace.

As it passed, Li leapt and landed on the bird's back. Helene jumped on the next loop. Angrier and no less slowly, the bird came around again and Kai vaulted the banister.

He crashed onto the bird. Fingers clutched for handholds, surprisingly warm, heated by body and sun. Feathers were smooth, except where stiff bristles jabbed. Under Kai, the muscles of the bird tensed and stretched and fought.

Before the creature could settle and peck them to death, Kai crawled, stick still in hand, towards the bird's neck. He whipped the stick, thrown off balance. The smack of meat made the beak snap in response, changing the roostrich's course in that direction, distracted.

An impromptu plan—Kai swung the stick to direct the roostrich's path. It was imperfect. The creature bucked and twisted with renewed fury, sometimes ignoring directions, but Kai did the best he could.

After a few loops, Kai jockeyed the roostrich in a suitable direction, but rather than being able to finesse their way out the construction site, it was a bit blunter.

Ostrich feet crashed through fence like brambles.

The bird ran onto cobblestone streets. People screamed. Wind rushed by. In chaos, the bird stopped bucking, startled by stone underfoot, trying to zigzag around goods, tents, and the parting, yelling hordes. The roostrich was surprisingly nimble. Four passengers clung on while the bird swung around corners like a ship leaning in a hurricane. Windows zoomed by. Clotheslines snapped on the bird's chest. The quake of a fat bird pounding down the street made people hide under doorways. Those in the beast's path leaped to the safety of brick buildings in a desperate lunge like a running of bulls.

Through mayhem, Kai tried and failed to keep calm. He peered over the side, struck by height and pace. Tracking progress was impossible. Buildings and markets and houses were indistinguishable. Each block was wood and brick and brownish-red blurs and that was all.

Until Kai saw the wall peering over houses ahead.

Over shingles and chimneys was unmoving stone, separating the city from the world.

Kai swatted at the roostrich, keeping it on track. As the wall grew taller and taller above; terror ascended with it. Kai searched for a new plan because the bird couldn't fly—it was all flap and no takeoff.

The bird ran without any plan, barreling down a central road where it could stretch its wings and run at speed. Buildings channeled them towards the end of the road, the wall looming and growing larger. Freed from obstacles, the roostrich charged, furious at failed attempts to throw its passengers and seemingly desiring mutual destruction.

"Do we jump?" Cara yelled over the buffeting noise.

"At this speed?" Kai planted his face into the feathers, away from the harsh winds that tried to eat his words.

Li was enjoying himself, sitting with a smile on his face. "Maybe it'll have a hard-enough head."

Kai hoped so, but he couldn't bear to watch oncoming doom.

The wall eclipsed the horizon. A few soldiers on the parapets parted.

For all the chaos, there seemed to be silence. An expectation of collision. Adrenaline pushed out sound. Clenched muscles tightened airways and ears. Eyes closed and waiting was terrible.

Then, the inevitable.

The roostrich burst through a stone wall without slowing.

It had been so fast, so sudden, the sound only came after. Crunching. Crushing. Crumbling.

As stones tumbled and rolled, so did ostrich legs, stumbling and faltering to nothing. The bird leaned and tilted until knees buckled and skidded.

A rooster head, colorful as sunset, dipped into the earth.

Stunned, Kai slid off the stalled bird, knees similarly buckling into the earth. When he and the others regained themselves, still shaken, they looked back.

A whole section of wall exploded out. A trail of stones followed them, splayed, ranging from boulders to pebble sized pieces. And at the end of the wreckage, the bird rested with its head stuck into the ground like an ostrich. Peaceful, almost sleeping.

Cara asked what they were all thinking. "Is it dead?"

"Like a bird hitting a window," Li said. "Neck's broken."

Cara's lips quivered. "Are you sure?"

The body lay still and unmoving. Feathers wavered in the wind. No breath passed through.

"They'll be feasting for weeks." Li motioned down a length of wall where a group of people were gathered, carrying a tall ladder towards the wall.

Cara shook her head. "That's awful, Li."

Helene frowned. "Why didn't we use a ladder?"

"I thought this would be easier," Kai said.

"Well, you were wrong."

"The bird wasn't very smart, but it was kind of beautiful," Kai said. "If you have a time machine, we can go back and fight the soldiers instead of using the bird."

"What do we do now?" Li asked, ever-pragmatic.

"You and Cara are going back." Kai's head throbbed from the rush and collision. A headache muddled his thoughts, but he knew what had to be done. They had to do as Helene suggested and deal with myths in his stead. That was the only way he could justify leaving.

"We're not going back," Cara said, livid. "We came to help you."

"I can't stop Helene from coming with me," Kai said, brushing off a bit of dust from his hair as if that would clear his head. "But I'm your brother and I can't—"

"You can't tell us what we can and can't do." Cara flushed with insult. It was the rage of a good-natured person and darker for it.

Helene came between them. "Someone needs to stay and deal with the myths."

"Exactly." Kai took a deep breath. "And the rest of the family."

"We're not children." Cara's anger was more sadness than rage. "We won't be treated like it. I risked my life to save you and now you want to leave us behind?"

"You're not children." Kai smiled at Cara. She was no longer the little girl he adored, nor the rebellious teen he had tolerated, she was grown and he admired who she had become. "It's for that very bravery that I need you to stay behind. You and Li must protect the family and do my job while I'm gone. You might be better at it than I was—your concern for the bird shows you have what it takes to not only face myths, but also empathize with them—and that is far more important. There's still a lot you have to learn, but you can talk to Rollo. He helped me when I first started, and he's the only one of my co-workers that's the right sort of hero."

"It's what you wanted, Cara," Li said. "Maybe between the two of us, we can fill Kai's shoes."

"It won't be long before you outgrow them," Kai said, confident they could balance each other.

Cara collected herself. She bit her lip, eyes on her twin and taking a deep breath of midday heat. She gave her bag of supplies to Helene. "Don't let Kai do anything stupid."

"That's an impossible task," Helene said, smiling with comradery. "You have one, too—watch out for your twin."

Li snorted. "I heard that."

"Good," Helene said. "Remember the talk we had earlier, Li."

"How're we going to explain this?" Cara pointed at the mess they had made of the ancient wall.

Without the rush, the wall appeared less dominating. It was feeble, looking more like placed rubble than a solid barrier. No binding held it together, rocks were simply stacked and stabilized by weight, ready to tumble. It was more symbolic than functional.

"We'll figure it out," Li said, unworried. "After all, we did what we're supposed to—deal with a myth. And wait one second." He cleared his throat and with an over-exaggerated tone, said, "Kai, please don't go." He grinned. "There, we tried to stop Kai from leaving."

"Was that necessary?" Kai asked. "Couldn't you have lied?"

"I'd prefer to, but Helene said it's easier to stretch the truth."

"What else did you tell him?" Kai asked, suspicious.

Helene shrugged.

Guards on top of the still-standing sections of wall began to move towards the gap.

"You better go back," Kai said and gave Cara a hug. More gingerly, he hugged Li, who returned it stiffly.

"Don't worry." Cara beamed at the faith placed in her. "We'll make you proud."

Together, Cara and Li walked away, shrinking from Kai and back towards the mess he'd made.

"I already am proud," Kai whispered. He turned to Helene. "Why don't you go back, too?"

"Not a chance."

"Why not?"

"Why would I?" She led the way past the dead roostrich. "Neither of us like it, but our fates are tied together. Helping you helps me."

"Why do I think that's the only truthful thing you've said?" Kai followed. He was not unwelcome to company, ceding to stubbornness, but he was also wary of what she would want in return for her help.

The world ahead flattened. Tree stumps left mounds of greying wood, which were the only remnants of an old forest. Where stumps were cleared, croplands struggled, lining the path to nowhere. The fields ahead were not stretches of green and gold rustling in the wind; rather, these were bleached and stiff.

The horizon was a grand mirage, wavering in the sunlight. As Kai aimed towards uncertainty beyond, he knew there would be more than drought to withstand, more than walls to destroy, more than men to escape, and more than monsters to make. In the empty horizon, there lay more opportunity and danger than anywhere else.

Kai disturbed a dusty path. Energy and elation welled by making it this far. He was on the path to Sophia, leaving the past behind.

If only all steps were as easy as the first.

SEVEN

NOT ALL INTENTIONS

EVERY STEP ONWARDS was harder than the last. Kai and Helene walked for hours without a word. Tension was the only thing that tied them together.

Around them, fields browned. Decay became desolation. Beauty accompanied it. Sun dipped into the oncoming golden waves of sand dunes. Shadows grew over the copper land, and the sky streaked purple.

Their pace slowed. Kai appreciated the respite from heat. Yet, soon, heat would plunge to frigid frost and impending darkness would impede their progress. Night was a more solid wall than those they left behind and what lurked in the unknown was more dangerous, too.

The path split about a rocky encampment, and a copse of grey trees cast long shadows. Kai stopped, uncertain. With no map or sign in sight, there was no way to tell which was the way he wanted—there were no convenient directions to Sophia.

When there was only one path, Kai couldn't be lost; however, at the first obstacle, he realized how unprepared he was. Even if Irkalla was east, was it northeast? Southeast? He was willing to search every corner of the world, travel as far as his feet could carry him, but an uncertain path towards a certain purpose left room for doubt. In hesitation, there was too much time to think. Too much time to feel. A sneaking dread that he might falter and fail crept in.

Helene's glare fell upon him. "Well?"

Kai nodded towards the rocks. "We can escape the wind there. Tomorrow we can argue on which way to go."

"It's a good thing there's only one shelter. Otherwise, we'd argue about that, too."

Kai mumbled loud enough that she might hear him, "Or we could go our separate ways."

The last steps to the outcropping were the hardest. With a destination in sight, legs struggled. The circular outcropping guarded against the ever-chillier wind. So long after muscles had known rest, it hurt more to stop than keep going.

A glow came into view around the boulders—a campfire. They were not alone.

Two men sat on a plateaued rock. Kai tensed, prepared for a fight at his unintentional intrusion.

"Welcome. I'm Al."

It was not the response Kai expected. Good nature bellowed from a bubbling belly to words and the man's demeanor. Al introduced himself as one of those people with effervescent light and infectious energy, holding onto warmth and offering it to all they come into contact with like a warm stone.

"Come sit down," Al said and patted the uncomfortable-looking rock, scooting closer to his companion.

At the genuine welcome, Kai's hesitance thawed by the trust Al showed to let him and Helene join without question. The flattened boulder was cut crescent about one side of the fire, and under Kai's backside, the rock was rough and uneven. He stayed a few feet from the two men, and the excitable fire danced in front of him, burning tinder and gnarled bark, sparking and popping with dry wood. Heat was exuberant. Despite Kai's feet roasting nearer, it was his forehead that felt the brunt of the fire. Still, after the boiling day, no sweat remained. Kai drank from a waterskin and offered a sip to Helene; however, she refused and stayed standing.

"I'm Tom," said the other man. He had a reserved smile that was little lip and all teeth. Polished would be the right word for both the smile and the man. From teeth to hair to clothes, everything was in line, despite nature's best attempts to skew it. Next to Tom, there was a medical bag, organized with white wrappings and little tinctures. He pressed a gauze pad against Al's robust arm and a bit of blood glistened through.

Tom's eyes refocused on the wound. The focus saw life as serious, the injury, too; it was not a life-threatening injury by any means, but by the intensity Tom paid to his patient, he made it seem so. When Al moved, Tom moved with him, in tune with fidgets and twitches.

Tom wrapped the arm and satisfied, he got to other matters. "Who are you?"

"Just some travelers. I'm Kai and this is Helene. How'd you get that wound?"

"Oh, this? This is nothing." Al shrugged and watched the playful fire with the delight of a child. "I fell."

Tom, the doctor, clarified, "He hit a branch."

"How do you fall into a branch?" Kai asked.

"You know. I'm just dumb sometimes." Al spoke with Kai as if they had known each other a long time. "We were running and I slipped down a dune. The tree was half-buried."

"Why were you running?" Helene asked, dark eyes absorbing firelight.

"We were being chased." Tom kept his words sharp and pointed like the medical tools in his bag. "You came from Asphodel?"

Kai nodded.

"Running from something?"

"Aren't we all?" Kai managed a faint smile before it faded in the shadows. "We're heading east to Duat in hopes of finding Irkalla."

Al laughed, hearty and full. "Irkalla? Sure. Why don't you just ask someone to slit your throat and save time?"

Tom tutted.

"Sorry," Al said. "But he's either lying or joking."

Kai watched shooting embers launch from the fire, burst, and extinguish in the cool night air. "Afraid it's neither."

"A death-wish, then." Al prodded at his wound and winced.

"Don't do that." Tom put the remaining wrappings in his bag and zipped it. "For what possible reason would you try to go there?"

"Love," Kai said.

Tom tensed. "Not searching for your child, I hope?"

"No." Helene laughed, echoing around the boulders. "Hell no. Kai and I? What a kid we'd make."

"You're friends?" Al asked.

"We're married," Kai said. "Or, we were."

Tom threw a bit of kindling into the fire. "Sounds complicated."

"Yeah." Kai's melancholy enveloped with the darkness. He fought against it with hope just as the solitary fire flickered at the shadows. "We're going to find my second wife."

"Ah," Al said, and then, with more dismal a tone, repeated, "Ah."

"See," Tom said to Al. "Love makes you do stupid things."

"And where would we be without it?" Al asked.

"In less pain."

"A worthwhile pain." Al returned to Kai, intrigued. "Your first wife is helping you find your second?"

Kai glanced askance at Helene. "She convinced me to go, actually."

"Either she still loves you or she must be very special."

"Thank you, I am special," Helene said, flames twinkling in her smile.

"Why would you risk your life if you don't love him?" Tom asked.

Helene's smile died on her lips. She fiddled with loose strands of hair that had gone astray during their journey. "Just because I don't love him doesn't mean I want him to be unhappy."

Kai inspected her and realized he didn't recognize her; rather, he recognized who she acted as. "We seem to be tied together. Helping one of us helps the other."

"I couldn't agree more," Helene said.

The wind howled. Purple-black sky loomed. Drawing closer to the fire, the group closed in, and despite initial hesitations, there was no doubt of comradery, as a collective enemy—nature—threatened them all.

Kai shivered at night's caress as it seeped through the rocks. "Why are you going to Asphodel? Pardon the assumption, but you both look like you're getting along fine. Nice clothes, nice equipment."

"We go back and forth between Asphodel and Duat," Tom said with a professional sternness.

"Then you must know the way over the sea?" Kai was relieved that they might be able to point him in the right direction.

"There's waves where you're going, but I doubt a boat will be of any use." Al chuckled. "You could row, but you won't get very far."

Kai said, "I thought there was a vast sea between Asphodel and Duat? Unless all the stories about sea gods fighting happened on land?"

"Do they not talk about it in Asphodel?" Al asked.

"Talk about what?"

"The sea has dried out." Al pursed his lips, and as he said this, he swept his view across tired faces and, with his bandage flexing at the tension of thought, came to a decision. "You'll never make it across alone."

"Al, we can't—" Tom stopped with a sigh. "It took us five days to cross, can't we take half that to rest? At least until you heal?"

"This?" Al rolled his sleeve over the wound. "See, it's nothing. I'm always ready for another trip. We can go with them."

"You don't have to come with us," Kai said. "I don't want you to trouble yourself on our account."

"It's no bother," Al said.

Tom frowned. "It is a bother. But I suppose we can't let you cross the swampsand without a guide."

"Swampsand?"

"What does it sound like? A sea doesn't become desert in a day. You'll see it. Hopefully, the bridge that used to cross the sea is clear."

"Just show us to the bridge, then," Kai said. This didn't feel very heroic at all. He needed directions—that much he was willing to accept—but he wanted the bare minimum of help. Saving Sophia was solely up to him. It was his failure that had gotten her into this, and it had to be him that would save her. That was the only way he could be a hero. That was the only way guilt would rest.

"If you don't want our help…" Tom said.

"Nonsense." Al shook his head. "They need our help. There's more to be wary of. Without a guide, they'll be buried by noon."

"How much is it going to cost us?" Helene asked.

"Nothing."

"Pah," Helene scoffed. "No one does anything for free."

"And you're helping your ex-husband unselfishly?" Tom asked with a sharp smirk.

At this, Helene scowled, trapped and insulted by her own words. She was stuck unable to be contrary without contradicting her stated motives.

Al ignored the negative energy, dusting it away with a natural, easy mood. "It's not my job to help, but we have nothing for Asphodel. Might as well go back to Duat. Besides, it'd play on my conscience to let you wander alone."

Kai smiled at the good-natured man. The straightforwardness brought comfort, and Kai drifted from alertness to exhaustion and ease. Still, he maintained his senses. "In any case, we should get some rest and an early start before it gets too hot. Which one of you wants to take the first watch with me?"

"Keep watch if that makes you feel better." Al yawned wide. "The nights are safe out here. No one goes wandering in the dark and the monsters like their prey scared, not sleeping. It's the daytime you have to worry about."

"No offense," Kai said. "But I'd rather keep an eye out. We don't mean you harm, but if we did, that's a very trusting strategy."

"It's a well-calculated one." Al stretched. "Tom with his puny surgical tools is more armed than you. And no offense to you either, but if you tried to strangle me in my sleep, I think I'd overpower you easy."

"That's a great reason to make them keep watch," Tom said.

"Sorry." A true, uncomplicated smile spread on Al's face. "I didn't mean it to sound so threatening. Sometimes, I'm a little too blunt."

"I'll take the first watch," Helene said. "You look tired, Kai."

Kai found no reason to argue with the truth. His muscles ached, focus wavered like the fire, and his mind was bleary and drained. "It's been a long day. Thanks."

As conversation simmered down, the constant crackle of roasting wood chattered into the night. A warm, golden aura blanketed them from a frosty desert night. Al and Tom took one side, settling into the open earth near the fire like it was the most natural thing in the world. Kai, meanwhile, was not opposed to a bit of dirt, but he had to get accustomed to sleeping on it. Underfoot, land seemed smooth, but it broke under him with pebbles and coarseness. Sand and dirt seemed soft, but lying on it, it was stiff. His body cushioned nothing, bone against stone. He understood why it was called terra firma—it was terribly firm.

Even his bag, which he thought might make a decent pillow, was surprisingly lumpy. It crooked his neck and poked into him. He gave up on it and set it aside, pulling a thin fleece from it and covering himself. Instead of the bag, his arm became a functional pillow, bicep warm against his cheek. Restless, he tossed and turned, repositioning himself, scooting further from the baking fire and back again when a bitter wind bit, closing his eyes and finding the same discomfort that distracted him during the day—thoughts of Sophia. Daydreams and yearning kept him walking during waking hours, and he only hoped that when the drifting sands of sleep carried him away, she would be waiting in his dreams.

However, after much anticipation, he sunk into a deep, dreamless sleep, only to wake what seemed like a moment later.

The fire was still burning. His breath frosted. A campfire-winter night. Nose and fingertips tickled in crisp air, but the rest remained pleasantly warm. Eyes remained shut, aware of the glow of firelight and wanting to drift back to the sweet tranquility of amber sleep.

A rustle. The amber petrified in his veins. Something was nearby, something searching his pack. He was sure of it.

He froze between fight and flight. Not wanting to startle the scavenger, Kai did not confront his alarm. Dread grew into caustic terror. Curiosity at this mysterious danger forced him to act opposed to better judgment. He threw off the fleece, rolled over, and sleep-stuck eyes pried open, uncertain if they wanted to see reality.

"Helene?"

She was just as startled and released Kai's bag. "Kai?" A calm, uncaring demeanor regained itself. "I was looking for water."

"Don't you have some?" he whispered.

"Mine's still hot. I was hoping yours would be cooler. Wishful thinking, I suppose."

"It's right there." Kai pointed at his bag. "I can see it from here. Just leave it away from the fire and it'll cool."

"Ah, right in front of my eyes." She chuckled. It was surprisingly convincing. "The fire's playing tricks on me. Thanks."

She sipped from the waterskin.

Kai struggled and sat, stiff from sleeping on what plants called bedding. "If you can't even see that, maybe it's better if I take over the watch. I'm up anyway, get some rest."

She yawned, as if the reminder of sleep made her realize tiredness. "Alright."

She set the water away, stretched, and lay down, taking his fleece and sleeping on her side, resting her back against the rocks. She did not toss and turn, and after a minute, her breathing slowed and tension released. Steady breath and a throbbing fire glowing, Helene's hair varied auburn and chestnut with shadows. Her face relaxed and became gentle. Kai smiled at her as she slept—everyone looked more innocent as they slumbered. Al and Tom looked similarly peaceful. There was a bit of jealousy in seeing everyone so restful and tranquil; however, Kai felt quite content by the fire, staring out into the dark night of dreams.

The fire danced at a brisk wind. Goosebumps rose on Kai's arms. Seeking refuge, he dug hands into his pockets.

Something pricked him—the familiar prick of a feather quill.

He withdrew. At the reminder of the phoenix feather, his eyes swung with a gust of suspicion to Helene's sleeping figure and distrust haunted the darkness.

EIGHT

THE PASSIVE-AGGRESSIVE HERO

CARA KNOCKED THREE TIMES at a sturdy oak door. The noise barely faded when she knocked again. Li crossed his arms and leaned back on a stucco white wall.

Above the door, a sign—'MC-HQ'—was spelled out in gold letters nailed to a wood board. Cara always imagined being called to be a hero; she would finally step out of Kai's shadow, protect Elysium, and most importantly, do her family proud. However, no one had called her here and no one answered.

Beyond the blocky building shade, the sun bore ever harder on the backs of Elysium's residents. The cracks of drought were starting to show, even here. Faces flushed red under the sun. Some still reveled in sunlight, taking it as an opportunity to go for a run, kick and throw balls in a variety of sports fields, only to retreat for a cold drink or a crisp shower. Elysium still smiled.

Li had a smile, too, but it was quite different. It was ironic. "I don't think they care enough to answer."

"Surely they must," Cara said and crossed her arms, still staring at the unmoving door. "Kai was the best hero they had."

"Yeah, but we're not Kai."

Cara knocked, if only for the echo. She knocked again to disturb whoever ignored her. She knocked again and again out of frustration and failure.

That, eventually, was heard by a passerby.

"You know they're out for lunch, right?" asked a man built like the building—upright and imposing.

"When will they be back?" Cara asked.

"Hopefully never," the man said, motioning for Cara to move.

She stood defiant. "I'll wait here."

He pulled out a key and, again, motioned to Cara. "Then I'll just stand out here and sweat with you. Or, perhaps, you want to have this conversation inside?"

Her cheeks reddened and she pivoted, moving out the way of the heroic-looking man.

"Feisty as a first instinct, they'll like you." The man opened the door. A waft of fresh, dust-free air escaped and drew them inside. Cara took his comment as a compliment and beamed as she entered. The man held the door, ready to close it while Li still stood outside. "Are you coming?"

"I suppose," Li said.

"How enthusiastic. Come on, then."

Li strolled into the shady respite, and no sweat covered his burning neck. As he passed the man, they sized each other up. Whether it was the look Li gave or the brush of a sudden breeze, the brawny man shuddered and slammed the door to keep the ballooning temperature outside.

The headquarters for heroes was hollow in the middle. Desks and bamboo-screens lined the perimeter as informal detective offices. Two palm-leaf fans spun around on the ceiling, attached with ropes and pulleys, connected like cogs.

"What's powering the fans?" Cara asked, trying to start a conversation.

The man kept walking. "We have a ninety-nine-armed Hecatoncheires in the back; he feels a bit shorthanded, but he makes do."

Cara chuckled, assuming it was a joke.

"Well…." The man let his word linger, letting it draw them further into the room. He sat at a desk and motioned for them to sit. The chairs were once red-cushioned but had become a faded pink-white where many bottoms wore at it. "Sit down and tell me all about it."

"About what?" Cara asked, sitting.

"What myth is the problem this time? What goes bump in the night? Do you want us to stab it or burn it? Slice it to pieces or chain it up?"

Cara shook her head. "We don't want any of that."

"We could've eaten chicken for days if we had something to slice it up with," Li said, standing with his hands on the shoulder of the wood-arched chair and eyes focused on the man.

"Is that a joke?" Cara was unsure at her twin's intention, but she nudged him. "Stop staring and sit down."

Li remained. "We're Kai's siblings; he's gone, but we want to take his place."

"You're Kai's siblings?" said the man with an over-excited smile. "It all makes sense now. You must be…" The smile vanished. "Oh wait, I don't care."

Half-heartedly and still hoping the man was joking, Cara said, "I'm Cara and this is Li. Kai told us we should find someone named Rollo."

"Of course he did."

"Any idea when he might be back?" she asked.

"I have a pretty good idea."

"When?"

"About a minute ago. He's sitting in this chair, and in case that isn't clear enough—I'm him."

"You're Rollo?" Cara brushed dust off her dress. "You taught Kai?"

"Indeed, and let me say, you have big shoes to fill." The tone was serious sass. "Kai didn't act as bad as the rest of these fools, but he was worse than the whole lot of them." An eye-roll. "He tried. But he should've known better. I can't blame him, though. It's a rare talent to care so much about appearing heroic that you're willing to ignore your own morals."

"And you think you're better?" Li asked, finding a hint of a real smile.

"Not half as much as I want to be."

Li sighed and sat, but something Rollo said seemed to spark his interest, and the subtle grin returned. "What made Kai so bad?"

"He was bad because he was so good."

Cara and Li cocked their heads in opposite directions.

"Be careful, your heads might crash back together like that." Rollo continued, unabashed, moving on to serious matters without pause. "The rest of the heroes—the rest of

Elysium, now—think myths create all the ills of the world. When bread goes missing, it must be gluten-fairies. When a goat is eaten, it must be goat-eating werewolves. And when people disappear, they argue whether it's a minotaur or manticore."

Cara nodded along with him, but she responded logically. "But a lot of those cases are true. That's the point of myth control."

"Right there is the problem," Rollo said in an aha-type gotcha moment. "The very thought that we should treat them like monsters."

She repeated what Kai had said, "Some are dangerous."

Rollo remonstrated with his finger. "Exactly—some. Not all. Not most, even. I used to think myths were monsters before I met Kai. He showed me the light, even if he doesn't act on it. Not all myths are evil; they come into this world scared and confused, surrounded by people who scream and run at the sight of them. They're scapegoated for everything that goes wrong until they are hunted for sport and heroism, when, really, they just need someone to hear them out."

"But we can't understand them," Cara said.

"You don't need to speak the same language to have empathy," Rollo said. "Fear, sadness, joy—you'd be surprised how alike myths and humans are."

Li laughed. "Then myths are evil—humans are."

"Evil? Actions and intentions can be evil, but I don't believe myths or humans are completely evil. Some of my co-workers put that theory to the test, though."

The door fiddled open, and in walked three men marching with merry moods. If these three men were heroes, they were the idols of joking, laughter, and playfulness. The first man was a miniature sun—round, jovial, and hard to look at, but inevitably hard to avoid—he engulfed the room with a bright, ugly smile, which was charming as a lopsided cloud. His friends, who followed and almost disappeared behind the girth, were left in his orbit. One laughed like an intoxicated dolphin might at a terrible pun. The third man was stern and taciturn; however, an uptick of the lips at the jokes indicated more amusement than the dolphin-like man.

This stern man was the first to speak with a teasing and light tone despite a scarred and brutal face. "When the skunk-monster sprayed, the crowd checked their own armpits for the stench."

The rotund man laughed, hearty shoulders bouncing along with expansive lungs, a sword jangling at his waist. He was the least armed of the men, but between unsuitably, comically, large fists and his own heft, he seemed ready to wrestle a hydra. "Disgusting. Maybe it wasn't the skunk and it was just you, Achilles."

Achilles' dolphin-pitched laughter faded at the insult, and the only impression was of immeasurable beauty under an unkempt facade. Torn, stained clothes. Curled, tussled brunette hair. Clear and complex eyes, with curves and contours of the face that reminisced of chiseled marble. It was as if sweat and disheveled clothes were to distract from natural beauty. Achilles returned the insult. "At least I'm not more massive than the masses, Ajax"

The round man frowned, taking out his sword. For a moment, it was as if he would strike, but he simply placed it on a desk, before taking a considerable load off by sitting in a creaky wood chair and bending the back as he leaned.

The scarred, stern man noticed Li and Cara sitting with Rollo. "Stop joking, both of you. We have guests." He was blunt in greeting, arriving with short, heavy handshakes. "I'm Hercules."

"*The* Hercules?" Cara asked.

"No." Rollo rolled his eyes. "But can't you see the resemblance? The nicknames don't even do them justice; they'll take care of any problem you have with heroic force."

"You're in a good mood today, Rollo," Hercules said. "That's the spirit to have with clients."

"You didn't close the door." Rollo scowled and pushed his chair back with a strong scrape and sulked past the heroes to the door. He slammed the hot air out. "They're not clients—they're Kai's siblings."

Ajax propped his big feet on a desk. "Shame about him leaving and all."

"Thought himself too much of a hero," Achilles said, his dolphin-like laugh ringing out.

"That's the problem with heroes," Rollo said, laying a muscular hand on Li's shoulder and drawing close, sharing an inside comment with him. "Real heroes act heroic instead of thinking they are."

"What're you doing here?" Ajax asked, lackadaisically taking an apple from a drawer and tossing it up. He caught it and crunched his teeth into it, before juggling it once more.

"They've come for your job," Rollo said. He walked over and caught the apple as Ajax tossed it again. "Did you check into that cyclops?"

"I will, don't worry about it."

Rollo dangled the apple beyond Ajax's reaching arm. "And the paperwork?"

"It's all done."

"Glad we have our priorities in order." Rollo tossed the apple into Ajax's cushioned chest.

Achilles leaned up against the wall, studying the twins. "I see the resemblance. But this is dangerous work, can't succeed on looks alone."

Ajax laughed heartily. "If looks were all it took, Achilles would be better at it."

Achilles frowned. "Kai looked pathetic, but he did good work and we could use the help. It makes our job easier."

"We could use the extra time to help the people of Asphodel," Rollo said with his usual passive-aggressive tone.

Hercules grinned and the crinkles of his scars made it look pained. "Leave that to soldiers. They get rations for that; the people of Asphodel won't pay us enough to risk our lives for them."

Rollo sat and leaned on the armrest with his elbow, judgmental eyes disapproving of the heroes. "And the special assignments you keep accepting?"

"I'm not going to complain to them. They pay with more than gold."

"Who's them?" Cara asked.

Despite Cara's curiosity, Li looked very bored indeed. His boredom was a special sort of frustration and rage, which turned his face sour and the air around him, too. He turned to Cara. "The council, surely."

"He catches on quick." Rollo smiled, but it faded as the other heroes took it as an opportunity to talk about themselves. Judging by Rollo's practiced look of disapproval, the other heroes' egotism often distracted them.

This distraction, however, gave Li the opportunity to whisper to Cara. "I don't think this is for us."

"We can be useful here," she hissed. "Kai told us to take his place, and I intend on doing so."

Li crossed his arms. "That's not what I meant." He shrugged, sighed, and gave in. "But if you're not worried, why would I be?"

She gave him a questioning look, then followed up, "I'm not scared."

Deathly silent, Li brooded. His dourness left a glint in his eyes, which expressed a sort of twisted satisfaction at being rebutted. But he shook the look away, and whispered an explanation. "The council is the reason Kai isn't here. I don't have any qualms with the job, but do you really want to work for them?"

Cara dimmed into a pensive frown. A 'no' ran silently from her lips.

Hercules' loud voice broke into their conversation. "If they're half as good as Kai, we'll be in good shape."

Achilles said, "Yeah, there's two of them."

With a chuckle, Ajax bit into the apple, and while his mouth was full, said, "Gonna have ta' do the pap'a'wor' for em'." He swallowed. "Who's going to teach them?"

"I will," Rollo volunteered.

"No," Hercules said. "You gave too many ideas to Kai and now he's run off."

"Hopefully, it doesn't *run* in the family." Achilles laughed at his own, terrible, joke.

A double-beat knock at the door.

"Come in," Ajax yelled, not willing to leave his seat.

The door peered open and a small man with a whiskerless face and bright-red sunburnt cheeks poked his head in. "Delivery."

"Who for?" Ajax asked, a hopeful expectation in the hearty voice.

The delivery boy fumbled around with his satchel, pulling one envelope after another, only to return them back into the bag. "It's for Li and Cara. I was told they'd be here."

"For us?" Cara asked, approaching the delivery with an unsure expression. "What could it be?"

"A summons," Li said, unmoved.

"If you knew, why did I have to come?" The delivery boy shoved another envelope back in. "I've got another nine more deliveries today. Don't waste my time with useless ones. Oh, here it is."

He threw the envelope at Cara and skedaddled. She shut the door, looking as if the boy had delivered the plague.

"What did you expect?" Li asked, still sitting. "We'll go and explain why we were in Asphodel—trying to get Kai to come back. We even took down a myth while we were there. Then, we'll talk to the council about joining myth control and we hit two targets with a single arrow."

"Not two birds?" Achilles asked with a wry smile.

"No," Li said, glaring at Achilles. "I wouldn't joke about that. I love birds."

Achilles gulped at the ferocity, his recently-shaved Adam's apple quivering.

"It's not a summons," Cara said, stuffing the letter back in the envelope. "It's a punishment."

At that, Li raised a brow, more interested than concerned. Cara, though, drowned in worry. She had already failed.

NINE

PAVE THE ROAD TO HELL

I N THE DESERT MIDMORNING, sand played the role of reaper, slicing across dunes, twisting dust in droves, and splattering over Kai, Helene, and their two new companions as they crossed a formidable bridge. Like the desert that was made up of infinite grains, this soaring flyover was built of infinite stone. Snake-trails of dust weaved side to side on the sun-faded stone road. Occasionally, a ladder like a fire escape teased an exit from the bridge's tormenting heat, but it was only from one fire into another. The desert below was torturous and inescapable.

Kai battled sweltering sunlight, sweat, and aching muscles as much as thoughts of failure and doom. A hateful existence was his mortal enemy. Contrary to the campfire the previous night, light did not protect him. It destroyed. It incinerated muscles, cleaved lips, and addled his mind.

Sand bubbled into sky as hot oil did water, tainting blue sky like his visions. To anyone else, his dreams were delusions.

Yet, Kai seized upon his end goal as tangible and in his hands. He did not see truth—he saw what he wanted.

He could not imagine what lay between him and Sophia, but he could clearly see the legendary act of venturing to Irkalla. Then, the council would forgive and forget, welcoming him back as a hero. His family would embrace him in relief, the people would congratulate him deservedly for once, and the newspapers and novelists would eternalize an epic journey for the noblest purpose—love. In Kai's vision, the image of him and Sophia was vague; they had never walked the glorious streets of Elysium together, but even dying in the desert, Kai found the hope to go on because of this joy.

Before him, the false friend of the future was already in sight, whispering sweet, sweet fictions.

Heat burned golden dreams away, and Kai realized nothing had been accomplished. Not yet.

The idea of reaching Sophia threatened to sink into the surrounding desolation, seeming increasingly impossible as his body suffered. Purpose went from lofty love to something incredibly base; he wanted a rest. Yet, he kept going, focused on making it one more step.

Helene, Al, and Tom stopped, much to Kai's relief and annoyance. They sucked in dust-thick breaths and drank hot water.

Tom moaned and spat out a bit of boiling water. "This is life—nothing but labor and toil. Struggling on and on from one moment to the next that it's hard to tell whether life is getting better or worse, until a new affliction arises and reminds us how unbearable and tiresome living is. Just sand, hellish, hard sand. Heat, too. The same sights, the same effort,

the same desert, killing us and making it torture the whole
while."

"And yet you still come back and forth with me," Al said.

Tom managed a smile. "If I didn't, you'd be dead, and
you're the only reason I'm alive, too."

"I think the desert's beautiful." Al swallowed hot water
with unaltered optimism. "The desert looks the same, but it
never is. The wind varies. Harsh and hot. Smooth and
refreshing. The dunes wave at me constantly. And under us,
we pass countless unseen lives. Bugs and snakes chase each
other. Maybe it's just me, but I like to imagine it. This isn't a
struggle—it's life, and it's ugly, but isn't that more beautiful
than nothingness?"

Tom grunted. "It looks like a whole lot of nothing to me."
He looked over the bridge and laughed. "But it looks like we
found the sea."

Kai stuffed his waterskin into his bag and rushed over to
the concrete barrier. Far below, glassy water was broken by
occasional splotches of foliage. There was a swamp in the
desert; blue sky and golden mountains in the distance reflected
on clear patches.

However, like the reflections, the water was an illusion.

"Is that glass in the sand?" Kai asked.

"From lightning storms," Al said.

Blustery winds rippled and broke the mirage. The pristine
top layer scattered. Gusts lifted, broke, and swept away glass
shards, trapping them in nets of what looked like algae but
was actually the tops of buried trees. Kai saw the name
'swampsand' as fitting—the sand swamped everything.

Kai had only seen the like in a burying blizzard. Looking
down from the bridge's vantage point, the swampsand was flat

like arctic ice, but with the perspective of distance, bright sun-seared ridges and black shadowed valleys rolled. Dune after dune, the world was an endless mountain range.

"You got my hopes up for nothing," Kai said.

Tom thrust the water back into his bag. "Hope will do you no good here. Like everything here, it turns to dust. Better to not have it than lose it."

"Why do you have to be such a pessimist?" Al asked. "If I lost hope here, it would be me that'd be lost."

"We all can't be as unfalteringly optimistic as you." Tom shook his head and chuckled. "It's astounding you don't float off like a balloon."

Hurt splayed on Al's face, but he tried to make light of it. "It's a good thing I have you to drag me down to earth then."

They stared at each other, tension balanced.

Tom cut the hot air. "I'm sorry. It's this heat."

"I know."

And as if they argued quite a few times, they went quickly from hurt to remorse. Tom took out a piece of stale flatbread, split it, and handed the other half to Al. With survival at stake, they did not let argument cloud how they needed and cared for each other.

While Al and Tom ate, Kai pulled Helene away, intent on trying to clear the air between them, too, as suspicions from the past night still lingered.

In the middle of the road, they stopped. Unsure how to start the conversation, Kai glanced at her and looked away.

"What do you want?" she asked, temper short-circuited by temperature.

"Want more water from my bag? It might be cooler." He hadn't meant it to be so passive-aggressive, but it came thoughtlessly in the heat.

"I'm fine." A wry smile. She gazed at him with a stinging, provocative gaze. "Getting along alright? You're looking a little pale."

He glared back from under sweat-laden brows. "I knew exactly how dangerous this would be. I'm not going to stop at a little heat."

"A little?"

"A lot." Kai didn't need the reminder. "But it's worth it. Are you regretting coming with me now?"

"I'm still here, aren't I?"

"Good. It's great that you're here."

"Of course." She smirked. "That's why you tried to leave without me."

Kai was unsure how he'd lost control of the conversation, but old feelings of fogged argument stirred. Anger—as general an emotion as the vast desert and specific as a grain of sand—welled to the surface.

"How long are we going to keep up this charade?" Kai's feeling burst into an inferno of hurt and suspicion. "You're risking your life being here. You'd never do that unless there was something worth more than that, and there's little, if anything worth so much to you."

"What about you? I died because of you once before." She laughed. "Worth it? No. But only because it didn't accomplish what I wanted."

"Of course not!" Livid anger scorched where Kai was sunburned, blood pumping painful in his cheeks. "The gods decided we're soulmates. We'll be reincarnated as swans and wolves and every other animal that's joined for life." He tried to spit, but nothing came. "Whether I succeed or not, you'll be happy." He laughed, spiteful and pained. "Maybe that's why the gods kept us together—you survive on my suffering."

"You never knew me." She said it with a tone more hellish than the day. "You still don't."

Her words echoed Sophia's concerns and hurt Kai more for it. Stung, he withdrew and anger quieted. "It's not for lack of trying."

A death-blow grin. "Trying is never the issue, it's succeeding."

Leaving with a forced, ironic laugh, Kai left Helene behind, but even in the expanse, he could not escape emotion. He tried nonetheless. And for a long time, he went on alone, not caring whether anyone followed.

Thoughts of Helene and Sophia, Elysium and Asphodel, Cara and Li drifted by him as the sands below.

Hubris crushed him with the heat. He had to be a hero. He had to be great. Perfect. Focused on not showing weakness, he kept going until his world went static and weakness churned his stomach and legs into mush. Like seasickness, he anchored to a banister, burning stone under his hands holding him.

Pride could only carry him so far.

A mirage made Kai's mind wander and wonder. A shadow, delusion, or more? The movement stopped and he spotted an enormous bearded lizard sunning on a dune.

Anxieties and ill-feeling anchored to this one, simple reality. The lonely creature lay without concern. Scales glittered under sunlight. Kai thought back to all the myths he had encountered. They were imagination that became truth, and had Kai not seen life in this desert, he would've thought it impossible.

That lizard settled Kai's spiraling suffering. Suddenly, his impossible dreams seemed less so. Skittering and sliding down a slope, the lizard snuck to the shade of a half-buried pine tree. Like the reptile, Kai cast himself onwards focused on a single image—Sophia.

Where pride could not move him, love did. The memory of Sophia's hand slipping from his at the fence could not be the last moment they were together.

The others caught up with him, but silenced lasted. Each mile repeated. A constant glow of sun and drifting sands passed like indistinct, brief sleep. The only thing that lasted was the bronze-gold dust underfoot, filling the zigzag cracks between stone.

But that dust tremored and shook, flying into the air by a tumult of hooves.

Tom grabbed Kai's shoulder, stopping him. "We need to get off the bridge."

Brutal neighs blasted from beyond. Tom motioned at an escape ladder, draped over the edge of the bridge. Al, Tom, and Helene went down, but Kai lingered to the last.

Curiosity, or stupidity caused by heat exhaustion, kept him with an eye on the horizon, where four celestial horses galloped across the bridge. The horses, white with manes of sun-orange, pulled a regal chariot. Standing as tall as the horses was a man, or rather, something with the shape of a man but skin of glowing, burning orange. And as much as Kai wanted to bask in the radiance, there was danger.

An animalistic tingle shot down his spine unto his legs, and in a panic, he scampered down the ladder.

At the bottom, the bridge stood grand and towering, sheltering them. However, its shadow did little for the heat, as baking gusts brought it scraping across the desert.

"Was that a god?" Kai asked.

Al shook his head. "No."

Mixed disappointment and relief in Kai's voice. "How can you be so sure?"

"Gods are not like that."

"The gods left after the war," Kai said. "Besides stories, no one would even know they're real."

Al sunk against a vast, dominating pillar that held up the bridge. "Some gods broke the truce. They speak, but what's up there doesn't."

"It's a myth?" Kai asked.

"Shh," Tom said.

Hard hooves cracked against stone, the sound soaring like a parabola as it approached. Chariot wheels bounced and bucked while the horses' gait was smooth. Then, the sound passed, drifting away.

Al said. "Myth or not, it ferries people across the bridge."

Helene picked up a pile of sand. "Then why didn't we do that? I've had enough sand."

"It ferries bodies."

Helene let the silt slip through her hands. The sound of hooves had stopped in the distance. Not faded, just stopped. A creaking-door of a re-approach followed. The myth was coming back.

"We can't risk it," Tom hissed.

Al nodded. "I know." He smiled at Kai, as the good-hearted do when they try and relay bad news. "We'll have to get away from the bridge and cross the dunes. If we didn't know the way, it'd take weeks, but we've made it through the sands before and can retrace our steps."

"Probably," Tom added.

Kai bit his cracked lip, bleeding a bit. "Probably?"

Al was suddenly soft-spoken. "The sands always shift. At its shortest, we can make it in a day."

Kai gazed up towards the myth, his confidence shaken. Usually, he would've faced the myth, but what he learned from the success with the snow leopard had been unlearned with the roostrich. "Are the dunes more dangerous than that myth?"

"Depends. There's no good choice."

Helene acted abnormally accepting to suggestion. "We'll go whatever way you think is best, Al. You know what you're doing."

A rare frown, unnatural and shallow like a footstep on a beach that could easily be washed away, crinkled on Al's face. "We'll cross the sands."

With a background of whinnies, sharp and piercing above, Al led them across the desert. Unease followed with the threat of the myth behind and what remained in their path.

Across plateaus, one misstep might send them sliding to perilous sinkholes. Sand sunk underfoot, gobbling ground sucking them in, sucking them back. The effort was unbearable. Sand penetrated the obvious places like toes and feet, but it also went as it willed, gritting between clenched teeth, invading the recesses of ears, and, worse, clinging to nose and filling lungs.

"I don't trust them," Helene whispered to Kai. "We have no idea where they're leading us. The bridge is an established path, but now we're following them to the middle of nowhere."

"Keep your wits about you."

"You agree with me?" Helene stopped on top of the dune, a steep embankment threatening on either side.

Kai looked back towards the bridge shrinking in the distance. "Most people are good. And they seem to mean well, but I don't know."

"What happened to seeing the best in people?" She followed his gaze. "What happened to the Kai I knew?"

"You mean why didn't I want to face the myth?" He didn't let her stir him into a rage again. "I don't know." He sighed. "You were right. I don't know you, that's true."

"When am I not truthful?"

"All the time."

"Maybe you know me better than I thought."

Kai kicked distractedly, but the plateau gave way. He clawed as gravity dragged him down the embankment.

A muscular arm grabbed him and hoisted him back up. It was Al. "Argue later, now's not the time."

Kai nodded and trudged after Al. Like the drought-filled desert, Kai didn't feel red-hot rage against Helene, but a simmering emptiness. There was no way to fight Helene. Nothing got to her. She was an unknowable void, and she knew how to wear him down.

He buried feeling further and kept going.

They didn't make it anywhere fast. A few hours passed without incident until they came to a stop at a crest, looking down to what looked like a raised road cutting through the dunes.

"This is new," Al said with a bit of worry. "I'm a little more lost than I thought. I usually avoid roads."

"A trader who avoids roads?" Helene's eyes widened, realizing this cheery, good-natured man was more than appeared. A resounding chuckle followed. "You're a smuggler."

"I guess we could take a road for once," Al said.

"You're a smuggler?" Kai's trust for the man fell quick, and instinctively he clenched his fists. "What's in this for you? Leading us to slavers for a quick bit of coin?"

"What kind of monster do you think I am!" Al calmed, but his face still showed hurt and insult. "Yes, I run a little contraband, but we are not what we do—just look at Tom, he's a doctor and a killer." Al's smile returned, warm and full-hearted. "Not of people, but he loves to kill a good mood." His voice still had a slight sharp tone. "Judge me for breaking the law. But you know what we transport? Medical supplies that Asphodel and Duat hoard from each other. Have I given you any reason to distrust me? As you said earlier, most people aren't bad."

"That doesn't mean they're good," Kai said, twisted at the turning of his words.

"We're strangers in the middle of nowhere, if we wanted to rob you, we would've."

Kai digested what Al said, and, more importantly, what Al had done so far, finally returning the smile.

Al laughed, apparently finding what he was about to say funny. "However—I don't think I'm going to help my case by saying this—but it might be safest to take the roads near the mining camps."

Tom exhaled deeply. "You think so?"

"You were right about the sands last time. That myth could still be out there, and I don't want you pulling another branch out my arm. I think you'd die of worry." Al was hesitant facing the road. "I'm not sure the mines are any better. I'd rather die than be in one of those pits."

Kai agreed. With such hellish heat, he couldn't comprehend such a fate, just as he couldn't bear to think of Sophia's plight in a similarly harrowing underworld. Yet, Kai did think of it, and he couldn't help but feel that he shouldn't let anyone suffer so.

TEN

REFUSE

HELENE HISSED, "COME BACK."
Tense and impatient to escape the desert and be nearer to Sophia, Kai couldn't explain why he was standing at the lip of a wretched pit. "I have to take a look."

Sand drained into a shadowy underworld; this was one of the malicious mining camps Al warned of.

An outback-orange dirt road spiraled down to where tiny figures worked. The sun was receding, dragging a shadow-blanket up the other side of the hole. Behind Kai was the road that would take him towards his goal. In the distance, colossal dunes shrunk to smooth sand-flats. Although arid dust clouds covered the vast seas of sand ahead like fog over an ocean, there was progress in sight.

Kai, however, focused on something other than that. The people below were suffering, and their plight tempted him with the selfless glory of their rescue. Liberation seemed an idyllic heroism, which whispered that this, like venturing to Irkalla, was noble. These people were faceless strangers, but maybe because of comparable underworld fates, when Kai saw them, he thought of Sophia. Kai could almost hear her whispers on the desert wind saying that he couldn't leave these people to suffer on her account.

Helene tried to pull him back from the edge. "You'll get us caught."

Kai shrugged her off. "I don't see any watchmen."

Al snuck over to them, his good mood entirely gone, destroyed by the severity of the situation. "They're in no position to fight back."

"There's shade," Helene said. "They're better off than us; I can hear my sunburn."

Al shook his head. "I'd rather be up here. Down there it's—" He shuddered.

"Hot and hellish?" Kai asked.

"At least it's not as bad as Irka—" Al stopped himself. "We should go."

Kai lingered, his fingers clawing into the dirt as he knelt, trying to get a closer look. "This isn't right."

Tom climbed the slope to the lip and said, "Nothing about this world is right. You were in Elysium and now you're suffering like us."

"He makes himself suffer." Helene scowled. "And now, me, too."

Civility between them was under a very thin guise. Kai looked away when their eyes met. "How much daylight do we have?"

Al took a sidelong look towards the sun. "A couple hours. We should set up camp soon, there's still at least another half-day to Duat, but let's make some progress."

The group filed away from the pit, yet Kai remained unable to tear himself away.

Helene turned back towards him. "We have enough problems, Kai."

"I can't leave them down there to suffer."

"You can't do anything about it," Helene said. "You were never good at dealing with men, just myths. And even that you seem to struggle with."

"Do you want me to go back to the bridge and face that myth?" Kai balled his fists at his own helplessness. But he took a deep breath, sucking in anger. "Sometimes, it's better not to fight."

"This isn't your fight or your problem."

"You're right, but I'm making it my problem. I'll just add one more to my list."

Helene pushed him. "The only problem you have is yourself. Do you think by pretending to be a hero and ignoring your real problems, you won't feel them anymore?"

"I was trying to be like you for once…" Kai said with a sharp grin, not unlike the one Helene gave him when she said something particularly cutting. "Unfeeling."

He, however, did not get the same response from her as she did from him—she smiled at the confrontation. "How sweet. But even at that, you're a failure."

"Maybe I am! Maybe I fail at love, family, and friendship. So what? Does that mean I shouldn't try? Should I let Sophia rot in hell!" He let the anger stretch. So often feeling failure, he needed one success to spur him on, and he knew what he had to do. "I have to try and help these people. I'm supposed to be a hero."

Helene rolled her eyes and went quiet.

Kai heard the pit's toil. He had tried to ignore the torturous grunts and groans, but like his own thoughts, he couldn't.

His jaw clenched with vitriol. "We can choose to do what's best for us or do the right thing. You might only think about yourself, but I don't."

"Is that what you think?" Helene's confrontation was a cold calm. "Even your heroism is uniquely selfish—it's vanity—only a way to make yourself feel better."

"This is called being human." He was hot and bitter. "You wouldn't understand caring about anything other than yourself."

"And Sophia?" Helene grinned. "I thought you loved her? But here you are, going—"

"I love Sophia more than anything." Love and pride and anger became an impassioned tempest. "But just because I love Sophia doesn't mean I should weigh her over everyone and everything else…no matter how I want to." A pang of heartache seized him. "I can't. She'd hate me for letting those people suffer. If I didn't try to save them, it'd haunt me. I thought you knew me."

"That's why I want to save you from yourself." She sighed. "You can't say I didn't try."

Al finally found the courage to reengage, having pretended not to listen to the argument. "We're running out of daylight."

"I'm going to free them," Kai said. "Find a place nearby to spend the night, and if I'm not back by tomorrow midday, go on without me."

"We shouldn't wait that long," Tom said. "If there's a—"

"Don't say it." Al crossed thick arms. "It's bad luck."

"And this is a bad idea," Tom said.

"For a good purpose." Al nodded to Kai. "Midday. We'll make it to Duat tomorrow with that much daylight."

Tom sulked, kicking at sand as he acquiesced with silence.

"I'd like to go with you," Al said, but he looked at Tom. "He'd kill me though. If you need us, make a signal and we'll try our best."

"Thanks." Kai was grateful for the offer of aid, but he didn't intend on taking it. This was his responsibility.

"If you're going, I'm not letting you go alone," Helene said.

Kai huffed. "Are you kidding?"

"It doesn't make it less heroic if you have help."

"What can I do so you won't follow me?"

"Throw me off the cliff." Helene smirked, the air of civility recovering. "And even then, I'd be down there before you."

"Are you just hoping to watch me fail? I'm not sure what I did to deserve you."

"Or I, you." She was back to her frosty self. "Our fates are tied together."

Kai stormed off.

Helene followed him around the sinkhole. The road spiraled down like an orange peel. The path was deserted, and no one watched the way. Guards didn't look for people breaking in, only those who tried to escape.

Wood supports held the quarry together, bending in strain, rotting and splintering. Beams split with age-cracks, but the hole held. The further they went, the more nature was constrained by manmade structures. Nature's vengeance was baking heat. There was no sun, but it was a convection oven filled with sand.

The air grew serious. Towering sidewalls between levels of roads left long shadows. Sand flew off the upper reaches and upon them.

The closer Kai got, the smaller the workers appeared. Skeletal figures mined with taut skin at the point of ripping. Bodies consumed themselves, redirecting muscle to where it was needed most, away from the core to the extremities of legs and arms.

Then, there were the guards, who stood and sat and looked out like sleek black dogs, guarding what they saw as a pile of bones. They wore black hats and clothes, teasing the heat and working against it, sitting and fanning themselves.

While the guards held fans, the workers held pickaxes, and both swung at a similar rate. Chiseling resounded. Hard sounds. Heavy sounds. Horrible sounds. Workers drew things from the earth, and while it was impossible to destroy the chunks, only make them smaller, it was easy to destroy the earth. As they changed the landscape, people were changed by it, too. Wrinkles buried into bodies as dryness cracked reddened earth.

It was a mess of people, moans and groans, yells and encouragements—dozens of workers and five guards. Although pickaxes could've been weapons, people worked nonetheless. Will had been broken by whip and chain, which now lay idle.

Kai would've given up had it not been for a belief that hope, like mined earth, could be broken smaller but not destroyed.

A curious occurrence. A worker checked where the guards were—he had discovered something, but did not alert them. Under chiseled rock was bark.

Unlike the trees buried in the swampsand, this was older. Emerald moss grew on deep-brown bark. The man clawed at the moss with purpose and intent.

It was only when he stepped away that Kai could see what was drawn into the wall. Where it was bare, the bark became a dark "R" in the glowing green moss.

"What's that about?" Kai was curious and strangely inspired by this act of defiance, regardless of meaning, as it was the man's spirit that instilled a sense of hope that was lacking before.

The guards came and seized the man. One guard, furious, scraped at the moss and bark with a commandeered pickaxe, muddling the drawing.

Helene's mouth was a bit agape. "Is that a tree?"

Kai felt it necessary not to let the rebellious man's effort go in vain, watching the guards lead him away to a white-wood shack. This fanned Kai's purpose. Only when the man was out of sight did he address Helene's comment.

"It's only a patch of bark."

"No, over there." She pointed.

A single gargantuan man pushed carts into a tunnel made of bark like a massive, hollow branch. This vast tree was brightened by the same glowing moss, which pulsed bright and angry as people mined.

Kai was not particularly surprised by a myth being true. "The stories of a tree—Yggdrasil—supporting the world are true. Looks like a tunnel under the desert."

He marked where the guards were. One at the entrance to the tunnel. One wandering, pacing behind a group of digging workers, having gotten weary of trying to clear the drawing, only leaving a filled-in outline of an 'R'. Meanwhile, another guard sat in a lawn chair, fanning himself. Then, there was a barn and the pleasant-looking shack, which had at least two guards in it.

"I think we can take the guards," Kai said.

Helene shook her head. With the sun lowering and the temperature decreasing, tempers flared less. They were back on more pleasant terms with each other. "You sound more like yourself—a bit daft and a lot brave."

"Are you saying we shouldn't do it?"

"Do it smart," Helene said, fidgeting with her pack to see if they had anything that could help. "We don't have any weapons and you're not strong enough to overpower them."

Kai was steady thinking. "If the workers helped, it'd be easy."

"I'm sure they'll join in with some random stranger who shows up trying to start a rebellion."

"I'm not going to be a stranger. I'm going to work with them."

Helene shook her head. "You can't build that kind of trust in a day."

"Then what do you suggest I do?"

She was quiet, but after thinking, she whispered, "You're an idiot." She said it with a demeaning tone, but it certainly wasn't demeaning in the way she looked at Kai—a strange look, more suspicious than anything thus far—she looked at him like a hero, radiant as the sun, and she turned her eyes downwards from him, as if he was too bright now. "Whatever. Good luck with that."

"That's it, then?" He asked, pleased at her leaving. "You only wanted to come this far?"

"Manual labor isn't my thing," she said.

"Well, you've been so very helpful."

Helene was unphased. "What happens if Al and Tom decide to leave?"

"So be it." Kai looked to the ridge. "What about you?"

"What about me?"

"What happens if I don't come back? Will you leave without me?"

"Depends. If you get stuck in the mines, I suppose I'll see you in the next life. If not, I'm stuck with you anyways."

"That's very reassuring." Kai stood more confident than he felt. "Guess you'll just have to wait. I'll escape." He nodded an assurance to himself. "There're no chains. They probably assume people wouldn't make it far in the desert."

"Without Al and Tom, you wouldn't either. You haven't thought this through."

"Are you done?"

"No, this is exactly like you," Helene said. "You remind me more of how you were before. Caring way too much about saving people and having them love you."

"What a flaw," Kai said, sarcastic.

"It's your worst flaw," she said. "But I wouldn't want it any other way." She smiled and pointed at his bag. "Won't it be suspicious to have supplies? If they're going to believe you came here on your own will, you'll have to look really desperate."

"More desperate?" He chuckled and swung the bag off his shoulder. He handed it to her, watching her face carefully. "Go on, I'll be fine."

She slung the bag over her shoulder and the smile faded as if forced to disappear. "I know, it's other people I worry about."

Kai didn't know quite what she meant, but he faked a smile and waved her off. Then, he waited until she was far up the road and reached into his pocket. He was comforted that he still had the leopard's feather. In an emergency, that was all he needed.

Or, at least, he hoped that was all he needed. Surety was left behind, and yet, he pressed on nonetheless.

He decided on a dramatic entrance. Or, if not dramatic, believable.

To make it seem like he was desperate, Kai decided to roll down the hillside. It would hurt. Hot, caustic sand would tear at him, and with the forbearance of pain, he hesitated on the edge.

The road back was the simple choice, but that's why being Elysium's hero was so unsatisfactory—it was easy. This, like saving Sophia, was absurd and heroic. With looming difficulty, though, it was insane not to doubt.

However, before he could change his mind, Kai slid off the slope, barreling and rolling down the hill in a tumult, swirling and twirling in the whirlpool of sand and self, unto pain and servitude. But he had to try.

ELEVEN

THE NEW LEADER

WITHOUT KAI, CARA HAD to be strong. Marcus complained. Li quarreled with him. Parents prayed. Grandparents stayed silent. And Cara, well, she tried her best, but her best was never enough.

Elysium was lost to them.

Their new Asphodel apartment was on the corner of what can only be described as prime real estate in a slum. The one-room tenement was smaller than their old living room, and nowhere near as nice. Mildew creeped out the cracks of the ceiling. The faucets spurted air and leaked in the walls, dripping loud each night. Rats were the only beneficiary, the critters' little paw-steps echoed, presumably drinking from the pipes as a hamster did from a water bottle, while the family left a glass in the sink, hoping that more than a drop would drip out.

Cara's father and Marcus lost their jobs. As moving boxes began to empty, everything was unpacked and sold for pittances. Trinkets were sold first. Except, that is, for the piece of jade that Kai had bought Cara. She kept that. She hid that. It was the hope that she held onto—that Kai might return, and that although things were dreadful, difficult, and worsening, she might turn their destitution around.

After the move-in and sell-off, there was a settling like sediment being compacted; the family fought for space, but floor was all they had to fight over. Beds and furniture would come later. Maybe when there was space. Maybe when there was money. And in the night, the family slept restlessly and kicked at each other.

These quarrels culminated in the burning late-afternoon when a second letter arrived. The letter was from a man named Victor, and he offered Cara and her family an opportunity to reverse their punishment.

The whole family except Kai sat against the room's four walls, backs sloping off the floor and shifting uncomfortably. Arms wrapped around knees and torsos, containing themselves as they devolved into factions.

"You're not going to meet Victor," Cara's father said, his authoritarian voice rattling the paper-thin walls. Although his voice shook the walls, he, too, looked shaken. The move made him look older. The usual straight-backed posture was gone, and he sat with his wife holding his hand.

"I just want to meet him, uncle." Marcus was alone on a wall; no one sided with him. "Victor was just elected to Asphodel's only council spot. There's so much buzz around him. Some even say he's a demi-god."

"You'll take that back," Cara's mother said, shrill. "We must worship the gods, not deify mortals."

Marcus shrugged. "I didn't say it. I'm just saying he wants to change things. Hopefully, he can get rid of the myth problem plaguing us."

"You're the biggest problem plaguing me right now." Li gazed out the tiny window with a view of a faded pastel blue wall next door. It wasn't a good replica of the sky; however, it was better than the dreary earthy undertones of the apartment.

Cara's father ignored animosity. "Without Kai, it's my duty to plead our case. If Victor is as fair as people say, he wouldn't offer us a way to Elysium if he didn't mean it. Just because Kai left does not mean we should be punished this harshly."

"We were only rewarded because of Kai." Li crossed his arms. "We deserve nothing."

"How can you say that?" Cara's mother asked, an accusatory scowl deep in a plump face. "We have venerated the gods and been model citizens. We earned our place, and I've done my best to lift us, even when some of us have been vile and naive."

"Am I the naive one?" Li asked.

"That smart mouth of yours doesn't help." Cara's mother firmed with frustration. "But they're punishing us for Kai's choice. It's one thing to be selfish, but he had to drag us down with him. And the two of you helped. I'm disappointed, Cara. You were supposed to be the good one. The reasonable one. But you're as faithless as Kai and as bad as Li."

Li growled. "Blame me. I don't care. But Cara helped Kai because she loves him—unlike you. You only cared that the gods loved him. I wonder how your precious gods would feel about a parent who would sacrifice their child for personal interest? It might remind Zeus of his father, Kronos, who ate his children to protect himself."

Speechless, Cara's mother elbowed her husband to respond.

Surprise stumbled his rebuttal. "We can—she just wants—you will respect your mother."

Li crossed his arms. "She should respect me, too."

"Yes, mutual respect," Cara's father said, scratching his chin. "Your mother cares for the gods because they watch over this family. But rather than pointing fingers, we need to come together. I don't think it's you or Cara's fault—you were only helping your brother."

"What?" Redness rose on Cara's mother's fleshy cheeks.

"We all love each other," Cara's father said, watching Li for a reaction. "We're a family. Surely, you must respect that?"

"I don't respect blood for blood's sake." Li side-eyed Marcus and went pensive. The taut coldness in him thawed and became his version of softness, a nod to his parents. "I respect those who love and care for me. Mother wants the best for the family in her own way, and I recognize where I could be better." The soft words re-hardened, and the inevitable contrast came. "But no one should blame Cara."

"Did I detect a bit of emotion there?" Marcus said. "I thought I'd see stones cry first."

For an instant, there was a tinge of embarrassment and Li looked away. But when he returned to Marcus, there was only star-distant fire and apathy.

Cara laid her hand on Li's shoulder. "It is my fault, though. I snuck out with Kai, encouraged him, and helped him leave, which has brought us here. But Kai told me to take care of the family. So, I will. I'll talk to Victor and do whatever it takes to get us back to Elysium. I promise."

"What are you going to do, beg him?" Marcus laughed. "He might be merciful, but leeches don't go to Elysium."

Li fixed a dead stare on Marcus. "Anything else to say before I sew your mouth shut?"

Cara reined her twin in. "It's not worth it. I don't hear a word he says, anyway."

Cara's father offered her a sympathetic smile, filled with parental tenderness, but his words were subtle daggers. "I know you mean the best, but this is our only chance. I've dealt with people like this before. I'm the head of this family, and I will act as such."

Cara flickered between hurt and defiance; her father's lack of belief hurt her more than Marcus' words.

Li glanced at his twin, saddened, and went cold. "Kai was the head of this family. Without him, we're headless. But he gave Cara and I this responsibility. Two heads, regrown like a hydra. Twins, opposites, and together, we'll be better than him."

"And what about me?" asked Cara's grandfather. "I'm the oldest one here."

"No disrespect," said Cara's father. "But you passed that torch down to me long ago."

Marcus butted in, "I agree with—"

"No one asked you," Li said.

"I still have a voice here."

"You're all squabbling children," said Cara's mother.

The room twirled and whirled with shouts and assertions, bouncing back and forth as a ball between confined walls. Arguments overlapped, went without reason, and went from one group to another, fighting one insult to the next, hurled and echoed, replied and forwarded.

Then, a voice cut through it all.

"Enough." Cara's short stature stood above them all, silencing them with blossoming resolve. "Wasn't losing Kai enough? I can't stand to see us fall apart like this. We're supposed to love each other. We tried to defend Kai, but the council's cruelty strung him along with promises of Sophia until they could betray him. But it won't happen again. Li and I will not fail this family. Together, the council can't con us with empty promises. We may be miserable, but we also have nothing to lose. Li and I will do anything to save us."

Cara wavered, threatening to break under the burden she willingly seized, but instead, the pressure compressed blame, guilt, and the failure of family into strength. The shaking stopped and composed into a solid resolution, not ending the quarrel with passion, but by logic and determination.

Cara brandished the letter. "This was addressed to Li and I. It was meant for us. You mean well and I love you all. But this is our meeting. It is our responsibility. We won't let you down." She strode to the door. "And that's that."

The argument was silenced by her resounding voice and the letter itself, which fluttered to the floor with finality as Cara left.

Li followed her out into the fading day, and as he closed the rust-squeaking door, he got in a final word. "Don't underestimate her. She's the best of us."

When Li caught up to Cara, walking through a burning world, he had a strangely beaming smile, which cracked a usual stone-stuck demeanor.

"Was I too harsh?" she asked.

"You did well. They may not see it, but I do."

"It?"

"You." He nudged her, and uncomfortable with feeling, spoke sarcastically. "How hardhearted you are."

"They say twins are alike. I never thought that was true." She shrugged, hiding a blush under the shadow of a tilted head. "The least we can do for Kai is give the council a piece of our minds."

"I would quite enjoy that. And what of the appeal?"

"Start with that." Cara flashed a brow mischievously. "It'll be worthwhile either way."

"And what do you think about what Marcus said?" Li asked.

"I told you, I don't listen to him. Victor's just a politician vying for power. When Kai and I were here, the people didn't seem fond of Elysium or the council. But we're part of Asphodel, now, and this is their representative. Maybe he does want to help us. But you need to be careful. The gods could do worse to us yet."

"Not much. Yet, I think it's people, not gods, we have to worry about." Li's ironic grin glinted. "I'd quite like to see a god, or even if this man is a semi or demi-god. I'll believe it when I see it. Anyone or anything who's truly good."

"Trying to replace Kai?"

"No, not at all."

Cara hesitated, but asked anyway, "When you were with Helene, what did she say?"

"Nothing…too much. I'll tell you later."

They were at the gates to Elysium, which they had passed what seemed so long ago. Soldiers stood at either side of an open gate, expressions flat as the leaf-blade spears they carried. It was not a promising sign to see the same guards they had tricked.

"You two?" asked the wolf-like soldier.

The brutal eyes were more unpleasant than before, and the welcome was a shuffling of feet, armor, and weapons, which was like the ruffling of a metal bird's feathers. Neither soldier, though, expanded plumage to block their way.

Cara tried to break the tension with a familiar smile. "Can we go through? We have a meeting with Victor."

"We're not going to stop you. Don't be late. I don't know why he's dealing with you two, but I hope it's for a new punishment. Just don't get lost."

"Don't worry, we won't," Li said.

"You got us extra duty," said the other soldier, Albus. "Do you know if Kai's alright?"

"Hurry up," demanded the unfriendly soldier, pointing with his spear and not letting them answer. "Best not be back any time soon."

Li brushed by the spear, unafraid. "We'll have to pass back into Asphodel. See you in a bit."

"I'd be happy to kick you back down the hill," mumbled the man.

Cara and Li left the soldiers behind. With old steps, their path was assured and they forgot the discomfort of Asphodel. Cheer and comfort returned. And yet, their familiar home's every small and subtle change in their absence was an enormous, earth-shattering affair. As they walked down the street, absorbed by new whitewashed shutters, the latest-dressed mannequins, and fresh potted evergreens that looked a bit brown, they barely noticed how silent and empty the markets were compared to the nostalgic memories of times before the worsening drought.

But one change dominated all others—the construction of the grand spire was complete, with its gold and engraved design of a curled dragon swirling about the tower.

It was at this newly completed temple—the Root, as it was called—that they were to meet Victor.

The Root's base was Greek. Red columns and delicate carvings. Old, but repainted. The grey-marble upper half, tower, and golden spire were cleared of bamboo scaffolding, which lingered in little piles around the grounds. The illustrious spire stood above the rest of Elysium, and here, it was to be a new, glorious beacon to Asphodel and the rest of the world.

Beneath the building's long shadow, Cara and Li were tiny. As they entered enormous oak doors, they struggled against the inclination to bow, so accustomed to doing so in front of others, especially their mother. But when she wasn't around, it became a matter of habit and choice to follow this convention. That was the sign of an effective tradition—it was done regardless of belief, regardless of desire, and whether anyone was there to witness it or not.

As they entered, Cara bowed and Li did not.

No one waited for them. The hall was empty except for columns. Pews were not put into place yet, and the vast space was highlighted by what was missing. Yet, the central feature stood out more—at the front of the room were smaller arched wood doors, engraved with the glittering gold design of a two-sided tree growing up and down to an invisible circle, with roots or branches dependent, totally, on perspective.

The scale of the room was magnet-focused on the small, but outstanding, doors, and Cara and Li were drawn onwards as if in a funnel towards a focal point. Exactly as intended.

Standing before the simple, elegant doors, Cara and Li wondered what was on the other side.

"Sometimes, you get so focused on the end that you forget what's around you," said a man with eyes running over them like a crisp Scandinavian stream. "If only hope accomplished something, I'd stand here for days. Cara and Li? I'm Victor."

Cara turned. Victor had snuck up behind them, and yet, did not startle her. As she appraised him, feeling bounced between anger at the council in general and a ritual smile at meeting a new person.

Victor certainly reminded Cara of what others saw as great, charismatic leaders. But more than any politician or leader Cara had seen before, this man had a look of genuine care, not looking down or even at her, but with her towards the doors and room. And, as Marcus had mentioned, Cara could see how this man might be a demi-god. The aura of power and grace extended from waterfall eyes flowing forth kindness and strength.

Cara needed his help to lift the family out of their destitute situation, but it was hard to contain the anger she had for the council—for what they had done to Kai, and to a lesser degree, to her.

All her preparations for what she would say to Victor vanished into the cloud of anger. "After all Kai did for Elysium, how could the council keep Kai and Sophia apart? And why send Sophia to Irkalla? What gives you the right to judge people like that?"

"I have no right to do that. No one is perfect, least of all me." Victor smiled. His smile was like all other charismatic smiles—unique. It was not about his mouth, but the way the smile lit his whole face and demonstrated a rare imperfection—profound laugh-lines and worry wrinkles in a young face. "I wasn't on the council for that decision. Kai might've disobeyed the gods, but he did what he had to. I don't blame him. I only hope I would do the same for the people I care about. I heard you both intended on taking his place in myth control?"

"Indeed." Li was sizing up the man, and at first impression, it seemed that he was pleased. He did not look with ambivalence nor disdain; rather, he picked apart every detail, dissecting mannerisms and minutia, examining and probing for flaw and weakness. "We did get a rather rude letter from the council that stopped us from helping, though. I assume you were on the council for that decision."

Cara's anger cooled, having to, as she could feel the familiar confrontational aura come upon her twin. "Li," she warned.

Li focused on Victor, daring him to be thrown off balance, but Victor's kind look did not waver, and at the insinuation of the rudeness, the man did not flinch.

"I was. But I can see my word that I didn't vote for your expulsion to Asphodel would mean nothing." Victor motioned for them to follow. "I hope we're not too late."

He led them to a door on the outskirts of the room and onto an old, rickety staircase. The first steps, old and weary wood, coughed weakly underfoot, and as steps changed to stone, the wheezing stopped and filled with the clarity of footfalls.

As Victor went, his voice echoed, bouncing about the grey-stone spiral staircase. Resounding. Reverberating. Lingering. They followed the man, trailing and engulfed by his voice.

"You're new to Asphodel, but I'll give it to you frankly. People are dying. Walls are crumbling. Long-lost terrors are crawling out the darkness, while new ones run rampant. If you really want to help—both your family and Asphodel—I have a proposition for you."

They stepped through an archway and onto a balcony, where a majestic sunset awaited. The sky blushed with a streak of savannah-orange at the horizon, while pale blue and a falling, fainting purple loomed. Cloud-wisps dipped into the painted sky and pulled color towards the city. The final rays of light dazzled through dust—imperial, energetic, wonderful. Bronzing with the rapid descent of the sun, what was left became amber and darkening fire, extinguishing in the coming night.

Victor looked upon the magisterial sky and back at Cara and Li.

"But we'll get to that proposal in a moment," Victor said. "I wanted to meet here for a reason. Look out there and tell me what you see."

Annoyed by this delay, Li swept his gaze across the sky as if he was sweeping away cobwebs. "I see the night approaching."

Cara took Victor more seriously, grasping the iron railing and staring out at Elysium and Asphodel under the conclusion of a smoldering day. She tried to be eloquent. "The eclipse of the day is godly. Spires reach for the sun, and the sun reaches for us."

"I agree with what your brother said." Victor did not look to the horizon, he looked down to the twin-cities and more specifically, the iron fence below. "The night is coming. But night is necessary." He paused, seemingly distracted. "Do you want any water?" He offered them a leather and gold-laced waterskin.

"No," Li said. "I'm allergic to gold."

Cara shot Li a questioning look and was rebuffed with inexpressiveness. Her lips were dry and cracked, and she salivated over the thought of water and still shook her head. "I'm fine, thanks."

"Alright," Victor said. "If I mess this up, it'll be a long, embarrassing walk."

"A walk?" Cara asked.

With an outrageous and athletic toss, Victor sent the waterskin flying and tumbling through the sunset air and over the fence to Asphodel. Satisfied, he smiled again.

"What'd you do that for?" Cara asked.

Victor scanned the rooftops of Elysium, which built on the old, upwards and onwards. "Towers. Temples. Symbols and calls to the gods, asking for hope, asking for help. And so far, unheard. Meanwhile, Asphodel prays by surviving. Is it better to hope, survive, or try and find a solution that might not exist?"

Offering no answers, Victor stared over the city. Cara was caught off guard by the insinuation that the gods did not care, as she had only made her statement because it was a reverent thing to say.

Victor's eyes glittered in the final rays of sunlight, and he flowed from one thought to another, coming back to the beginning. "When I see the sunset, all I see is the reflection of sunrise. Without one, we'd never have the other. Darkness is falling in Asphodel, but the question is whether we will hope, survive, *and* find a solution. Then, we might see the sun rise again." Victor turned a hopeful expression towards Cara. "I threw the waterskin because that small act is all I can do right now. It's little, but someone will find it and look up, wondering where their good fortune came from. People down there need something to believe in."

Cara prepared for the logical next step—that Victor would say that he'd make the world better, that people might look up to this hope-inspiring man, and that where the gods failed, this godly man might not.

That's not what he said; instead, he smiled at her. "I want *you* to answer their prayers."

His smile was warm under the affectation of the last god-rays of sun, beaming directly at her. It was hopeful, inspiring, and produced a similarly brilliant feeling within her.

"I want you to make the world better." Victor nodded at Li. "Make yourselves better. You can make this world safer for your family, for your neighbors, for everyone."

Despite Cara's certainty earlier, this seemed too much, too soon. "Why us?"

"I heard about a little incident with a mythical chicken." Victor chuckled. "You scrambled a few eggs, but sometimes, that happens. I won't judge your mistakes, but I will judge inaction. And so, I am giving you the opportunity you desired."

"To join myth control?" With excitement and the twilight wind, elated goosebumps rose on Cara's skin.

"Not quite," Victor leaned on the railing and cast hopeful eyes to the city. "To make your own—a department in Asphodel."

"By ourselves?" Cara's voice was unsure, but she remained jubilant at the opportunity.

"You'll need help at first." Victor attempted another smile, more subdued, but it soured with what he said next. "Rollo and I may not agree on many things, but he would be the natural choice, since he trained Kai."

With the mention of Rollo, Cara saw it as an easy way to express her own view on the subject as someone else's. "He won't agree to killing myths."

"That's not what I want, either." Victor shook vehemently. "I don't want bloodshed." He crossed his arms. "All I want is to know what is out there. Knowledge is our greatest strength, and as the sun heads into darkness, we may find our solution in such darkness."

Apprehension and fascination fluttered through Cara as she followed his gaze. "You want us to go to the ruins?"

Victor nodded.

Li's eyes narrowed at the man. "And what do we get in return?"

"I'll lodge the petition to have you and your family reinstated to Elysium."

Cara went to agree, but Li's hand landed on her shoulder.

"And what happens after this mission?" Li kept his expression solid, being the cool-head to Cara's quick decision. "What proof do we have that you'll keep your word?"

"A careful, thoughtful man. We need more of those." Victor nodded. "That, or you dealt with too many 'gods' and not enough certainty." He seemed amused. "The council's voice will ring true in the only way they know how—writing. A contract. Definitive terms for reinstatement. The council is quarrelsome, but they will do well to listen to me. They may think that Asphodel is weak and divided, but we make up the majority of this city. People are angry. I am angry, too. I won't deny it." He scowled, and it was deeply upsetting after the usual cheer. "I'm sure you've seen how wonderful Asphodel is compared to Elysium already. But change is coming, and I hope that the rest of the council will see it before it's too late. They may hide behind the mention of gods, but they cannot do so forever. The gods are distant and we are here."

Cara nodded along, while Li was unmoved.

The sun set, leaving the outline of spires on a purpling background. Victor sighed and shook their hands. "I'm glad I got to meet you, but I have another less pleasant meeting to get to—something about an incident at a mine. I don't agree with the rest of the council, but just like most people, I have no other choice but to do my job. I can only try my best. I'll send you the contract as soon as possible, and next time we meet, I expect you will have more to say to me than I will have to say to you."

And with a small flourish of a bow, as if the twins were the presiding members of this meeting, he left them alone on the balcony. He did not ask them to leave, letting them linger in Elysium as long as they wanted.

His steps could be heard echoing down the staircase, and when they were gone, Cara asked, "What'd you think of him?"

Li shrugged. "He likes to talk."

"He seemed reasonable enough."

"The most dangerous people usually are."

"Are you saying you don't like him?" Cara asked.

"No, I'm not saying that," Li said, calm as dusk. "I don't like or dislike him. There are only a few people I have such feelings for. He doesn't sound like Elysium's councilmembers, but I'll believe he's different when I see real action." An amused smile, if only for Li—a slight inclination of lips. "We should use him, before he uses us. You liked him, though, didn't you?"

"Stop smiling like that," Cara said.

"I thought you wanted me to smile more."

"You're insufferable," she said, but smiled, too. "Victor was nothing like I expected—I expected high and mighty, cruel and arbitrary, or just spitting out the usual politician promises."

"He promised a lot."

"All he promised was to petition for us," Cara said.

Li fell to shadow as he looked past the fence to Asphodel. "Is that not a lot?"

"To us, I suppose." Cara joined him, enjoying the cooling air while it lasted, before they had to return to the dank apartment. "We can't go on like this."

"Are you sure about going to the ruins?"

"We made a promise to Kai, to our family, and this is the only way we can survive. We're pariahs in Asphodel. Would you rather starve and die?" Cara frowned, deep and sad. "Do we have a choice?"

"There's always a choice. But sometimes, the alternative is too impossible to imagine." Li's distant eyes focused on Cara. "You got all teary-eyed at the death of a bird, what'll you do if we have no other choice but to kill a myth?"

"We don't know what's in the ruins." She played with her hair, fighting herself and easing tension with nervous movement. "But we'll do it our way—the way that Rollo wanted Kai to do it—with empathy."

Li laughed. "I'm not good at that."

"Then be thankful I'm around." Her good mood faltered even as she joked. "You can be my sidekick."

"Come on, hero," Li said, barely acknowledging her jest. He was pensive as night fell and wrapped an arm around her.

It was forced and stiff, but the effort was what counted. "Don't be sad. The night can be beautiful as day."

They huddled together, staring towards the ruins, not because it might save or destroy Asphodel, but because it might save their family.

TWELVE

RESIST

A CLUNKY METRONOME RESOUNDED as Kai swung his pickaxe into stubborn rock. He tossed the dislodged stone into an iron cart. Everything was hard—the rock, the effort, and the sound, which was broken by random tidbits directed towards Kai from his two neighbors while working in the pit.

"Keep going, don't let *him* see you slacking," said the wiry man to Kai's left, veins more prominent in sweat-drenched arms than the dark-bark latticed in sandstone.

The man on Kai's right agreed. "Save your energy for when *he* passes, so it looks like you're doing a good job."

"Don't do that," said the first man, whose dirt-covered face cracked with warning. "He'll notice your production is down, and then you'll be sent to work in the tunnel."

"I wouldn't mind the shade," Kai said with a joking smile, but his co-worker's seriousness went unaffected.

The line of workers hushed, but the pickaxes swung faster. An enormous man, even more colossal up close compared to when Kai had seen him from above, pushed an empty minecart like it was a toddler's walker. This man—the *him* the others referred to—was mythically large. His bald head and cheeks were sunburned, except where scraggly mutton chops shaded skin. A meerkat popped up on a mountain-ridge shoulder. The black snout sniffed and its head twitched on the lookout. Satisfied, the critter laid down, blending into muscles and brown dust on the giant's shoulder.

When the giant took a full cart, his fingers were thicker than the iron-rod handle and a single push clogged the wheels with dirt. Yet, the cart was shoved along by the truculence of the man, leaving a long trail.

"What's with that?" Kai asked.

"He's doing his job," said Kai's neighbor.

"I meant the meerkat."

"It's his pet, I guess. He catches crickets and bugs to feed it."

Kai's less-talkative neighbor coughed at a splattering of dust. "Maybe he's fattening it up."

"Doubt it," said the other. "He cares for it better than he does for us." Kai's neighbor heaved his pickaxe with a sharp smash, even as he spoke to Kai. "Just do your work and you'll get a meal, a place to sleep, and no trouble. If you're good, they'll put you on moss duty."

"What do they want moss for? And who wants it?"

"You ask too many questions."

Kai was unsure how to balance caution and how little time he had to be subtle. "I get it, slaves aren't supposed to ask questions."

"We're not slaves," the man said. "We're employees. We get paid."

"We do?"

"Based on the weight of stone and bark you mine," he said, striking the rock again with a particularly hefty blow, tearing away a chunk of hard sandstone.

Kai looked both ways, only seeing a barn and the small manager's shack. "What is there to buy? Sand?"

"Rent for a roof in the barn and food in your stomach. Man, you're slow."

"And that's not slavery?"

"It's a living," the man said. "It's not so different from the job I used to have in Duat."

Kai's caution compressed with the constraints of time. "Don't you want more?"

"We're free to leave if we have the money for passage," the man said. "But this is my home."

"So, slavery by circumstance," Kai whispered to himself, making sure he didn't say it to the man. But he couldn't help but ask, "How do they keep people in line?"

"If you do your job poorly, you deserve punishment."

"Does everyone here feel the same way?" Kai asked his other neighbor, a rather shaky man. "What about the 'R' drawn in the wall?"

The man's pick missed the rock wall. He jerked back into work, wordless, and that gave Kai an answer. With a sigh, Kai resumed mining, leaving the other two men to work, suspecting them a lost cause.

Sweaty and exhausted, Kai hoped that the sun fading over the lip of the mine would lessen the temperature. Yet, the heat baked with the sky. The orange clouds matched the dirt, and Kai stopped working, absorbing golden light that tormented his muscles and delighted his eyes. The others ignored both heat and beauty as if already dead.

Kai had to help these people.

But for now, he had to work. There was no other choice. Manual labor plagued Kai. As he tried to break rock, so did it try to break him. He struggled, and tired by the desert already, a willing mind fought an unwilling body. There was only the *clink* of pick and stone, lifting the heavy tool with beleaguered sinews and pulling stone from stone, piling heavy rocks into a cart behind, only for it to be wheeled away and start again.

"This is heroism," Kai muttered under his breath, taking a particularly violent swing at the uneven sandstone. Hard, solid dust splattered out about him, cascading off the wall and into his lungs. He coughed and continued. On the next blow, a chunk as big as Kai's foot came dislodged and there was sense of relief as it *clunked* to the ground. "What an epic victory."

But it was short-lived.

Rock remained. Kai's neighbor seemed pleased when he split stone, smiling with delight as he placed it in the cart. But Kai did not relish some small victory, and only grew more disheartened by the menial, repetitive, and futile task.

In the throes of dusk, the dying of the light, Kai felt like he was dying along with the sun. The angelic-beams of evening—a commonality to mountains, tall cities, and the deepest holes where the rest of the world obscures sunset and leaves only the trace of the escaping light—did little to lessen the labor. The work was a violent slumber.

When the time finally came to end the effort, Kai left the wall and surveyed the results of his labor. Earth seemed little different. Nothing changed without a great deal of effort.

Yet, there were scars. The slightest destruction still left enormous wounds. Under the stone where others had worked harder than Kai, the world tree was exposed, moss taken, and bark cried golden sap. Remaining moss glared angrily, lighting the darkness around Kai a foreboding green.

As Kai retreated with the some of the crowd for dinner, Kai's wiry neighbor stayed behind.

Seeing the man still working, Kai muttered to himself. "If I have to do this again tomorrow, I'll ask him to hit me with the pickaxe, since he seems to enjoy it so much."

Kai left his pickaxe by the barn, hearing those still working as a background noise of blows like crickets in a summer night—annoying at first, and then, vaguely comforting.

Since he was new, the guards started Kai with credit, which was explained to him by a rather tedious man at the barn doors. And like the first hit of a drug, or in this case, more like the first breath of oxygen—something needed to live—Kai figured that credit was meant to be a method to keep the workers trapped in a cycle.

Inside was a simple barn with hay beds and rafters, but it was protection from the elements, an escape from dust, sun, and the toil of workday.

After getting their food from an assembly line and paying a clipboard-holding guard, people talked and ate and drank, congregating in time-tested ways, as barn animals, tavern-goers, and a king's court all did—in comforting groups. Conversation flowed as the food did; both were sustenance and nothing more.

Kai lingered alone. Two men noticed him and beckoned him over to a floor-seat. Hard under his rump, Kai's sore muscles hurt more when finally at rest. He took the first few bites of his bland food. There were two tiny potato squares, smashed beans, and rawhide-looking jerky, which Kai ate as he ached in silence.

His two companions sized him up, leaving food untouched. His dinner-mates could've been twins, if they looked any bit alike.

One looked brutal. A tall figure with tight-coiled muscles in a rock-hard jaw and razor-short black hair. The other man looked like he had been brutalized. He had the face of a misshapen mishap—a nose broken to the left, scars, and beautifully hopeful eyes. Despite differences, the brutal and brutalized man had a kinship in how they looked at Kai.

Aware of scrutiny, Kai attempted a smile, which faltered with exhaustion. Still, his eyes held the purpose that brought him here, a desire to help.

The man with the broken nose spoke, "I'm Mushmouth. This is Tiger."

Kai was about to ask about the nicknames, but the man revealed teeth like a vampire that had been punched in the mouth—two sharp canines bent at acute angles.

"You shouldn't be here," Tiger said harshly, sinewy arms crossed. However, his voice wasn't aggressive or accusatory, just a statement. "Why'd you come?"

Kai knew his time was short, and he would have to take risks. But he didn't trust these two yet. "I got lost and ended up here. I guess it's not—"

"Too bad?" Mushmouth interrupted. "Have you been talking to Silvertongue? Gave you all that employee nonsense?"

"Look, I've only been here for the day. I don't really know what's going on."

Tiger, this time, interrupted with a smile. It was jarring. "At first, it's not bad. Then, they get you stuck. Sure, you're free to leave if you're debt free, but that's how they keep people here."

"Why not leave anyway? There's only a few guards."

"And *him*," Mushmouth said.

Kai assumed the tone referred to the behemoth. "Is *he* a myth?"

"Can't be human." Tiger, who a moment before looked quite strong, became feeble in his words as he continued. "People try and escape, but he always finds them. Last week, someone escaped and found a smuggler with a horse. Both the escapee and the smuggler were dragged back. *He* tossed the horse from the top of the pit, and the way it crumpled—" He shuddered. "The smuggler was still in the saddle."

"And the person who escaped?" Kai asked, taking a nervous bite of food.

"He's eating the horse with you right now." Tiger picked up a stringy bit of jerky from the tray and plopped it in his mouth.

Kai pushed his plate away, unsure whether he could reason with myths anymore. "But you still want to escape?"

"Are you kidding?" Tiger asked. "That was the fifth time I tried. Mushmouth has tried more than me, and despite the lost wages, it hasn't stopped us."

"That's good," Kai said offhandedly, unsure what else he could say. His thoughts of his own escape were becoming muddled as his meal. "I saw someone draw an 'R' earlier, what was that about?"

"Doodler?" Mushmouth frowned lopsided. "He wasn't eager to work. It's too bad, I doubt we'll see him again."

Kai gulped. "What did they do to him?"

"I don't know." Mushmouth said. "They'll say he wasn't a good employee and left."

Kai scrapped at the wood floor with his fingernail. "What if I can get you out?"

Mushmouth chuckled. "I knew you were dumb."

Kai nodded, acquiescing it might be true. "I came to save you."

"You're even dumber than I thought." Mushmouth phrased it as a joke, but it only came out sad. "Almost as dumb as Doodler."

"Probably." Kai drew an 'R' in the dust on the cracked wood floor. "I know this won't be easy, but I had to do something."

"You came with a plan?" Tiger asked with renewed vigor.

"Of a sort."

Tiger set down the horse jerky. "How can we help?"

Under the sound of grim laughter and the crash of forks, they planned. As dinner and leisure finished, the barn quieted and candles were extinguished.

All the people prepared for another long day by sleeping early.

All of them, except Kai, who lay on the barn floor with his eyes open, excited for what was to come. Even awake, he dreamed glorious images. Him, leading the people against their captors. He heard chants, felt the adrenaline, and prophesized victory in his imagination, even preparing a speech for the moment they ascended, transcendent, out the mines together. He was not the only one in the vision, just one of many, but he was leading the pack, the face of such resistance—the hero.

Not being able to lull himself from daydream into real dreams, he decided on a walk, weaving through the hall of snores and sleep. He slid the barn doors ajar with a loud creak, as if an alarm to the guards.

But outside, everything was quiet.

No one stopped Kai, and he went out into the crisp desert air, closing the door behind him. Goosebumps rose on his neck, caressed to crests by the chills that swirled about the night air, the cold a complete opposite to the daytime desert as darkness was to light.

Sneaking was easy, except for his clouded frost-breath that he tried to hush between the slit in his mouth. The wafts matched the shy night above, painted by a few wisps. Staring up, he wished for such comfort to be within his reach, but he was left with the vague reassurance of his arms wrapped around himself.

Across the pit, a dull glow of green moss.

"What're you doing out here?" whispered a voice. It was Kai's neighbor during the day, who Mushmouth had called Silvertongue.

"I was—" Kai stopped, not having any excuse prepared, and thus, could only return the question. "What are you doing here?"

Silvertongue grinned, and with a slightly parted mouth, there was a glow behind teeth like a trapped firefly. "You're wasting time."

The man walked off and Kai followed. They went to the wall. A bit of moss grew at the bark scars, a dim green nebula illuminating Silvertongue.

Silvertongue's calloused fingers dug at the moss, dragging a bit away. Silvertongue stuck it in his mouth like cotton candy.

"Can't do that while the guards are watching," Silvertongue said, eyes piercing through the shadows. He took more.

"I thought you like the guards?" Kai asked, confused.

"Appearances. It does no one any good to look unhappy and rebellious when you're trying to do something sneaky."

"And you're not worried about me turning you in for...whatever you're doing?"

"You're an open book, my friend. Think you're smart, but really, you're not all that clever. Figured you for a rebellious sort. Especially hanging around with Tiger and Mushmouth. You said too much earlier, and that's why I know you won't say anything about this."

Kai kept his mouth on a tighter leash. "What's with the moss?"

"With normal hours, no one can get out of debt. The moss is like coffee. Keeps me working and hope in sight." Silvertongue grinned again and his teeth were radiant with the background light.

"That's why they call you Silvertongue."

He nodded, scratching at the moss. Finished, he backed away, leaving an 'R', brown bark in the glowing green.

Kai hesitated. "And the 'R'?"

"Resist, as Doodler insisted. Fairly obvious, really. But that's what makes it easily digestible." Silvertongue's grin turned to an ironic snarl. "It's a lost cause, but it makes me feel a little better."

"Why not do something more?"

"Because it's useless. What don't you understand about that? People are selfish. Both us and the guards—we're doing the best we can. Sometimes, that involves speaking out, and other times, it means staying silent."

Kai's face tensed, defying the words. "Better to die loud than die silent. What about morals? About what you believe in? Dignity, even?"

"Dignity is a luxury I don't have." Silvertongue shook his head. "You're talking about ideals, and I'm talking about life. My life. I've only got one, and I won't waste it for nothing. If sacrificing it freed everyone, I'd die happily. But that's not how this works."

"Consequences don't matter. The fight for freedom is noble in itself."

"You know, you have the mentality of a martyr."

"And I thought I was just another employee," Kai said, sarcastic, then added, "They can't kill us all."

"They don't have to." The man sighed with a big plume of frost. "Doesn't mean they can't make you disappear, and with you, everyone else's bravery. See how that worked for Doodler?"

"The guards are outnumbered; people won't let them get away with murder. No one is above justice."

"Except those who define and enforce justice."

Kai's fists froze with certainty. "Then people will rise up against them—I'll rise up against them, even if no one joins me."

"I'd suggest you don't back the guards into a corner. There's a reason Tiger and Mushmouth are still alive and others never return." Silvertongue looked at him sadly, with the sympathy of someone headed towards the gallows. "But if you're so intent on finding reason to justify your own death, go to the guardhouse. I can't change your course. I can only wish you a successful death."

Silvertongue walked off, leaving Kai at the wall alone. The tiny halo-glow of the man's fog-breath lit the air as he strolled to the barn.

Kai headed towards the guardhouse, which was wrapped in a blanket of rocks. In the window, the flicker of a candle was distorted in frosted glass.

Two guards were awake, indistinguishable from each other, fogged shadows and well-trimmed faces. They stood in somber light about a low table. Kai slid beneath the windowsill, listening best he could.

"What are we going to do?" asked a guard, his voice low and unsure.

The other's voice was louder and more serious. "They say the corruption's getting worse. We have to increase production."

Hesitant, the first guard paused. "What if that's the reason it's getting—"

"They know what they're doing."

"I'm sorry, I didn't mean anything by it."

"We're doing an important job here," the stern guard lectured. But he stopped and there was a bit of shuffling. "It's one thing to disobey us, but to disobey the gods, that's wrong."

It didn't seem like the two guards were talking amongst themselves now, and Kai snuck a better look through the window, finding a spot where the haze was clearer. The two guards looked down at the table like curious dogs at a trapped fox. However, the table was not a table—the object moved.

It was the man Kai had seen earlier, the man who gave Kai hope in the afternoon by drawing an 'R'—Doodler. His clothes were dirtied, long-hair disheveled, and a bit of blood dripped from thin lips, spluttered onto the floor.

The more imposing guard leaned over him and asked, "Will you get back to work tomorrow?"

Doodler whispered, his voice hoarse and short. "I'm not your slave."

"You're right," said the guard. "But we are all the gods' slaves."

"Whatever you have to tell yourself."

A violent smile. "Do we have to go through this again?"

"Go to Irkalla," Doodler said.

The guard stood, sighed, and shook his head. A boot swung.

The blow *thumped* into Doodler's chest and he cringed in pain. As more kicks followed, Kai did not want to watch, but he froze in terror. It was like the sacrifice of the chimera—Kai was helpless and weak, but this time, Kai would not let them get away with it. He could not.

As Kai considered how to approach, the hesitant guard did not join the beating, but when Doodler cried out, instinct sent a stifling hand upon the helpless mouth. Doodler pushed and writhed harder, biting and scratching. Fingernails drew blood on the calmer guard, and hands wrestled each other, until the small guard wrangled Doodler and spun him face down. Meanwhile, the violent guard grew more so. The struggle was a flailing awfulness. Worse than the blows themselves, Doodler pled and cried, struggled and fought, wriggled and slowly and surely, fell to acceptance, tranquility, and a sort of violent peace, where the blows landed and he moved less and less, until there was nothing but pained eyes, asking for help and then, there was a blow to the head and no more pain.

Kai watched as the eyes lost life. It happened too fast, and Kai was horribly still during it.

Doodler was still, too.

The guards stopped beating a limp body and were too distracted to see that Doodler was looking out the window at Kai.

"Is he?" the reluctant guard asked.

The violent guard poked with a black boot, and upon getting no response, there was a look of worry. Hands went to Doodler's neck, and as if struck by absence, the violent guard backed away, drew out a cloth, and began to wipe the scratch marks off his boots. "Help me clean this up."

Kai ducked down as the guards began to search for a way to clean up. There were rustles and scrubbing, byproducts of cleaning, and then the light went out, while further rustles followed. The night was truly dark.

Kai remained under the window a while, wondering why this had happened, what could make men do such things, putting the brutality and actual act to the furthest corner of his mind. He tried to wipe it clean, but the violence stained his memory with feeling more than image. There was a feeling of crimson.

Pain and rage.

And as feeling called for retribution, he regretted not being more a hero. Kai was no Hercules, but he also didn't feel himself.

He began a muffled sob, sitting in the leaf-bare bushes and surprised at his own tearfulness. Tears froze and dried to flecks of salt and frost on his cheeks. But not forgetting the man's suffering, he cleared his eyes and clenched his fists, resolved at what must come next.

The guards opened the door, peering to make sure the coast was clear. One carried two shovels, while the other dragged a man who looked to be asleep. Had it not been for what Kai had seen, he would've thought Doodler to be peacefully dreaming. Maybe he was.

Kai followed, silent and breathless. He swallowed anger. It was not time for it.

The guards went across the grounds and into the bark tunnel, Kai slipped in behind. Wood was ancient, dark, and knotted. A damp smell permeated. The tunnel split into three directions, one which was taped over with yellow rope and had a sign placed on a pile of fallen bark and rocks that said, 'Danger, cave-ins possible'.

The guards went under the rope and over the debris, lugging the body along. Kai went to scramble after them, but he stopped at the sound of shovels and voices.

"Dig faster. We've got that early meeting tomorrow."

Shovels hurried. Kai decided it best to wait around the corner and plan—letting his rage take over action would end well only in his imagination. However furious he was, attacking the two guards straight-on was a tough task. Without strength, he had to be smart.

"Should we say a few words?" asked the trembling voice.

"We're the ones who killed him." The loud voice was emotionless. "It's better if we don't."

"I didn't—" said the uncertain guard. "Yeah, it's better if we don't."

"No one will miss him." The voice echoed. "They'll think he left like the others."

"I wish we could've let him go." Sadness rung through the weak-voiced man.

"Times are different. No one can leave anymore. We're short-handed as it is."

"It's insane." A shuffling of feet. "Five guards for this many workers. Why not get more?"

A solid *thump*. "They don't have to pay workers as much. Besides, it'll be fine. We have *him* on our side."

"*He* scares me as much as the workers."

"More." Even the louder man shuddered. "At least we can understand people. They're not monsters."

"*He's* not the worst monster out there."

"But *he* does smell like it."

"I think that's just the meerkat. Little thing, surprisingly big smell."

There were further sounds of digging, and then the patting of shovels on flattening earth. The guards scrabbled back and went past Kai.

He did not leap on them as he intended.

It would've made him feel better, but it would not accomplish what he wanted. Kai didn't know how to feel or what to think, but he knew what had to be done. And he only hoped he was strong enough for it.

THIRTEEN

REVOLT

T HE BARN STIRRED and Kai did too. Whispers rose in the morning, and sleep-sand eyes were cleared by hands or a look outside. A dreadful awakening. People investigated the commotion, only for some to return like they'd been dipped in ice—shivering or numb. Curious to know what the disturbance was, others exited.

Kai, however, already knew. He knew all too well.

As he crawled out his corner and joined the crowd, flashbacks of burning fury and chilling flesh woke him like caffeine. Yet, besides eyes darkened by his long night, the only sign of the night before was dirt under his fingernails.

Outside the barn, dawn's rays leapt over the rim of the quarry. Darkening clouds mirrored the ring of onlookers. Kai broke to the front, and at the sight, his throat clenched as if struck.

A mound of blankets, but Kai knew that Doodler would never wake and throw them off.

The crowd was haunted by the shadow of death, a primordial discomfort. There was a horrible, near-silent shuffling feet and held breath.

The quiet vigil was broken by a confused bustling.

The five guards carved into the circle, investigating the cause of concern with whips and swords ready. One of the guards—the one who had held Doodler down—dropped his whip at seeing the body he thought he'd buried. Another black-clad guard grabbed the whip and handed it back.

Although Kai didn't know the guards' names, each one of their wants and desires were hateful to him. But he did not give in to this hate. He had not the night before, and he would not do so now.

"Get to work," one of the guards directed as if nothing had happened. "Just an accident."

The crowd remained stunned. However, the guard's words seemed to restore feeling in the morning air.

Anxiety rippled through the crowd. "Is he dead?"

"I think it's Doodler."

"No need for alarm," said one of the guards. "He must not've been able to handle the work. Give us some space and we'll clean up here."

The guards held whips between their hands like crime-scene tape, blocking the crowd from the sight. Precarious, the crowd stepped back as if from a cliff edge. The gathering and the guards stared. Neither wanted to show fear, but as both groups shot looks at the body, both began to. And that was the start of animosity.

The guards urged workers towards the barn. Kai went with them, simmering as the crowd did, still shocked that the body was not a dream.

"Why are you pushing us back?" asked one man, fearful.

"Do we still have work today?"

The turbulent sea of people shifted temperamental, black-clad figures against the crowd.

"What happened?"

"This is ridiculous."

"Stop pushing."

The crowd compressed too far. Volatile, the situation teetered at the barn doors, crowds churning like the clouds above.

A whip cracked like thunder. "Go inside."

Someone shouted, "Did you kill him?"

Kai was squeezed with the crowd, and in the pushback, there was a scuffle to Kai's right.

Another *crack*.

A man yelped, stumbled, and fell. His white shirt was ripped by hard-leather at the shoulder, raw and red underneath.

Kai split the crowds as he made his way to the front. The five guards stood before him, huddled and holding up hands in a vain attempt to diffuse the push-back.

"Calm down! Get back!" shouted a guard, threatening with a whip, glistening at the tip like a bloody sunrise.

This calmed no one. "Murderers!"

A single man's word rippled through the crowd. Chaos followed. Shouts. Profanity. Objects were thrown at the guards, and, outnumbered, they backed towards the body, frightened. The crowd pressed in. It was as if a den of lions had been surrounded by wildebeests—lions were better equipped for the fight, but because of a united horde, the lions would not last.

Disorder tumbled towards rebellion.

However, anarchy calmed with a single arrival.

It was *him*—the giant—pushing through to come between the guards and crowd.

The mythical-sized man stared at the crowd, and workers broke eye contact and backed away. Guards stepped forward; however, they were unwilling to go beyond the safety of the giant. They cracked their whips at the ground for terror and intimidation more than any real purpose.

Fists unclenched and the crowd simmered into discontent rather than physical conflict.

Somehow, this violent-looking colossus had prevented further violence. But for how long could not be known.

Kai stood his ground, ready to fight the guards and the giant. He expected more support than he got. Mushmouth and Tiger stood with him, but the crowd scuttled off.

"Where are you going?" Kai asked people as they passed. "They killed this man."

A *crack*. His upper body stung sharp, a light, fleeting whip-tap that reddened and did not break skin. Kai leapt at the guards, scuffling before another blow could come, grabbing at the whip's harsh sandpaper-like leather that tore at his palms.

Kai readied his fist, but he never got to land his own blow. Meaty hands grabbed his collar and he was lifted into the air, shirt rubbing against his newly-raw skin. The ease at which the giant picked him up was comical.

"No violence," said the giant.

Surprised at the man's first words, Kai was shocked into obedience.

The giant held out a fry-pan sized hand to stop the guards.

Wavering, the guards lowered the whips, and one said, "Get them back to work. We'll dock his pay later."

The giant let Kai down, leading him, Mushmouth, and Tiger towards the wall.

Kai was furious. He didn't care about pay. He'd just expected—well, he didn't know exactly what—but some sort of final confrontation where the people would rise up against injustice.

While the guards circled the body, keeping it out of sight and shuffling it away for re-burial, Kai stood at the mine with Mushmouth and Tiger. With pickaxes nowhere in sight, they dug in with their hands.

"How're we supposed to do this?" Kai asked. He slapped the rock, palm pulsing afterward like his stinging shoulder.

Mushmouth looked up at the looming clouds. "Just dig with your fingers."

"What just happened?" Kai asked.

"People are scared," Mushmouth said. "But until they're more scared of what will happen to them if they don't revolt than what might happen during that revolt, nothing will change."

Kai clenched his fists. "I refuse to believe that freedom isn't worth the fight."

The rage from death and injustice burned in Kai's eyes hotter than the desert sun, but Kai found himself in chilling shade; Kai turned to see the giant looming larger over him than the coming storm.

Mushmouth and Tiger worked faster, but Kai stood his ground and confronted the giant. "I won't work anymore."

"They don't understand," the giant mumbled to himself, leaning against a pickaxe that groaned under his weight. The meerkat stood alert on his shoulder. The giant rubbed at the meerkat's neck with a pinky half the size of the creature, whispering, "They don't listen to old Joe. The guards are lucky to have me, and I'm lucky to have you."

"It doesn't have to be like this," Kai said to the massive man. "Because of you, these people live in fear. Although you may be strong-armed, you're weak-hearted."

"And you? You're just weak." The colossus huffed, his chest swelling to explosive proportions, but instead of anger, he laughed, hearty. "I've heard worse. If only you could understand me."

"You're a myth, but I understand what you're saying."

"You do?" The man-giant stared at him with inquisitive eyes. "I suppose it changes nothing. You want a solution? The solution is here." He cast the pickaxe down before Kai. "Get back to work."

"No."

The scene between Kai and the giant finally got others, including even Silvertongue, to stop working.

Kai tried to stir the crowd. "Are you going to let them get away with killing a man? All you're doing is paying off a debt created by those who do nothing except live off your work. Their only tool is fear. But I'm not afraid. Without fear, they have nothing. Without us, they are nothing."

There were smiles, but little more. As his words fell short, Kai saw he was missing one crucial aspect—belonging. Kai was an outsider. He felt it. The dim faces staring at him made it obvious as the approaching storm that revolution was not a single speech or man.

Rebellions did not happen overnight; they built on continued abuse, swinging closer and further from a flashpoint until a single or series of acts unleashed the tension like a rubber band snapping. Kai demonstrated such an inciting incident. But it was not time. Tension had released and would have to build again. So, as much as he wanted to help, Kai realized that his position was hopeless.

However, Kai defied failure, smiling at the giant and hoping to create a lasting impression in his escape, which might encourage and boil the tempers of others faster. "As I said, I'm not going back to work."

"It's my job to keep people in line," said the giant. "If you won't work, they'll do the same to you as that poor soul."

Kai challenged the man, despite the mismatched size. "But you're the only reason they're getting away with this."

"Please, will you just get back to work?"

"No."

"What am I supposed to do?" the giant asked the meerkat, accustomed to having only it for conversation.

Kai grinned. "There's only one good path available for those who try to be the master of a man accustomed to freedom."

"What's that?"

"Give them their freedom back."

"I can't do that," The giant said. "*They* won't allow that. They need the moss. If no one works, the drought continues and the world dies."

"I can't stay here." Kai was definite and absolute. He needed to save Sophia. She would appreciate him trying to save these people, and even though he had failed here, he could not fail in finding her.

The giant's lips tensed. "It's not a choice."

"You're right."

Kai bolted. The giant blocked his way and shoved him back. They shuffled, and although Kai tried to dodge and duck, the giant blocked him with embarrassing ease.

Feeling foolish, feeling weak, fury swelled within Kai. He was angry at the guards, at the workers, at himself. How could he risk Sophia for people who did not want his help? He could fail a million times—but he could not fail her. Helpless, fearful, and filled by purpose, Kai's fists went to strike, more to distract and escape than beat the myth.

The result was obvious. Kai punched the man's absorptive stomach like a tennis ball thrown into a pool. A splash-back. The myth compacted a black-and-blue drubbing into a single fistful, and Kai was splattered against the wall with blood and sound.

Discarded like the pickaxe next to him, Kai lay in in the dirt. Dazed and bruised, he still got to his feet.

Thought and feeling fell under a fog of crimson. Life came in flashes of scarlet lightning. Fingers around a splintery handle. The weight of a heavy pickaxe lightened by adrenaline. A sudden swing, metal streaking through the air. Then, a sudden stop.

A thump of blood and a body into a crater of dust.

The pickaxe followed into dirt. Nothing more until the haze lifted.

People's silence told Kai what had happened, and Kai supposed it had. The meerkat sniffed at the giant's cavernous nose. The tiny critter's black-circled eyes questioned Kai's guilt, before turning back to the giant and nuzzling the nest-like mutton chops.

Kai stood stunned, feeling as if he should've been horrified at the fragility of life. But he was not.

He thought he should run, and run he did.

After watching the giant be felled, guards watched Kai go, hiding whips behind their backs. Kai sprinted past. He left Mushmouth, Tiger, and Silvertongue—he did not know what would happen to them, whether they would escape or not— he only knew that his feet had to carry him away before the guards overcame surprise, and so, he ran and ran, up the dusty path, around the spiral quarry, chased by his past, ascendant to the desert, where he hoped to find sun and light, but only found coming clouds.

A dark brown wall of churning sand smothered the sun. Only once he emerged into the desert again did the first bits of emotion gather in him as the looming sand-clouds built in the sky. He feared what he had done would only make things worse for the people below. It certainly made him feel worse.

If he hadn't tried to be a hero, this never would have happened. But if he hadn't tried, wouldn't that have been worse? Self-defense or not, justified or not, Kai had killed. The mythical man was dead, but guilt lived.

Kai wished it hadn't cost a life, but nothing and no one would prevent him from saving Sophia. Certain in his path, Kai put the mines behind him. In the flatlands, it was easy to find Al, Tom, and Helene at a small campsite.

"You're back," Al said, offering Kai a waterskin, which was refused. Al returned it to his satchel and offered a smile instead. "With the storm coming, I thought we were going to have to leave you behind. But we're closer to Duat than I thought, and I made you a promise to stay until midday."

"We're not close enough to make it in time," Tom mumbled, checking to make sure all his medical gear was accounted for. "Can I say sandstorm now? It can't be bad luck to say it because all we have is bad luck anyways."

"What happened?" Helene asked.

Kai shook his head and walked on. That was all.

FOURTEEN

THE RUINS

A LINE DIVIDED ASPHODEL from the unknown. Cara and Li waited, a small bridge and a dry river bed separating them from the slow-crumbling buildings beyond. Sepia sands were a film over resting ruins. Dead trees and daytime apparitions, mundane or fantastic, lay ahead; Cara was not sure which she feared more. Imagination, excitement, and apprehension swelled.

It was past midday, and Rollo was late.

Adventurous enthusiasm diminished. Cara crossed her arms, but despite rising doubt, she faced uncertainty nonetheless. Li was a comfort—he looked calm, unmoved as the line of dust between Asphodel and the bridge. Safety lay behind in the bustle of the city and the savory, tempting smells of a market asking them to turn back. Cara knew that was impossible, although she wished otherwise. If they wanted to survive—if they wanted to indulge in any of the sweet pleasures of life—they had to face danger. That was their job.

It was what Cara always wanted. But now, standing at the edge of the ruins, it seemed less like a good dream.

A smile of cracked ruby. "Are you two waiting for someone?" asked a woman. She had a chalky complexion and sharp features. Her eyes, though, were warm and dark.

"A co-worker." Cara welcomed the woman with an equally warm smile. "We're part of the new myth control division for Asphodel."

"The ruins are dangerous," the woman said.

"It's our job to face danger." Cara stood straighter, solidity restored by pride.

"My statement stands."

"What would you know of it?" Li asked, side-eying the woman.

"I'm the well-woman over there." The woman pointed down an alley. "I hear all the rumors. They're stories, but sometimes, stories are just well-told truths. I wouldn't intrude in the ruins, if I was you."

Cara crossed her arms. "We can handle ourselves."

"I'm sure you can," the woman said and walked away. "Listening isn't the job of myth control, I suppose. I just thought—never mind."

"What?"

The woman shook her head and looked back. "The ruins don't like being disturbed. Just don't start any trouble and you might be ok." She went down the alley towards the well.

Cara and Li agreed with a frown. Hope for an easy, simple stroll through the uninhabited city was a lie they told themselves. Myths were stories, after all. But both knew better—myths were real. The only question was what kind of myths lay ahead.

When Rollo arrived, some of the hesitation dissipated with his presence. He strode confidently, but he did not look entirely pleased, constantly looking over his shoulder at something, but he returned a half-smile towards Cara and Li. He brought two scabbard-belted swords with him, and at greeting, he handed them over.

The twins unsheathed the blades and tested the sharpness. It was an instinct, and also childish, as if checking out a toy; from kid to adult, some things didn't change.

"I thought you were all about non-violence?" Li asked, pleased by finding hypocrisy.

"I am." Rollo grinned. "You two aren't, and therefore, you'll need the swords."

Cara asked, "If we need to defend ourselves, why don't you?"

"Because my life is meaningless. In case of an oh-so-hungry myth, I might be meaty enough to satiate its hunger."

"You sound a bit like Kai." Cara sheathed the sword, wavering whether to attach the brown-leather belt or throw it away.

"Kai isn't as funny, but who do you think he got his humor from?" Rollo laughed. "Only thing is…I'm serious." For once, he looked it, too. "I won't use violence, even to defend myself."

Li latched the sword around his waist. "Is that not violence against yourself? Some sort of self-destruction?"

"It's my life. I can destroy it if I want." Rollo motioned for them to follow and went into the undisturbed dust with a light, confident stride.

Despite Rollo's lack of pomp and circumstance to such a dramatic step, Cara did not follow. "Aren't you going to teach us anything? Tell us anything to watch out for?"

The hero rotated and walked backwards, arms out, questioning and careless. "I've never been to the ruins. How could I tell you anything? Myths here may be violent. They may be peaceful. They may be any number of things. There is only one way to prepare for uncertainty, and that is your only lesson—learning how to learn." He turned back around and was across the bridge.

Li whispered to Cara. "The more he speaks, the more I think we'll get along."

"The more he speaks, the more he gets on my nerves. He's nothing like Kai." Cara frowned. "Aren't you worried?"

Li answered with action. He stepped onto the bridge, dust clouds cascading away from him. "It'd be idiotic not to be worried—but you can call me an idiot. Worry might be appropriate and even helpful, yet, it's something I lack. I thought you wanted to do heroic things? Like Kai? Isn't this heroic, going where no one else dares?"

Cara followed but glanced back to the inhabited mayhem of Asphodel, aware of the disparity between what was behind and in front. "I want to protect people, but there's no people here. This feels like searching, not saving."

"We're searching for knowledge. Understanding can save lives. Better that we're learning than burning."

Li's logic calmed Cara's emotion. She grinned, comforted and confident again. Together, they traced Rollo's steps across the divide.

Across the bridge and onwards, the houses and rubble swallowed them. Carcasses of long-lost destruction decayed.

The fallen and broken bones of a city cratered into dust. Crumbling supports remained. Walls were shattered brick-teeth, as if some beast crashed through. Some of the holes did look rather bull-sized. Trees that lined the main boulevard were dead, barren, and uprooted. The sand-dank alleys dug on either side, narrowed by still standing city-skeletons.

"Should we stop and paint a picture?" Rollo asked, waiting for the twins at an alley. "As nice as this wide, bright street is, I think it's time we venture into the real ruins."

Their path led from the wide road to the somber side streets. Bricks spotted the ground like puddles. While there was no murky water to step in, the air was thick with basins of dust. Particles hung in the air, illuminated by sun-slits between buildings. But mostly, the tilting towers cast hulking shadows, covering twisted debris, gnarled trees, and them. It was dark and dreadful; nothing was on a grid, and they went in circles, met dead ends, and in general, got lost.

But besides their imagination, they encountered nothing.

Li simmered, impatience growing. "Another dead end?"

"Only if you can't bend your knees." Rollo shimmied under a leaning, half-broken archway. He whispered, "They'll be hiding, trying not to attract attention."

"Why?" Cara asked, no more than a murmur.

Li slipped through. "They're scared of us."

Cara ducked under the brick and hung closer to Li's confidence as they walked down the dirty street. "We haven't done anything to them."

"Not yet." Rollo stopped, listening. "Doesn't mean all the people of Asphodel don't scare them."

A pitiful cry wafted towards them. It was quiet, barely audible, but an entirely soul-shattering moan of pain. Not asking for help, just suffering. Whimpering. Weeping.

Rollo crept forwards, cautious. He ducked in a red-brick building through a shattered hole in the wall. Pity brought bravery, and Cara went in ahead of Li. In a room of grey rubble, broken tiles, and twisted metal, there was a colorful kicking in the corner—a rainbow-colored sheep.

The creature was lying, and tufted kaleidoscopic wool twitched under the painful convulsions, shimmering and shivering with technicolor. Blood broke the divide between the vibrant animal and barren world, trickling from the creature's underbelly. Crimson liquid stained pale tile and the grey grass that had sprouted through grout and died. In pain, the small lamb struggled with *clicks* and *clacks* of desperate hooves, trying to distance itself from these new intruders. But it could go no further. The fluffed sheep looked between Cara and another hole in the wall, wondering whether it was better to retreat. Cries grew more desperate.

The creature raised its tiny head. Two fangs, sabretooth-like, curled from the upper mouth and over the lower black lip. If the creature was bigger, it might've been threatening, but the display was almost kitten-like.

Unable to let the piteous creature suffer, Cara approached, hands out in an unthreatening manner, trying to display care and wanting to help the poor thing. Like finding an abused puppy, there was dual-sided feeling—warm compassion and anger at what had hurt it.

"Careful," Rollo said to Cara. For all his talk of compassion, he kept cautious.

Hypocrisy angered Cara, and she hissed soft and passive-aggressive, "What, do you know what it is?"

"Seems like food for something bigger," Li said.

Rollo was taken aback by Cara's spirit. "I don't know what it is. But that's why we should be careful."

"We've got to stop the bleeding," Cara said. "Li, give me part of your shirt."

Without hesitation, Li used the razor-sharp sword to cut off his sleeve.

The sheep bleated and barred its teeth.

Li's uncaring demeanor broke to sadness as he handed over the fabric. "It doesn't want our help."

"Don't you see it's bleeding to death?" Cara approached with the fabric to stem the bleeding. "We need to do something."

Rollo crossed muscular arms. "Check it over, but if it's going to survive, let it be."

The creature's fumbling legs stumbled, but it found footing and stood. Blood dripped to the ground. The sheep's lightshow beamed, changing the blood-pool deep purple and orange and blue, shimmering brighter when rays passed through and glistening black when the lights moved away. Again, the creature bleated.

"Seems to be healthy enough." Li glanced at Rollo. "Are you not going to stop her?"

Rollo shook his head. "It'll outrun her, and if not, she can help it. If it's suffering, it'd be heartless to do nothing."

"Sounds like an argument to put it out of its misery," Li whispered. But despite usual callousness, there was a crack in his demeanor—worry was written over his face.

Cara was within arm's reach, bright beams dancing over her figure, but the creature did not dart away. "It's okay. I want to help you. Just let me put some pressure on the wound and you'll be alright. I don't mean you any harm."

If the creature understood, it did not believe. Big black orbs of eyes stared her down.

Cara persisted and tried to charm the creature as Kai might, with a cautious charisma and reasonable words. "You're scared." She knelt to its level and laid a palm out towards it. "We came to help you."

The sheep lowered its sleek, color-changing head, icicle-like teeth afire with color, tangling into chest fur.

The whole creature went scarlet. Warning.

Rollo was calm with panic. "Back off."

There was a sharp inhale, a piercing *baa*, and the sheep spun, leaving a furry red backside facing Cara.

Li leapt and pulled Cara away, expecting a kick.

What came was not a kick.

The sheep sprayed squid-ink like a skunk. Black, seeping goo streamed. A scream. There was blood and a blinding flash of chaotic light. The creature shimmered like an iridescent octopus, such limitless color, the world overwhelmed white.

The dazzling sheep bounded out the room, but ooze still sizzled.

Coughs and chaos.

Li pulled Cara out the room. Tears streamed. Noses burned. Throats convulsed. Noxious gas seeped after them, and they ran. That's all they could do—instinct instructing them to get away.

But there was no getting away—liquid gunk clung to Li's arm, sizzling and rotting, following them with a cloud of streaming smoke that wind did not extinguish.

"Wait," said a familiar voice.

Firm hands and a soothing liquid poured over the goo, draining onto dry dust below, staining ground dark. The goo simmered on Li's shoulder, drying dark black. Cringing in pain, Li was kept upright by Cara. But as they realized who had helped them, they both almost fell.

It was Kai.

"Follow me," he said, ushering them into a building.

Safe inside a simple wood-floored room, Kai capped a waterskin and smiled at them. Cara and Li were so shocked by what had just happened and the sudden appearance of their brother that they did not return the smile.

The only sound was a bit of sizzle on Li's shoulder, still burning. Li cringed and went to wipe it away.

"Don't," Kai said. "It'll fizzle out on its own, there's nothing you can do now except stop spreading it."

Overcome with her twin's sacrifice and brother's return, Cara cried. "You saved—thank you—I'm sorry—thank you."

Li's guard was up, and he took a deep, pained breath. "What're you doing here?"

"I heard you were coming here. It seems I'm a bit late."

Joyous as it was to have Kai back, after the sheep, Cara was infected with a little of Li's suspicion. "But how did you get back so quickly? Where's Sophia? Helene?"

"They're fine." Kai sighed. "Take a minute and rest."

They were in an old apartment, a respite from the outside world. The room lacked furniture, but with three solid walls, it was a safe cave. The way they came in was jagged stone and drywall, jutting like stalactites and stalagmites.

"What about Rollo?" Cara asked. "We have to go get him."

"In a minute." Kai held up his hands and nodded. "We've got to plan our next move; they'll be more danger."

"You can't be Kai." Li gritted his teeth, charcoaled flesh cracking his bicep. A mound of the goo stuck on solid, surrounded by fissures. "Kai'd never leave someone out there in danger without wanting to help, no matter how stupid it was."

Cara went to argue, but found that she couldn't. Li was right. Adrenaline pumped fire out of her. "Kai can't be here. What sort of monster are you? A doppelgänger? Skinwalker? Wraith? Demon?"

"Calm down," Kai said. "They'll hear you."

"Don't tell me to calm down. It's impossible that you're here." Cara continued louder. "How dare you take his form!"

Li flicked his eyes around. And with the preemptive cringe of coming pain, he grabbed at the black goo on his shoulder. The lump sizzled on his hand anew, smelling of burnt flesh. Decisive, Li threw it and hit Kai in the chest.

The room rumbled.

The disguise fell away, and a monster writhed in pain. They were inside a monster's mouth—the triangular and jagged walls were teeth, blending like a chameleon, while the fake-Kai was an angler-fish lure.

Cara reached for her sword, but Li dragged her away, leaping over the serrated drywall and into daylight. The whole building quivered. A wall-jaw snapped behind them.

They ran. Desperate. Terrified. Directionless except to escape, unsure of what every wall might be, what every bit of rubble might hide, and what might lurk around each corner. Whether they were going further towards fiends, frantic eyes and limbs darted one way and another, adrenaline numbing cramping lungs and the caustic burn of sinews. They dashed through flickers of shadow and light, debris and dust, alleys and finally, a garden.

They stopped.

Surprise. The garden bloomed with flourishing flowers, thriving bushes, and luscious-looking trees.

"Everything should be dead," Cara said, shocked by this drought-haven.

Li's wide-eyes opened wider. "I wish it was."

"How can you say that?"

The garden answered her. Flowers awakened. Not flowers, but myths. The pink orchids were praying mantises, dancing with claws and pincers. Red-roses were jellyfish that bloomed and constricted, while little white birds pretended to be lilies, yellow pollen-beaks tweeting. Nothing was as it seemed. By the wrinkled tree trunk next to them, there was a butterfly with an eye-design on its wings, a usual imitation of a predator; except this was a real predator—an ocelot with the design of a butterfly on its face.

It was wonderous. It was amazing. It was frightening.

Cara set off on a dead sprint.

Li blistered down the garden path after her, dirt spluttering like breath behind them.

Thousands of eyes watched, startled by strange intruders running through their garden. When they ventured too close to the flowers, a praying mantis instinctively lashed out, quick and precise, scraping as rose-thorns do.

They burst through the garden and into a park surrounded by trees. Grass was dead, but animals strolled without leashes and owners. A herd of golden-antlered antelope bounded, and a unicorn-horned rabbit hopped after them. Boars and bears cuddled under grand oaks filled with more scuttling creatures than leaves. The idyllic scene, filled with hybrids and myths, was peaceful and evolving and dangerous.

But for the most part, the myths did not pay attention to Cara and Li, except for a horde of birds sitting on the dead lawn. As the twins focused on them, beady eyes focused back, and that's when they realized it was not bird-eyes watching. Bulging orb eyes were surrounded by fish scales. They had fish bodies, feathered wings, and the awkward waddle of geese feet. It was a horde of goose-fish. Startled by the sudden appearance of the twins, a few took off. Others followed, taking off in a swarm of literal flying fish. More followed from the lawn, from the trees, from everywhere. A whole gaggling swarm of fish-birds flew frenzied.

Cara and Li were chased back through the garden by chaos. Shimmering scales and rustling, falling feathers. Honks and dolphin-like squeaks. Back through the garden, they ran and ran, through alleys and destroyed buildings, knowing no direction. Cackles and growls threatened from dark shadows unseen.

The sky went black with goose-fish.

Finally, they saw hope—the main street, leading back into the rest of Asphodel.

Relief washed over them as they dashed across the line in the sand, causing perilous trails of dust behind, which were only further churned by the wind of what followed.

Clouds of goose-fish filled the sky, circling about the ruins and further still, causing just as much bedlam below.

Asphodel was mayhem, the sky was chaos, and the twins did not stop running until they crashed through home's door, much to the surprise of the rest of the family. It would be a long time before the goose-fish settled back to the ruins, and in their time over the city, they left a hailstorm of feathers, scales, and white-black guano, which was precisely aimed at stores and sidewalks and upwards-staring heads. While no one died, any doubt that myths lived in greater quantities than ever known in the ruins died that day.

Cara and Li hid from what they had seen. What they had run from. And how they had failed. Rollo found them a while later; they were both wounded, just in different ways.

FIFTEEN

FALLING FURTHER

A SANDSTORM. COPPER MELTED in the cerulean sky and dried dark. Thunderheads joined, swallowing blue, greedy and growing greater. Clouds were like the bristles of the feather in Kai's pocket—sparser towards the tip with a dense, compact base. The smell of rain was absent. It would not come.

A plunging golden lightning bolt connected the choppy sky and tranquil desert. A still moment. Then, black velvet shadows swallowed sleek sands.

Thunder. Roaring quakes cascaded dunes, and sand rained upwards, feeding the hungry beast. The inescapable wall of a sandstorm engulfed the horizon.

"We can't go further," Al said.

"We have to." Kai clenched his fists. "We can't go back."

The group of four gazed upwards. Winds stirred and bit. Sand followed, scattering and scraping against them.

The approach of dooming nature seemed appropriate. Desert and tempest were punishment for Kai's failure; nature's wrath mirrored the disaster of the mines.

The storm lifted and stretched to meet them, tumbling into a boulder-roll of churning brown and black. The world watched, hushed, until thunder shook the very earth they stood on.

Helene shouted over the discordant winds. "Should we start digging our graves or do you have a plan?"

"I have a plan." Kai stopped. His head tilted at the gusting sands. As the storm closed in, he held his resolve against the instinct to turn and run. "For now, shelter in place."

Helene hissed, "That's not a plan."

Devastating lightning spearheaded the storm, and where firebolts struck, sand crystalized into glass, creating petrified towers of silica. Violent winds followed. Glass leaned, careened, and broke back into sand.

Gusts greeted Kai with a sensation of sandpaper. "We made it as far as we could. Now, we hope." Kai took out a white shirt from his bag and wrapped it around his head. By the time it was secure, it was already freckled.

Eyes open in the slit between fabric, a barrage of sand burrowed through, but Kai could not tear himself away from beautiful, boundless nature—he imagined it like the gods—so stunning, it burned.

Dark tendrils twirled, like some gargantuan beast reaching to engulf the earth, sucking everything into the vortex. The storm-wall cascaded closer.

"We never should've come with them," Tom said to Al.

Al shrugged. "We've been through worse."

"We have?"

"Maybe not." Al handed Tom a shawl. "But as long as we're together, things never seem that bad."

Tom took the fabric with a rare smile. Sand splattered, and the spluttering of trying to expel it stopped the smile.

The wall hit.

Sand swallowed them. Breath without air. Heat without sun. Blasting bolts flashed, firing once and twice and thrice, halos in the haze. Lightning reflected life. Violent. Short. Beautiful. Thunder rumbled and boomed, shuddered and shook; some strikes went quick and some lingered—but it was life lived loud.

A godly bolt struck near Kai. His soul trembled, feet wavered, and he fell.

He sunk in sand. Exposed skin screamed at the elements. Breathing was thick and heavy, like sucking in burning water and coughing after. The howl of wind flapped against the cloth on his face.

Squalls broke. The storm's temper was fury. Kai was stranded in a bombarding barrage of baritone. He called out for Helene, who couldn't have been more than a few feet away but was shrouded by sand. "Where are you?"

A yell of thunder responded and a chorus of wind echoed. Glass shards, crystallized bits of sand from the nearby bolt, sliced about.

In fear and instinct, Kai prayed. But Kai did not count on help from the universe, he anchored it on the belief he'd held since the beginning. He hoped it would work.

It had to.

Kai felt the feather in his pocket. That feather—the one from the snow leopard—was not so much a plan as desperation.

He pulled it out and stuck it to the wind, wishing for the cold that would come with it. With a strange poignancy, he understood now why the leopard was made in the first place.

The feather tore from his hand and flew off. Wind dragged the blazing red twirling into the air, spinning by an invisible hand.

As hope was wrestled away, Kai couldn't watch and instead bowed to the sand, bearing the storm's fury.

CRACK.

Thunder exploded nearby. A wet thing touched him on his exposed hand, sending shivers down his spine. The last thing he wanted was something wet in a storm of sand and glass—it was probably blood.

But it wasn't, the touch was cool and comforting.

Kai looked up.

A furry, white face on a background of black. The snow leopard was a beacon in the storm, its tail bursting with star-red light. But instead of the regal big cat that had greeted him at the spire, this version was surprisingly small—a kitten.

Still, it spoke with great authority. "I should scratch your eyes out for getting me into this."

"Get us out of here first."

The snow leopard's pink-black nose twitched. "How many people did you bring into your predicament?"

"Change the weather and ask questions later."

"I can't do that. I'm only a kitten."

"You can't? You're useless?"

"No, you're useless." The cat kicked a paw-full of sand at him.

The divot in the desert struck him more than the sand, reminding him of the mine. "What about Yggdrasil? The tunnels."

"Probably too deep." The cat's blue eyes stared, eyelids flicking away sand. "Not on the wrong track, though. Where are we?"

"Does it look like an ocean?"

"This isn't the time for sarcasm." The leopard snarled. "Are we near Duat?"

"Maybe? Probably? Would that help?"

The leopard kneaded at sand, moved a few feet, and dug, scratching at the sand with little paws as it might do in a litter box. However, it made surprisingly fast progress and soon drilled a hole bigger than itself.

"You're trying anyways?" Kai asked, watching the blue-white pelt pick up more and more brown sand.

"There are other tunnels." The cat coughed sand like a hairball. "A good idea only gets us so far. Are you going to help, or are you going to make a kitten do everything?"

Kai crawled over and dug at the hole.

The cat watched. "Hurry."

Kai thought he was digging his own grave, but he dug faster. Then, he stopped. Under the sand was something hard.

The cat pressed an ivory claw against the sandstone.

The sand slumped, slipped, and sunk. A sinkhole. Like escaping from a broken hourglass, Kai fell with the cat.

Three other figures slid and landed beside him with quiet *thumps*. In the tunnel, the wind was less loud and thunder did not come with booms, but with the rumbling of the floor and walls.

The tunnel was rectangular, sloped slightly down. As the clouds of dust settled, it was still. The only light was a comforting red glow, emitted from the phoenix feathers on the leopard's tail tip.

"Is that a sand cat?" Helene asked, scraping the stubborn dust off.

"I'm Shebu," said the leopard, shaking the desert from its fur. "And you are?"

Helene made no inclination of understanding, keeping dark eyes matched with the cat's blue. "Interesting feathers. Useful in the dark."

"I was already useful," Shebu said. "But I guess I get no thanks for saving you."

Kai unwrapped the shirt about his head, stuffed it back in his bag, and picked up the kitten in his arms. "She can't understand you."

The leopard growled. "I know, but that doesn't mean she can't thank me. Sometimes I hate being a cat." The kitten curled in Kai's arms, leaving the fluffy tail draped over his forearm to light the way. Eyes closed for a cat nap. "And sometimes, I love being a cat."

Kai grunted cheerfully before addressing Helene, "This is Shebu, a myth of some sort."

Fangs playfully bit onto Kai's forearm and growled, "I'm not a myth."

"It's so cute," Al said, unwrapping Tom's head-covering before his own.

Kai stroked the leopard's back so it'd release him. "Then what are you?"

"Cute, for now. I suppose." Shebu settled. "I'm just me. How would you like to be called a myth? Like you don't exist?" The cat pouted into sudden sleep, but ears still twitched and swiveled, listening.

"I know it sounds crazy," Kai said. "But I can understand…beings like Shebu here. Some, at least. That's why I did well in myth control in Elysium."

"Maybe you can understand myths because you are one," Helene said.

Kai's frown changed to a grin. "I don't think I'm a myth."

Tom asked, "Sorry to break in, but how did we get here?"

Al elbowed him. "Was that an intentional pun? Did we discover your humor down here, too?"

Tom smiled. The mood was better, having escaped the storm.

"Shebu," Kai said, as if the one word would explain everything, but he only got confused looks. "She dissolved the sandstone and we fell through."

Tom stared blankly at him. "Uh-huh. And where'd she come from?"

"My pocket." Kai was being short, busy thinking. "We're near Duat."

Shebu nuzzled its soft chin on him as a nod. "The pyramids nearby, not the city."

Kai dug sand out the recesses of his ear. "You should thank Shebu. We'd be lost without her."

Al came over and scratched Shebu behind the ear. "Thank you for saving us."

"Thanks." Tom patted Shebu on a fuzzy head, before looking at Kai. "Which way do we go?"

"I don't know," Kai said.

"Don't look at me," Shebu said, one sleepy eye peering open. "We're in the pyramid. I know the way as well as you do."

"What'd it say?" Helene asked.

"I'll tell you after you thank her."

"Thank you, cat," Helene said.

"Shebu said she doesn't know. But that I should lead the way."

The others followed Kai and the light he held. Shebu's tail was enough to see five, maybe ten feet ahead. As Shebu snored, the tail-light waned, pulsing dimly with each cute breath. The walk was dreamlike, the rhythmic tapping of feet on sandstone lulling with a *click* after *clack*, falling into line until four sets were one and dwindled into a soothing constancy.

Yet, at each step, they all knew it could change. They were walking in the unknown.

The further they went, it became increasingly undeniable that this was part of a pyramid. Tunnels split. Chambers were filled with nothing but cobwebs. They stopped at dead ends and backtracked. The darkness was always ahead.

Kai stopped and let Shebu down to take a drink from his waterskin. Then, he took a drink for himself, dust still itching his throat, and water washed it down.

Helene stroked Shebu. "I didn't mean to sound ungrateful earlier." She looked at Kai. "She's actually quite majestic. This is the leopard from Elysium?"

Kai accidently squeezed the waterskin too hard and it went down the wrong pipe. He coughed up a bit of sand. "It is. She was bigger then."

"I'm sure she was ferocious."

Shebu purred, pleased at the apparent compliment. As Helene stroked again, the tail raised rigid.

"Can I pick you up?"

Shebu nodded and found a new home in Helene's arms.

"What if I lead the way for a bit?" Helene asked.

Not fully recovered from the mines, Kai's arms were shaking and aching from holding the cat, who looked perfectly content with the suggestion. Kai figured it would be fine. It was not like Helene could run off in the dark, since Shebu's light would be an impossible beacon to disguise.

"Alright."

Kai suspiciously eyed Helene during the uneventful walk, and eventually, they stopped in a short hallway illuminated by Shebu's dome of red light.

The sandstone tiles here were well-defined. The grout lay shallow between the ridges, and Helene looked serious. "It must be a trap."

"Scared?" Kai asked, surprised at her hesitation. "If you want, I'll go first."

"I'm just thinking it through, unlike you." Helene studied the tiles. "Step where I step. If it's safe for me, it'll be safe for you."

Helene tested the stone. It was sturdy. And convinced, she prodded her way forward, keeping close to the wall.

Kai followed behind. To lessen the chance of setting off a trap, he balanced against the wall.

His weight touched and the wall gave way. Off-balance, he stumbled over himself and fell. He tumbled down a steep chute, flailing and trying to right himself, spinning and struggling, until he wriggled and slid down the embankment feet first.

When he hit bottom, his fall was cushioned by his tailbone, leaving an extremely unpleasant bruise that left him limping and shuddering as he tried to stand. Shaking the pain off, he realized he was alone in another section of the pyramid.

Helene's voice echoed from the slide. "Are you alright?"

"Yeah. Wait up there. Keep Al and Tom close." Kai frowned, hoping more that they would watch her.

"What's down there?" came Helene's echo.

Kai said, "There's only a door."

Before he could try it, there was a knock. A repeated rap-tap-tapping from the other side.

Someone asking to come in. With each tremor of the hinges, Kai's rickety spine trembled with a deathly chill fitting the tomb. He was cornered.

The best defense was silence, lacking other options. Despite fear, bravery was not lacking, and Kai was ready for a mummy or miscreation to burst through the door.

The door creaked open, and a flicker of flame furrowed through the crack. A halo of crackling wicker and melting wax entered. A man slipped in behind.

He was no mummy, but he had a petrified look about him. His dull eyes had a glaze over them, which focused on the candle and only peered from it to Kai for a split second thinner than the frail and failing hairs on the man's head.

At the sad state of the man, Kai helped with the door. "Are you okay?"

"You're in the wrong place," said the man.

Kai shut the door after the man, in case anything might follow. "How long have you been here?"

"This is a tomb. The dead live here."

"Right." Kai wasn't sure the man had all the sand left in his desert.

The man pinched the candle flame. There was smoke and a dulling orange wick. "Don't get smart with me." A draft swept through the chamber, and they were in renewed darkness, left with the lingering halos of light. "Temba's my name. This crypt is mine. The chill you feel is mine. The darkness and light, too. Did you bring friends?"

Worried this was a myth, Kai let the question fade, as if the silence illustrated there was no one else. "Are you human?"

The man grinned, his teeth a faint outline, reflecting dull embers of his near-dead candle. "I'd like to see you be so human after…" He mumbled and went quiet. A rustling of fingers echoed unnaturally. "It seems I still have ten fingers, two eyes, a nose, and about the right number of teeth. So yes, I am still Temba. The desert was harsh and the crypt was welcoming. Spiders and rats prefer it outside. I am hungry. Very, very hungry. But no, I don't want to eat you. Wouldn't have the strength anyway." He staggered and sat, back hunched again the stone. "I only have the strength of a faltering old man who's been here too long."

From his bag, Kai pulled out flatbread and cautiously, ever-so-cautiously, handed it over. Fingers brushed against his, and there was nothing unnatural except the ghoulish boniness.

"Thank the gods," Temba said, munching on the bread.

Kai kept his distance. He was not certain, but this man did seem to be only a man.

"Is there any way out?" Kai asked.

Bread crumbled to the floor and sharp hands clawed at what fell, letting nothing be wasted. Temba pointed with his thumb towards the slide. "Only if there's someone up there.

The door to escape from down here can only be opened from the outside."

"It really is your lucky day," Kai said.

Temba smiled. "Yes, this is a gift from above."

"And from me. But you're right, we might get a gift from above. I do have friends up there."

Temba stopped mid-bite, his teeth stuck halfway through. They unclenched and he spit out the food. "Why didn't you say so? We can dine at the table of the gods instead of eating bread." With new energy, he was on his feet and pulled out a match, striking it on the wall and producing flame. Candle caught and the room was bright again. "I can afford to use the light instead of crawling through darkness." He called up the slide. "Hello up there."

Without confirmation, there was no way to tell whether Temba was a myth only he could understand, and Kai followed up, "Helene, can you hear someone else?"

"Who was that?" her voice echoed down.

Kai relaxed, taking a deep breath. "Just an old man named Temba."

"Everything okay?" Helene asked.

"Everything's great," Temba replied. "Go further and you'll find a petrified wood door. Let us out."

Kai caught the man's excitement. "Just do what he says, but be careful."

"Alright," Helene said.

Temba pulled at Kai's arm, leading him past the door and into a corridor. The tunnel split, but Temba did not hesitate and brought Kai down a series of twists and turns until, finally, they reached a thick door with no handle, preserved and sleek amber.

"We'll wait here," Temba said, cheerful to marinate in the candlelight and only nibble at the bread, rather than scarf it down as he had before.

Kai asked, "How'll she know which door to open?"

"There's one wood door, this old one. The builders left an escape in case they ever triggered a trap. Without help, people like me are stuck. After all the other traps and tricks, complacency got the best of me. Makes me feel better that I wasn't the only one to fall down that last trap."

"What other traps?"

The man's filmed eyes focused on him. "They're all over the place. No way you could've made it this far by luck."

"We just broke in to escape a storm."

"Is that the only reason you're here?"

"We're trying to get to Irkalla," Kai said. "But I'm not sure we have any idea how to get there."

The man's glee cracked grim. "What do you want with Irkalla?"

"Do you know about it?"

"Of course I do." Temba grimaced. "It's under us. If you listen to the walls, you can hear the screams. But why would you go there?"

"My wife, Sophia, is there."

The man laughed hollow. "No one goes there that isn't welcome, and no one returns. If all you came for was that, you've wasted your time. And here I thought you were a thief or spy. You're only an idiot." Temba shook his head sadly. "I'm sorry for you."

This frail man, looking down at Kai like he was a lost cause, while the old man himself was trapped, did not sit right with Kai. He didn't appreciate the pity, and the man's sorry look broke Kai's good nature. Pieces welled within him as seditious shards. Containing himself would be the best course of action. This was only an old man. He didn't know what Kai had been through. Kai knew this and tried to keep thoughts within. But Temba's ironic pity made an unnatural feeling simmer and thoughts hissed free of their cage.

"You shouldn't pity me. I'm trying to save my wife, and what are you doing here? Breaking into the gods' domain? Stealing from a crypt? Trying to get away with whatever you can lay your hands on, only to end up trapped, exactly as the pyramids were intended to do to thieves? Apparently, a bit of coin and food is worth more than your life. How selfish can you be?"

"And what you're doing isn't selfish?" Temba asked.

Kai shoved Temba up on the wall, the bony shoulders hard as the stone. Dust rained down. Breath between them clouded.

"I'm not doing this for myself." Kai didn't mean fury but somehow, he couldn't control it. "I was a hero in Elysium. Yet, I don't want to save you!"

Temba chuckled, unsettling the mood. "You think you're so smart, do you? A bit of pity and you're ready to trust me. When the pity is returned, pride burns you up. You're easier to move than a marionette."

Kai knew better, but pressed the man harder. "What do you mean?"

The man ignored him with a radiant smile, which stretched with a stellar star effect like a supernova.

This was not a man.

The chamber filled a deep, dark blue like tender midnight on a full moon. Walls vanished into a rotating galaxy. A serene night sky became an expansive cosmos and at the center was a warm, orange glowing man. A sun—the sun.

"I think I've learned enough about you," said the voice. Papery skin felt of reassuring lifeblood underneath, safe and ancient. Golden.

Kai released Temba, but the man floated where he'd been held. Under them was a black hole, a stretch of space that was nothing but darkness.

"You're not human."

"At least you have eyes, if not a brain. My name is Ahu-Ra. You should've trusted your first instinct and not frailty, a made-up name, and smiles. Too good of a heart will get you into trouble."

The man's beard appeared as interlocking crescent moons. Candlelight ringed into a halo above the man's head. He was not an animalistic Egyptian god, and besides a hawk-like sharpness to pupils, Ahu-Ra was a human figure.

"You're not a myth," Kai said, excited. Then, in a low, unsure tone. "You really are a god."

SIXTEEN

THE NEXT STEP

THERE WAS SWEET NOSTALGIA drifting in Asphodel's market, and Cara wished she could conjure the exciting memories when she came here with Kai. Times were different now. That fond recollection dimmed at the prospect of what happened and what came next. She glanced at Li. He was walking, stoic as ever, but she knew it was a front. Under his sleeve, a black char branded his shoulder like a cracked tattoo. His hand bore marks from where he had thrown the sheep's goo. The fleshy outers of his palm were blackened and his fingerprints were constantly visible, marked by a dull grey like ink. But the hand injury was just a discoloration, whereas his wounded arm swung strangely, rigidly, and every once in a while, an echo of burning shook his stoicism.

Li grasped at his shoulder, the tendril of pain burrowing deep. Cara's frown grew; his pain was the fault of her naivety.

"I'm sorry." Cara laid a hand on his good arm.

He grimaced more. "Stop saying that."

Cara knew how bad it was, or how bad it looked, but Li pushed through pain. Asphodel's dusty, disorderly market was teeming with crowds, but Cara and Li weren't there for the goods.

The twins were meeting Victor before his speech. Rollo was joining, too.

The twins arrived at a pristine glass-fronted jade store. Li led the way, and a pleasant silver bell rang at their entrance.

Inside, there were white-tiled floors, blackwood shelves, and tin-cupped ceilings that spouted light like rain. The shine made color pop, radiant jade sparkling and dancing under crystalline illumination. Yet, Victor and Rollo only glared at each other, standing in front of a display case with the most expensive pieces depicting gods and myths with diamond eyes and ruby-topped staffs.

"Asphodel is in chaos," Victor said, leaning on the rectangular counter, jade staring up at him. "The council wants someone to be responsible. I know what happened in the ruins was tough."

"Yes, I'm sure you know how tough it was." Rollo gave an encouraging smile to Cara and Li as the bell over the door chimed subdued at the door closing. "How're you two holding up? How's the arm?"

Li crossed his arms, making sure that the wound's fissure could not be seen under his sleeve. "Fine. Just a bit of ink."

"You don't have to act so tough." Cara kept away from the shelves of jade, not wanting to accidentally break something she couldn't pay for.

Rollo chewed on his lip, thinking. "I'm not sure how a sheep, wolf, and octopus mixed, but I suppose when the seas dry out, myths don't die, they adapt."

Li shrugged and added, "At least it wasn't a bull-shark."

"This isn't the time for jokes." Cara looked at the strange replacement for a twin beside her. "When did you even get a sense of humor?"

"I always had one. It's just a bit black and unfit for usual company."

Taking Li's new demeanor as an unintended side effect of his injury, Cara accepted it in stride and greeted Victor, which occurred with the usual pleasantries that Li did not partake in.

Formalities finished, Victor's absorptive smile straightened, serious. "I have good and bad news for you. Probably best to start with the good—I got you an advance on your salary, and I also found your father and cousin jobs."

Li rolled his eyes. "Giving Marcus a job sounds like bad news to me. What's worse?"

There was uncommon hesitation from Victor. "I should've never sent you to the ruins." Victor looked sympathetically at Li, who deflected his gaze. "It's ridiculous, but the council wants there to be consequences for the swarm of goose-fish, or Geesh, as some call them. There was a lot of chaos. I think it's just a bunch of crap. To be fair, there was a bunch of bird crap. But people believe the myths will come for them at any moment, and the council needs someone else to blame."

"Us of course." The coolness in Li's eyes did not fan into fire. "How surprising."

Victor nodded. "The brave are the first to be blamed by the cowardly."

Li stared at Victor, trying to find some crack in the honest demeanor, but there was none. Uncrossing his arms, Li gave up on hiding the thin pencil-mark fissure that trailed below his sleeve. "I understand, some good acts have painful side effects. It doesn't bother me."

"Well, it does bother me." Victor tried to grin, but for once, it was forced and he gave it up. "But I agree. Doing the right thing is never easy—a lot of the time, you don't even know if it's the right thing." A brief discomforting glare shot between him and Rollo, before Victor asked Cara, "I just hope you learned something about the ruins? In a way, I suppose we all did."

Cara gritted her teeth. "I tried to help the myth, but—"

Rollo laid a sturdy hand on her shoulder. "You don't have to take the blame for me. I was the one in charge. It was my fault that the Geesh—if that's what such inventive people are intent on calling some oh-so-scary flying fish—were startled and decided to swarm."

"Is this true?" Victor asked Cara, seeing her hesitation.

Cara questioned Rollo with a look, and he nodded, smiling as if to say this was exactly what he wanted. "We weren't ready to face what was there."

Victor smiled. "I always appreciate a good half-truth." But it faded into a frown as charismatic as his smile. "You want to help, Rollo. I don't think we'll disagree that's one, if the only thing, we share."

Rollo nodded, genuine and non-ironic. "You're finally right about something. The only question is, who actually helps people?"

Victor was quiet, and finally said, "Guess we'll find out."

Rollo and Victor contemplated each other.

Rollo filled his frame with a vast, fresh breath. "It was their first day. You know I have to take the blame. It doesn't matter. I'm going to the ruins again."

"What?" Cara exclaimed with dismay.

But Rollo didn't look afraid. He'd always been honest, if only through sarcasm, but now, he looked certain. "If I survive, maybe we'll see each other again. At least then, we'll find the answer to whether the myths truly are evil."

Cara shook her head. "But after all that, how can you say they're not dangerous?"

"I think you need to find a dictionary." Rollo deflected serious words in humor. "Not everything that's dangerous is evil. You won't change my mind. I'm a big hero, remember? And you're just my students. I taught you what you need, and the choices you make with that are up to you." He bear-hugged her and Li together, and the twins struggled away.

"What did you teach us?" Cara asked.

Rollo chuckled. "Nothing. The best lessons can't be taught, only learned."

Victor offered a hand to Rollo and they shook. It was cordial. Neither, though, broke eye contact, intent on some internal battle between them, which could not be settled at such a moment.

"I hope your ill-advised decision turns out well," Victor said.

"Hope is one thing. The result is another." Rollo shrugged. "I'm not sure what I'm hoping for though. I'm a hypocrite. Cara taught me that. I'll let them tell their story without me. With time so limited, I have better things to do than spend more of it…here."

Rollo slipped out the store to the sound of the bell and walked through the massing crowd.

Li watched him go and returned with skepticism. "What's the deal between you two?"

Victor said, "We're trying to cure the drought, and we have different methods for the same end."

"Cure a drought?" Cara asked.

"Something like that." Victor shook off a thought like the shaking of the doorbell. "I'd be an awful doctor—I'm trying a solution before knowing the cause. However, if Rollo finds the cause, it may be too late for the solution."

"You don't like him," Li said, accusatory.

There was no lie. "No, I don't. And he doesn't like me either. It's a respectful dislike. That happens when you want the same thing." Victor met Li's dissecting eyes, but unlike others, he did not shiver. "Still, I'm sad to see Rollo go. Elysium's other heroes know how to do a job, but none of them have the same humor." The standoff broke, and Victor warmed. "This is my opinion, not the council's—but I think the two of you did well." Victor knelt and looked through the glass counter, where a scene of mythical jade figures was frozen, his focus on a foot-tall figure of Hercules wrestling Cerberus' slobbering dog-heads. "Satisfy my curiosity. I've always been interested in myths—beyond the Geesh and this sheep-thing Rollo described, what else did you see?"

Cara managed a small bit of previous humor. "You wouldn't believe me if I told you."

"I wouldn't believe you if there wasn't something unbelievable."

"We saw Kai."

"I didn't realize he was a myth." Victor's reflection on the glass fragmented between jade.

"It wasn't the real Kai. It was a myth's lure. The building was a camouflaged creature."

Cool eyes left the figurines and focused on Cara.

She continued, "And there was a garden of smaller critters pretending to be plants. And a park of bigger myths, too. Tons of them."

"None of them attacked us," Li said. "They seemed surprised we were there."

"We didn't stick around," Cara clarified, and with a gentle gaze at her brother, seemed to apologize again. "The one that attacked us was plenty."

"Would you call the myths a threat?" Victor asked, peering through the display's glass and still kneeling.

"However strange and interesting they were, yes, they are."

Li was stern. "I disagree."

"How can you say that?" An echo of fear—the terror at pain, screaming, and running—panged through Cara. "One of them scarred you."

Li distanced himself from feeling, even-headed. "It was afraid. We were, too. But that wasn't an attack, it was an escape. Some of them might be dangerous, but I'm not going to say they all are."

"Maybe not." Victor stood back up, mediating the tension between the twins by becoming the focal point. "But at least we know more about the ruins."

"That's good, isn't it?" Cara asked. "People will be less afraid if they know."

Li remained fixated on Cara. "But we only know part of it. And that's worse." He looked at her as if she was the example.

"It's not being scared if it's justified," Cara said, her voice biting.

Li scowled. "If I didn't know better, I would think you're the one who got hurt."

"You said this lure posed as Kai?" Victor asked, returning to the subject with serene ease. "Presumably it talked, then?"

Cara calmed and nodded.

"And I thought myths couldn't talk to us. Maybe I was wrong. Wouldn't be the first time." Victor ran a nervous finger along the dust-free glass, leaving a smudge. "There's something else I would like you to do. Just this last thing and I promise I'll do more than petition for you—I promise to get your family back to Elysium, provided you don't give up on Asphodel afterwards."

"You want us to go back to the ruins?" Li guessed, still tense.

Cara's fire returned. "It won't be like last time. We won't take it lightly or treat it naively."

"No, not that." Victor glanced out the window, where a full crowd was gathered. "I want you to reassure the people of Asphodel. Imaginations are running wild. I don't know whether it's someone camping or something more, but there's a strange light in Asphodel Park. It only burns in the wooded area at night and extinguishes before anyone can find the source. Maybe it is a myth. If you find it, I want you to try and bring it back. Then, we can show people there's nothing to be afraid of."

Vague relief washed through Cara at not having to go back to the ruins. But the relief did not last, the emotional scar of worry reopening as quick as it closed with the thought of encountering another myth. "And if it is something to be afraid of?"

"If you need backup, don't hesitate to ask," Victor said. "I don't want any more chaos or you to put yourself in unnecessary danger. Sometimes, the most heroic action is asking for a bit of help."

Cara nodded. "We'll check it out and if we need assistance, we'll ask."

"Good. Now if you'll excuse me, I think it's time for my speech. I invite you to stay and hear me out."

"I'd love to," Li said with a sincere-seeming smile. "But my arm is killing me, and I think I'd better go home. Are you coming Cara?"

She looked between two inviting smiles, which were so similar and so different. Victor's seemed to drag her in, while Li's seemed to drag her away.

"I'll stick around," she said.

"Excellent. I hope you feel better soon, Li." Victor shook his hand and exited the store. People immediately crowded around him, and there too, he was busy shaking hands and commenting to everyone he came across as if they were old friends.

"Are you alright?" Cara's asked Li.

Li shook her off. "I'm alright."

"You're mad at me. How many times do I have to say I'm sorry?"

"It's not about that."

"You can't lie to me."

"I'm not," Li said. "I just don't like this. There's just a sense that everything is getting worse, not better."

"It's hurting, I know." Cara lifted his sleeve and cringed. "We should put more ointment on it, and you should let it have some more air. It's ugly, but you shouldn't be ashamed of it."

"I'm not hiding it." Li snarled at her pity. "I'm used to being marked. I've been marked since birth. People, even my own family, look at me like I'm a freak. Maybe that's not as visible, but what marked me inside, that darkness, has always been there. But this?" He pointed to the hideous coal-like scar. "This is a good mark. I don't regret it. This was the best thing I ever did—protecting you. But I don't want to fixate on one good deed and the scars it gave me. I don't want to be afraid. I want to be better. The past changes us, but I'm tired of it defining me. I'm moving on and so should you."

"That's what we're doing," Cara said. "We won't make the same mistakes."

"Don't confuse consequences with mistakes."

"I'm not."

Li was about to retort, but he stopped, and with a groan and sigh, he said, "I really am tired. I'll see you at home later?"

"Alright," she said, not wanting to argue anymore, saddened by the strained connection with her twin. Unsure what else to say, she returned to an echoed call of mundane nature. "Have mom put the ointment on it.

"Mom and I aren't speaking."

"You don't need to. She still loves you. She'll still take care of you." Cara frowned. "We'll go to the park tonight."

Li exhaled a sharp breath, shoved the door open, and bustled through the crowd. Cara watched him go, holding back tears before joining the masses and waiting to hear what Victor had to say. She didn't know how to fix her relationship with Li; it was never perfect, but it, like her life, was more broken than ever before.

However, she held onto the belief that it would get better.

SEVENTEEN

FOR THE GODS

MYTHS HAD PREPARED KAI for everything except a god. Even during boring sermons, Kai thought of the gods with awe. He had never seen one. He had expected much. And not once, never in his wildest dreams, was a god what paced before him.

After appearing as the center of a galaxy, the god lost his radiance. He was vaguely reminiscent of the sunlit figure. His face was regal-bearded, curled with wisdom. Once scraggly hair was sunlight white instead of moonlit pale. With the renewal, cheeks plumped like swelling dawn clouds. But god or not, he did not look godly.

Ahu-Ra was incredibly, ineffably, human. He limped, coughed, and had it not been for the lack of real imperfection and symmetry of his face, Ahu-Ra would've just been a feeble old man.

In a crowd, the god would've blended in. He was so normal, in fact, it was abnormal.

Humans tended towards oddity. Deformities. Defects. A mole here, a dimple there. Quirks could be charming or unseemly, but normal was an impossible standard except for the gods.

Yet, because of the human element, Kai couldn't help but be conflicted by his past idea of the gods and what stood before him. It gave him chills.

"What was the point of that display?" Kai asked, standing in the stone crypt by the only door out.

The god ignored him; rather than answer with words, Ahu-Ra stood straighter, trying to look godlier, but a cough bent him and he paced.

"Why're you like this?" Kai asked.

"Ask better questions." Ahu-Ra turned and smiled. "You're running out of time to ask them."

"What am I supposed to ask?"

The god grinned. "That's a better question, but one I can't answer. Only you can answer what you need to ask."

"You talk like a…." He paused, avoiding the word 'myth', and continued, "Besides being vague, what are you planning?"

Ahu-Ra coughed, and where there should've been lines in the face, wrinkles lessened instead of deepened. "It's almost morning. It's time for the others to wake up."

"What did you get my friends into?"

"A tomb."

"If you hurt them, I'll kill you."

"Brave, brash words." The god chuckled, hollow and clear as space. "But if you're helpful, betrayal might be forgiven."

"Betrayal? You tricked me, sent my friends into who knows what, and—"

"We're all in a tomb. Can't a god have a sense of humor? I told the truth—I sent them to open this door. As you can see, no handle on this side." A mischievous grin. "When we're out, my starlight will wake the others. They left me here, but I think it is time for a great slumber to give way to a feast." Ahu-Ra scratched at his beard and seemed to have forgotten about Kai being in the room. "It seems like eons since we were together. Some will be surprised to find ourselves a little closer than expected." The god frowned. "But we are cultivating our mistakes. Everything has changed and nothing has. Humans are used to change—gods are not so good with it. The world moves at a pace past the gods. That's why we rely on humans. That's why gods fight over mortals."

"Gods fight for humans?" Kai couldn't ask more, perplexed at the absurdity of what the god had said.

"I hear your friends. What comes next will create an echo of wars past—a small tremor, an aftershock and pre-shock for what is to come. But in instability, the old crumbles and the new builds stronger to be ready for the next quake."

The door cracked open and Shebu's humanistic expression, a cheerful smile on the furred face, peeked through. Helene was here, but Al and Tom were nowhere to be seen.

Kai was not pleased to see Helene. He wasn't sure what, exactly, she had released by saving him, but he felt the world might've been better off if he was left to rot with Ahu-Ra.

"Where are Al and Tom?" Kai asked.

Helene shrugged. "We got separated."

"Beautiful company you have here," Ahu-Ra said.

Helene smiled. However, it was Shebu that Ahu-Ra was staring at.

An awkward introduction awaited. Kai went simple. "Ahu-Ra, meet my ex-wife and a magical snow-leopard that popped out of my pocket. Helene, this is a god, and I don't think any of us can comprehend what you've done by saving me. So yeah, shake hands and he'll take us to meet some other gods, I guess."

Shebu wagged a long tail back and forth. "Two gods fused into one. Fascinating. And such a clean joining. You can barely see the seams."

Ahu-Ra snarled. "Watch your words, cat."

The snarl was returned. "And I thought it would be a nice welcome. What happened to liking cats?"

"I'm only half Egyptian."

"Doesn't mean you have to take that tone," Shebu said.

"You can understand each other?" Kai asked.

A nod, and the god's glittering smile was the only star-like thing left about him.

Helene eyed Ahu-Ra with a strange fixation. "You're a god?"

"You're a human?" the god asked similarly.

Without waiting for another question, the god walked away. Figuring the god wanted them to follow and it was better to not be lost here, they trailed Ahu-Ra down the pyramid halls until they reached a burial chamber.

Nine stone thrones surrounded a black slab sarcophagus the length of two giants that acted as a sort of table. The thrones were simple, as to not distract from the purpose of this place—the mummy. Glass covered the top of the sarcophagus, allowing a view inside. Cast in a dove-white shroud that glittered under candlelight, the lying figure was godly. A pristine ivory headdress sparkled with gold and

Egyptian-blue striped sidings shaped like two imperial feathers. The death-mask rested as a façade of powerful gilded features.

As stunning as the god-mummy was, it unsettled Kai, and he couldn't look at it too long. The walls enthralled him instead.

The first glance mirrored the horizon over a sparkling sea—shining gold and turquoise acrylic walls. More than just drawings and pictures, the walls told a story.

The four walls were divided into eight frames, two on each wall, but part of something larger—a cycle of day and night. The first frame was a boat breaking through rocky waves. Aboard the boat were gods, one with the light of sun on his head, bringing light to a dark earth. The next frame was a lake of fire, and the boat plunged into the shimmering sea spray. Sunset.

Contrast. A dark pane lurked across from Kai, an underworld hushing the god's light. The boat passed the lands of the dead, a throne, and a pharaonic god. Danger awaited. At the heart of the story was the task and trial—a great snake, a chaotic force, eager to swallow the sun and gods. Paint peeled and cracked in the next frame.

The snake devoured sun. Darkness. Slit eyes snuck through the cracks in the wall and through Kai, a shudder made by paint and gemstone, passing from myth to reality.

But the story did not end there, for while darkness may consume light for a time, shadows cannot destroy light, only contain it. The sun burst forth from the snake, unable to withhold fiery brilliance. Finally, the boat burst free with life-giving radiance, renewed and restored as a brilliant, yellow sunrise.

Ahu-Ra moved past the frames, and the wall shimmered as the sun does in a piece of glass. Wordless, he sat at a throne at the head of the sarcophagus.

Ground quaked. Dust hopped, flying into the air and incinerating like dying fireflies—lit, streaking in the sky, and then dimming to dark.

Under the glass-topped sarcophagus, the mummy stirred. Faceted marquise emerald eyes glowed. The headdress remained unmoved, but spotlight eyes turned to Ahu-Ra, and then, to Kai and Helene. The crypt rumbled—a deep-seated chuckle.

It faded and stilled. The light died out of the eyes.

And for a moment, Kai thought that was all. He dared to peer at the peaceful cross-armed figure, a colorful crook and flail over its white chest, but as he did, hidden tunnels opened across the hall.

Imperious footsteps. Heat waves and icy chills. Rattling and rustling, tremors and tantrums, smells of ocean-salt spray and dusty catacombs.

The gods were coming.

A gladiator-arena opening of warriors and predators arrived. While Kai had expected a zoo of human-animal gods—given the tendency of the Egyptian pantheon for such creations—what arrived was not as animal, but just as chaotic.

As with Ahu-Ra, the other gods appeared human; however, they entered like a stampede, streaming into the room as a collection of shoving, shouting, and heavy-handed rudeness. Taller figures trampled the fallen. Enormous figures trundled along. Men and women of every shape, size, and demeanor piled into the expansive room, filling it like Asphodel's busiest markets, except without any flow, stagnating. Where the gods' appearances didn't match a zoo, the variety and manners might have. Competing constantly, they fought over the few seats, pushing each other off like children. All the while, the smells of earth proliferated. A few gods smelt of burning. Others, forests. Some, oceans. Kai smelt and felt odd sensations as he was pushed from the discordant center and towards the golden walls. A hot hand brushed him. A cold breath chilled his spine.

The wall reassured him, the last pillar of normality. In chaos, Kai lost Helene and Shebu.

Ahu-Ra's sunbeam pulsed as a gavel of order hammering down—flash, flash, flash. And in the ringing halos, noise settled, a few gods seated, and the rest stood. The room stabilized.

"Thank you for your silence." Ahu-Ra's fiery gaze at his fellow gods seeming to say that he shouldn't have needed to restore order. He looked fully-awake, younger than before. But a cough racked him again.

"Is the sun a little low on fuel?" one of the crowd asked.

"He's certainly dimmer than before."

"Like you should talk. You're not that bright."

Ahu-Ra beat a fist against the glass-topped sarcophagus. "Silence. I know there is a lot of bickering left to do, but that must wait."

"It can wait till the imposter council is cast into Tartarus," said a sand-skinned man, whose hair seemed to shed sand, too.

"More futile wars are not the answer." Ahu-Ra frowned. "That's why we are here."

A woman at the other side of the sarcophagus-table smiled kindly, dark hair over her slender shoulders like a warm embrace. "He's right. We've got to consolidate, get our affairs in order, and get back to ruling our lands."

"Consolidate? We've already melded with other pantheon's gods," someone protested in the crowd with a light voice, and in the same breath, said with a deeper voice, "I can testify to that."

"Not combining gods, consolidating power," Ahu-Ra said.

"And you'll be the first one to offer yourself?" asked the sand-shedding god. "Osiris didn't go so easily."

Silent fury shook the motherly-goddess' face. "Offer yourself, traitor."

The sand god grinned. "Never."

"Then, who would offer themselves? And more importantly, who would receive the power?" asked the motherly-goddess.

The room devolved into finger-pointing and shouting. It made Kai feel at home—the argument felt like the familiar family quarrels he had left behind.

Still, Kai knew he could not feel safe with that similarity; if anything, it made him feel like something dreadful was going to happen. Kai slipped beneath raised arms and clenched fists, finding Helene and Shebu in a corner.

"Where's Al and Tom?" he asked again.

Helene shook her head. "I told you, we got separated in the tunnels."

"At least they're not here." Kai knew it was not time to question her further. "I don't think all the gods are as civilized as Ahu-Ra."

"They may look human," Shebu said, curled up in Helene's arms. "But some are animals."

Another sunbeam restored order, and this time, Ahu-Ra coughed uncontrollably, echoing deep into the crowd. "I'll be the first one to offer myself if it comes to it, but it'll do us no good. We can't do what we always have. The humans have moved on in our absence."

The sand god sneered. "How would you know? You haven't left this pyramid since the war."

"We can all feel how sick the world tree is," Ahu-Ra said. "The changes are enough to know that belief is moving quicker than ever. Ask the humans who released me. Where are they?"

Kai froze. Gods searched, trying to figure out who didn't belong, and it didn't take long.

"Here's one."

The sand-haired god split the crowd and grabbed Kai's arm, his hand coarse as sandpaper. "You woke me up from a nice nap. Better have a good reason why."

The god Kai displaced at the table was an agile man with a hawk-beaked nose that glared at Kai like prey.

But Kai did not have time to fear. Kai found himself among the gods. Cold, metal features of the mummy stared lifeless under his hands. Others watched him, too. The air crackled with the collective power of their gaze.

Uncertain, Kai maintained bravery. He always figured the gods were watching, and now that he knew they were, it strangely did not bother him; instead, it invigorated him.

"What are mortals doing here?" asked a snakelike, man-god at the table, keen eyes dissecting Kai.

"We were on a journey when we were caught by a sandstorm—"

"We don't care."

"No wonder people don't believe in you," Kai spurted without thinking. "If you don't listen to people, why would they listen to you?"

The god hissed, venomous. But another sunbeam blinded the room.

"He's blunt, but he's right," Ahu-Ra said, straining under the weight of another instillation of forced order.

Kai counted himself lucky that Ahu-Ra was around.

"Who would think the gods worthy of belief if they saw us?" Ahu-Ra flourished his hands about the room. "We're near-powerless. Without power, we can't have belief. And without belief, we can't have power."

"We have done enough for mortals," said one of the crowd.

Another said, "Humans are ungrateful. Do something and they take it for granted. Don't, get blamed."

"Let them rot with Yggdrasil."

"It is our fault that the tree is rotting." Ahu-Ra remained calm and waved someone away who tried to whisper in his ear. "The corruption will come for us all. If we fail, the world tree will die." Ahu-Ra stared at Kai. "What we need is a bit of good gardening." A contemplative breath. "Humans are the soil and nutrients. Gods are the gardeners. But there are too many gardeners digging and harvesting. The plant is dying, and in death, the corruption thrives, making sure nothing grows back."

The sand god growled. "Some of us don't mind a dead garden. Besides, we've buried the corruption below us."

Ahu-Ra ignored the other god, imploring Kai with starlight eyes. "We must do our part, and so must you, human. Since we are not supposed to leave, we need a mortal to deliver a vital message to Elysium. It might not be the most heroic act, but it is necessary."

As the god's words sunk into Kai, bladelike, it entered a wound that was already open—his last attempt and failure at heroism—and instead of drawing new blood, the blade filled the gap, patching past failure. If he trusted the god, this was better than the symptom-bandaging he had done in Elysium. Already, he was imagining restoring the world as he had imagined leading people out the mines.

But this time, it wasn't about him. He did not feature in the visions. It wasn't about heroism. He wanted to remedy the drought, the suffering of Asphodel, his schismatic family, and lastly, a bare afternote, create a better world for himself; yet, it was only because it would be better for his beloved.

All such dreams died with that. How could he think about anything else until he had Sophia?

Kai knew this, and yet, that didn't mean he couldn't be curious. "How do you intend to fix the tree?"

"Let it be lost," said the sand god. "I like the desert."

Some of the gods whispered and argued. Raising into debate, the cacophony created chaos. The room devolved into factions and buzzed.

This time, Ahu-Ra did not silence them, speaking only to Kai and those few who bothered to listen. "We don't fix it like Elysium's council, taking the tree's moss to make themselves gods but killing the world in the process. We learned the trappings of searching for power long ago. We dug too deep and the world suffered from our ambition; that's why people are sent from all over to fill the hole their forebearers dug." Ahu-Ra sighed, breathing harsh reality before continuing. "Irkalla is doomed, but they stem the tide of the corruption.

Even the gods of Irkalla are not immune. They'll decay slower than mortals, but it's a terrible fate. Before it spreads, we must fix our realm and Elysium must fix theirs. But Elysium needs to know how. It sounds strange, but fixing this is not up to the gods."

Kai stood. "What do you mean 'decay'? What happens to mortals in Irkalla?"

"Rot down to the soul."

Kai sunk back into the chair, a drowning dread dragging him down. "No next life? My soulmate, gone?"

"Oh, to be in love," said the motherly-goddess at the table with a somber tone, one of the few listening. "It gives you such selective hearing. Forget about the world dying—all thoughts are about one soul dying."

Ahu-Ra gave a paradoxical grin to the goddess, before returning his usually light eyes to Kai. But now, the godly eyes were mournful as dusk. "I wish I had better news for you."

Kai shook his head. "You said Irkalla is below us? How do I get there?"

"I like him," the motherly goddess said. "A grain of hope in a beach of dismay, and the fleck of sand, no matter how impossible to find, is all that matters to the single-aimed mind."

Ahu-Ra sighed, saddened. "I'll show you the hole to Irkalla, but put any idea of going there out of your mind. Maybe it'll make you feel better to say you got closer than most. However, there's no saving the doomed and no use in venturing to where there's no return."

Kai clenched his teeth. "Is there any use in anything then? Unlike gods, whether mortals try and fail or don't try at all, the end is the same."

Ahu-Ra laid a flat palm on the glass coffin. "There are more similarities between gods and mortals than you know." Eyes lingered over the mummy before he tore himself away. "If you want to do your wife justice, make sure no one else suffers her fate. Bring this message to Elysium's gods. Then, maybe, we can heal this world."

"Find someone else." Kai shook violently. "I'm not a delivery boy. I'm not even a hero. I have to go to Irkalla, even if it kills me."

Wanting to argue more, Kai was stopped by a hand on his shoulder—Helene's.

"This isn't the time for telling the truth," Helene whispered into his ear, her calmness and surety cooling Kai's fire.

Kai nodded. Gods seemed no better at listening and changing their minds than mortals. "What's the message?"

"It's not for your eyes." Ahu-Ra motioned for a scribe. "Trismegistos, give me a scroll." A god with a blue-feather quill brought parchment, and Ahu-Ra scribbled over the glass-top, hiding the words with his arm, as a schoolboy does to protect the vital test answers that he wants no one else to take.

While Ahu-Ra wrote, Kai focused on the scribe, concerned and intrigued by what Ahu-Ra had said. "Trismegistos is a Greek name."

"Oh, you think I am one of your gods?" The scribe-god pondered him as a bird does seed. "I must disappoint you. Like many, I am a fused version of similar gods. Yet, some subtle contrasts keep pantheons apart. In Elysium, you might find a god like me. The closer we appear, the more the smallest differences divide us."

Ahu-Ra rolled the papyrus and sealed it with a bit of wax, superheated by a flash of light from the god's hand.

Imbedding back in the conversation, Ahu-Ra said, "Should you be tempted to open it, it will burn you to a crisp."

"Give it to Helene, not me."

"No."

"And why not?"

Ahu-Ra's eyes were enigmatic. "I trust you. You were a hero in Elysium, and the gods may grant you an audience. Will you deliver my message?"

"What choice do I have?" Yet, Kai knew his choice. And it was not delivering the message.

"Do you not want to know how to find the gods?" Ahu-Ra asked.

"I assumed you'd tell me."

"And I thought you knew—the council are the gods I speak of. While some lesser gods may've broke the truce, the old gods were sealed away as I was. Who knows, you may even find a god or two among the council."

Ahu-Ra rose without addressing the throng and motioned for Kai, Helene, and Shebu to follow with calm dignity.

The sand god called from the table, a venom seeping through words. "I assume you will tell me the message later."

Other gods hushed and stood at attention as Ahu-Ra left down a tunnel. Kai was glad to be out of the mess of gods, keeping an eye on Helene, who strode with him, Shebu in her arms. After a short walk, they stopped.

A vast chamber with a sinkhole in the middle. The sandstone path circled the hole, crumbling at the edges and falling into a brown-gold vortex. From the ceiling, sand rained like a waterfall and into the depths.

"Is that the way to Irkalla?" Kai was mere feet from the sweet abyss that promised him a way towards his goal. It pulled him, dragging him inch by inch towards the void, so he might slip in and slide down, taking an easy way towards an uneasy path.

The god recognized eagerness and rather than stopping Kai, Ahu-Ra held out an arm to stop Helene from intervening.

Ahu-Ra said, "I've been assured your two other friends are outside, they'll be waiting, as long as you cooperate."

Realizing the soft-worded threat, Kai struggled against himself. Having come all this way, with his quest-goal in sight, he could not bear to let the opportunity slip as the sand did. Sophia was down there, and love tugged, wanting to alleviate her suffering. However, Kai knew that would mean betraying Al and Tom.

The heroic act would be to dive in. The noble act would be to not betray those who had helped him.

Capturing the image of falling sand and the entrance to Irkalla into his memory, Kai wavered between the hole, Ahu-Ra's pity-filled frown, and Helene and Shebu's concerned looks. His heart beat further and further towards his beloved. Muscles tensed and shook. Life hurt. The decision hurt more.

Kai released pain to nothingness with a sigh and the choice fell away. "I can't repay good-heartedness with betrayal. You win."

Ahu-Ra said, heartfelt, "No one is winning here."

"Let's go," Kai said, leading around the sinkhole, and not once did his step flicker in the direction of where his heart wanted. Logic overcame emotion, and the rational part of him made a sincere promise to Kai's heart that it would be satisfied, even if it hurt now.

Ahu-Ra retook the lead with a fastidious step and a shaking head. The god looked as distraught as Kai. Helene tried to smile at Kai and patted him on the back, stiff.

Shebu leapt, scrabbling up onto Kai's shoulder. The cat said, "I'll do whatever I can to help."

Kai nodded, not feeling particularly comforted by any of them. Nothing would placate him after coming all this way and falling short. Nothing would make him feel better. Except finding a way back.

They reached a dead end. Ahu-Ra touched the cold wall ahead and the sandstone slab swung open, letting in a blinding blister of sunlight. The redness of a burning sun over sand blasted away the remnants of darkness. Outside, two shadowed figures waited with worried looks—Al and Tom.

Stunned by the ease at which Ahu-Ra had let them out, Kai asked, "The gods can leave at any time?"

Ahu-Ra said, "We follow a truce I'm not sure exists anymore. If I were to say this back there, I'd probably be in a sarcophagus with Osiris: but I quite think it's time we sent the truce to the wind and all left this hole. And powerful as I may be—or once was—that only gets me so far. My allies are slim, and I'm not sure how well they stood the test of time. Gods may not age, fade, or change much, but our relationships are always in turmoil, whim to belief. Politics, eh? They inspire nothing except flip-flopping hatred and backstab-ready friendships."

"Sounds like god problems," Helene said with a sarcastic tilt. "Immortal life and power are such curses."

Ahu-Ra chuckled, and then turned deadly serious. "They certainly are. More than you know."

Shebu leapt onto desert sand and stretched. Helene greeted Al and Tom with genuine relief, and Kai noted this, wondering whether it was an act for his benefit.

Meanwhile, Kai was alone in the pyramid with Ahu-Ra, leaving a brief moment in which two people can say so little and so much.

Kai said, "You're going to break the truce."

"If you deliver the message, I won't have to." Ahu-Ra offered the scroll. "I hope you remember what I said."

Kai took the paper, which crumpled in a tense hand. He wasn't sure if what Ahu-Ra said was about opening the scroll or something else, but he already knew what he wanted to say. "Thanks for your hospitality, but I hope to never use it again."

"I wouldn't be so certain that we won't see each other again." Ahu-Ra veiled tone and a well-rehearsed smile.

Kai stepped back to the desert, "I'm not certain, just hoping."

"I wish you luck." The slender smile of a god disappeared behind a slab of marble as it swung on easy hinges and shut. The sloping pyramid was smooth surfaced.

"Are you okay?" Al asked.

"I'm fine," Helene said, taking Shebu into her arms, who seemed to be taking to her presence. "Kai, I'm not so sure. The gods have an errand for us, like we're some sort of messenger service."

"What's the message?" Tom asked.

Kai laughed. He couldn't help it. "It's too important for us." He handed the letter to Helene, eager to get rid of it. "But the gods' will, will have to wait. I have unfinished business— I came all this way for a reason. It's a good thing the god doesn't know about Shebu's power."

Kai smiled wider than he had in a long time; he was happy that he was getting closer, even if Sophia was so terribly far away.

EIGHTEEN

THE LIGHT IN THE DARK

ASPHODEL PARK WAS QUIET and dark. Life was asleep, and the sky rested watchful eyes with clouded eyelids closing in. Nightmares might lie in darkness, but so far, Cara and Li were the only disturbance of the nervous night.

In the colorless world, the park seemed less dead. Unlike drought-destroyed days, sunlight did not glare and scorch. There was only the glow from the surrounding city. Trees hung with shadows instead of leaves, and the spindly reach of their stretching, sagging limbs descended into long, mournful drapes.

Entering dreary woods, Cara and Li tried to cast away ominous air with a lantern. The soft flame illuminated them and little else.

"This is dull," Li said, carrying the flickering black-iron lantern between them. Light was cast on the closer half of his face and shadows encroached from the other.

Cara stared into darkness, fearful of what was there, but convinced she could face it. "You're bored?"

"I meant the wick is low." Li frowned. "Are you sure about this?"

"No." Cara shivered at the frost-dew air of the night park. She tried to reassure with brighter words than the candle. "It's worth it, though. I don't think I've ever seen Mom so happy as when the new mattresses were delivered."

"That was a nice gesture by Victor. I can't deny that."

Cara said, "You should've heard his speech. But I understand your—"

"Stop." The lantern rattled. Li paused, Cara frozen a step behind. "It's nothing…" Li carried on. "My arm's doing better."

"Maybe you should hold that lantern in the other arm."

"I'm sharing the light," Li said with a strained smile.

"Then stand on my other side."

"I'm fine."

Cara didn't argue with her twin. There was no winning, and instead, she reverted subject. "The crowd was enormous."

"I know. I walked through it."

"When Victor started speaking, the energy was crazy. And between the bobbing heads, I heard him call my name. My heart stopped. But when I got up there, it was intoxicating. Like ambrosia in my veins. Victor asked me to tell the crowd about the ruins." She exhaled, pleased. "They looked at me like a hero. But the way they looked at Victor." She shook her head, paling at the comparison. "They loved him. Almost like a god."

"I'm sure Victor's alright."

"Alright?"

"Well-intentioned," Li said. "Look, I just want you to be careful."

They looked at each other, caring all-too-much for each other, but concern swung serious.

Cara teased with the truth, "Of course, Mr. Skeptical."

Li's knuckles were moonlight-pale around the lantern-handle. "Even Rollo believes Victor wants the best for Asphodel. But you had the best intentions helping that myth, and that was one myth, not a crowd of desperate people. A speaker can intend on leading a crowd's emotions, but sometimes, it can be the other way around."

"You just can't believe anyone can be so good."

The mood soured like the darkness abounding, and Li hissed, "Because no one is *so* anything."

"Right," Cara whispered her anger. "Because then you have to accept you're not normal."

"I accepted that a long time ago."

They stopped and the sibling-struggle halted, too. Cara held her breath hushed. "Is that the light?"

There was the city-glow peeking through tree limbs, but also another light between tree trunks close by.

Not wanting to admit danger, Cara and Li looked and pondered in tune, where did this light come from? Some random luminescence? Their own light, reflected back? Or the lights of the city reflected on something else?

Any might've been true, but unlikely. The rumor Victor had told them to seek out seemed more truth than any other explanation.

Li extinguished the lantern and they snuck along in the dark towards the light.

Night's cold draft tingled dangerous instinct into goosebumps. The halos of the extinguished lantern-light left the world dark, hanging like a ringing in their ears. A branch crackled.

The light took off.

Cara sprinted, desperate to catch the source before it escaped. Li struggled to keep up. Branches hung about, scraping subtle fingers over shoulders and hair. They followed the light, ever-elusive, ever out of grasp. A glimmer. A streak between trees. The twins caught only the trail and not the thing itself.

The light stumbled and dimmed as it hit the ground.

The twins vaulted a thick root, and in a clearing, they stopped. White ash-trees spindled fingers around the area, and mythical light spooked away darkness.

"It's you?" Cara asked, accusing and confused.

The light was familiar—the well-woman with ruby-red lips that had questioned them at the border between Asphodel and the ruins. The woman brushed dead leaves off and looked to leave. But at the sound of Cara's voice, the woman hesitated, recognizing the twins.

The woman shone a spectral sheen. No lantern, no fire, just her. An incandescent silkiness of youthful skin radiated liquid silver, an incarnation of aura. Awe stunned the twins like watching an auroral moon escape clouds.

The woman glowed brighter. "Leave me be."

"You're a myth," Cara said, her hand going to the sheathed sword.

The woman stood and snarled; two long canines peeked out, red lips glinting on ice-ivory fangs. "I'm as much person as you are."

Cara paused, her trembling hand pulling away from the blade at her waist. "Do you need a mirror? People don't glow and have teeth like that."

"Gods might," Li said, letting the lantern hang unlit; it was unnecessary.

"You didn't know any better last we met," the woman said.

"Now I do," Cara said. "You're a creature prowling in the dark."

"I am not a creature." An irritated pulse. It cooled, contained. "I have a name—Grace. But you're exactly why I'm hiding—not prowling—in these woods."

Cara fought fear, resorting to compassion. "We're not here to hunt you, just to bring you back and talk."

"Bringing? More like dragging. You'd put me in a cage like an animal or trophy—but I'm not either. I may look a bit like a monster—some myths are monsters—but that doesn't mean I'm one."

"I'd consider you super-human, if anything," Li said. "Like a solar-powered vampire."

Grace smiled, unsubdued fangs. "You're not wrong."

Weary of perilous teeth and emotional light, Cara flashbacked to terror. "We saw what lies in the ruins. We know how dangerous it is."

"I told you the truth, didn't I?" Grace asked. "I told you not to go there. Myths keep to themselves, why couldn't you do the same?"

"Myths appear even in Elysium," Cara said, calling out the lie.

"There's more worth dying for there. And like you, some myths don't listen." Grace pursed bright lips. "They put the rest at risk and that makes it more dangerous for those suitable to walk among humans." She bit her lip, fangs drawing blood that blended into lipstick. "This life has cursed us. We didn't ask to be made different, but we are. Leave myths be, and we'll leave you be."

"Come and tell that to people." Cara crossed her arms, clenching tight with struggle. "Or are you trying to trick us? Have us turn our backs and pounce?"

"That would only bring more bloodshed. Human wrath is the last thing I want."

Li brought logic to the emotional conversation. "If you just want to speak for peace, come with us. Show people there's nothing to be scared of—that myths can be logical like you."

"I cannot and should not do that. They'll make a side-show out of me at best, and at worst, they'll burn me alive." A solemn nod. "You were brave enough to go into the ruins, you're willing to hear me out, and I thank you for that, but those more fearful will not. It's happened before and will do so again."

"When did it happen before?" Cara asked.

The woman whispered, "I defended myself."

Cara grasped the sword hilt. "You killed someone?"

"Not now. Not here." Grace motioned for calm. "Even defending myself makes things worse. When people go missing, I have to, too. It's not like I ate them. I eat animals, and now, dead meat, unpleasant as it is."

"You eat live animals?" Cara asked, disgusted.

"Do you not know where your dinner comes from?" Grace shivered at a cold breeze. "I buy my meals. When I figure out which myth is stealing…" A rumbling growl and clenched fists. "We're all hungry. The less civilized myths eat each other, but that is preferable to getting us all killed."

"You believe the humans are that much of a threat?" Li asked, and for once, he showed a bit of emotion that was not anger; it was compassion.

"How have other humans treated you?" Grace asked. "I can pass as human and they still treat me like dirt. I'm not sure if humans hate myths or other humans more, but they're allowed—encouraged—to kill myths. If all the mortals in the city want us dead, we won't survive."

"Those bird-fish blocked out the sky," Cara said. "There's an entire park of monsters."

Grace laughed. "There's an entire city of humans, and they're a different sort of monster."

"Better equipped, too," Li said. "It's not like numbers prevent ants from being eaten by anteaters."

"You're not helping." Cara frowned at her brother and addressed the woman. "We can argue semantics all day, but you need to come with us."

"Why, exactly, would I need to do that?"

"Because it's the only way to figure things out. Fix things. Deescalate things."

"Is that why you have the sword?" Grace asked.

"I don't want any—"

"Spare me the nonsense." Grace grinned, but threatening fangs were unavoidable. "Your heart isn't in it. You're scared."

The sword hissed out a scabbard. "I am not afraid of using this."

Grace's long teeth glinted. "We're not so different after all, are we?"

"Stop it." Li pulled Cara's arm down. "This isn't you."

Cara shrugged him off but didn't raise the sword again. Tension ran taut, and struggling between choice and nature, Cara was paralyzed.

Li put himself between Cara and Grace. "You don't want to fight any more than we do."

The sharp-toothed threat disappeared.

Li continued, "What if we come with you to the ruins? As a show of good faith? We can learn more and relay the information."

Grace hesitated. "I don't know if the others will welcome you."

"I don't care. People believe I'm a monster. Maybe I'll fit in." Li implored her with usually cold eyes. "But I believe you—I believe that not all myths are monsters. All the stories say there's things to be afraid of, but I want to know for myself. I want to give myths that choice. And I hope I'm not wrong."

Grace thought a moment and sighed, the frost of midnight exhaled from the cell-bars of teeth. "I can't go to the ruins with you. But if you're serious, really serious, go tomorrow afternoon and take the first left. The house at the end. Ask for Dain."

"That simple?"

"That simple." Grace sat against a tree, content that no fight would ensue. "Goodnight."

Li nodded and took Cara away. She sheathed her sword, but she was seething. Li struggled to light another match, and finally, flame sparked. He lit the lantern, leaving the smoking husk inside the metal container with the other wither-black sticks.

"You're just going to let her stay out here?" Cara asked. "She might hurt someone."

"Only if they try to hurt her." Li trudged through the woods; without the rush, it was a long and quiet walk, except for their own talk. "Are you going to tell Victor about her?"

"I have to, don't I?" Cara crossed her arms in the cold. "If Grace is being truthful, we have nothing to be afraid of. But people won't accept that until they see it for themselves. They'll see myths can be reasonable."

"Do you really want to do this the right way, or are you only saying that? Because the Cara I knew wouldn't draw a sword on someone. We're not talking about a monster we can't reason with. She's was just trying to live her life and do the best for herself, as we are."

"We're not doing this for ourselves."

"We're not?" Li smirked. "Could've fooled me. You're trying to be like Kai—seen as a hero, not an actual hero."

"Kai is a hero."

It was now, in the tension and solemnity of the dreaded, dark path, that Li finally let off the shackles that barred him. It was not anger that had brought him to such a point, but a realization that Cara needed to hear what he had to say, regardless of the pain it would bring. Before, he feared how Cara might take it. But he decided to give her that choice. "No one is a hero the way you think. People are not infallible. Kai, especially."

"He's your brother and a good man. A true hero."

The lantern shivered in Li's hand and cast ghostly reflections in his anxiousness. "I'll treat him as he is—a flawed hero. Admirable, but he makes mistakes. Not only mistakes, he's done evil things. None of us are good or bad, we all do good and bad. No matter how we like to think of ourselves as heroes, it's not that simple. It's a constant struggle, and for some, it's easier than others. Intentions may be good. Actions may be good. Consequences may be good. I won't determine how morals should be judged; however, I do know that no one is perfectly good or evil. Even the gods. When Ra goes through the underworld, Set, who killed Ra's father, protected the sun god. When Prometheus gave humanity fire, Zeus chained him to a rock. In myths, monsters and beasts eat their children and protect strangers. No one is perfectly anything." He stopped, both in his thought and in his tracks. There was no going back, though. "You see Kai as a noble hero, but he got Sophia sent to the underworld, failed as a husband to Helene, and when Kai said he wasn't a hero, he wasn't being modest, he just felt guilty."

Cara was afraid to ask. "About what?"

"For what made him a hero in the first place." Li wavered, wondering whether it would help. "Kai didn't just kill a traitor. He killed his friend."

Cara paused, considering a response, trying to come up with some explanation. "Is that what Helene told you?"

He nodded.

"She's lying." Cara chuckled caustically. "That's all she ever was, a liar."

"For the most part, you're right. But even a liar tells the truth sometimes."

Cara's incensed voice blanketed the forest. "And you could tell? Who made you the judge of such things?"

"No one." Li was calm in the face of anger and did not rise to meet it. "I believe what I believe. It may not be truth. It may not be completely reality. But I do not live in a dreamworld like you, stuck behind preconceived notions of who people are. People change. Me included. You and everyone else always thought I was a monster. You made me think I was, too. Just because I don't show emotion like others doesn't mean I don't feel it."

Light dangled between them. "I never said—"

"You never said it, but you thought it. And it's not true. I can choose to be good or evil, just like the myths. I refuse to treat them like monsters. I know all too well what that's like. I'm going to give the myths the choice between peace and war, love and hate, good and evil. They may kill me; they may've already killed Rollo. But I will not condemn them without giving them a chance." He paused. "Are you going to bring Grace to Victor?"

Cara calmed. "He just wants to learn from her, what's wrong with that?"

"You're going to drag her before a crowd?"

"Victor will get us back to Elysium."

"Yes, as such glorious heroes," Li said. "You can be just like Kai then. And I'm the selfish one...."

"If we don't do this, we'll be stuck starving is Asphodel." Pained eyes. "Victor won't let anything happen to Grace."

"It's not Victor I'm worried about." Li laughed angrily. Spitefully. "Would you rather just drag me up on stage instead? Would that be easier? Or would you not do that just because we're too alike?"

"We are not alike." A common refrain of distance, but Cara's uncertainty made it ring hollow.

"I used to think that, too," Li said. "But we're too much alike. We made different choices on how to go about, well, almost everything. And I'm making my choice now—I'm going to the ruins. You can choose to protect innocent lives or our family."

"I want to do both." Cara held back tears. "I want to do the right thing."

"There is no right thing. Every choice is damned. Own it."

Li handed her the lantern and walked off into darkness.

NINETEEN

DESCENT

FOUR FIGURES AND A KITTEN sheltered under the shadow of a pyramid in the desert daylight. It was as hard to ignore the pyramid as it was a boulder breaking a river. Yet, while Kai planned his break-in, Al and Tom were scouting the distance.

"That speck has to be Duat," Al said, pointing.

Tom shook his head. "The city is over there." He pointed a slightly different direction.

"Then we just head in that general direction till we see it for sure." Al had a big-bubble of a smile at finding compromise. "We can pick up supplies and head back to Asphodel."

"You make it sound so easy."

"It's not far. I don't want to camp out here again." Al motioned to Kai and Helene to head on. "Coming?"

Kai didn't move. "Helene is. I'm not."

"I can answer for myself." Helene was on edge, contemplating the pyramid and horizon, the kitten in her arms flicking eyes open from a nap.

"It's not a question," Kai said. "You can't come with me."

"Of course I can," Helene said, impenetrable eyes hardening. She released Shebu from her arms onto the sand, letting the cat stretch. "I've come all this way. I don't want to go to Irkalla, but I feel like I have to."

"You feel?" Kai knew a quip wouldn't get to her, and he was right; Helene didn't even react. He tried again. "How, exactly, did you lose Al and Tom in the pyramid?"

That at least got some reaction, a dismissive, but charming lip-curl of a smile. "It's a pyramid; it's supposed to confuse intruders."

Reasonable as the explanation was—Kai felt there was some game. She did not want to help him. Maybe she never had. "Don't lie to me."

Delicate arched eyebrows did not bend or move. "It's not a lie."

"Am I just paranoid, then? You never used to lie to me, did you?"

"Things change. We change." She brightened, personifying hope. It was like a siren song, saying what Kai wanted to hear.

Even though Kai knew it was a trick, it was hard to argue against. But this time, what she said stopped him. "I've heard that before." There was an unpleasant feeling deep within, prodding him, warning him, but he couldn't quite grasp it— like sand, the tighter he grasped at the memory, the more it slipped away. Nothing was wrong with what she had said, but it reminded him of the past.

"She's not lying." Al came between them, mediating. "I don't know what problems the two of you have with each other, but you're wasting time arguing. We got separated by accident. I know you've come this far, but it's crazy to go back. If it hadn't been for that goddess coming along, I think that sand god would've eaten us."

Kai ignored him, whispering words she had said to him so long ago, "Everything changes but us."

Helene smirked, the slightest sliver, which returned to a stony demeanor.

Kai said to Al, "Bring Helene with you to Asphodel. She can deliver Ahu-Ra's message to Elysium. I have to do this alone."

"Don't lie to me. Don't lie to yourself." Helene grinned, devilish. "I have to go with you because I don't know what happens if your soul dies in Irkalla. Maybe only the gods could save me then. Once you save Sophia, we'll never have to see each other again."

Kai frowned. She had revealed a reason for being here—a rare truth—but he knew it could not be the whole truth. She would never admit that.

Al's demeanor grew serious. "You can't go back."

"You're right, I can't," Kai said. "Not to Asphodel. Not yet."

"Maybe not ever," Helene added. "One way or another, we're not going back as soulmates."

Now, Kai was certain. "Helene's too good at this."

"Kai doesn't care that gods will stop him. He doesn't care how far Irkalla is. He doesn't even care if he dies."

"If I don't go, I might as well be dead," Kai said. Saying it reassured him; having backtracked from Irkalla, it was harder to restart towards danger, but he had to all the same.

"You want to die? Fine." Al raised his hands and walked away. "I can't stop crazy."

Helene confronted Kai. "He's stupid, not crazy."

"You're the crazy one," Kai said, light-toned.

"Together we're crazy stupid," Helene said.

"This is like old times," Kai said. He meant it, too. They were an arm's length away. The pyramid's shadow darkened Helene. Cedar braids draped over sun-reddened collarbones, loose strands blowing over desert-tanned cheeks like snake-streaks in a dune. But there was only one tempting focal point that fought for Kai's attention—bright hazel eyes.

Engrossing, the glisten in her eyes cast light on him like he was a hero. But lips did not match eyes, and like a spider after a trapped fly, Helene's words bit. "Maybe going to Irkalla is not so much about Sophia as it is getting away from me."

There it was. Drawing him in, then pushing away. It hurt more that way. But this time, Kai did not budge. She made a mistake—her lie was too close to the truth.

"Why would I want to get away from you?" Kai took Helene's frosty hands and locked eyes. Her pupils widened. She hadn't expected this. Good. "We can go back to Asphodel and spend eternity starving together. We made vows to each other, didn't we? Till death do us part?" A grin. "Maybe you took that too literally."

She dropped his hands. "What did you say?" A crack in the well-considered front, an insecure frown.

Kai pressed the advantage. "I don't know why I loved you. Reason said love was because of intellect, humor, whatever—

an after-the-fact rationale. We made mistakes. We quarreled. When I realized we weren't working, it wasn't because I couldn't find a reason to be with you—no, I loved you. It wasn't until love found a good reason to die that it broke everything. You broke everything."

"Me?" The crack resealed, and she pointed at herself. "You think I was the problem?"

"I didn't." Kai chuckled at his naivety. "But there's the same feeling that something is wrong here. You play games with my emotions. You take pleasure from seeing me suffer. From having me fail. From having power over me. I don't know what else you want. But I know it's dangerous, and that you are, too. Love won't tint my view. It can't. Rose-colored glasses are only red warning signs."

"All I've done is help you." She spat into the sand, leaving it shadowed.

She waited for a reaction—expecting him to say, 'how?'. Cara had helped him in Asphodel, Al and Tom in the desert, while she had left him alone in the mines. Unless she counted opening a door and releasing a potentially world-ending god, she had done nothing. Kai felt familiar pride well within him, but he refused it, and instead, he said, "Fine. Come with me. Let's go die together."

She hesitated, trying to read him. "What a heroic couple we'll make."

"Is that the best you've got? Just stop."

"Stop what?"

"This." He let the façade fade. "Stop pretending. By offering your help, you were only pulling my strings, knowing I'll do the opposite. Then, I don't and you decide to use my pride, saying we'd be a heroic couple. As much as I want to believe the offer was genuine, I know better."

"Am I not entitled to change? You saw the best in me. You loved me."

"Things change. We change. Everything changes except *us*." A dreadful recollection. "That's what you said to me *that* night. It was the last thing you said to me. I thought it meant that the two of us might change, but we'd always be together. That's not what you meant, though, was it?"

"What?" The cracked frown was back.

"For better or worse, richer or poorer, sickness or health, but not death." Kai frowned, too. "Death didn't part us, though, did it?"

Her frown erupted into anger. "It was your fault!"

Kai's voice was even. "You died hating me. Most people have happy reunions in the afterlife. Imagine your surprise."

"I don't hate you—that would require feeling something about you." The anger in her face hushed.

A chuckle. "For all the time I've known you, I'm not sure you've expressed your true feelings. If you did, I couldn't tell the difference. But I never thought you felt nothing. Maybe it's better if you just keep telling me lies."

Helene contained herself, fists clenched in concentrated effort. Cold fury simmered away slowly, silently.

"For so long, I hated myself that I couldn't save you," Kai said. "But that's why I have to save Sophia now. Maybe that'll save you, too. It may be impossible, but then again, maybe it was impossible to save you before."

"Impossible? It was easy!" It was as if all her rage concentrated into the center of her face, but the violence flash-froze into icy words. "Excuse me if I say something I mean: screw you."

She stormed off into the desert, and a shallow silence lay thinly over unstirred sand.

Shocked, Al said, "That was unpleasant."

"Al," Tom said, a tone of reprimand in the simple naming. "Don't get involved."

"I'm just saying." Al shook his head. "What was all that?"

Kai bit his lip, reveling in pain, words still ringing through him. "Make sure she makes it back safely and doesn't drown in sand or something. Knowing her, if she gets the message to Elysium, she'll negotiate a deal and our souls will no longer be tied. Either way, we're done."

Al nodded. "For what it's worth, I hope you don't die."

They walked away, and Kai was left with Shebu, who sat and watched him, her tail and feathers flicking the sand behind her like a snow angel.

"Helene was getting along with you so well, I'm surprised she didn't take you with her," Kai said. "I thought you were what she wanted, but I think she just wants me gone."

"I don't think she's an animal person." The cat licked itself with a big, pink tongue. "She ruffled me the wrong way." The licking stopped and big blue eyes gazed at Kai. "Do you have a plan?"

"I'm going to jump in the sandpit."

"And if the gods try to stop you?"

"I'm a kicker, and I could take a few scratching lessons from you." Teasing turned serious. "I'll fight. That's all I have left. Success or death, Helene will be happy either way."

The cat pawed at the sand. "This is the world's biggest litterbox, and somehow your idea is still the biggest piece of—"

"I don't need your opinion. It doesn't matter that I have no idea what I'm doing or what's down there. All I know is that I have to try and save Sophia…I'll probably die trying."

"You have more important things to do than getting yourself killed." Shebu dug claws into soft sand. "The gods gave you a task. And the myths, as you like to call them—you can give us a voice. Other people need you."

"They needed me before," Kai said, furious heart still beating. "But Sophia does, too. I can't help everyone. And until I get her back, there's nothing else."

"What about your friends and family?" Shebu asked.

Kai pursed his lips, suppressing guilt and worry. "Can you open the pyramid?"

"I'm not a pet," Shebu said. "I don't take orders."

"Cats usually don't." A brief playful grin. "But I'm asking you. What can I do to convince you?"

"It's not about what you can do." Shebu's whiskers curled. "Sometimes, it's about what you can't."

"Are you saying you can't open the pyramid?"

"That's not what I meant." Pupils expanded in deep-sea eyes intent on Kai. "I told you that people need something to believe in; you may not see it, but people believe in you. If you come back—when you come back—you have to think of more than this obsession with being a hero. You can do more."

"So, you can open the pyramid?"

"You hear so well, but listen so poorly."

"I do listen, but there's nothing more I can do," Kai said.

The cat cast its head down, trudging to the wall. A single claw outstretched and a block of stone disintegrated before the translucent ivory. "I know it's impossible to come back from where we're going, but if we do, I hope what we see gives you a better perspective."

"There is no 'we'. You're not coming with me."

The snow leopard leaped into the pyramid. "It's my choice."

"No. I can't risk anyone else's life doing this. Helene didn't need to try and convince me—I already knew this is something I need to do alone." Kai picked up the fluffball and placed Shebu back outside.

The leopard hopped back in. "We've been through this. You can't order me to do anything."

Kai investigated the darkness, checking that no one was lurking. "Why would you want to come with me?"

"You're the only one who can understand me."

Kai pursed his lips and crossed his arms. The two stared at each other, waiting for the other to break, but Kai was every bit as stubborn as the cat.

Shebu frowned. "Is this the game you're going to play?"

Kai made no motion of hearing.

"And I'm the kitten?" Shebu's red-feathers tremored like a fan. "The silent treatment?"

Shebu's ears flicked in annoyance. "You're going to make me leave?"

"I'm not going to make you do anything," Kai said.

"But if I come with you, you'll ignore me?"

"Make your way back to Elysium. My sister, Cara, will take care of you, whether she can understand you or not, she'll try her best. I'm sure you can smell her out."

Shebu's silver-blue sheen rippled with frustration. "Maybe Helene can learn to listen to me better than you."

"Don't trust Helene."

"I'm not getting involved in your marital issues."

Kai glanced into the desert and Helene was out of sight. "We both know you're no ordinary myth. I caught her looking for your feather. She only cares about power. Over me, over everyone she meets. But most people are not as stupid as I am to always fall for it. I think she came all this way for you."

"I'll take that as a compliment that you think I'm that important, but then why did she leave without me?"

"It's a ploy. Angry as she may be, she's not crazy. She's always got a plan."

"You were the one that called her crazy," Shebu said.

"Crazy manipulative."

Shebu's whiskers curled. "She could've just run off with me when we were alone. Why'd she let you out?"

"I don't know!" A bitter exhale. "Maybe I'm letting our problems color my perception. But in your current state, it's safer not to risk it."

Petulant, the cat barred its teeth. "I may look like a kitten, but I can take care of myself. You lost your say."

"That's not what I meant.…"

The cat hopped out into the desert, kicking sprays of sand behind it, burying Kai's feet with a thin layer. He shook it off and took one final look at the world, where the snow leopard padded away.

A bittersweet loneliness fell upon Kai. He was glad for the freedom of being by himself, especially after the horrid feelings sifted to the surface when arguing with Helene. Yet, he was saddened by lost companionship. While Kai hesitated at what he had to face alone, he was excited by the prospect of achieving it.

A solid purpose dragged him into the pyramid. He retraced steps to the pit. There, someone was waiting for him.

Ahu-Ra.

Kai was not surprised; instead, there was only an exhilarating rush burning in Kai's heart. He was here—the entrance to Irkalla.

The god was staring into the pit, having not noticed Kai and focused on the hypnotic draining sand, which spiraled into the underworld. The desert drained into this hourglass of the world. However, while time was running low, sand was not; the world was making a feeble attempt to rid itself of this plague. The god tried to help the effort—Ahu-Ra shuffled sand into the pit with his feet.

The god noticed Kai. "I was wondering if you'd be back."

"If?" Kai looked skeptical. "You knew. That's why you're here."

"Fine, you caught me. It confirmed what I thought about the cat. And also, about you."

"Are you going to stop me?"

"I could."

"You could," Kai agreed. "But you'd have to kill me. Might as well let me do it myself."

The god chuckled, bell-like, which echoed in the chamber as a metronome. "This is not a task to take lightly—"

"I'm not—"

A hand raised. "Let me finish. What's down there is worse than death. Even if you find Sophia, she won't be the same as you left her. And by some miracle that you don't die and escape a worse fate, you won't come back the same, either."

"Are you trying to save me?" Kai hadn't expected that. "Spare me divine guidance, I've had enough of gods thinking they know better. That's what separated Sophia and I in the first place."

"No divine guidance." Ahu-Ra's stroked his curled white beard. "I don't have any for you. I'm not that divine. We're not so different, and many times, I think gods are less wise, as petty, and more extreme than mortals. If anything, gods are the caricatures of humanity."

"You're immortal."

"Many humans think they are, too." Ahu-Ra's eyes glimmered. "At some level, though, I believe we know our time is limited. All that comes with the illusion of infinite time is infinite procrastination. Gods don't learn. We don't change. But we are just as wrong as humans. Gods still die. Except, we have a better idea what awaits us, and your fate is a little less sure."

"You're right." Kai joined the god at the edge and stared into the hole. What horrors lay inside was irrelevant to the hope Kai held onto in his heart. He smiled. "As much as I love our chats, my time is limited."

Ahu-Ra smiled back at him. "I hope you get her back."

With the ease of descending a flight of stairs, Kai stepped into the sinkhole. The first step, solid. The second snuck away. The third was gone. He went freely into the fall, not gracefully, not like a diver, but like a ragdoll, no expectation or worry of what lay at the bottom. He did not flail, did not falter. He let go of tension, lulled and sinking.

A jerk like that of falling asleep too fast. A last reaction against release. Adrenaline sparked. Eyes opened to the sand around him, an impenetrable wall of sand cascading around him like a waterfall.

And he heard the final words from above—echoing with the voice of a god. "One bit of divine guidance: don't eat or drink anything you didn't bring with you."

Kai registered the words, but there was nothing else he could do. There was no point in fear. No point in struggle. The fall itself didn't hurt, the stopping at the bottom would.

However, his fall was caught by a bed of sand. Sucked down, he drowned in thick, cough-inducing earth and grasped for help. To his surprise, he found something solid. A knotted stick clung in his hands, and as he pulled, it pulled him too. The sand shifted and the saving pole dragged him, hand by hand, pull by pull, out the mound.

He spat and shook and shivered, sand spluttering. And finally free of the live-burial, he felt safe enough to let go of his aid, only to see the staff was attached to a man.

"You're not supposed to be here." Shadows covered the man's face, despite an eerie green glow in the cave.

"I appreciate the help," Kai said, dusting himself off. "I don't think I would've escaped without you."

Darkness hid features, and this hooded man seemed more shade or shadow than a real person, except for two bloodshot eyes.

"Gold?" the figure asked.

"You want to be paid for saving me. Alright." Kai fumbled at his pack, which was filled with sand as much as the remnants of food and gold. He pulled out a coin for the man, but his savior did not go for the coin.

"Do you want more?" Kai asked.

In a flash, the staff crashed into Kai's breastbone, his bag flying away as he shot back into the mound of sand.

Anger, as much as a desire to survive, got Kai out the sand before he could be dragged down.

Kai went to confront the shade, ready for a fight, rage pounding through his aching chest, but the man, and Kai's pack, were already gone.

Kai was unconcerned, even though he had lost everything he had brought with him—except for the singular coin in his palm. Where he was going, he wasn't sure he'd live long enough to need food. He wasn't quite sure why he held onto the coin, but he was glad he had. It was a souvenir, a reminder of Asphodel and Elysium, somewhere to go back to and a place besides this underworld.

Kai looked ahead and found a wood tunnel like he'd seen in the mine. Moss grew on the bark and lit the way through this branch of Yggdrasil, the tree that supported the world.

As Kai went, the tunnel tightened and moss dimmed. Hair brushed over the knots and bumps of the surface, making him nervous that he would hit his head. He slouched. Grainy wood kept him on a singular path through the twisting branch. Hands caught random splinters. Finally, he reached a stairway, a set of black, petrified wood. A tactile, gold grip line embedded at each step down, declared where one step ended and the next began. In the darkness, that bit of feel helped.

Kai rotated the coin through his fingers, keeping himself distracted from the tiresome descent.

Moss curled and dried the deeper he went, crumpling in brown patches and leaving only the faintest aura of green to see. The eerie echo of light befitted a land of spells and magic, foreboding. Kai dismissed thoughts of such things, worried it might make them real.

Eventually, he reached the end of the tiresome, lonely descent and passed into another notch in the world tree.

A large, lit hall. Illumination came with gut-wrenching fear. Crocodilian eyes stared him down. Open-mouthed jaws and teeth basked by a long, rectangular table.

But there was more to the beast.

The mythical creature had a head of a Nile crocodile, but there were two other heads connected to the same body—that of a lion with glorious flowing mane and a long-toothed brown hippo, snorting. All three predators connected to the black body of a Doberman, lean but large, with abnormally long claws, sharp as the violence in the six eyes. Under other circumstances, Kai would've laughed at the stitching together of such animals—crocodile, lion, hippo, and dog—but as the reptilian eyes focused on him, cold and calculating, with a hunger all their own, Kai couldn't help but shrink back towards the stairs.

The Egyptian-Cerberus creature hissed, violent and sharp, somewhere between the throaty pitch of a crocodile and the angry tone of a lion.

"Quiet," said a man sitting at the white-clothed table, resting a black-clad elbow on the clean fabric.

Without dissent, the miscreation laid the central crocodile head on a paw and pouted like a pet. The other two heads remained alert, not quite so threatening. This allowed Kai the slightest relief, and a moment to take his eyes off the animal and judge those at the table, similar to how they judged him.

There were three figures, one seated at each section of the table, leaving great leaps of space between them, and although they appeared human, they were like Ahu-Ra—caricatures of normal humanity.

"Welcome to the underworld," said the man in the center, a white-bearded, but bald man with a judicial, impartial manner. "We will be your judges today. I'm Rasnos, and this is Masura and Daefet."

"Welcome, puny one," said Daefet, whose harsh voice had held back the beast. Spindly fingers played over the white cloth and a crown of thorns circled his head, as if to create the illusion of regality, or even, to replace real horns that had once donned the sardonic-smiled god's head.

"Come closer," Masura said, with a far sweeter smile. She sat diligently with a blue ostrich feather upright by her ear in swooping black hair. "Ammerus bites, but we don't."

The crocodile snapped its jaws in response.

Not reassured, Kai came closer, standing by the table nearer the sincere goddess, and further from the creature and other gods.

"Is this Irkalla?" Kai asked. "And what judgment?"

"We ask the questions." Daefet grinned with dark pupils.

"This is not Irkalla." Rasnos straightened in his chair. "You will have to cross the bridge beyond. We determine your punishment. It's all bad, but we determine how bad." The judge stroked his beard. "What's your name, mortal?"

"Kai"

"Well Kai, if you answer two or more questions with 'yes' and have no acceptable justification, Ammerus here…" Rasnos pointed towards the creature. "Will attack, gnaw on you a bit, rip off a few limbs, tear you apart, and then devour you."

"Couldn't it just eat me?" Kai asked, a grim joke.

Serious, Rasnos shook his head. "That wouldn't be painful enough. You have to suffer for your crimes."

Kai gulped. "What if I've already done that to myself?"

All three gods did not look pleased by his humor, and ignoring Kai's rhetorical question, Rasnos said, "Let's start easy."

"You forgot something," Masura said, drawing the blue feather out of her hair and held it in her elegant hand.

"Right," Rasnos said and turned to Kai. "Do you vow on your soul to speak the truth?"

"Sure." Kai wasn't here for judgment, but if it got him to Irkalla, then so be it. They could make him the poop-scooper for Cerberus and he wouldn't mind, he wasn't actually going to do the job.

"Come up and sign," Masura said, offering the feather.

"Oh," Kai said, grabbing it and examining it for a moment. "You know, I once rode a myth with feathers bigger than this." The texture was familiar, reminding him of a wild ride. "What happens if I lie?"

"The cloth will know." Daefet rubbed his finger over tablecloth fabric again, finding sick joy in it.

Rasnos frowned. "We're fair. After you leave this room, you may lie again, although I don't suggest making a habit of it."

Kai signed and it vanished into fabric. And although they had said he couldn't lie, that didn't mean he had to tell the truth. "Let's get on with it."

Daefet grinned. "Well, have you ever lied?"

"Who hasn't?" Kai said.

"One yes already." Daefet leaned forward.

Ammerus licked its lion lips. Before Kai could protest that there might be justification for lying, another question came.

"Have you ever stolen food?" Daefet asked.

"Food?" Kai was more careful this time. "Do we include borrowing?"

"Not this again." Daefet rolled his eyes. "How do you borrow food?"

"Can I have a cup of sugar? I'll bake you a cake with it."

"Not a morsel," Masura said, eyeing Daefet with distrust. "Farmlands, crops, means of production. That kind of food."

"Can you define that further?" Kai found small joy in the back and forth.

Rasnos intervened. "Let's keep it simple. If there's any middle ground or interpretation issues, we can go deeper into it, but I just want answers, no more questions."

Kai reluctantly nodded.

"Have you ever cheated on your wife?" the old judge asked.

Kai had no need to lie. "No."

"Betrayed your family?"

This gave Kai pause. Had he betrayed them by coming here? The truthful answer was that he might've, but he believed it was not—he had not deceived his family and tried to make sure they were taken care of, even if it put the responsibility on Cara and Li. Eventually, Kai settled on a middle ground. "I've only done what I thought was best."

The judge went onto the next question. "Have you ever betrayed the gods?"

Kai had defied the council. No god had ever given him orders, only men—except Ahu-Ra. "I've never betrayed my gods."

"Besides in defense, have you ever killed someone?"

There was the myth, but that was not what Kai thought of. Silence. Desolate avoidance. Until, with a gulp, Kai's dry mouth mustered a word. "Yes." There was no denying that.

"Ah, so that is why you are here. I guess we'll have to go further—"

"No," Kai interrupted.

"You don't want to go into mitigating circumstances?"

"I have no excuses, but that's not why I'm here."

Rasnos crossed his arms. "You've killed someone without justification, but that's not why you were sent down here?"

"I can't justify what I did," Kai said. "But if I could go back, I wouldn't do it again. Although, it's not for a reason I would've expected at the time."

"Because you were caught?" Rasnos looked bored.

"At the time, I turned myself in." Kai found it strange, but he was smiling, his guilt satisfied that he might actually get punished. "Before it happened, we fought together. Ate together. Watched over each other. And just because he betrayed others, I betrayed him. At the time, it was such a simple act, a simple choice, but afterward, it was so hard to explain. Why did I care about honor? Or about the gods?" Kai stopped, realizing he was speaking to gods, but he kept speaking the truth. "I killed a friend, and that earned me Elysium—but I chose wrong."

"You were a hero?" Rasnos asked, pondering him.

Kai didn't hear, and once releasing this well-held secret, remorse spewed forth painful memories. "I tried to find him in the afterlife. But I only heard rumors, a spell in the Fields of Punishment, and then, Asphodel. If I asked too much, there'd be too many questions in return. I never told my family about him. And after leaving Elysium, I didn't get the chance to find him because I had to save my wife from Irkalla. Maybe I didn't want to find him."

"What?" Rasnos asked.

A memory of waterfall eyes asking Kai 'why?' tortured him. He bit his lip, painful for body as well as soul, and Kai continued, "Everything I've done since has been to do better—for a guilty man, sacrifice is the idea that keeps things from falling apart." As the gods and god-beast stared him down, Kai felt relief. For so long, Kai kept what earned him Elysium vague, telling only the official reasoning: killing a traitor. Maybe this time, he would be punished by someone else besides himself. "If, or when, I make it back, I'll make it right. But it'd be fitting if there was some justice for that mistake here. Even if he might not want that. But there's no explanation for...." He struggled with a haunted name. "For killing a friend...for killing Victor."

TWENTY

THE SCHISM

CARA SPUN A JADE LION, the stone cooling burning hands. A roaring icon and regal mane questioned her whenever it came around. Doing nothing was unthinkable, unheroic, unbearable. She either had to speak to Victor or join Li in the ruins. Under the weight of this choice, thoughts spun like the trinket.

The morning was warming and the few birds that had not abandoned Asphodel Park tweeted hoarsely. Cara had been here all night, and with sunlight, it became a pleasant place to think. The park was deserted. She sat on a hard bench. The sun moved slow. Cara moved less than it did. Heat crept on her neck, baking black locks. Jade caught the light, spinning and sparkling.

When the sun was fully risen, climbing into the heavens and vaulting over layered clouds, Cara still hadn't risen. People avoided her; she was a wrathful monument of herself, and no one wanted to approach her aura of indecision.

No matter how she prayed for the right answer from god or hero, the answers did not come as they used to. All that was right in the world became wrong—the image of Kai she held for so long was tarnished. She didn't want to believe what Li had told her about Kai, but the suspicion itself destroyed the image she had of Kai, of heroes, of everything good.

When perfection cracked, however small, it broke completely—it was no longer perfect.

The soaring sun swam through the cerulean sky. Cara lifted her eyes from the statue and across the dead park. Dirt paths were barely distinguishable from dusty, disintegrating grass. The city struggled against decay. Despite the charm of Elysium, it was the depths of Asphodel that struck her—the fading paint, crumbling columns, and choking red dust. People pushed through sand, moved rubble, and rebuilt at the same time the city fell. Everyone knew the situation was desperate. Regardless, they survived. Cara no longer cared for Elysium; rather, she wanted a new Elysium for these hard-working souls, including her family, who in their resilience and refusal to bend to a cruel world were true heroes to her. She made up her mind to do whatever would help them, and she chose with the best of intentions.

But she chose a terrible option, and she knew it. Both options were dreadful, and she felt this with all her heart.

When Cara left to walk the streets, a jade lion was left lonely on an iron bench.

❖ ❖ ❖

At home, Li worried that Cara hadn't come home since their argument. He reasoned she needed space and figured it was too early to go to Victor.

The family was sleeping on the new mattresses strewn on the floor. Where the family saw this as a step towards normality, Li only saw the cost—how he had suffered for them to sleep soundly. His shoulder ached. However, each time acidic agony dug into him, a smile entrenched itself upon his face. It wasn't masochism, but a peculiar sort of pride—a reminder. He was glad that his family was better off, but that wasn't what he was pleased by. The act itself—protecting Cara—was what mattered. Unselfish and good, the thought made him feel warm. He wanted to feel that way all the time. He wanted to feel less hollow.

With a final look around the moldy, cramped room, Li realized the family might lose more. Unsure whether going to the ruins would lead to his doom or his family's, Li didn't care. If he died with that glorious feeling that was strange and unknown to him—doing a good thing without regard to consequence—that would be fine. That choice was all he could control.

Nonetheless, he wouldn't die for nothing and had no intention of doing so. He strapped a sword to his belt. He could defend himself. And yet, as he went to leave the apartment, carrying it felt dirty.

When he stepped out the door and onwards to the ruins, a pure glow spread through him. Behind in the apartment, the sword was left in the corner by the door, just as one might leave an umbrella after looking outside and seeing the clouds clearing.

❖ ❖ ❖

After wasting the rest of the day with excuses and hesitation, Cara finally made her way to where she knew Victor would be—the grandest of Asphodel's temples. It was enormous and old, but not as grand as any of Elysium's. Still, there was a charm as Cara entered, especially because of the enormous stained-glass archway at the front of the room, which danced with kaleidoscopic light as the sun plummeted, burning the whole way down.

Under the weight of a stone roof, rotted wood beams strained and creaked. Whispers and prayers the wood had heard now echoed back to the crowd, who spoke too loud to hear.

Pews sank where backside after backside warped wood. Carpets blushed on less-traveled sides, while the center paled under further feet. The temple was filling. With such a crowd, there was the gambit of emotion, but laughter was little. Collecting in such numbers was a rarity, and it was like olden times where people congregated for the gods, except this was for something more tangible. *Someone* more tangible. It was for Victor.

The purpose, though, was quite similar to the temples of old. People came to listen. People came to experience. People came to hope.

Cara was here for Victor, too, but she was here for another reason.

Needle-knitting her way through the crowd, she cut to the front. Pure intention kept her path, and breaking through the amassed mayhem, she reached the altar. The rectangular stone was cracked and details on the side had worn away by the blunt chisel of time. The sun turned purple in a pane of blue-stained glass, cresting at the archway and shining triumphant over unwaxed floors and tired wood and stone.

It was too late for Cara to turn back now. She went to knock at the priestly door beyond the altar, but before she did, the door opened.

Victor ushered her in and closed the door. This backstage area was filled with a random assortment of icons and junk, chalices and trinkets, gold and rust. Busts of old gods hid under cloth coverings, noses and features poking and seeking to be free. One remained uncovered—a human-sized marble statue of Zeus with a golden toga and scepter, sitting on a mythically engraved throne. Regal, fair, and benevolent, the statue of the god stared at Cara with a golden eagle perched on his ivory shoulder.

In every way Victor was like the statue, except that he didn't have a bird perched on his shoulder.

"I expected you," Victor said, glowing with a cheery and natural disposition.

"You did?" Cara smoothed her hair, which had become tousled by her tussling with the crowds.

"Of course." He said this seriously and then returned to a light-hearted tone. "I opened the door for you, didn't I?"

Cara acquiesced the point. Her heart pounded, and she wasn't quite sure why. Or, rather, why it had chosen this moment. On the way over, she had practiced what she wanted to say, and it was only when saying it aloud that it prompted the bewitched pumping of blood.

"We found the light in the park. Or, rather, who. It's—we—I—" Cara's words got jumbled. Mind raced, tongue ran dry, and she bit at her dried lip. It felt like an awful betrayal, and she wasn't sure why; she had no loyalty to the myth, but it still felt wrong to mention Grace.

"Water?" Victor asked. He handed her a waterskin, not gold-engraved like the one he had thrown to Asphodel, or even fine leather, but plain and patched.

The water was cold and crisp on Cara's lips. She continued, "We found the source of the light. It is a myth, but I'm not sure exactly what she is. Some sort of vampiric woman that glows at night but appears human during the day. Li and I actually met her before. I know you wanted us to bring back the myth, and although Grace didn't seem like a threat, she wouldn't come with us. She was scared."

"I would be, too," Victor said. "Even when I speak in front of a crowd, I feel like I could die. I couldn't imagine if that crowd hated me for what I was. But I promise I won't let harm come to her."

"I told her that, but she didn't want to come. After the ruins, we felt it was better not to engage."

"That is for the best. Is she still in Asphodel?"

"Yes."

"I'm sure we can reason with her," Victor said. "To think, I might've even talked to myths without knowing it. There're so many stories about myths—but I want to know what stories myths could tell." He paused, a bright look in his eyes. "Sometimes, I wonder if anyone will remember any of us. We try to come up with a story about our lives, but life is not as linear as a story, it's messy and almost never mythical. I wonder if, for the myths, it's the same way. But if this drought does not stop, there won't be any myths or anyone to hear about them." The light in his eyes dimmed, saddened, but his words were resolute. "I won't let that happen, though. I can't."

Cara hadn't thought how the myths would be affected by drought, too. She hadn't thought about their story, but it was too late to change her path now. "Grace said the myths were starving. It was like she was working to feed them." A pang of guilt. "The last thing I want is her treated like an animal—I don't want her hurt or caged."

"Of course not." Victor met her eyes, a waterfall of sincerity. "If she's as human as you say, there's no reason for that. We'll treat her with the dignity we would show anyone. People will make their own judgments of what she says and whether she can vouch that other myths aren't a threat."

Cara hesitated and returned to what swayed her decision. "Will this make Asphodel safer? Make people less afraid?"

"I don't know." Victor radiated a warmth that demonstrated he knew his words weren't the assurance she needed, but it was the truth. "The gods don't know what people will do. People don't know themselves. That's free will. Life is nothing but choices, and even if we can't choose everything, the small choices make us human." He looked to the door, a general whisper of hubbub seeping through. "The gods were mistaken to retreat from the world. To leave us here like this. They, too, became myths."

"What's there left to believe in?" Cara asked, hoping for an answer.

"Whatever gives you hope."

She smiled at him. But she didn't say what she thought, only an extension of it. "The people out there give me hope. Li told me that we should give people a choice, and in the face of death, these people have chosen not to give up. They're holding onto a thread. They believe in you. And maybe out of that, this time of division and anger and toil can end. I can feel it."

"We can only do our best." Victor frowned. "I think it's time to go out there, people are getting restless. Speeches make me nervous, but it's better to think of it as excitement, though." He waved away his concerns, hands trembling subtly. "I guess someone needs to go talk to Grace. Where is she now?"

Ashamed, Cara looked at the floor and saw her reflection in the cracked marble. She hated the dirty reflection that stared back at her. "Grace works at the well near the ruins."

❖ ❖ ❖

Late afternoon. Li watched hope fall with the sun. Waiting set him on edge, threatening to crack a stony façade. Shadows lengthened and shops closed for the day, rotating signs in windows and throwing down metal gates with resounding bangs. Many places were closing early to go for Victor's speech. While it was the end of their workday, Li's work was just beginning. The ruins remained undisturbed, but Li didn't want to disturb it alone.

However, he realized he must. Although he thought of going back home, if Cara had chosen him and the myths, she would've been here.

He kicked at the line of sand separating Asphodel from the ruins. "Cara really has changed. But so have I."

He clenched his fists and chased the sand cloud he'd stirred across the bridge. Taking a deep, thick breath, filled with the pollutant of his own doing, he took the first left as Grace had said.

The ruins leaned over him, bent shingles curling and bricks blown outwards. The alley tightened. In the cruel shadow of towering remains, Li walked a lonely path between ever-changing houses—the red brick, the grey brick, the gutters and the gullies, old graffiti and broken windows, a transparent red-tint of dust covering it all.

Li didn't scour rooftops or windows for peering eyes. If he was being watched, there'd be nothing he could do. Confidence was his only weapon. Danger was all around, simmering in a sense of unease that myths might lurk anywhere. He posed no threat by clenching fists or angry eyes. There was no emotion at all in Li. He just walked.

Unlike before, Li was not unfeeling; instead, there was a certainty outweighing an apathy of a lifetime.

A door at the end of the alley.

He knocked and dust answered, shaken over the entrance. Rotted wood stood sturdy. Li stared. Behind him, a wind gusted down the narrow way, brushing his back. Goosebumps rose, but Li didn't shiver.

"I'm here to see Dain. Grace sent me."

The door creaked open and a gruff man peered out. This man did not appear monstrous, and like Grace, this myth could pass as human. If there was one aspect that set the man apart, it was that he was almost a werewolf in a butler's outfit. Full beard, eyebrows, and head of hair. Thicket-covered hands. But he posed no threat and ushered Li in.

"Are you Dain?"

The man shook his head and was eerily silent, lips stitched together. He pointed down the corridor through the rickety house.

Li nodded and smiled, passing by. Candles hung on walls, smoking flames leaning with the draft. Following smoke across pale, peeling wallpaper, Li felt as if he had wandered into another age older than what he left behind. Air thickened with mystery. Panels were knotted by time. The smell of ancient books drafted out side-rooms, where shelves of newly-dusted tomes rested. At the end of the hall, Li descended the only set of stairs towards the basement and held onto the banister tight. The stairs squeaked. Smooth railings became rough bark, and the dull light of quiet fire became a vibrant, lively green glow.

Moss hung on the sloping ceiling.

The building was left behind, and Li followed the cracks in archaic bark. The steps ended and he came to a chamber—a knot in a bigger branch.

But he was not alone.

Two formidable creatures examined Li from either side. Both had dragon heads, one had antlers and the other had a single ivory horn. They had the bodies of muscular horses covered in gem-glittering scales. Ox tails flicked back and forth, clearing the lingering smoke from dragon mouths. However formidable, the green, piercing eyes were peaceful. Tranquil. And although the myths were fiery, they smelt of calm, meditative incense.

The Qilin read Li as he had read stories of them, and he bowed with respect before proceeding down the center of the dark-bark room, focused on a platform molded from the tree itself, where a single myth stood.

"Dain?"

A robin-breasted deer exuded a godly vigil over him, arching sculpted neck muscles to a chiseled muzzle, while sharp antler tips pointed to the ceiling.

"Can you speak?" Li asked.

"Of course."

"How was I supposed to know? You're a deer."

"I am not a deer, I'm the lord of a branch of Yggdrasil."

"The deer lord?"

Rather humanlike, the deer looked quite cross. "Did Grace send you for our entertainment?"

"I've been told I don't have a good sense of humor. I only came to talk."

"Not many would walk into a den of monsters," Dain said.

"You don't seem monstrous to me…" Li paused. "Lordship."

The deer shook its head, dew leaping off antlers in a mist. "After your last escapade to our city, I didn't expect you back. But those who confronted you have been reprimanded."

"We were the intruders," Li said, casting a shameful gaze towards the bark ground.

"Indeed," Dain said. "But I made it clear not to engage with humans. It only brings trouble."

"I think they were just hungry." Li found it strange that he was the one arguing for the innocence of myths who had tried to hurt him, while a myth argued otherwise.

"Ever-open mouths. These new myths are more trouble than they're worth."

"Aren't you related?"

Disgust, the deer snorted. "There are old myths and new myths. Ones with power, and those concocted out of nothing but a bit of belief."

"Does that make them any less real?" Li asked.

"I never said they're any less real, but it's like comparing gods to mortals."

"Gods seem a lot less real to me."

The deer grinned. "Perhaps, in my old age, I am too harsh. These new myths are the product of the dying tree spouting seeds as it burns. Nothing lives forever, not stories, not even the gods. One day the great tree of Yggdrasil will die, too. Maybe one day soon. Until then, I will do as I have since the tree, and I, were merely seeds." As if this reminded him, Dain stretched its neck and nibbled at a patch of moss at the ceiling.

"But why is the tree dying?"

After finishing chewing, the deer said, "Because mortals don't believe."

"Have you looked outside?" Li's cold manner was incredulous. "There are tons of myths. People believe."

"They believe in too much. When everything is godly, there are no gods." The deer snorted. "Whatever you believe about the world becomes your world. Whatever the world believes about us becomes us. And whatever everyone believes about the world becomes *the* world."

Behind Li, the Qilin rattled their scales, clear as windchimes. The deer nodded towards them and the two myths left, heralding their exit with plumes of smoke.

Li was unphased. "Then why not show yourself? Plenty of people would believe in a talking deer."

"They believe enough. But it is not love nor reverence—it is only hatred and fear."

Li was anything but scared of the myth in front of him. "Why would people fear something that they can reason with? Like you or Grace."

"Because they don't bother to reason," Dain said. "The world has judged us already."

"That doesn't mean we shouldn't try."

"You are not like most. That is a good thing." Dain considered him and seemed to come to a decision. "You want to know what myths are? Come with me and I will show you. I think there's a person you know who'd be quite pleased to see you, even if he won't say that."

"Rollo?" Li smiled.

The deer nodded.

That was answer and truth for Li—not all myths were monsters.

❖ ❖ ❖

Victor strode on stage to astounding cheers. His calm was the eye of a frenzied storm. The clapping thunder whirled to the reverberating rafters. There was such energy, such passion, that it was impossible not to get swept up in the consuming current.

Cara stood in the front row, and the cacophony behind her ran goosebumps up her arms and neck. She clapped politely, excited, but not carried away. Victor smiled, and it seemed that shining grin was for her alone; it struck her with a jolt and made her smile, too.

"When I first arrived at Asphodel, I only had one reaction," Victor said over the quieting crowd. "Nothing." Eyes washed over the crowd from the podium-altar, his figure framed by a backdrop of arched stained-glass, a simmering golden sun resting over his head like a crown. "I passed through the gates and stepped into this city, speechless. I'd never seen anything like it, and I knew there was no other place I ever wanted to be again." Hands emoted energetically. "This city was a tapestry of beautiful chaos. There was garlic and onion simmering in woks, bread fresh out the oven, and jars of spices that dragged me stall to stall, jar to jar, from basil and rosemary, cumin and turmeric, and then, when I sniffed out dessert, I filled myself on cake and cinnamon buns. Goods were sold from every corner, coloring this city from rugs to rooftops. And then, there were the voices—people hawking, whispering, laughing." His eyes were bright with the memory of better times. "I wanted to be part of it. I wanted to make it better. And I still do." He paused, mournful. "But that tapestry is unraveling. The smells, drifting away. The goods, scarcer. And laughter, gone." Statuesque conviction gave the audience certainty in an uncertain time. "While we suffer, Elysium remains a parasite. The mistakes that brought us here seem destined to doom us with starvation, division, and death. The heroes of Elysium make mistakes, gods make mistakes, and how is it then, that only normal people suffer for them?" A shake of the head. "I came here to be part of this tapestry— I am one of you." He leaned on the altar. "The only question is whether Asphodel will become a myth lost to the centuries, or if we will be able to tell the story of its survival."

A commotion broke into his speech. Attention swiveled from Victor to the open doors at the entrance of the temple. Light shone over the heads of eager, restless crowds.

Seas of people parted, and Grace walked in, flanked in a triangle by three heroes. Cara recognized the heroes as the ones from Elysium, who went by the nicknames of Achilles, Ajax, and Hercules. They were disguised, wearing the garb of normal soldiers who might be expected in Asphodel, but still, it was easy to tell them apart. Ajax was too round, Achilles too beautiful, and Hercules too scarred. Their weapons were not drawn and Grace seemed unharmed, but the situation put Cara ill-at-ease.

As they walked closer, Victor met them at the stairs that led to the stage, and Cara heard Victor whisper, "This is not what I meant."

Ajax, round and jovial, whispered back. "What? We didn't hurt her. Just a bit of convincing."

Victor hid displeasure. He tried to smile at Grace, but there was also doubt at confronting a myth. He offered a hand to lead her up the stairs. She looked at him coldly and refused. Victor shrugged this off and returned to the podium-altar, while Grace stood nearby, defiant. The heroes kept a watchful eye.

"It seems we have a special guest," Victor said. "This is Grace."

She rolled her eyes, and the crowd was uncertain at the reception they should give her.

"Keep an open mind." Victor looked between the crowd and Grace. "She is an ambassador from a part of Asphodel."

Grace shrunk from the crowd's scrutiny. Her hand went to her mouth as if to bite her nails, but she stopped herself and shook, deciding it was not a good idea. Even if teeth went unnoticed, it was not a good habit.

"You see, Grace is quite extraordinary," Victor said. "While gods no longer walk among us, something not quite god and not quite mortal does. We know them as myths."

There were gossiping whispers and slightly shocked gasps, which died to the concentration and nitpicking of Grace by the hall-full of eyes.

"We've all heard stories," Victor said. "Myths are synonymous with monsters, but I want to know if they escaped our nightmares or if they are as victimized as we are."

Cara gulped.

However, Victor did not go down the route she thought. Victor was optimistic and bright. "Like Grace, there are myths capable of logic and reason. She's walked and worked with us, without us knowing the difference. Maybe like humans, can myths be good or evil?"

"Evil!" yelled out a few people who did not understand rhetoric.

Victor said, "Do not be quick to judge. Give them a chance. Give Grace a chance to explain."

The crowd shrunk into seats. More than ever before, Cara saw goodness on the stage. For most of her life, Cara had measured herself to Kai. Now, that image was tainted and Victor positioned himself higher and higher—as a leader, as fair, as heroic. In this temple, Victor was not only preacher, but idol as well. He seemed reasonable, where the crowd did not. But that worried Cara.

"Myths wouldn't give us such a chance, they'd gobble us up at the first opportunity," argued someone.

Victor heard the comment and honed in on the individual. "We don't know that. We make mistakes, too. That's why we're in Asphodel. That is why we should give myths the same opportunity to change. If they mean peace, we will not destroy them. We have enough problems with Elysium. But if myths betray us, we will fight back overwhelmingly."

There were nods and agreeance to this.

A temporary wince on Victor's face as he turned to Grace. "I know you didn't want to be here, but I hope that you take this opportunity."

"Was I given another choice?"

"Tell the people a little about yourself. What you do, what you are."

Grace looked terrified before the horde of unidentifiable masses, who threatened her with ice-cold eyes. But she steeled herself and attempted a sure tone, "I don't think there is a name for what I am. Call me a myth, call me a monster, call me what you want. I've heard it all. For my entire life, I've been hunted and feared. I know nothing different." She attempted a hesitant smile, fangs half-obscured. "But most of you know me as a well-worker. None of you noticed the difference. I live as one of you, and for all purposes, I am. I'm trying to live my life and make enough money for food and my family."

"You have a family?" Victor asked, eyebrows raised, speaking with genuine surprise.

"What, because I'm a monster, I can't have family?" Grace said this harshly, but she calmed herself. "My family are myths. Just as you care for other humans, I care for other myths."

"Family, or monsters?" said one of the crowd.

"Are no humans monsters?" Grace asked back.

The crowd rankled.

Victor interrupted the rising tension. "So, you have sway over other myths? What about the myths that steal or kill? Or what about the bird-fish that caused so much chaos?"

Grace looked right at Cara. "Have no humans hurt myths? I haven't hurt anyone."

Victor followed Grace's gaze. Cara bit her lip, keeping back words, but by the look on her face, she accidentally gave a clue away, and Victor read her easily.

"You say you've never hurt anyone," Victor said. "Is that what you told Cara?"

"I've hurt no one in Asphodel." Grace snarled at Cara. "I changed. So have other myths. But apparently, that means nothing."

Victor asked, "Why lie if you're not worried about changing back to more violent ways?"

"Because I will not get a fair trial. This is not." Grace stayed tranquil, trying to be logical, but her voice increased at each penetrating stare at her, looking at her like a freak. "Do you think I'm blind? I see how you're looking at me, ready to pounce at my first mistake so it will fit the narrative you tell yourself. But I'm not a monster. I'm not an animal. Any one of you could've been born into my shoes."

"I don't think you're a monster," Victor said, but as he looked at the accusing crowds, he had to change his tone. "But you've hurt people and still might be dangerous. And what happens to dangerous humans?"

The crowd responded.

"We chain them."

"Imprison them."

"Kill them."

Grace snarled. "I am not the dangerous one."

Victor focused on Cara, hoping she'd have better answers. "Cara was the one that found this myth. What do you think? Do you think Grace is dangerous?"

Cara froze as Grace's hard eyes stared into her.

But before Cara could speak, Grace went cold and said, "She's already judged me by her actions."

"That's not true." Cara stood, staring defiantly back. "I only wanted you to come here and plead your case."

As in the woods, Grace barred fangs. "I was dragged here. You made my choice for me. You betrayed me. At least your twin is better than you."

Cara's pride mirrored Kai's. "You threatened me. All I wanted is to talk. This is supposed to make things better."

"Just here to talk? Oh, let's talk, then." Long teeth glared. "You waiting to pounce on any excuse for your fear. I've seen your type. 'Heroes' they say. All I see is someone who fears what is different and tries to destroy rather than understand. Your older brother and your twin didn't see me as a monster. Who's the real monster here?"

"I am trying to do the right thing."

"By betraying me," Grace said. "And you call yourself good?" Venom and bite rose. "There'll be blood on your hands."

Cara heard violence building behind her and approached the stage, positioning herself between the whispering masses and Grace. "Calm down."

Sharp fangs shone and Grace tinged red with violence, reminding Cara of the glow in the forest. There were rising hysterics in the crowd at this display, which left an ethereal tint over the crowd like diffused stage lights.

"Get the myth out of here," Victor said to the heroes in the corner.

Three heroes came to restrain Grace. When the first hand met her shoulder, teeth spun and bit. Blood spurted. Old floors soaked in the spectacle. The other two heroes dragged Grace away. The crowd yelled and jeered.

Victor stopped the crowd with his presence, and then attended to the injured hero. "Are you okay?"

Hercules held his bicep, where a chunk of flesh had been torn away. "What's one more scar?"

Wrapping and treating the wound with donated supplies, Victor aided the hero. Cara stood shell-shocked while Grace was dragged out a side door by the other two heroes.

Raucous whispers resounded until the air buzzed with anger. The crowd wanted blood to be paid in blood. Violence followed violence. The imagined threat of monsters had become very real indeed. It had only one incident, but it only confirmed ages of fear and anger.

"Beasts! Animals! Monsters!" said the crowd.

However, the crowd waited for Victor. In such a moment, words were the precursor to directing feelings, and Victor did his best to control it.

"This is the last thing I wanted," Victor said, calm and orderly at the pulpit. "But regardless of what seeks to starve us, destroy us, and divide us, I believe we can come together." Victor's voice trembled with emotion. "I believe we can change. That we can be better. We won't be heroes, but together, we can be heroic." Victor's passion flowed like fire amongst the crowd. "The gods have forsaken us. Elysium has forsaken us. Everything we believed in has betrayed us. It's time to believe in what's actually here—us."

Victor glanced over his shoulder, smiled towards the crowd, and raised his arms. With a grand clap that echoed off chamber walls and in every ear, he drew his hands away. Unclasped, the sun exploded between his palms.

A prismatic wall of rainbow-lit color split on either side of the crowds, beaming through and cradling them. Rapture. Shards of laser-like glory burst from the sunbeam schism. Wonder-struck eyes shimmered in the reflection of a definite and astounding miracle—rainbows leaped over their heads. The hushed reverence in the room was deafening. No one dared move, lest they break the rays. Pure, angelic awe burned in every heart the moment that Victor held the sun in his hands, splitting the air into shining spectrums of celestial color through divine-sparks of dust.

As Victor lowered his arms, the rainbows receded. The room took a collective breath.

"The drought will end, and together, I believe we can change this world for the better," Victor said. "Have hope."

Victor raised his hands again. There was a sound at the window—the pitter-patter of rain clinking on glass. Small at first, but with the ticking seconds of held breath, a downpour began, clinking against windows and roof.

The crowd stood, ears cast towards the window, doubting and disbelieving what they heard. The sound grew as whispers did through the hall. Uncertainty became excitement, words grew louder, rising as a violent elation through the jubilation of drought-downtrodden people who had found salvation.

The doors of the temple opened and resplendent rain poured in the street outside. The rainfall was drowned out by the roar of the crowd, cheering and rushing to the doors to bathe in the respite of long-overdue rain.

Cara followed the jubilant crowds. Cupped hands and open mouths caught crisp rain. There was dancing and spinning and bathing in the rain. It was a bonfire of laughter and joy. After so much pain, exuberant crowds soaked the moment in, overwhelmed by anarchic emotion. And with so much belief, there was a self-righteous happiness that boiled under the surface, simmering and rising higher with every drop of water.

Cara's confused tears blended with the freeing rains that poured over her. In the blinding, beautiful deluge, a glow kindled in the haze—belief sparked torches and the downpour threatened a downfall.

TWENTY-ONE

TO THE EDGE OF

T HE THREE-HEADED PREDATOR, Ammerus, was on all fours, about the same height as the judge's table and long as Kai was tall. Although the beast wasn't colossal, the combination of predators was terrifying.

Lion-whiskers curled beside a blood-hungry nose. A hippo's gaping maw yawned with teeth like tusks. Meanwhile, the Nile-crocodile head was eerily still; ambush eyes narrowed, ready to pounce, latch, twist, turn, and snap. No matter how slender the soulless-slit pupils were, they cut into Kai like sabers.

Ammerus might've had three heads, but there was only one desire—to devour Kai.

The old judge, Rasnos, considered Kai. "We weren't supposed to have any deliveries today. Did Elysium's council send you?"

"No."

"Then this is not a trial." Rasnos put his hand flat on the table like banging a gavel. "He's yours, Ammerus."

"You look delicious," said the crocodile head of Ammerus, and the lion head continued, "You can beg. It's always sweeter when they beg."

Kai faced the god-creature, which reminded him of so many other myths he had faced over the years. "You won't hear begging from me."

Rasnos held his hand up towards the beast and asked Kai, "You understand Ammerus? Wait, did the pyramid gods send you about the corruption? They've been promising action for ages."

Kai grinned, telling selective truth. "Ahu-Ra gave me a mission. Personally, I'm here to save my wife."

Rasnos stroked his long beard. "I've met gods that understand myths and less-civilized gods, but you're not a god."

"I'm just a human who made a promise to my wife—I'd do anything to be with her—but to do that, I needed to deal with myths. And now, I need to go to Irkalla."

The demonic-god, Daefet smiled, teeth spiking from chapped, fleshy lips. "She's in Irkalla? How safe."

An impassioned scowl. "Nothing will stop us from being together." Kai softened his tone, but the burning within remained. "I released Ahu-Ra, and after this, I'll do whatever it takes to help him fix the corruption."

"The only help you'll do is for my stomach," Ammerus said.

Kai ignored the beast. "I'm only asking that you let me try to help. If I fail, the result would be the same anyway—death."

"It's not the same to me," Ammerus hissed.

Daefet patted the lion head and joked harshly, "You're getting a bit chubby anyway."

The crocodile head snapped, but the god's fingers retreated out of range. Ammerus growled. "I don't want to fix the corruption. I want food. And he's the best on the menu. Humans are selfish. He'll leave us with nothing but gnawing hunger."

"That's your curse," Rasnos said. His fingers seized, twitching and rumpling the white tablecloth in the crack between sections of the thick wood tables. The god held on harder, trying to stop the arthritic spasm. "Blasted corruption." When the seizure stopped, tension migrated to his face. "We'll vote on what to do with him. If Ahu-Ra gave him a mission, maybe we shouldn't interfere. Those in favor of Ammerus eating him?"

Ammerus raised all three heads in ascent, obstinately showing chins as a child would raise both hands to try and sneak two votes into a classroom poll.

"That's one vote," Rasnos said.

For a moment, Daefet's devilish eyes met Kai, probing and pressing for weakness, pondering and wondering at the mortal before him, with the judgment of a god and the anger of a devil. Kai stared back, unflinching and undisturbed.

Daefet showed dissatisfaction at the lack of reaction—a raised hand. "This mortal doesn't believe in us." Long fingernails straightening further. "He's the kind that would forget about us as quickly as save us, and all he has in mind is his singular goal. Such single-minded people are impossible to control. Impossible to predict. He can't tempt me with vague promises of helping with the corruption."

"Like you should talk of temptation," Masura said, long hair swaying as she shook her head at her counterpart.

"Which is exactly why I know what it looks like. And when not to fall for it."

Masura sighed. "I'm not sure we have a choice. Those opposed to eating him?"

There was one vote—Masura—leaving the old god, Rasnos, pondering Kai, not having voted either way.

"Well, I guess death it is," Rasnos said.

Kai trembled, suppressing rage. It seemed unjust to be doomed by Rasnos' apathy, but instead of anger, Kai had to create logic from bitter emotion. Yet, when he dug for logic, he only found the raw bedrock of his soul—love. "How can you sit there without an opinion? The world is dying. My world is already dead. All that's left is hope. And yet, that's all I need. That's what dragged me from Elysium, across the desert, and down here. I'll never give up. I can't." Invigorated words burned caustic, an echo of pain. "Haven't you ever loved and lost?"

The judge contemplated him, lips pursed.

"Of course you have," Kai said. "Even gods know loss—alliances, fleeting beings they love, and now, mortals that loved them. But it's not too late. Both gods and humanity might be saved by holding onto hope. Despite injustice and loss, I've never lost faith in what I believe. If I can do what is supposed to be impossible and rescue my wife from Irkalla, we can still believe in saving this world."

Rasnos' resolute face broke to sympathy. "The humans did love us, once. We used to be fair. Merciful. It's time we went back to who we were. It's time we cared." The old god raised a frail hand. "It appears we have a tie."

Calmed, Kai took a deep breath. "What now?"

"Technically, this is our second judgment—I said you were Ammerus' earlier—and since this was a tie, the first judgment stands."

Kai's calm receded. "You're still going to let Ammerus eat me?"

Three animal heads grinned.

"There's a reason I didn't bother to vote in the first place." The old god stood and pushed his seat in, walking towards the exit tunnel. Masura and Daefet joined him in walking away, but as they entered the tunnel, Rasnos turned and gave him a final, piteous look while the others continued onwards. "However, I'm glad I voted. We haven't sentenced you to death—just that Ammerus is allowed to eat you. So, if you find your way out of this room, we won't stop you."

Rasnos left, the shadows and footsteps of gods retreating into the darkness of the tunnel beyond.

Kai spit at their receding shadows. "What a stupid consolation."

"Bitterness is good," the hippo head said.

The lion growled. "A bit of anger makes them spicy."

"I just want to hear his bones snap." The crocodile clicked its jaws to accentuate the point. "They crackle with fear."

Kai thought this was like myths he had faced before, except this might be more dangerous; this was a god after all. "You won't get any fear from me. If I die again, I will do it for love. I am not afraid of dying, and I'm definitely not afraid of you."

The Doberman body's black fur shook as it chuckled. For such bulky heads, the rest of Ammerus was sleek and muscular. The smoothed fur at the neck met with mane, skin, and scale, clean-cut like on the nape of a well-trimmed man. Order and grace only added to the god-beast's threat, and each padding step forward on bending paw pressed down on stone and Kai's heart.

"I've fought worse." Kai's boast was surer than how he felt. When confronted with the thought of violence, danger was new, fresh, and awful each time. He waited for his body to take over—the fight reflex and instinct—when there was no time for thought. Yet, this time, fear accompanied movement.

Ammerus leaped, snarling and biting and chomping. Kai rolled, finding his feet under him. Although reflexes kept him alive, his mind raced. He was defenseless, he couldn't go back, and with the narrow hallway onwards, he'd never outrun the beast.

The monster leaped. Another close call. The hindquarters brushed by, twisting to redirect and claws scrabbling to spin the beast around. Desperate, Kai saw the tablecloth and yanked at the fabric, but it refused to come. Imagining whether it would be lion, hippo, or crocodilian teeth that would grab him, his thoughts were accompanied with instinct. He jumped onto the table, buying time and hoping the height might keep the creature at bay.

The monster thrashed at the cloth. Fabric tore, giving way to teeth and claws, slobber and hissing. Kai kicked. Boot. Head. Other foot, other head. Solid contact, sliding him back. Again, snapping jaws, only to be beaten back. It was the worst game of whack-a-monster he had ever played.

Kai misjudged and his foot fell between hippo's gaping jaw. Panic-flailed arms got enough traction to send him back, and he tumbled off the table.

A crocodile snout poked through the tablecloth, lifting the fabric like a tease, knowing its prey was close and defenseless.

The monster was only toying with him. Ammerus was in an amiable, playful mood, enticed by desperation. The predator was having fun with its food before devouring it.

"Not afraid of death?" The lion barred four fangs. "Good, you should be afraid of life. Soon enough, you'll be praying for mercy."

At this inopportune moment, Kai smiled, the lines in his face cracked by the unique and ultimate invigoration; there was no more appreciation of being alive than at the brink of death.

An idea came clear through fear. While the creature crawled under the table, chomping and biting and hissing—in general, showing off and trying to instill fear—Kai was relieved at the egotism of the dog-god, who thought Kai was easy prey, when, really, he was about to turn the table on the god—literally.

A gold coin flew from Kai's hand between the three heads. The fast movement whizzing by enticed animal heads to turn, following the flight.

Kai grabbed the table, adrenaline and fear flipping it over.

The edge landed on the dog-god's back, pinning it. Straining, Kai rolled the table flat over the beast. Claws scratched at the ground, an audible struggle like the click and slip of a dog scrambling over hardwood floor.

Kai heaved himself onto the table and pressed down, finding sick satisfaction in the three angry heads trying to reach back and bite him, but mostly, he found joy in besting a god.

Ancients had left many poems and stories about battles such as this—the struggle, triumph, and heroism, but in the moment, there was only toil, the awkwardness of a teetering table, and the relief of survival. Even to the most ambitious, to the most wanting of glory, the epic was lost to the moment. As it had been in previous fights, Kai saw nothing epic about a victory over this god. Especially since he hadn't achieved anything but a stalemate; the creature couldn't eat him, but neither could Kai go anywhere without letting the beast go free.

"What do we do now?" Kai asked.

The creature growled and spat.

A grin. "Can we be civilized?"

Ammerus' crocodilian-head said, "Let me go, so I can eat you."

"Apparently not," Kai said. "And obviously I won't be doing that."

"There's no escape," the lion-head boasted.

"Very confident for a dog caught under a table."

"You can't laze there forever," said the hippo-head.

"I could. You're rocking me to sleep with all that moving." Kai relaxed, sitting on the table. "I would've thought a god would be stronger."

"How about you let me out from under here and we see who's stronger?" said the lion.

"I guess the gods aren't what they used to be." Kai wobbled a bit. "I know the angle of your legs makes it a bit difficult to get any push, but I didn't expect this to work so well."

The crocodile tried to turn, but its snout gave up and rested on the cold stone, while the lion and hippo kept trying, inching with every desperate stretch, to reach any part of Kai.

"Tired?" Kai asked and followed with a yawn. "Am I really worth all this effort? Don't you want easy, defeated prey, rather than such a struggle?"

The crocodile snapped its jaws. "The struggle is half the fun and well worth the wait."

"Suit yourself."

Patient, Kai let his mind wander. He seized upon a common feeling, the same feeling he had when talking to Rasnos—love. At this point, it was similar to desperation. Yet, love was as instinctual as breathing. But there was a different kind of love he thought of now—the awe and respect he had when dealing with pleasant creations like Shebu. When dealing with the monster under him, it was inexplicably difficult to justify any semblance of sympathy. Still, Kai did try, and as he had with many myths before, he tried to find compromise.

"How about we make a deal?" he asked.

The lion growled exuberantly, but relented to the possibility. "What kind of deal? You have nothing to offer me."

"I don't? What about releasing you? In exchange, you do the same."

"Why?"

"Because it's the only way we get out of here. Otherwise, we'll both go hungry."

The hippo gulped air, exerted to exhaustion by the effort. "You'll keep your promise and reverse the corruption?"

"I'll try." Kai lessened the vindictive pressure. "I don't want to hurt you. And if you're hungry, I'll find you better food than a stringy chew toy like me."

"Fine." The crocodile hissed. "But if you fail, I will tear you limb from limb."

"Naturally." Kai's idea came just as naturally. "Now, I'm going to get off, grab the coin, and go."

Balancing back to his feet on the middle of a precarious seesaw, Kai kept himself heavy on the powerful back legs, wanting to add pressure there and give himself the most time possible when the dog-god slithered its way out from under the table.

The coin was lying near the entrance and opposite from where Kai wanted to go. He only hoped the stairway was narrow enough to buy him time. This was a leap of faith.

Kai stepped off the table and tried, as best he could, to calmly walk towards the coin—he didn't want to be the one to signal some hesitance on their deal.

But he expected betrayal.

Ammerus clambered out from under the table and snuck behind him, yet Kai heard the creature and knew when the strike would come—when he bent for the coin. A subtle scrape of claws readied to pounce. Kai picked up the coin, and without looking, dodged.

The monster leapt past and slid into the stairs leading back. Bumbling, four scraping paws scrabbled over wood and then, slick stone. Kai was already halfway to the tunnel onwards. Three mouths lusted after him.

Hanging moss spotlights flew by. Monstrous snarls hounded him.

Something—someone, blocked Kai's path.

Rasnos.

The god filled the tunnel. Between beast behind and god ahead, Kai was trapped. Confined. But he had to try.

Rasnos pivoted like a door, letting Kai pass as a bull-fighter might. The god boomed, "Enough, Ammerus. You made a deal, and our deals bind us. Let him go."

Running, Kai dared to look over his shoulder, seeing the old judge blocking the dog-god's path.

The three-headed god growled deeply with bellowing vocal cords, but it followed no further. As Kai increased the distance, sound dimmed. Adrenaline faded, and the strain of running led to a slow down, lingering to a cruel march.

Kai laughed, crazed excitement warming his fear-cold spine. "I can't believe I outwitted a god. That might've been heroic." He took a lasting breath of thick, sweet air. "I'm still alive. That's more important than heroism. I'll savor that."

Failure after failure, the simplicity of survival seemed an astounding, fantastic success. Pent up sadness vacillated into a form of happiness, glad at the opportunity of reversing his fortunes. It was easy to take having a future for granted and look ahead—that was Kai's natural way of thinking—but after mistakes, trials, and beating a god, this slight pause gave him the chance for appreciation.

It lasted a brilliant, glorious moment. Then, he carried on. That was the welcoming committee, and true trials lay before him; anticipation spoiled the moment.

Battle won, his war remained.

TWENTY-TWO

THE FLOOD AND THE FIRE

THERE WASN'T MUCH to pack, but Cara took all the time she could. Her grandparents, cousin, and father had already left, leaving her with mother.

"It was awful," Cara said, clenching the top of a box tightly and tucking it closed. Somehow, this recollection was the easy part, repeating only what she witnessed, not felt. "After the temple, some went to Elysium and some went to the ruins. The sound that followed was rage, fear, and death. Asphodel overwhelmed everything."

"At least we don't have to worry about more myths," Cara's mother said, leaning against the drywall and smiling at the empty room, glad to be moving out. She tried to sympathize with Cara, but there was no understanding the horror that had happened. "The drought's over, the myths are gone, and we get to move back to Elysium."

"Injustice comes home to nest." Cara intended it to reference Elysium's treatment of Asphodel, but that was not how her mother understood it.

"It wasn't injustice. You did good."

"It's not—" Cara went to say it was not good, but at her mother's proud look, Cara couldn't break that. It would accomplish nothing. She had already destroyed too much. "It's not Elysium anymore, mom. The fence is gone. The council is gone. There's only Victor now."

"We're better off with him," Cara's mother said. "He's someone we can believe in. After helping us with the mattresses, I knew he'd help everyone." A slight pause. "I just wish you hadn't seen…."

Cara shut her eyes with a terrible flashback. "The floods and fires? The blood and water? I'm glad I saw it all." She sighed, then continued. "Because of the fire, the world was all red. It was only when the morning light rose that people realized humans and myths did not bleed so different."

"The ruins were already ruined."

Cara bit her lip. She had to say something. "Everything burned. Myths and mortals."

"What's important is you're safe. We're going home. Have you seen your twin yet?"

There it was. Existential absence, ripping Cara in two like a zipper that snapped at the bottom. "That's what I wanted to talk to you about." A pause. Their eyes met. Cara held on, trying to separate thoughts from bitter feeling.

"What?" her mother asked.

"Li was in the ruins."

Cara's mother gave her an indistinguishable look, picked up the last box, and walked towards the door. It opened and shut. Nothing else.

Cara was left alone in the Asphodel apartment. Everything was gone.

Heroes.

Myths.

Li.

In the end, Elysium was Asphodel and Asphodel was Elysium. Drought over, more rainclouds gathered outside. The world seemed saved. But to Cara, none of that mattered. The world had never seemed so hopeless.

TWENTY-THREE

DEATH

A LIFELESS CAVERN. No breath or breeze broke the stillness, except a rhythmic lake lapping against a cold stone shore, but even waves made no noise. The dark waters absorbed the sparse jade starlight of moss on the tree-bark ceiling. That little light warmed nothing. Kai was cold, lulled by the silent sand underfoot, left lonely, tired, and on edge.

Quiet was deafening. Even what should've made noise—Kai's footfalls and breath—did not. The echoless cave was like a padded room, and it drove Kai insane.

This was wrong. All wrong. Between heartbeats, he heard his blood streaming through his veins. Bones grinded with every step. And as he couldn't cease the unsettling sound, neither could he pause. The flow of his life kept him from rest. Yet, that sound was his salvation, reminding him that he was alive and not cold and dead as the tree and cavern.

He gulped. The sound startled him. But as noise was consumed, he missed it. "Where is that bridge?" He asked himself. "Just keep going." His ears chased his voice, but it vanished. "What's wrong with this place?"

The crushing nothingness gave him his answer.

Petrified by the demoralizing mood of this eerie place and unable to find more to say, Kai carried on, hoping for a sign that there was a way forward.

An all-encompassing odor was the only progression. Smoke. Acrid and biting, the harshness curled his nose hairs in horror. Fog bogged his lungs with acidic vapor.

Kai thought of the most pleasant aroma he could, bound to a scene in his early life, kicking his feet back and forth as he lay on his parent's rug, content in a different world, reading a book about a bazaar where the smell of stir-fried vegetables cooked over an open flame, only to be absorbed by his mother tossing food in a skillet, making the book real as life. The world wound its ways into his memory; the tainted fingers of smoke strangled smell and taste. He gagged and coughed, the dying throws against the utter destruction of taste bud and throat.

Searching for reprieve, Kai knelt near the lake. Glassy waters waited and blackness devoured his reflection. A tired, cold hand reached into the cool liquid, wanting to wash away bitterness. Cupped hands drew the water out and towards cracked lips. The water drained warmth from his hands. He wavered, wanting to drink it down, but knowing he should not.

He un-cupped his hands and the liquid fell without a splash. Ahu-Ra's words echoed in his ears—he shouldn't eat or drink anything down here.

He scooted from the shore and sat, coughs lessening. He regained composure.

"Please. Just a bit of food, a bit of water. Anything. It's been hours…or days, I don't know anymore." Kai held his knees in. "Anybody, if you're listening, don't let me die on this shore." He tried to spit, but nothing came. "No. I'm alone. My life is in my hands. Sophia's too. I've got to get across. I must."

That was enough encouragement to get himself back on his feet and keep going.

As if an answer to his prayers, through dimness, there was a slate-grey bridge. Kai frowned at the sight, thinking it another musing of his mind.

But, as he drew closer, he saw that the bridge was real, and a small smile survived. The bridge arched over the water, a thin, grey rainbow. His smile faded. The bridge looked perilously narrow, ascending towards a bark ceiling, and one wobble looked like it might send him careening off the side to a perilous drop.

Kai hated heights, but he hated this shore more.

Keen to get across, Kai took the first step. The dark bridge blended with the dark waters below, making it difficult to distinguish the next step of solid ground from the air.

A bony finger tapped his shoulder before he could go further. "Toll, please."

Kai looked behind him, where a hooded man was camouflaged against the shadows.

"Didn't you steal all my stuff earlier?" Kai asked.

The man was blank. "Must've been a shade. I see the resemblance, but frankly, that's insulting. I am no doomed soul; count yourself lucky that the toll across is a fixed price."

"Charon?"

"Some might call me that. The toll for the Chinvat bridge is one silver danake. I also accept property deeds or well-forged weapons."

"I have one aureus," Kai said, pulling out the single gold coin he had left.

"I don't offer change."

The kinks and corners of the hammer-flattened coin clung to Kai's fingers. He felt bad letting the last of his possessions go, having nothing else to tie him to the world above, and down here, even the simple coin was a reassuring reminder that his past life had been real, and that, at one point, he had a house and family and enough coins to give them away.

"It'll do you no good where you're going," the part-Charon said, holding out a bony hand, as if he had this same conversation once or twice before.

"I know." Kai handed the coin over.

"Watch your step and don't let your concentration lapse." The shade-god dissipated into the darkness beyond.

"You're not going to guide me across?" Kai got no answer. He was alone again. After a horrible spell in enveloping silence, Kai even missed the shade-god's words. Trying to fill loneliness, he spoke thoughts aloud and was glad that there was the slightest echo off the bridge. "I'm glad I kept the coin. Otherwise, I might be lost on this shore longer. Maybe, that's why that shade stole from me." Kai climbed cautious up the sloping bridge. "Hell, if I saw someone with some food right about now, I'd take it from them too." He shook his head. "What's wrong with me?"

Distracted, his foot went too wide and towards the edge, clinging to the ice-smooth stone and teetering half in the air. Kai slid his feet together.

A glance down stopped his heart. The water was simultaneously right at his feet and catastrophically far away. The bridge and lake were the same texture and smoothness— a still Scandinavian grey. There was no visible difference, just a deadly one.

The dim glow of moss did nothing to help. The green glow was the same on bridge and water alike.

Vertigo twisted pernicious claws into him. Trembling, he took a deep breath. Fighting fear, his only choice was to search for solidity with his feet, asking for the reassuring pushback of ground. Relying on touch, his feet missed the bridge less than his eyes. Like smell and taste, sight was useless. Whatever this eerie place was, the petrified wood, vacuous waters, and unmoving air were unnaturally still. Kai felt as if he was, too.

His arm hair perked up, hoping for a gust to knock them down with further chill, but the cold came without movement.

Halfway up, Kai started to feel surer, even as his arms and upper body seesawed for balance. To anyone watching, he would've looked to be imitating a strutting bird. Despite how crazy it looked, it was working.

Kai reached the top of the arch. Around him, the bridge and water seemed a flat floor. With a wood roof overhead, the world was strangely normal. He had to tell himself not to trust it. He was on a sliver of safety. The water was not close. The wood above was. Huge knots were dotted in the bark like handholds. Even small branches and twigs grew outwards toward him, offering help.

Kai reached at a branch.

It cracked at his touch. Off-balance, he wobbled and almost toppled off the edge. With breath frozen in fear, he dropped the twig and watched it dive into the depths of the lake below. The bark and petrified wood were not there to help; the tree was as brittle as his limbs felt.

A fog rolled in, responding to the twig and covering the path forward.

Kai laughed at the encroaching mist, not knowing how else to deal with the prospect of death. He hoped the laugh would warm his bones, but he remained numb.

"This is ridiculous," he said to himself. "Let me face a monster. The gods, even. Something I can talk to or escape. But nature? Cold and gravity? What am I supposed to do?"

Mist obscured the lake and bridge. The slope down disappeared into a fog, and he was frozen.

"Every step is a step of faith, and right now, I could use a little faith. Zeus or Ra or whoever, guide my step. I don't want to die to a stupid bridge." He tried to clench frozen fists, but his fingers were stiff and unresponsive. "I want warmth. I want solid ground. I want anything but this."

Kai prodded with unfeeling feet, hoping for surety and getting nothing. He retracted.

"Why am I praying to the gods? I need Cara, Helene, or Sophia; they would know what to say to sturdy me. Cara would tease me that I've forgotten how to step like a baby and laughter would un-numb me. Sophia would encourage me, and her certainty would be mine. Helene, well, she'd challenge me, making fun of my frailty. That, even, would be preferable to standing here alone; defiance would force me forwards. And yet, when I tell myself any of these things, it does nothing. No words I say will. But if I can't overcome fear, I must go through it anyways."

Kai unfroze himself and took a step—brave, headstrong, terrified. Safety only came when his foot hit the ground and he did not fall, and only then, barely.

But the bridge did not slope down. There were steps in the fog—a set of stairs down.

This was a rather strange development, and Kai clicked his heel on the backstep, making sure it was real, but the solidity of touch reaffirmed the change. "I wonder if underworld health and safety made that change." Kai grinned. Stairs allowed him to use the ledge to find where the next step was. Embarrassing as it was, he shuffled his way down, glad for steps, rather than a slippery, icy slope.

After many awkward side-steps to the bottom, Kai was joyous at being off the bridge, finding himself at the bottom, cold and tired, but with a sense of accomplishment.

Away from the bridge, fog cleared.

Black sand, speckled with sparkling silver-grain of mica, stretched as the night sky does in the quiet places of the world—brilliant, bright, breathtaking.

Yet, Kai couldn't shake the numbness, his arms trembling with the remnants of fear and fright. Unlike so much of the world, which was so hellish with heat, this underworld was a frigid numbness, as if it was a condensed freeze at the center of the earth that the rest of the world was trying to warm.

Walking the beach, Kai left craters marking the pristine sands until awe anchored him. Ahead was what could only be the obsidian underworld of Irkalla, an imposing outline with parapets of shadow, towers of darkness, and only illuminated by the faint auroral-green moss dotted across a bark night sky.

A feeling shivered through him like he wasn't supposed to look at such a place.

However, the success beamed like a star; it felt visible to the world. A great burden that dragged him down disappeared. The relief was astounding. Everything else paled in comparison to the feeling. Overwhelmed, Kai sat in the sand, impressed by accomplishing what seemed impossible and wondering how after such failure in his life, he could know such success.

There'd been so much in his life. There was yelling for the sake of love, fighting for the sake of peace, and doing evil for the sake of good. Other moments from what seemed a different lifetime streamed by him. There was the greatly unselfish—a mother starving so her children could eat, strangers protecting strangers, and simple everyday smiles. Some of these events changed lives and others changed the world.

But despite all Kai had seen, nothing was like this. Kai felt different. Cooler. Calmer.

He thought of how he was—chasing the idyllic—thinking that was how he would be remembered. He had fought to be one of the individuals others idealized like warriors, kings, and mythic heroes. But that ideal was not real. These well-revered people did not change the world as Kai thought they did. Like the sand around him, the heroes might've been like the sparkling flecks in a vast sea of sand, but they were only an infinitesimally small part of a larger, more beautiful picture.

As Kai looked around, there was a sense of something out of place. Sand closed in, Irkalla seemed smaller, but it was still magnificent.

An illusory night sky sparkled and shimmered with starlight on the ground around him, Kai did not try to understand how or why. Instead, he picked up a handful of icy sand, letting mica twinkle intertwined in the black waterfall. He understood the scale of the beach like he understood the universe and himself—simply. The simple purpose of love brought him this far, directing his body as gravity directed celestial bodies.

But this moment was as if gravity had reversed. He had always wanted to be loved; now, he only loved. Pride faded. He did not want to be remembered as a mythic hero, he only wanted to be Sophia's.

Nothing in his life had prepared him for the kind of clarity he experienced at this moment.

If he could've bottled the feeling, he would've been a god. And for a moment, lost in the depth of the everlasting darkness around him, Kai tried and failed to hold on.

The feeling drained from him and he was lost.

The bridge-master's warning echo in Kai's ears. 'Watch your step'. That much was obvious.

But the bridge was not the only thing Kai had to be wary of.

'Don't let your concentration lapse'. That warning was more cryptic and only now did Kai understand. His focus had lapsed, thinking he had accomplished his goal. Similarly, Kai's body had lapsed and he hadn't even noticed.

Lying flat on the beach, Kai's eyelids crackled as he blinked, frosting over. Skin on his calves burned in the black sand. Frigid fires crept up his legs, twanging through fingers and shooting through forearms, while cheeks and nose tingled with frost.

Hell, it seemed, was filled with the feeling of fire—but only by the biting sawtooth of a deep freeze. It was too late.

The pain became numbness.

Surrounded by blackness and moss-stars and tree and Irkalla in the distance, Kai drifted. And ever-so-slowly, he was rocked to sleep by the tiny vibration of sand settling under his weight, the stillness of the shore, and the subtle movement of the world.

The ground had been a false friend. His final sight was the dark, untouchable bark-sky that would be his crypt. Eyes closed. He was left with the feeling that he had made it to Irkalla and still failed.

A few footsteps and voices broke into his dreams.

"There's someone." Cloth scraped over sand. "Too bad, the tree took him."

"Better him than us."

"It couldn't be us. But what a peaceful, enviable death."

Kai's thoughts whispered. *Am I dying? Am I dead? No, I can't be. But it's not up to me, is it?* Again, he heard his pulse. This time, slowing. The final rhythm of his life was peaceful, reassuring, and resounding. His heart was saying to him—let go, let go, let go. And in return, his mind boomed. *Not yet. Not yet. Not yet.*

TWENTY-FOUR

THE REVERSAL

PEOPLE COULD NOT DETERMINE whether the new combination of Asphodel and Elysium should've been called Asphium or Elysodel. Neither could Cara determine whether Asphodel or Elysium was better or worse off, only that it had changed at great cost.

And although Cara was treated as a hero, she didn't feel like one. More than that, she knew she wasn't.

Now, she understood Kai better. If what he did to earn Elysium was anything like what she had done, it was worth only its weight in guilt—a feeling that crushed her.

Back in their family's original, luxurious house in Elysium, it felt no better than the poor tenement in Asphodel, serving only as a constant reminder of what had happened. Everything she cared about was lost. Nothing mattered.

After *that* night, Li still had not returned and was presumed to have been lost—that was the only way Cara could phrase it. Other people, and more myths, died. Cara blamed herself for every lost soul. Especially Li.

Cara could not go back. She didn't know how to move forwards, either.

Unable to stand her house in Elysium—inhabited by a silently-sobbing mother who lost a son, a smug cousin who lost a nuisance, and a hollow father who lost his pride—Cara sulked in Elysium, a shadow of herself, wandering the days away without her other half.

The sun was out. But it was not harsh like before. Rain cooled the land and dust had begun to settle, clumping back into dirt.

The foundations of the city remained unchanged. White-brick sidewalks still existed, but in places, there was litter. When Cara made it to Elysium's market, all such brick-and-mortar stores were stocked with goods but vacant of people. Street stalls like Asphodel dominated. Jade and fruits and tapestries were sold side by side. Rainbow-colors and smells and textures flitted about; however, Cara saw grey and smelled the faint remnants of unpleasant smoke and fire. Mid-way down the street, one of the stores had been vandalized and goods inside burnt. Ash remained.

Cara stopped in front of this store, feeling an echo of what had occurred here. Possibly someone had insulted Victor. Or Asphodel. Deserved or not, Cara couldn't tell, she could not judge anyone except herself.

Hawkers called out, trying to sell her food. She had no pleasant memories left of Asphodel or Elysium's once-spellbinding food market; they had been painted over. In truth, the foods here were not the juiciest fruits and meats as hoarded by Elysium before, but it was still a solid selection.

Cara knew already—Elysium and Asphodel were not heaven and hell, only a single place, somewhere between either.

Turning the corner, she traced her past and wound up at the temple where her family used to worship.

The temple she had unwillingly been dragged to by her mother was another victim of destruction. Charred black wood was heaped in piles. Wrecked altars and charcoaled stone crumbled. The smaller pieces were swept away by nature's fastidious hand and wind churned ash. A few large pillars remained standing. It would take more time for those to be cleared.

The death-dark destruction of mankind's construction stood in harsh contrast to the blooming greenery in the garden. Earth was pockmarked by divots of solid rain. In recesses and cracks, rain pools shimmered under sunshine. Droplets glimmered and fell pleasantly from buildings and trees. Leaves sucked in dew, grass grew through remnants of dust, and a few flowers peeked out, wondering whether to bloom.

The first few birds and bugs returned, singing and buzzing a renewed song. Although there was rejuvenation, a smile was impossible for Cara, and as she watched a sparrow flitter between two trees that were no longer dead and brown, she should've been hopeful—the world seemed to be healing—but despite new life that sprung from the ashes, Cara's hope did not.

Smoke twisted in the cooler winds, drifting from a bonfire in the middle of the street between the temple and a garden connecting Elysium and Asphodel. A group of ten or twenty circled the raging fire. Cara stood at the back, unable to see but the faintest of flickers from the fire, dancing over the crowd.

She couldn't bear to see what they were burning, but she heard the crackle—maybe it was old books, idols, or a myth that had once lived and was now no more than stories and statues.

At the thought, emotion bubbled to the surface; yet, Cara's eyes had run out of tears to cry and only hurt.

Feeling empty, Cara's feet took her to Victor. She did not trust him. She did not like him. He had abused her trust. Yet, she blamed herself for what happened and found it hard not to return to Victor; that was the only familiar direction still left. She tried to hate herself more for retreating to him, but she could sink no lower. And as many times as she told herself what she did was wrong, she could hear Victor's seductive whispers telling her that her intentions were good. And when Victor said that he didn't mean for such a tragedy to happen, Cara even believed him.

She had little other choice.

To believe he could've intended such evil was unthinkable. She couldn't imagine he was that manipulative. He might be godlike, but he was not omnipotent. Cara chose her path—he had never forced her. All she intended was good, not evil. But in the end, her intentions didn't matter. In her head, good didn't exist. Evil, though, did—and it was her.

Her world was dead, and the only reminder of a past before consequence was Victor's temple—the Root.

It was the only temple left in what was Elysium. The rest were remnants and destruction alongside newly-popped up stores and fledgling trees and hopeful grins.

She paused in front of the Root. In the past few days, the old-style Greek bottom half had been renovated. The scale was impressive but not superbly ornate. No columns, no fancy façade like the old places of worship. A pure grey-stone wall, rectangular and enormous, was spotted with stained glass windows of red and blue and black, with simple shapes of diamonds, squares, and such. A single spire rose from the rooftop towards the heavens. The most impressive gods were those who did not require grandeur. What was impressive was inside—Victor—a god that could be seen and talked to.

At first, anyone could go 'pray' to Victor. This created problems; people had unreasonable, unanswerable requests, and a god that was too available had pitfalls. Now, Victor kept to private audiences.

However, Cara was welcome any time. She didn't know what she wanted to say to Victor, whether to scream, cry, or just sit in silence. Without Li, she had lost part of herself, too. Sarcasm, sass, and fire were gone. So were care, love, and joy. While the world had overcome drought, there was a drought within her.

She had no idea how Kai had gone on after losing Sophia. Where he had found purpose in loss, Cara was a phantom. She sulked to the massive arched oak doors, which even a roostrich might've been able to squeeze through. Normal-sized double doors were outlined in the bigger ones and there was an iron door handle for less titan-sized people to use.

The door opened before she got there.

She expected Victor—he had a habit of preempting her. But it was not.

It was Helene.

Closing the massive door with a subtle click, Helene saw Cara. If Helene was surprised, she did not show it. Cara was surprised, but there was not enough feeling to react. They stared at each other for a dull moment.

An ember sparked in Cara. "Where's Kai?"

"He's not back," Helene said, deadpan, with her habit of saying such things in a manner indeterminable.

"Is that a question?" Cara asked.

"Is that?"

Cara was in no mood for banter. "What're you doing here?"

Helene stared past Cara at the smoke rising from other temples. "Victor told me you did well."

"How do you know Victor?"

A subdued grin. "You never met him, did you?" Helene glanced over her shoulder and returned with an uncertain grimace. "Before all this. When he knew Kai."

Cara searched for a lie. "Victor and Kai knew each other?"

"They were friends."

"Unlikely friends, it seems," Cara said.

Helene laughed. "Maybe. Kai killed him."

Quiet, Cara flickered between distrust and realization. "Kai became a hero because he killed a traitor."

"Only those who lose are traitors." A self-reassuring nod. "Victor won in the end. You know, we have similar tastes." Helene's deep brown eyes found comradery with Cara.

Cara cringed, expecting her to say 'Victor' and dreading it.

But that was not what Helene said. A sly smile. "We like power."

"I don't like Victor."

"And I don't like Kai." Wistful, Helene exhaled deeply. "But sometimes, I might've loved him." She shook her head, clearing feeling. "Victor wasn't after vengeance, but no one believes in a god they once killed, so he made sure Kai left. To be honest, I didn't expect Victor to succeed so quickly or be so clever." Uncertainty etched itself in Helene's face. "He made himself a god and anyone that might discredit that story was conveniently sent away."

"Then you should watch out, too," Cara said, spiteful. Pieces of a puzzle were falling in line and it added up to a picture she didn't like.

Helene shook her head. "In that manner, too, we're alike. But Victor understands who his friends are. You should be glad. We'll be rewarded with power."

"Power isn't well shared." An unfamiliar feeling bubbled from nothingness—rage. "What did you do to Kai?"

"I didn't do anything. Kai made his own decisions."

"Did you kill him?" Cara was fire and violence, presence pressing forward.

Helene backed up against the marble wall. "He's alive."

"Liar!" Cara hissed. "All you do is lie!"

"It's the truth. Why would I lie?"

"Then why isn't he here?" Cara's fist clenched.

"Because he failed."

Rage simmered into uncertainty and Cara backed off. Helene regained her usual cool demeanor.

"I helped," Helene said, brushing a bit of disheveled chestnut hair out her face. "That's all I did—I helped everyone. Victor, Kai, myself. Everyone got what they wanted. Victor wanted Kai gone. Kai wanted to be with Sophia. And I…" Helene sighed, sad. "Maybe none of us liked what we got, but we got what we asked for. Kai went to Irkalla. Last I knew, he was alive. I don't know anymore. But Victor will make sure Kai's dedication is never forgotten. He'll have stories told about him."

"Witch!" Renewed tears streamed down Cara's face. Hateful, hot tears, turning cold on her cheeks. "How can you be so unfeeling? How can you not care? As if it makes it better that Victor tells his story?"

"I think you've forgotten what your brother's like." Helene chuckled. "He wants to be great. He wouldn't accept my help—and to think I actually wanted to. Ha. He's got an infectious way of making you care. I felt bad for convincing him to go in the first place, but it's what he wanted. It's what he needed. All he cared about was being a hero."

"Kai cares about the people he loves." The past, perfect picture of Kai returned in a flash and vanished just as fast. "He even cared about you. And all you did was spite him. But he'll be back. I know he will."

Helene bit her lip. "If he does, Victor will probably kill him. Might be fair. I don't know. Maybe you can convince Victor otherwise."

Cara went quiet. A bitter tear escaped. Helene stood silent, too, the subtle redness of regretful eyes was with her as well. Aching eyes directed towards the door. Victor's manipulation became clear to Cara. He had used Helene, just as he had used her.

Helene asked, "Are you going in?"

"No," Cara said. "I'm going home. If Victor wants me, he can send a message."

Spinning and heading back, Cara strode livid. Fury exuded in solid steps on the foundational stone of Elysium. She had done no one proud, but she would reverse course. She could not change what she had done, but she could change what she did going forward. She would do Kai proud. She would do Li proud. She would do herself proud.

TWENTY-FIVE

ASK

WITH THE SUDDEN SHIVER of breaking out of icy water, Kai awakened.

A strange sight greeted sand-crusted eyes; an elegant woman knelt, her spring-green dress blooming on black floors.

The world around Kai was no less dead than he had almost been. The world was haunted by the green glow of withering moss above. Stalactites cracked through bark and pierced any illusion Kai had of escape. Hope, though, lay with the woman, who examined him as a gardener does a piteous plant.

"Am I dead?" Kai asked.

"You're awake. That's a good start." The woman's half-turned head displayed fine-cut features and gentleness. And yet, as she stood, tall and elegant, her face turned and revealed a more complex picture of what must've been a goddess.

She was living and dead, split down the middle. The schism started from a part in her hair. Midnight dark hair fell one way and moonbeam bright the other. Each side had a highlight of the opposite, a silver comet streaking through night and a shadow cast through light. And like the split in hair, the face, too, was a dichotomy. One side was a lively and youthful woman. But the other side was far from normal. Blue-black skin, the color of twilight, sunk sallow over languid bones. Like blush, a cheekbone, shiny silver, stuck out.

The contrast unsettled Kai, and he couldn't help but recoil away on the ground.

"Have you lost your words, mortal?" She left him and returned to one of two stone thrones.

"No." The moment on the shore rushed back and pacified any surprise for the goddess. "I just need a moment to get re-accustomed to being alive."

"You do seem alive." She smiled, the living side with a joyous beam of teeth and red lips, while the dead half had grey lips and yellow teeth. "Sometimes with you mortals, it can be hard to tell. You're fortunate some of Irkalla's inhabitants found you and had the…how should I say it, mental capacity—yes, that—to not touch you and call for me. Luckily, they thought you were dead and not simply dying."

Kai pushed himself to a knee, then with struggling, wobbling effort, dragged himself to his feet. "Why?"

"You don't have the corruption."

"Is that why you're like this?"

A spiteful scowl. "What's that supposed to mean?"

"I didn't mean—" Kai bit his lip. "It's—"

The vile look softened unto sadness. "Yes, because of that."

"But what exactly is the corruption?"

"It is death. Decay. It is—"

"Desolate," said a man's voice. "And I, am, Desalet. Though, if it is easier, you may call me Desolate."

The cold click of boots strode by Kai and across the courtyard—for what else could this court be called, besides a courtyard, being somewhere between a medieval throne room of grey marble and regal columns with the outdoorsy feel of bark and cave and unchiseled stone. The god was as the surroundings. Regal. Wild. Cold. Unlike the goddess, this god was not a dichotomy; he was, in many ways, like the beach that had taken Kai—fiery ice. Silver-blue eyes were orbs of indifferent pain. He was bony and hard-cut in feature, moderated slightly by a springy, curled beard and tangled head of dead-white hair. On his head was a crown of white gold, a circlet that blended into the locks, and even the gemstone, oval, was bleached and shone silver like magnesium-white flame. His skin was the color of fresh ice, but lightning-zags of brown skin still lived, peeling like the pages of a burned book.

"You don't belong here." The god climbed three steps to sit on his throne and callously stared down at Kai. "But the Maiden was good enough to bring you."

"Thank you, your majesty," Kai said. A bit of sweet words couldn't hurt, even if they tasted a bit bitter.

The Maiden drummed fingers over the throne, clattering them against the hard surface with the hand that was still lively. "Curiosity got the best of me. Somehow you're here and don't have the corruption." Her hand scratched at the blue-black skin on her face. "Where the rest of this world does not age, does not suffer so, we do. We killed the tree, and now, it is killing us."

"Well, not so much killing us per se." Desolate grabbed the blue forearm of the goddess with his long fingers, stopping her scratching. "Changing us. I kind of like your new look. Adds a bit of variety."

"I thought you wanted me for youth and beauty?" The goddess barbed these words with a bit of double-edged venom.

"Love cannot last for eternity on looks alone," Desolate said. "How boring that would be, stuck with the same person for that long. Ten years, sure. One hundred, maybe. But after a few millennia, it gets a bit boring, especially when gods don't really change in looks or personality. Why do you think the other gods are such lascivious cheats with mortals? But this whole ordeal has a few perks."

The Maiden withdrew her arm. "I see only curses, renewing scars and hatred."

"Come, dear. Let's not fight in front of company."

Despite awkwardness, Kai found the debacle entertaining. The gods were so overly human. Even their arguments were familiar. "I've had my share of marital issues. If I have any advice—"

"—I don't need a mortal's advice." Desolate raised a pale hand.

"Maybe if you listened, you wouldn't be here with the corruption." The words left Kai reflexively again like in the gathering of gods, but this time, the fire wasn't there. By the ferocious fury in the god's face, Kai certainly wished he could take back the words, not because they were untrue, but simply to avoid such hatred and anger. After his near-death ordeal, even the god's anger seemed inconsequential compared to Kai's fight against a peaceful death.

The god was cold. "Watch your words. Otherwise, we'll start you in the pit. Those down there have little humanity left, and I'm sure they'd see your…freshness, as appealing."

"Come now," the Maiden said. "You can't send him down there for speaking the truth."

Desolate smashed a fist on his throne and whined, "I can if I want to. This is my kingdom. Mine."

"It is our kingdom." The goddess glared at her husband with beaming eyes, one green and the other pupil-less.

Desolate shimmied his head sassily. "But it was mine first."

"We're partners. That's the deal." Even the decaying side of the goddess' face twitched with angered passion. "Unless you want a repeat of the ice age."

Desolate held his breath, tensed, before relinquishing with a sigh. "You're already chilly enough."

Kai kept his gaze triangulating between the two gods and the ground, embarrassed at being in this godly domestic dispute.

"Are you enjoying this, mortal?" Desolate asked.

Kai raised his hands, portraying innocence and keeping words careful. "Is there a right answer?"

Desolate's full spite turned towards him. "Which god sent you?"

"No—"

"Was it Ahriset? Harpocrates? Serapis? With all the new names, I might as well start making them up." Desolate scowled. "Unless it was Ahu-Ra? He might as well start worshiping humans like Prometheus."

"I don't think he—" the Maiden stopped and shook her head. "Whatever."

Shaking his head, Kai told the truth. "I wasn't sent to Irkalla. I came of my own accord."

"Did you come to check yourself into this asylum?" Desolate asked, his humor tinged with a chill. "You came to the right place to find crazy, but we only make people worse."

Unsettled, Kai shivered. "My wife is here."

The Maiden's bright eyes filled with the warm melancholy of a sunny morn after a surprise snow. "And you came to save her?"

"He came to join her," Desolate said.

"Pah—You don't understand love."

Pensive, Desolate sat stonier than his throne. "Not everyone loves like you do."

Kai intervened with a bowed head. "I came to save her. In Elysium, they called me a hero, but I only wanted to be Sophia's."

Desolate sighed. "A noble sentiment, but you cannot save the fallen."

"Don't tell me 'cannot'." Fierce mortal eyes met the god's sternness, but Kai averted his gaze, filled with shame instead of anger. "It's my fault she's here. We were parted because of the horrible things that made me a hero. And then, she was punished for my impatience."

Desolate frowned. "Once you're here, it doesn't matter what you did—right or wrong—we're all fallen and there is no going back."

"Send her back and I'll stay in her place."

"We don't do trades," Desolate said, as if he was echoing something he repeated robotically through the ages. "You, too, are fallen."

"He doesn't have the corruption," the Maiden said, taking Kai's side. "He hasn't eaten or drunk anything, and the tree decided it would rather take him than taint him. He can't stay here."

"Only someone crueler than I would part lovers." Desolate sighed, stoicism becoming remorseful. "He'll stay. He'll die. I'm sorry you came all this way for nothing."

Kai's instinct was to flare at the apology, but the usual anger did not come. Instead, he pondered the god, understanding him as he understood myths and men. A new coolness ran through him. "I forgive you."

Surprise tilted the god's crown askew. "You what?"

"You're doing what you must, and I'm doing the same." Kai empathized with the god in front of him. "If you granted my request for Sophia, it might put the world at risk by spreading the corruption." A solemn grin. "Before, I'd do anything to save Sophia. Right. Wrong. Impossible." Kai felt cold anger growing within, a vengeful freezing sadness, but the relief of fiery tears did not come to lessen the rampage of feeling. "But that was before. Now, I think you're right—I only want to be with her. Even one happy moment with her is an eternity to me. That sliver of bliss is worth more than immortality, more than fame, more than life. I loved her the first moment I saw her. She wasn't the most beautiful woman I'd ever seen, but there was something about her that latched onto my soul. I can't live without that. I can't live without her." His eyes burned. Now that emotion flowed, he tried to recoil from it. "Yet, there's this voice in my head that says I can't give up on saving her. That would be selfish. I don't have the corruption, so maybe we can figure out a solution. A beneficial deal—"

"Stop," Desolate said. The word was brutal, biting through the air, but the god's visage was quite different from the word. Cold-hearted eyes had warmed. They were bright as comforting fire and stony tears broke from the edges. "Don't cheapen what you said with—" The god stopped and took a breath, reining in underused softer emotions and the anger that came reflexively to counteract it. "I mean…I would never let a soul out of my care, souls are too important."

"Dear, you're crying," the Maiden said, bright as a spring day.

Desolate's tears dried with a sizzle. "No, you are."

The Maiden laid a hand on the god's cold arm. "If this is a time for change, maybe this is the perfect time for you to change."

"You're too soft, too easily moved." Desolate withdrew his arm from her. "No. Everything here is my domain. If I let go of one thing, more will seek to go with it."

When the Maiden huffed and turned away, the god glanced at her.

Desolate's eyes darted away as the Maiden suddenly sharp eyes returned and a smile spread on the goddess' skeletal mouth.

"You don't have to hold on so hard." The Maiden glared at her husband. "It's one soul, and the corruption can only be transferred once."

Desolate was quiet a moment, then said, "Until the tree overwhelms us and takes everything."

"Sophia isn't a risk to the whole world?" Kai asked, hope bubbling like new life from the depths.

The goddess shook her head.

Kai got on his knees before Desolate. "Please. Let Sophia go with me. You've lived for eons, but my time is brief and my world is fragile—my world is Sophia, and she is so little of yours. If I don't succeed, the whole world will be your domain. Think of it as a loan. Either I repay it by reversing the corruption, or we will be part of your domain again."

"If there is a way to rid of the world of the corruption, I believe you'll do it for your wife." Desolate nodded. "And if there is no way, you're right; this world will be my domain. So, maybe, I am willing to consider *loaning* the girl to you. What does a single soul matter to me, if it matters so much to the two of you?"

The goddess withheld a chuckle and laid a deathlike hand on Desolate. "Yes, do it for me."

Kai broke into their moment, elated and excited at the ease of which they were convinced. "You'll really let her go?"

The god bit at his lip with sharp teeth. "Don't think because I am a god of death that I have no feelings. I loved the Maiden as soon as I set eyes on her and I may not be perfect—"

"Or anywhere near," said the Maiden.

Desolate growled and shame cast his eyes to the floor. "But I've tried to make up for it." He smiled at his wife. "I love her, and I, too, have defied gods for that love. I understand what brought you here." He stopped, hearing words echo about the cave. "But I am a god, above reproach, and you're but a mortal. Don't get any lofty ideas that we are somehow similar."

Kai ignored this. "I can't believe it."

Desolate said, "There is one condition, though."

"Of course," Kai whispered.

"What was that?"

"What's the condition?" Kai said, unperturbed and expecting nothing less than giving something in return. Whatever it was, it didn't matter. No price was too high. He had paid so much thus far—leaving behind family, friends, and his past life—what was a little more.

"You must never touch her again."

"Hold on."

Desolate did not hold. "You've avoided the corruption thus far by a combination of will and chance. The tree can't or won't make you decay. Sometimes, people are given gifts or curses, but it is what you do with them that makes them one or the other. On your return to the surface, maybe you can find a way to channel—"

"That's not fair."

"Do not interrupt me." The air grew icy. "You're testing my patience. I gave you the terms for letting her leave, take them and be thankful."

Kai looked to the Maiden for help but got no such thing. The Maiden was stern as her deathly side and her smile had vanished.

"Be thankful for Desolate's mercy and give up on fairness. If you have not learned by now, you probably won't ever— the world, life, everything isn't fair, nor should it be. We make the rules here, and Desolate is granting what you asked. Do not ask for more."

Slowly, Kai nodded. He wanted to see Sophia—a sight he never thought his eyes would lay upon again—and that was enough. It was all he wanted, all he had wanted, and in this moment, it seemed all he could want.

Desolate snapped his fingers and a shaded figure with black robes and hood, cloaking whatever fate befell it, came to the throne.

"Find a Sophia and bring her."

"Not just any Sophia," Kai said, vigilant as to not be tricked by the gods. Somehow, this deal did not sit well. Distrust lingered, despite Desolate's mercy.

"Of course," Desolate said. "If it's the wrong one, we'll return her."

The shade asked, "Can you describe her?"

Temporarily lost for words, Kai tried to piece together anything that would do justice to the image of Sophia in his head. More than how she looked, what came to mind were memories: the sound of laughter at terrible jokes, smiles at the cuteness of stumbled words, and feigned sadness at playful insults. It was not a childish love, but a childish fantasy, innocent and joyous. Thoughts followed of challenge, compromise, and letting difficulties change actions but not love. Finally, instead of memory, Kai found a feeling tranquil as golden dusk. It was as if all other moments were slumber, where time passed with anticipation for waking. With only the thought of Sophia, Kai was alive. But trying to explain this to anyone else was impossible; in his mind, what Sophia looked like was a reflection of what he felt inside—golden, joyous, and youthful.

With anticipation, those were the words that came to mind, but he only managed to spit out, "She's blonde? Uh, always smiling. About my age."

"Doubtful," Desolate said, but he pursed his mouth at the Maiden's glare.

"Any distinguishing marks?" asked the shade.

"She's only got one dimple."

"Which cheek?"

"Left."

Desolate whispered, "Unless it's melted away."

The Maiden slapped him on *his* cheek. The god shrugged and went to apologize, but Kai had not heard the comment; he was too excited.

The shade went away, satisfied enough, or at least trying to avoid further tension. For Kai, the wait was excruciating. The final few minutes were longer than the rest combined. Where time flew during the journey, in anticipation, it creaked to a stop.

A tender pitter-patter of soft steps over stone. It bounced across walls before bearing towards him, and the whole while waiting, it echoed more and more in Kai's reddening ears. While his eyes searched, wanting wantonly to find rest on a well-awaited sight. As he looked for the source of sound, he saw an iron fence rising in the distance that reminded him of the fence that parted them before.

When Sophia strode into the court, Kai did not smile; this moment was too much to be encompassed in the movement of muscles; rather, his soul smiled, throwing off great shackles and beginning to live and love.

Sophia was stunning as the feeling. However, she was not as Kai had imagined. Her hair was not sunbeam-straight, but rather tangled and out-of-sorts. The sheen was smooth under the pale lights, but it was not brilliant. Features and face were not quite as Kai remembered either—she seemed older, was older, but this did not bother Kai. There was still the same bend of lips, the single dimple, and most importantly, the same soul still lived behind slightly beleaguered and tired eyes.

Her demeanor lit when she saw Kai and the single dimple deepened with her happiness.

Finally, Kai was happy, too. After the routine of heartache, when the tendrils of pain released their fastidious grip, Kai surfaced to an unrecognizable world. It was not magic and perfection, but a world that was what it was. He was in a cold, dark underworld with his beloved's loving eyes warming him. The moment was beautiful, she was beautiful, and he was timeless, wanting nothing, living everything, and desiring no more.

Past, present, and future mixed and melted in ecstatic sensation; every nerve and capillary wanted to jump, a tumultuous explosion of brimming feeling.

Kai was free to live.

For so long, the present slipped by undesired, thinking only of the next goal. And now, Kai grasped onto life with both hands, rattling it for every bit it was worth, and filing this moment away as something to be reenjoyed later. But with such fervent experiences, the afterglow was not as bright as the initial burst.

During the few steps that brought him and his beloved close, he found that rather than being overjoyed, beauty and expression were stymied, plagued by an invisible wall that separated him and Sophia. A reminder of Asphodel and Elysium's fence echoed.

Sophia's single dimple beamed with her smile like a spot of pure joy, and Kai's smile returned true. The height of amazement became the height of relief.

"I'm so happy to see you," he said, and he meant it more than anything he'd ever said.

She went to embrace him, but he stepped back.

"What's the matter?" she asked.

"I made a deal. I can't touch you." He met her eyes, and the desire to draw closer increased with magnetic yearning. The only togetherness they had at that moment was the expression of hesitation and confusion that Kai felt within himself. Yet, he would bear it. He had to. More than that, he would enjoy every moment. "We'll make the best of it."

Being within arm's reach was more painful than being separated by a thousand miles. He was still happy. But it was a difficult happiness, and he would find a way to make it less so.

TWENTY-SIX

THE MISSING PIECE

BACK AT HER HOME in Elysium, Cara sat in the middle of an empty couch. The chandelier's glass beads absorbed the light's embers. A layer of dust lay over table and armrests, stemming from loss and the sedentary lifestyle thereafter. In rocker and recliner, Cara's mother and father remained. Li and the rest of the family were not here.

Cara's mother tried to fill the silence. "Your grandparents will be happy—to think, they'll be owls and can sleep all day. I talked to Marcus yesterday; he seemed very excited about the assignment you got him—the first inhabitant of the reclaimed ruins."

Cara managed a grim smile. "I hope he doesn't run into any myths."

"Victor wouldn't send him there if it was unsafe."

"Just Li and I." Cara's smile stiffened, hardened by grief. The mention of Li forged her purpose. "Dad, do you know where Li's sword is?"

Her dad was hunched over, leaning head on hands, his pride bent. But at this, he looked up. "What for?"

Cara did not debate whether to lie or tell the truth; she chose both. "Mine ended up in the river, and now I need one for a job."

"My little girl," her mom said, smiling with a hollowness contrary to her usually full figure. Her rocker did not rock, as if the movement would shatter glassy eyes again. "I can't believe Victor chose you to be the head of myth control. It's wonderful." She sighed. "I just wish my other children were so lucky."

There was no anger or judgment in the statement, just sadness. Cara understood—her mother was conflicted. Having lost one set of gods, Cara's mother threw herself in full support of Victor. It didn't matter which gods, just that there was a god that watched over her and her family; except, now, this god only looked over a broken family.

"I'll fix things," Cara promised. She was likely unable to keep the promise, but she meant it with her whole heart. "At least what I still can. Helene's back. Kai will come back, soon, too. He may not be welcomed back as easily."

Her father stared at and through her in a way only fathers could. "What do you really want the sword for?"

Coy, Cara stared out the open window, where sunlight poured in, but the shadows of clouds passed about. "It depends on what Victor has to say." Thin-lipped, she decided there was no use hiding the truth, addressing her parents with adult seriousness. "When I saw Helene, she said that Victor wanted Kai gone and hinted that Victor was the one who determined Sophia's punishment. He's evil." Having spat this out, she went on, uncaring how her parents might react to dangerous, heretical words. "Victor made me believe I was doing good. He wanted power, and I don't care. Let him have it. But he messed with my family. What happened to Li was my fault, but I won't let Victor get away with hurting Kai. If Helene's telling the truth, I'll kill him."

Her mother was stunned by Cara's uncharacteristic violence. "You should be careful of that sharp mouth of yours." Sadness creased her face. "You can't kill him. He's a god."

"No. He's not."

Her father asked, "Do you believe Helene?"

"I believe she's a liar. However, if the truth is hurtful, she'll say it. And I'd be a fool not to believe it."

Her father glanced down. "That's cynicism I'd expect from your twin."

"That's not a bad thing," Cara insisted.

"I didn't mean it to be." A brief smile.

Cara looked to her mom. "You don't have any more to say?"

"What?"

"Not going to disown me for insulting your gods like Li?" Although the anger was directed at herself, it came out when remembering the last interaction between her mom and Li. Because of her, Li and her mom never got to make up.

"I love you. I love all my children." Her mother covered eyes with plump hands, but tears escaped nonetheless. Hands fell away and she shouted, "Do you think this is what I wanted?"

Then, sobs dried in absolute, desolate sadness.

"I know. I miss him, too." Cara held herself together. She went to the window, only shedding a tear when her parents couldn't see them. Voice breaking, she tried to sound stronger and more hopeful than she was. "Looks like there's more rain coming."

Heartbreak, both past and possible, shook Cara's mother. "Don't go. I can't lose you, too."

"You won't." Cara lied with a mournful smile. "But I need to do the right thing."

Shadows covered her father's eyes, tear glands crusted shut. There was more than one way of sadness; her father expressed it in a familiar manner to Cara—sarcasm. "You're going to just stab Victor? Even if he's not a god, he is a king. Surely you need a smarter plan."

"I'll let you know when I come up with a better one. Kai always protected us, regardless of the risk. It's time someone protected him."

"But why?" Cara's mother wrung her hands, as if questioning whether they were clean. For someone who always thought the gods had a personal interest in every act of the family, it was dreadful when that attention was unfavorable. "Why does Victor care so much about Kai? Why does he care so much about us?"

"Because Kai killed Victor." Cara laughed; she didn't know what else to do. "The afterlife is a mess. Apparently, it's a place for second chances. In life, Victor betrayed the gods. Here, he became one."

Her father stood. "Kai couldn't have killed Victor."

"Again, all I have is Helene's word. But I intend to hear it from Victor's own mouth." Cara gripped the sill of the open window, unaffected by the sprouting grass in the yard. "Maybe Victor saved the world. But he destroyed mine."

A flutter. Cara stumbled back. Cardinal feathers flew and perched on the window.

The crimson feathers were connected to a snow-leopard that was about the size of a normal cat.

Cara's mother leapt up and hid behind her rocker. "What is that?"

Her father answered, "A cat that took you are what you eat too seriously."

The snow leopard balanced on the sill, enormous paws covering the space and claws dug into the wood. Fur was ruffled and on end in spots. A couple brown-orange leaves were tangled in whitish fur. The cat shook, raining leaves to the rug. Blue eyes stared at Cara, and after a moment of judgment, the cat came to a resolution and meowed happily. It hopped down from the window and nuzzled at Cara's leg, wrapping a furry tail and feathers about her.

Startled, Cara recoiled, jumpy from past experience. "It's a myth."

The leopard hissed, tiny fangs attempting to be threatening. But black-trimmed lips covered it quickly and ears swiveled back to the window. It meowed again.

"Didn't Kai mention a feathered leopard?" her father asked.

Cara said, "That wasn't this small."

"We should report it," her mother said.

"No." Cara knelt to the leopard's level. She was unafraid of anything the leopard might do—she would deserve it. "Enough myths have died." Brown eyes met its deep-sea ones. "Do you want some fish?"

It shook its head and meowed again, more urgently.

"Milk?"

The cat paused, pondered, and shook its head.

"You can understand me?"

A nod.

She dreaded asking, thinking back to the dead roostrich; since, she hadn't eaten any poultry. "How about some chicken?"

The cat licked its lips, hesitating, and meowing again, louder. Tail-feathers flicked.

"I'll get some," her dad said and went to the kitchen.

"Did you come here for Kai?" Cara asked.

A nod, then a head shake.

"Is that a yes or no?"

The cat meowed, frustrated. Ears swiveled towards the window. Cara gaze followed.

Outside, it was bright, and the wonderous wisps of darkening clouds were gathering for another bout of life-giving rain, not dark and stormy, just a sprinkle. But there was a thunderous sound—the march of soldiers nearby. Cara couldn't see them, but she understood well enough.

She turned and asked, "Are they looking for you?"

The leopard nodded.

"As much as twenty questions is fun," Cara's mom said, rocking the chair in front of her with nervous hands. "Maybe we should hand it over. It's just a myth."

Cara gritted her teeth. "Li died for these myths."

Her mother went silent and looked down, ashamed.

Cara's father came back, bringing a porcelain plate of boiled chicken, hand-shredded. The kitten sniffed with a glistening pink-black nose before gobbling down pieces of moist meat with ravenous hunger. Cara's father stroked its back.

But the happy moment was interrupted by three sturdy knocks at the door. *BAM. BAM. BAM.*

Cara's mom paled. "It's the soldiers."

"Go to the bedroom," Cara said, a commanding tone sending her parents down an off-shooting hallway.

Cara hid in the hallway, around the corner from the door, the kitten near her leg. Both of them flattened against the wall, wondering what to do.

"Should I answer the door?" Cara asked.

The cat shook its head.

Cara wondered if she should go to her father for the sword, but her muscles were frozen in terror. She was not scared for her own life. She was scared that fighting the soldiers was useless, that she'd failed everyone, destroyed everything, and would have no time to fix it. Yet, she knew she had to get the sword in the bedroom and defend the myth, regardless of consequence.

But she hadn't made it a step before the door swung open. Growling and courageous, the kitten sprang around the corner and pounced towards the door.

The sounds of a fight did not come, though.

A voice. "Hold on. You're—" A confused meow, audible sniff, and a mew. "You managed to escape Victor? What a clever little myth." Another meow. "Sorry…not a myth. Come on, I'll translate."

The leopard pranced back around the corner and meowed at Cara.

"Kai?" Cara peeked out.

"You wish," Li said, smiling wide and true. "Guess you'll have to settle for me."

"Li?" Cara asked. Shock froze welling tears at the corner of her eyes, debating relief and joy. "Li!"

She sprung on him, hugging him with every bit of strength she had, squeezing him tight and never wanting to let him go, overjoyed at reuniting with her twin.

"I thought—we thought." Cara lost her words and blubbered her only thought. "I'm so glad you're alive."

"Me, too, I suppose?" Li hugged her tighter, for once not struggling from her embrace. But after the initial moment, they separated. Joy had healed a bit of the rift, but not all of it.

"But the floods? The fires? The ruins were a mess."

"The ruins were already ruined. They'll have to do more to destroy what's underneath," Li pursed his lips for a moment before deciding to continue. "Most of the myths went to the tunnels through Yggdrasil. You wouldn't believe what I saw down there."

A meow from Shebu.

"I heard a mention of it."

As she often had, Cara looked at her brother as a stranger. They were twins, but she wasn't sure she'd ever understood him, no matter how she'd tried. But she was determined to know better. "You understand myths?"

Li nodded. "I learned."

"But how?" Cara wondered how useful that could've been. There was jealousy, and she cast it away.

"There are things you're born with, and then, there's things you can learn. It required some empathy, but it was like a new language."

Shebu meowed. In response, Li contemplated, growing silent. Cara looked at him expectantly.

"What'd it say?"

"What *Shebu* said…" Li pet the cat. "Makes sense. Victor did all of this to stop the drought, and now, he wants to become a god so the drought can't return. Only, he's doesn't have all he needs."

"You got all that from a single meow?"

"No, I learned most of it from a deer. Shebu added the last bit."

After all the craziness, Cara accepted the deer comment without question. "Well, what is he missing? We've got to stop him."

"Two things—Shebu and power."

"How could he be missing power? Victor rules the entire city."

"Not that kind of power." Li was pensive. "He has belief and a story. Those make myths, but to become a god, Victor needs more. He needs the seed of Yggdrasil. That's where everything stems from. Even gods. And that's why he needs Shebu."

Cara gave him a questioning look.

"The deer gave me a lot of pointless history about tunnels and belief." Li shrugged. "But I'll save you the useless bits— under our feet is a tree that connects pantheons. The council thought they could become gods with the moss that grows from the tree. Gods used it to increase their powers, but it's not that simple. The only way to become a god is at the origin of the world. The origin of the gods. The seed. Gods fought wars over it. After the truce, it was locked away. But they made a key, and Shebu is that key." Li emptied the chicken from the plate onto the floor, holding the plate in front of the kitten. "Care to demonstrate?"

Shebu touched an ivory claw against the porcelain and it disintegrated into dust, a tiny pile of white ash on the wood floor.

"I don't care what Victor wants," Cara said. "We've got to stop him before he kills Kai."

"Why would he do that?"

"Victor was the traitor Kai killed."

"Interesting," Li said. "But it's not why I came here. I only came to say goodbye before I go with the myths." He looked at her, a little twinkle of care like she so often looked at him. "I suppose I can't let you go face Victor alone, though."

"You don't have to," Cara said. "It's my responsibility. And I didn't go with you when—"

"Enough," Li said, old anger biting with bitter cold.

"Is that Li?" asked a voice from the bedroom, leaving the twins suspended.

The door opened, and Cara's parents looked with shock at seeing Li. For a moment, eyes met and they just stood there, staring at each other.

Cara's mom leapt on him with an expansive hug, enveloping him with motherly love. Cara's father gave Li a manly bear-hug, which was just as sentimental. Despite fights and quarrels, parental love was firm, and Li, after so long of being treated as the black sheep, must've felt that—Cara even thought she saw Li shed a tear.

Li bit his lip. "It's good to see you."

"My boy," Cara's mother blubbered.

"Aren't you going to thank the gods?" Li asked, still tensed.

"No," his mother said. "The gods have done enough to destroy this family. I never thought I'd see you again. To have even two of my children...." She trailed off.

"Kai will come back," Cara said, trying to give her mother hope. "And we'll make sure he's safe. But to do that, we need the sword, dad."

He nodded and headed to the bedroom. "I'm glad I kept it."

"You can't be leaving already," Cara's mother said pleadingly and directed towards Li.

Li grinned. "I'm not leaving. You'll always have me in your heart."

"Don't joke," Cara said. "Not now."

Li ignored her, looking to his mother with new compassion. "We've had our differences. I never meant to hurt you, mom. It's just…sometimes, words come out my mouth, and as much as I mean them in the moment, that doesn't mean I should say it, and it doesn't mean that's what I feel, either."

"I'm as guilty of that," their mother said, and contrasting usual avoidance, she looked her son in the eyes. "I was scared you were too different, and Cara, too naive. The world is harder than me. All I wanted was for the gods to watch over you. I couldn't bear anything happening to you."

"We can take care of ourselves," Cara said.

"I realize that now. While parents teach their kids, the kids teach us, too."

"Found it," said their dad, coming out with a steel sword and appraising it. "Do you think the same advice not to run with scissors applies to swords?"

"Sure," Li said. "Just turn it towards the ground and at least you won't take an eye out."

"Only your foot." Their father handed it to Cara with a steady hand. "Oh, and take some chicken to go."

Shebu meowed.

Li smiled. "Shebu says you can't bribe cats into liking you as you would a dog."

"It's not a bribe. I just like animals." Their father knelt and scratched Shebu on a fuzzy chin.

Purr.

"Shebu says bribes might not work," Li said. "But she doesn't mind them."

"You're so serious usually," Cara said to her father, surprised by his gentleness. "What happened?"

"Where do you think Li got his sense of humor?" He gave Li a hearty pat on the shoulder, then looked to Cara. "You'd better get going."

Shebu meowed.

"We could use your help, Shebu, but that makes sense." Li translated for the rest. "Shebu's going to stay here. She doesn't want to risk going back to Victor. And I don't think the chicken hurts, either."

Shebu rolled her eyes but didn't disagree. The leopard leapt up onto the couch and curled, feeling quite safe and at home. Meanwhile, Cara and Li prepared to leave.

"This isn't goodbye," Li said to their parents, standing at the doorway that led to Elysium's streets. "I'll come back for Shebu before I go back to the myths. I promised I'd help them find a new home."

"You have a home here," their mother said.

A wistful grin. "I know."

They didn't dwell, knowing it'd only make parting more painful. There were obligatory hugs and goodbyes, and as the twins left for the depths of Elysium, they tried not to look back as their parents watched them leave, knowing that despite the hopeful words, it might be the last time they saw each other.

As soon as they were out of eyesight, unfinished feelings remained, and the twins returned to the conversation before their parents had intervened.

"You're going with the myths?" Cara asked. "Where?"

"I don't know." There was pain in his eyes. "But they know what it's like to be ostracized."

"You hate me," Cara said. "I let you go to the myths alone. I abandoned you. I won't again."

"I don't hate you," Li said. "I could never hate you. But I forgive you. And I love you. We both did what we thought was right. I'm sure you didn't mean for any of this to happen." He could sense the darkness at the edge of his words, almost biting her, and he tried to soften them. "It had to go this way—I chose one thing and you chose the opposite. That's how people tell us apart."

"Besides looking nothing alike?"

"We're twins," Li said. "Nothing will change that. You weren't perfect, but you always treated me better than anyone else."

"I still didn't treat you right. I didn't understand you. I still don't, but I want to. The difference between us is less than I ever wanted to admit. I'll never forgive myself for what happened, but I have hope again. You give me hope that I can be better."

Not entirely accustomed to sentimentality, Li changed the subject. "How are we going to get to Victor?"

"I'm still on good terms with him," Cara said.

Li grinned. "Maybe it's a good thing you did what you did."

"That's quite the silver lining to a dark cloud."

"I wouldn't be too down, most of the myths escaped into the tunnels."

"Most," Cara said.

Li examined her as he often did. "Yeah. But there's a certain hero I ran into down there you'll be happy to see again."

"Rollo?"

"Not all myths are monsters."

"Some people are," Cara said, thinking of herself and Victor.

"Making a mistake doesn't make you a monster." He understood and comforted her with newfound empathy. "Come on, we don't want to be late for our final meeting with Victor."

TWENTY-SEVEN

ANSWER

WHEN A FENCE KEPT Kai and Sophia apart, at least a hand might reach through, but now, love grasped by look alone. Kai's promise separated them. Words made the distance seem larger, as sound traveled slower than sight.

Their gaze asked the question: what do we do?

The chasm between them was only one of the problems that opened before Kai. How were they supposed to get out of Irkalla? Having undertaken the journey once, and almost having died, he was not eager to repeat the experience.

"How, exactly, are we supposed to get out?" Kai asked, looking to the gods on the shadowed thrones.

Desolate shuffled in his seat, bones cracking as he stretched his hands out together. He waved away the concern, and had a rather sour look, as if such mundane questions rather spoiled the moment. "You take the stairs."

"Stairs?"

The god's smile returned, but this time, it was at Kai's expense, rather than for him. "A series of steps to ascend or descend vertically, usually, but not always, leading somewhere."

Kai ignored condescension. "There're steps between Irkalla and the pyramid above?"

"We didn't build this place with the intention of being trapped. The sandpit is a way to prevent stupid attempts at escape. Only gods use the stairs."

"But you'll let me use them?" Kai asked.

"During your little reunion, I received word from above that you were given the task to deliver Ahu-Ra's message. So, although you may not be a god, you're doing important business, some might even call it *godly* business." Desolate flourished a hand.

"Then why not let me take it on the way down?" Kai asked.

"That godly business did not include coming down here."

That answered any remaining questions Kai had. Well, it didn't. He just wanted to stop speaking to Desolate. The god was getting all too much satisfaction out of this predicament for Kai's liking.

"I'll take you to the stairwell," said the Maiden, standing from her throne and limping away. The dichotomy of her youthfulness and decay was obvious in every step. And despite that, the goddess managed a certain gracefulness; the limp was rhythmic, dance-like in its stride, played to her own music and tuned to emotion. When she walked by the brown and grey rose garden at the entry to the court, the flowers perked into a salute and pale pink restored itself into a few petals at her presence.

At such a sight, Desolate had his most heartfelt smile yet, not condescending, not joyful, but a sad, reminiscent smile. Without a goodbye, Kai and Sophia left the death god, who wasn't paying attention and quite seemed to have forgotten about the mortals.

As they walked, Kai instinctively went to grasp Sophia's hand.

"I'd be more careful than that," the Maiden said over her shoulder.

His hand retreated to his side. "Habit. I made a deal, I know."

"It's for your own good," said the Maiden. "The corruption is a wretched sickness."

Sophia wrapped her arms around herself. "At least it feels better with the Maiden around. And you, too, Kai. It's hard to remember feeling this way."

The goddess brightened. "You're too kind, dear. Today is a rather good day for me, it must be said. With a bit of love in the air, even the roses try to bloom."

"What do you mean?" Kai asked Sophia, wanting to comfort her, but was unable except with his words.

Sophia smiled. "With you, I feel warm. Like it's been cold night after cold night and finally I'm in range of a fire."

"Like you can't remember warmth?"

"I remember how it is to be warm, how happiness is supposed to feel, to be safe, to be loved, but I can't conjure the feeling. Anyone who's lost in the dark knows what light is, but it doesn't help them see."

The Maiden tapped at a bark wall, which unraveled and revealed a spiral wood staircase that hugged a cylindrical wall. "Ah young love, always so focused on firsts and fireworks. We're here, and now you have the rest of your short lives to reminisce on the past."

"She's right…" Kai said. "Sort of. We should focus on the time we have."

"I'd suggest you keep your promise and return to Elysium safely," said the Maiden. "Ahu-Ra stressed how vital it was that you make it back, and how otherwise, none of us will be leaving the corruption behind."

"Maybe you should show me more before we go," Kai said, gazing back at the obsidian underworld. "I only saw the court, not what Irkalla really is."

The wrinkles in Sophia's forehead grew firm. "No."

"You don't have to come with me," Kai said. "I understand why you wouldn't want to go back."

"No," Sophia said, imploring him with her eyes. "Don't go. Don't leave me. Just let Irkalla be. For once, your imagination isn't worse."

The Maiden smiled in her own special, dual-sided way, which was sweet and sour. "Consider yourself doubly lucky. You get your beloved back and she's almost in the same state you left her. How much time do you think you lost, dear? They must've had you in the upper reaches."

"Yes," she said, unwilling to elaborate.

The goddess nodded. "I'm sure you'd rather leave here as quick as possible. So would I."

"Then why not leave?" Kai asked.

The goddess snapped like a flytrap and the roots around crackled. "I can't. The corruption is different with us, like we're an extension of the tree. Unlike a mortal, I'm contagious to everything I touch." The green and pure-white eye burned, but it was not angry, it was sad. "Get out and don't look back."

When the roots closed the door behind Kai and Sophia, the patch was not as before. Bark was black and petrified, and the dead tree demonstrating the infection.

Kai led the way up the rotted stairway, which creaked and groaned under his step, but this sound was reassuring after the quiet of the underworld. Since her soft steps were merely echoes, Kai glanced behind him all the time, wanting to make sure that Sophia was still behind him.

Seeing her and no gods, Kai thought about breaking his vow; the further they went and the more time they spent apart, the more his tired limbs called for some reprieve that might come from a touch of encouragement. The thought bubbled as he barreled his way upstairs, threatening to pop.

"I'm glad to have you back." He said this as much for her sake as to convince himself. "This might not be perfect, but I'm just happy to see you again. You've missed so much. Don't worry, I didn't leave Elysium helpless—Cara and Li took my place as heroes. And Helene, she actually came to the pyramid with me. It was odd. But maybe she does care. We met such helpful people on the way, you'd like them—a doctor and a smuggler. You'll laugh, I even created a myth, a roostrich—"

"Kai." Sophia stopped, and they faced each other on the stairs. "Why did you come for me?"

"What? How couldn't I?" He looked at her, standing a couple steps apart, the shadows lurking behind her. "You didn't deserve this."

"No one deserves Irkalla, but no one comes to save them."

"Would you rather I left you down there? I thought I could do something about it—I did."

Wrinkles tugged at her lips. "You couldn't have known that."

"I didn't. But I believed. Hope brought me here, but now I don't need to hope anymore. I have all I ever want." He held out his hand. "I don't care about being soulmates for eternity. I don't care about reincarnation. I don't care about an *after* to the afterlife. An end is preferable to never feeling the brush of your hand on mine."

She didn't grasp for him.

Kai continued, "The tree didn't give me the corruption. Even the gods didn't know why. So maybe I won't get it. But either way, this is what I want."

"I thought you kept your promises?"

"I made a promise to be with you."

Their hands stayed apart, inches separating them.

She smiled. Never had a smile so broken Kai's heart as this one did. It wrecked hope, and before she said it, he cast happiness to the abyss below.

"No," Sophia said, the wrinkles tugging down her smile. "I don't want you to join me in this. The more we want to be our memories, the more we become like them—lost."

Where his head had given up, his heart controlled his obstinate hand, leaving it outstretched in desperation. "I'm never lost when I'm with you."

"Who you lost is not the same person you found." She took her hand away and wanting to do something with it, ran her fingers through tangled hair. "Before I went to Irkalla, the change was not so visible, but you're still clinging onto an image of someone who I was without seeing who is in front of you. I can't be perfect. I never was. And now, I'll never be the same. But you can still have a life after me." She looked at him with hope in her eyes. "Was it not enough to save me? Is it not enough to be happy with that for a moment?"

"I am happy."

His natural inclination was to say 'was', but he was past that. He didn't want more, but that beast within created a terrible tension, and unable to stand there any longer, he started up the stairs.

He was startled by what she said about change—he saw the wrinkles that aged her, but that physical change meant nothing; it did not frighten him like emotional difference. If both of their personalities had changed, had their loved changed, too?

That uncertainty was rejected with heavy, certain steps. And it did not go unnoticed.

"Don't be upset," she said after him.

He stopped and looked back. "I'm not upset. I'm scared. I'm disappointed. This isn't how I imagined." By her quivering lip, he realized the pain he caused. "It's not you. The world changes, we change, but nothing will change my feelings for you. The problem is just this deal with Desolate. And not just him, but the other gods that brought us to this point."

"Not all gods mean us harm."

"I know." Kai thought of Ahu-Ra, who seemed decent, or at least not all good or bad. "The gods are not as I imagined; they're more like mortals. And I suppose that means they have imperfect judgment. That should make me hate them less for saying Helene and I were soulmates while leaving you in Asphodel, but it also makes me think that they can understand and know better."

"Maybe they can't change their ways."

"I don't know how either," Kai sighed and continued up the stairs, and under his breath said, "But I change anyways. I try. I choose to."

On the way to the top, Kai did not look back down. His body was, by all accounts, moving as he had on the way to the underworld—with purpose and conviction. Despite his epiphany, ambition and desire rose within him again. Although he wanted a single moment to change him, life did not work like that; instead, change required work.

After achieving the mythical feat of venturing to the underworld, heroism did not seem so heroic; the next step came regardless. The story of brave and courageous actions remained, but as Sophia said she could not feel the warmth of her memories, Kai could not reconjure triumph. His journey was more in memory, more in story, than present reality. And now, all he felt was frustration and hardship returning.

Hoping the fresh air would clear the negative atmosphere surrounding him, Kai was relieved to find an end to the stairs and an old, wood door.

The door tried to cling shut, but Kai's impatience beat it open. Amber and hardened sap at the door-outline was no match for his will. When the door creaked and smacked against another wall, a familiar sight awaited.

Kai was back at the sandpit where he had slid down into the underworld. Leaving was far easier than getting there. Almost too easy. He watched Sophia come to the threshold, the moss of the stairs clashing with the candles outside, battling for the coloring of the world and creating a vague twilight.

She lingered at the crossing, hesitant to leave the tree's embrace and step back into the world.

Expecting the worst, Kai grimaced, thinking, as she must have done, that she might fade away back into the shadows, unable to cross the border between worlds. Both, in deep recesses, were worried for the unheard-of possibility of someone corrupted returning to the world. They prepared that the gods might be tricking them.

Kai absorbed every detail about her, trying to ingrain her into memory. Just in case.

She was smiling at him. That smile, that little flicker of the bowed lips, stuck in his memory as a feeling like pleasant sunlight through closed eyelids. Golden ichor flowed until it filled him—until he was complete. He loved. He felt loved. And yet, there was a sense that it might drain away and while happiness coursed in his veins, it constricted tightly, trying to hold onto the present, clenching for everything it was worth, and adrenaline pulsed pleasantly and terribly within. His heart did not pound with the flutter of excitable love; rather, it beat with contractions of fear.

With love, there was always the dread it might be lost.

Sophia stepped over the threshold and onto pyramid sandstone.

She did not disappear. She wasn't lost. The only change was her once radiant hair was duller, and coming out into the world, she looked older. Wrinkles deepened in shadows. The aging that had taken place below was evident, far more, in the upper world.

Seeing her this way cleared his other concerns for a moment. Instead, he felt empathy. As looking upon a melted glacier, there was pity for what was lost. So too, did he feel grateful for what was left, and he looked upon her with renewed tenderness and the care in his heart was increased.

They breathed easier and Kai turned to more pressing concerns—the gods that might lurk in the temple. "Let's get out of here."

Taking the way out, Kai and Sophia retraced their steps to the hole Shebu had made. And, in no time, they were back outside to the burning blue hour before night fell.

"We'll head to Duat and resupply," Kai said, gauging the little light left by the heat. He figured there wasn't much time, but he filed that thought away, hopeful that they might make it. "Helene and some friends should be waiting for us there."

"It's incredible," Sophia said, eyes widened and bright at the ripples of golden sand, cresting into shadows as night fell.

"You won't think that about sand for long," Kai said with a knowing grin.

"No," Sophia said. "The sunlight, the wind, the warmth. I've missed it."

After the dark, cold underworld, Kai was inclined to agree. And for a moment, he appreciated the scene, standing with Sophia.

The pyramid was proud and painted indigo by twilight. Desert stretched towards Duat and rolled towards Asphodel, but with the heat haze, it melted to the azure horizon, settling into cold night. Soft sand, deferential to wind and elements and feet, returned absorbed heat. However tough the journey ahead might be, the peaceful world was a comforting, familiar place.

But Kai knew they could not stay forever. "If we can't make it to Duat, we'll have to spend the night out here."

"That doesn't seem so bad," Sophia said, exuberant at freedom.

"It freezes at night." As if to demonstrate Kai's point, a cooling gust swept away the heat.

Sophia's joy dimmed like the light. "Lead the way."

Leaving only the upturned tracks of footsteps behind them, the pair distanced themselves from the pyramid, until it, too, was absorbed by the desert behind them. Kai headed on the flat path towards where he thought he remembered Al pointing to Duat; however, a shadowed horizon made it impossible to see the city's speck.

Focused on keeping a magnetically-directed path towards his memory, Kai kept quiet, focused entirely on straight steps, rather than an indistinguishable horizon.

Sophia picked up on the silence. "You're still upset."

"No," Kai said, his feet scraping and muscles aching, but hope dragging him along.

"You can't lie to me."

"My heavy feet are the ones lying. I'm not." A gust of sand gritted in Kai's teeth, crunching with a clench.

"I was just being honest with you before," Sophia said. "I was only trying to think what's best for you. That's all."

The light retreated faster than they could chase it down.

"We're not going to make it." Kai spit sand, but still, a bit lingered. "I'm tired. I've crossed the world to get to you, almost died, and I'm trying to concentrate on pulling myself along." He met her saddened eyes, speaking with sincerity. "I really am happy. I'd hate to take this journey alone. Let's go a little further and find a dune to camp for the night."

She nodded in the peculiar way that feigned agreement, but still half-shook her head in doubt. A forbidding wind swept through the desert.

His reunion with Sophia was so opposed to previous dreams that it seemed a nightmare. He had expected elation. Laughs and smiles. Perfection.

Reality, though, was harsher than the night wind.

As shadows deepened, it became ever harder to appreciate the moment. The world, too, looked towards the future, a foreboding midnight blue being the last light before darkness.

The night marked a pronounced change upon Kai. As he stared up at a starless sky, he found nothing. Except, maybe, recollections of the underworld, of darkness, of gods. Before, he could blame invisible gods that determined the pathway of his life. It was one thing to be angry at the invisible hand, it was quite another to be angry at something that could be felt and touched.

Kai wanted to blame Desolate because of the deal, but the god had let Sophia go free. Instead, Kai still blamed the whole affair on the root of it all—the council and gods of Elysium. Because of them, Sophia ended up with the corruption.

He had to act—catch up with Helene, deliver Ahu-Ra's letter, and make sure no one suffered a similar fate as Sophia. Already, he was tempted into wanting more. He'd walk on through the night to pursue what he knew was probably further, fleeting heroism.

Kai looked back at Sophia, and that defeated pride and ambition. As soon as he faced forward, he swung between whether he wanted to be a hero or be happy. If either were even a choice.

Desperately, he wanted to be content with success, with being here, with saving Sophia.

It was too dark to go on, and Kai relented, indicating that the flat sand around was the only shelter they'd get. "Let's get a few hours rest and hope we don't freeze."

It was Sophia's turn to simmer, and she simply nodded. Her thoughts were impenetrable to Kai.

They sat, legs splayed out in the sand, a foot of distance between them.

She broke the pensive silence. "I'm sorry about being grumpy. You don't know what it was like down there."

"I don't." Calm, Kai gazed at her, his only sight in the dark desert. "But I do know what it was like without you. The corruption doesn't scare me. For all we know, the gods are lying. Maybe there are no soulmates. Maybe there is no reincarnation. Maybe this is all we have."

"For your sake, I hope not." She shuddered at the sudden breeze. The desert night was unforgivingly chilly for being so unbearably hot in the daytime. "I may decay, but you can still be a hero. You could earn a place in legend, a place in the Isles of the Blessed—eternal happiness, immortality."

"No place would be happy without you."

"Why can't you just let me go?" Sophia asked.

"Because I made a promise. And I may break a promise to a god, but not to you. Never to you."

"Is that it?" She looked at him for a reaction, not angry, not cold, just curious, as if trying to understand him. "Or did you come because you felt guilty? Or because it was heroic?"

"Couldn't it have been all of the above?" Kai grasped at the sand, which drifted out of his fingers as he recoiled.

She shook her head and grinned. "You can overcome everything except yourself."

He stared up at the blackness, but in the infinite sky, it did not impress upon him the same impression the ice-fire shore had. In that moment, he felt his life had been changed. Why was it so hard to think that way now?

"I wanted to be a hero," Kai said, returning to her and finding her eyes had never left him. "But not anymore. I'm free to join you in the corruption. I don't care about being remembered, about doing good, any of that."

"You don't have to say that. I know that's who you are."

"People change. I'd do anything for you—fight myths, brave the underworld, and even forgive myself. I can't change my past—how I've failed family, betrayed friendship, and refused hard truths—and I could sacrifice everything to try and make it right, but what does that accomplish? Only more mistakes, more bad choices, more to atone for. Eventually, though, the only way to redeem myself would be to save the world. But heroes like that are myths." A grin at reminiscent idealism. "At some point, I have to accept I can't be a hero. I never will be. That's the bitter truth." It pained him to say. And there was a voice in him saying not to risk the corruption, not to give up on a future, a voice of instinctual survival and hope—but he refused it. He refuted it and choose with certainty never felt before. "I choose you. Over everything. Everyone."

"You can't. Self-sacrifice won't save me. You belong to a larger story than just you and me. Other people depend on you."

"All I care about is you."

"At least care about us." Wrinkles deepened with pain, but she took a calm breath and crossed her arms in the cold, lonely night. "I'm grateful that you found me. I really am." An ashamed downward glance. "But you're not thinking." She brought her knees into a self-embrace, feet smoothing two channels of sand. "We've been through so much. However spoiled a honeymoon it is, I'm worried that if you get the corruption now, you might regret it later. You'll resent me for it, and then, well. I don't want it to be like...." She paused with a sigh.

"Me and Helene?" he asked.

She nodded.

"We make mistakes. But we learn from them." Kai found himself resenting her already for not wanting him to join her in the corruption. And although the dichotomy of love and resentment fought, the wounds left were filled in by further, overwhelming love. "When I was younger, my mom loved telling me stories of gods and myths. She always loved gods and made them seem faultless like perfect glass. And when I looked at them like a mirror, my reflection was like sand— same material, but only imperfect dust. And the more I tried to mold myself in their image, the more I crumbled. I tried to be perfect, and I only saw flaws. Then, I found myself not empathizing with the gods, but with the myths and monsters. And as I got older, I knew my failures, but that didn't mean I shouldn't try and make up for them—like heroes, like the story of Hercules. The real one. In a fit of madness, he killed his wife and tried to make up for his guilt by the twelve labors. And in the end, he becomes a god."

"He never gets that wife back," Sophia said, drawing circles in the sand with a finger. "He marries again. Hera sends him into another fit of madness, he kills more people, and he tries to make up for it. There wasn't a happy ending. He burns himself on a pyre before the gods take pity on him."

"I'm not Hercules." Kai motioned, self-deprecating. "But I've been thinking even if I can't be a hero, I can be a different sort of hero—the story of Hero and Leander. When Leander drowns, Hero leaps off the cliff so they can be together forever."

"Hero is a woman." Sophia's eyes were bright blue in darkness. "There is no forever. I can feel the age in my bones. It's a creeping certainty in me, knowing that I don't have all that much time left. Maybe it's a month, a year, a few, but it's like a cup filling with acid, dissolving, cracking, and eventually, it gives."

"Any time with you is more than I ever thought I'd ever have. I made you a promise—I'll do anything to be with you, even if that means dying together. That's immortality."

"That is anything but immortality." She didn't meet his eyes. "Even if I'd prefer a different way, I have no power over your decision. I've said my bit—I don't want you to die with me."

"And that's why you're nothing like Helene," Kai said. "I love you."

A single shooting star broke the dark orb overhead. The light it cast illuminated the world faint, and hopeful eyes looked out.

Sophia lay back, watching, and her hair rested like snake-trails in the sand. "This is the best gift you've ever given me."

"This?"

"This night." Her eyes were enamored at the rested tranquility of the dunes under the cover of deep purple-laden sky. The star faded away and it was dark again. "I just wish there were more stars."

"I see another," he said, too quiet for her to hear, eyes never leaving her.

"I'm so used to seeing bark and cave overhead, that freedom is so much more than I remember."

"Both are ceilings, only we can't touch this one."

"We might not be able to touch it, but the beauty can still touch us," she said. "I thought you would understand. It's about reaching for something, not actually getting it. If we could reach the sky, it wouldn't be so wonderous anymore."

"It might be," Kai said, happier than he had been in a long time. "It's all about perspective."

"I can't wait to see the sunrise." She lay back, hair billowed out. She tucked in the hair closer to Kai, careful that it wouldn't touch him. "Whatever you choose, I'll love you all the same."

He was silent. Laying back, Kai closed his eyes.

His soul was conflicted—for so long he wanted heroism and happiness. In order to have one, he had to give up the other.

Fear pricked like the cold air with such a decision. His whole life was defined by a desire to be loved; that was what drove him to help people, to make up for guilt, to be a hero. Now, he only wanted to love. More than anything, he loved Sophia.

She was already asleep, turned sideways, a dreadful foot separating them.

She shivered, and Kai wished nothing more than to warm her. At that moment, he truly believed that it was the best thing he could do with his life. He did not want for more. He knew he never would. His decision was made.

One tentative finger touched the heated radiance of a bare arm. Nothing changed. He did not feel different—did not feel cursed. There was no sudden aging, no darkness. Instead, the world was warm.

He wrapped an arm around her, and she nuzzled into him, comforted by his embrace.

All was good. The world was righted. His dreams had come true, and for once, he felt complete. Fighting and qualms fell unto the cliffs of the sand around them, and what remained was a beaming light in the dark desert.

He felt finer than a fairy tale. For so long, he felt little like a hero, but with her, he felt so. Like he had already accomplished everything he ever wanted. And he had. The whole world was in his arms.

Peace.

He closed his eyes, eager for the comfortable sleep approaching his calm mind.

Before he let sleep take him, he wanted one more glimpse of the dream that slept in his reality. She rolled in her sleep, and Kai went with her.

He reached and reached and reached, further and further. She kept withdrawing. Kept going further from his grasp.

Eyes opened, and she slipped through his fingers like sand. And there, she remained. She had gone. A faint shadow of her in the desert.

Kai grasped into the course remnants, picking up cold, hollow fragments and letting them fall through, trying to hold onto that moment of happiness, onto the bits of love and life, but it only slipped through his fingers. Wanting nothing, wanting something, wanting everything—it all ended the same way—death.

And all he was left with was memory and darkness.

TWENTY-EIGHT

ANGUISH

ANGUISH. PAIN. HEARTACHE. Kai was left lonely in the desert, wishing emptiness would end. There was no hope, no future, no nothing. Life was a vast void…

…until a voice of faint starlight filled the dunes, fighting against consuming darkness with a godly voice. "Nothing lives forever. Nothing dies for good. Unless we let it."

365

TWENTY-NINE

TILL LIFE DO US PART

WHEN KAI WALKED THROUGH Asphodel's gates, he did not walk alone. The difference between what he set out for and how he returned was as enormous as the distance between him and the sky. Kai's overwhelmingly bleak night—an engulfing, smothering emptiness—was broken by a bright afternoon.

He'd only been saved because of who found him; a wise-looking figure strode at his side, and they entered the new combination of Asphodel and Elysium as the rains cleared, which had surprised both Kai and his companion on the way here.

"More rain's coming," Ahu-Ra said. "Never thought I'd appreciate clouds covering the sun so much. It seems Victor has the drought under control. That's a start."

"I don't care," Kai said, nowhere as bright. He looked older, forehead wrinkles constantly strained and thinking, focusing on the future and wanting to forget the past. "Let Victor be a god. I just want Sophia back."

Ahu-Ra nodded. After being in a crypt so long, the god grew enamored by the laughter and haggling of the city. Although the food market was not fragrant as Elysium's had been, it was nowhere as dour as when Kai left Asphodel. But Kai barely noticed the change, marching with singular focus.

Ahu-Ra motioned behind them. "After the last time I visited, they built that wall."

"It obviously didn't work well. You walked right in."

"They stacked some stones to make people feel safe. Walls are signs. They thought it would keep me out; yet, I never cared what those gods wanted people to think. Now, no one does." The god grinned. "Nothing lives forever."

"And nothing dies for good. Unless we let it." Kai's hope generated the only reaction—a glint in his eyes as if the sun had struck them. "That's why I'm here. But I still don't understand why you're helping me."

The god skirted the subject as usual. "Love is the closest mortals have to magic. For all the power and grand acts, heroes and gods change the world less than a little love." The god's face brightened like a playful summer afternoon. "Or maybe, I'm just a sucker for a love story."

"This isn't a love story." Kai tensed, withholding the caustic echo of sand slipping through his fingers. "It's a tragedy."

"All love stories are tragedies in the end." The god turned stoic. "Some just have happier endings than others." Wiping the seriousness away with a hand on his beard, Ahu-Ra continued, "Speaking of, I had a wonderful final feast. The other gods could not understand how this world has changed, but mortals can. I'm quite looking forward to change."

Kai grunted cynically and walked through Asphodel, passing crowds of chaotic, cheerful people, while newly spouted trees and potted plants decorated sidewalks.

"Where do you think we can find Shebu?" Kai asked.

"Aren't you the one who was in myth control?" Ahu-Ra was quite enamored by a little hydrangea plant in a ceramic pot, flowers blooming in northern-light purple and blue. He stopped and smelled the flowers. "It's been so long since I've seen something so lively."

"Shebu's not a myth."

"I forgot," Ahu-Ra said. "I can't get off subject with you, but wasn't it you that sent the cat away?"

"Shebu was supposed to find my sister, but cats make their own decisions."

They passed into the jade market. Two rows of well-constructed stalls lined the street with a forest of goods inside. But Kai looked ahead to the end of the block, where there was a small clearing and crowd. A ring of laughter and someone he recognized.

It was Grace.

She stood bent and trapped in a wooden pillory, hands and head sticking out from the wood boards that locked together. Her ruby lips were just visible in the shadow of her downcast head and hair, trying to ignore the jests and laughter about her.

"What a scary myth," someone joked.

Another sarcastic voice, "Terrifying."

"What's the matter, freak? Not feeling too bright?"

Ahu-Ra put a firm hand on Kai's shoulder, leaning on him. "Do you know her?"

"She saved me once," Kai said, shamed by how others were treating her. "I didn't know she was a myth."

"Do you want to do something?"

Kai was conflicted by pain and the piteous scene, but purpose spurred him along. "We are doing something." He avoided the scene, turned a corner, and tried to comfort himself. "I can't be everyone's hero, and we can't risk getting caught. But if this works like you say, I'll fix this, too."

"I hope so," Ahu-Ra said. "It's an awful thing to repay good-heartedness with apathy."

"It's not apathy," Kai said, feeling horrified at himself for not at least meeting Grace's eyes. For not saying something. "But I can only do so much. I can only feel so much. I have to focus on saving Sophia. If stopping Victor and becoming a god saves others, all the better. But that's not what I care about. I can't."

❖ ❖ ❖

Cara leaned against the stucco wall of the myth control headquarters. People passed by, pretending not to know who she was, but it was evident that they did.

Rollo's heroic figure attracted little attention, but he supported the twins with a comforting, true smile. "It seems I need to collect half of a loan."

"What did you loan us?" Cara asked.

"Two swords," Li said. "But Cara threw hers away after what happened."

A sword swung at Cara's waist as she shifted her weight. "We only have the one Li left behind in the move."

"One sword, three people." Rollo couldn't help a sarcastic tilt. "My math might be off, but that doesn't quite add up."

Li tried to match the tone, but worry tinged sarcasm. "If anything, you need three swords. There are three heroes in there."

"Heroes?" Rollo stretched. "No. It's finally time I dealt with real monsters—the dolphin, the fake-Hercules, and the balloon. It's like the start of a bad joke. One even I wouldn't tell. But maybe I won't need a sword. If I tell a bad joke, it'll distract the dolphin, Achilles. And I'm sure I can find a mirror to make Hercules remember the pain of past wounds. All I need is something sharp to pop the balloon, Ajax."

"That's why you want the sword?" Li asked. "Just a poke? What happened to nonviolence?"

"I'm not fighting for myself." The veins in Rollo's arms ran strong as he clenched fists. "But you're right, swords couldn't be as sharp as my words."

Cara offered Rollo the sword. "I don't want it."

"I know you're a big strong hero now, but Victor's more dangerous than a couple of ironically-nicknamed idiots."

With stern eyes, Li smiled at Cara. "This time, we may need it."

A frown. "I don't want to use it. Only if we have to."

Rollo gave them a hearty clap on their shoulders. "You two taught me well."

"I thought you were the teacher?" Cara asked.

"And I thought I was a hero," Rollo winked and turned towards the door.

With Shebu hiding at home, Cara and Li couldn't waste time. As they headed towards the Root, they heard Rollo knock on the oak door.

"He'll be alright," Cara placed her arm on Li's shoulder, comforting him as he cast a glance back. "They won't be expecting him, and he knows what he's doing."

"I know," Li said, not shrugging her off. "I wish we did. This worries me more than the ruins."

Together, the twins passed through what had been Elysium, intent on their final destination, but also impressed at how the city was recovering. There was sprouting grass and dew, an absence of dust, and gathering sprinkle-clouds in the sky. It was not the home they had fought for, but one that had lived before the drought. Still, neither was sure if the means had been worth the end; the ground had been fertilized by blood and loss.

The Root was imposing and dark while a cloud covered the sun. The temple's shadow extended as the sun escaped. Even with daylight, stone walls were an unchanged grey; however, colored stain-glass windows glinted like the patches of sunshine through clouds.

At their approach, Cara hesitated. Two soldiers, who had not been there the last time she had come, were guarding the doors. But with Li at her side, Cara felt whole and ready for anything.

"Will you look who it is?" said the guard, who was the wolf-like one who had guarded the divide between Asphodel and Elysium before. "The opposite twins. One lovely and one not."

Albus, the S-scarred soldier, stood on the other side of the door. "Careful. She's a hero, you know."

"That was a compliment," said the other guard.

The defensiveness in Li's eyes was apparent as anger, but Cara took the lead, hiding a scowl. "We'd like to see Victor."

"You can go in, Victor's up on the spire," the contemptuous soldier said. "But not him." He motioned to Li.

Li rankled and glanced at the sword at Cara's waist.

Cara motioned for Li to settle himself. He listened. Finding old fire, Cara drew closer to the guard, watching as his eyes widened with her approach. "And why can't he go in?"

A bit of nerves. "Because he's untrustworthy."

"And I am trustworthy?"

The soldier nodded, helmet jangling a bit with the motion. Cara was within a couple feet, her breath so close that the soldier could feel it. She could see the fear in his eyes, whether of her or her reputation, Cara could not tell.

Cara continued, "How about I make you a deal?" She laid a hand on the soldier's armored shoulder.

The soldier smiled, backing a step towards the wall.

She smiled back. "Such a lovely face. A shame it's in this helmet." Her hand went to the helmet, as if about take it off, fingers curling under steel. "Oh, that's only my reflection."

A sharp motion. The *crack* of the helmet on a stone wall.

The soldier crumpled to the ground, out cold. His helmet rolled across the ground.

Cara drew the sword and pointed it at the other soldier, a rush of adrenaline sparking speedy motion. She felt fearless, if not heroic. She understood the danger she had placed them in, taking this drastic step, but knowing the risks, she chose to act.

"Kai once saved you, right?" Cara asked the other soldier. She lowered the tip of the sword.

Albus nodded, the S-scar on his arm straightened in tension.

"Good," Cara said. "We're trying to protect him."

"You're doing this for Kai?" Albus asked.

She nodded.

Albus shrugged towards his unconscious compatriot. "I warned him." Still, he held onto the spear tightly, struggling with a decision of duty. "But I have orders not to let Li or Kai in." A small grin under the helmet. "But I figure, if Kai didn't save me, I wouldn't be here to fulfill those orders. So, I'll do just that and not be here. Someone needs to take this lump…" He used the non-pointed part of the spear to point at the lying soldier. "To get that lump on his head checked out."

Cara put her sword away, trusting Albus to be true to his word. She was not naive, her hand still ready, and although she didn't believe in perfection, she still believed people could be good. "Thanks."

Albus went to check on the other soldier, while Cara went to the smaller oak door and opened it to the contemplative air inside.

Cara motioned to Li. "After you."

"Remind me not to upset you anymore," he said, walking past and into the temple.

The hall was devoid of people. The Root was the same as it was the first time they met Victor—there were no seats—except for a simple throne, white fabric and obsidian sidings, at the end of the hall. The throne was illuminated by the stained-glass winds behind, glimmering with subtle color and framed by the gold-engraved door with the design of a tree behind it.

Their footsteps echoed on the marble, expanding in emptiness. Victor was not here, and before they looked to the side door that led up to the spire, they both were re-entranced by the beautiful door at the end of the hall.

"What do you figure is behind it?" Cara asked.

"Shebu said the way to the seed was here. Over there's where she escaped." He nodded towards the side of the temple, where a glass window was auspiciously missing and had been boarded up by a couple of hasty wood planks.

"Victor might've planned this since the beginning." Cara smiled at Li. "But he couldn't plan on you. You're unstable."

"Sarcasm?" Li returned the grin.

"What a pleasant change," Cara said. "You get when I'm joking."

The pleasant mood between them decayed as they approached the simple wood door to the stairs. A sword seethed out a scabbard.

"Don't tell me you were born ready," Cara said.

"I wasn't," Li said. "But I'm ready now."

❖ ❖ ❖

Kai found it ironic that the fence that once separated him and Sophia was lying in freshly grown grass. Dust faded into dirt and iron rusted. This was the park where this whole ordeal started. It held such wonderful memories of their meetings, and also the one terrible, catastrophic awfulness that shredded those.

He had made Sophia a promise to be together. In that damning instant he had touched her, they had been. Kai would not let that be the end. He would not break that promise. Fence or death, nothing would part them forever.

But sitting on a bench nearby, he found a different wife— Helene.

She peered up from the shadow of amber hair, their eyes meeting and hardening. Strangely, though, her eyes were bloodshot and sad.

Kai had never really seen her cry before. There had been anger and there had been the tears themselves, but her eyes were never truly sad.

"You're alive?" Helene asked, sniffling back the uncharacteristic emotion into her usual sternness. "Where's Sophia?"

That was the question Kai expected, but it was not said with the same undertone of acidity.

"What happens between man and wife is not my concern," Ahu-Ra said, walking the dirt path through velvet-short grass. "I'll wait in eavesdropping range."

Ahu-Ra greeted Helene with a recognizing nod, passing through the iron archway that grew with refreshed ivy and into Elysium.

"You brought a god instead of Sophia?" Helene asked, trying to recover some semblance of composure. The tears were gone, but redness remained.

"I lost Sophia," Kai said. "But not for good. Ahu-Ra is helping me get her back."

"You trust him?"

"I have to. He saved me in the desert…afterward. He only wants one thing in return."

"What's that?"

"Not your problem," Kai said. "But I'm willing to bear any burden to get Sophia back."

Helene tinged scarlet, but she withheld emotion.

Kai asked. "Why were you crying?"

She held the façade for only a moment longer. "There's something wrong with Victor."

"There's something wrong with all of us." Kai sat on the iron bench next to her.

She didn't move away. "I thought he was off when he just stared out from the spire, but now, he won't see anyone. Even me."

"Is the reason you don't love me because you love him?"

"Jealous?" She laughed. "You should know—my heart is only for one person."

"A cold heart covered in fool's gold." Kai nudged her, disturbed by her seriousness. "I'm glad I wasn't the only fool."

A glance towards the fence in the grass. "Victor isn't why I'm here."

"Stop." Kai distanced himself on the bench. "I know what you're going to say."

"Care to fill me in? Because I'd really like to know."

"You're sad because of me." A stiff grin. "You'll draw me in, hurt me, and run away."

She nodded. It was an odd agreement. "I could say that, but it isn't what you think."

"You helped Victor and he betrayed you?"

Helene shook her head. "Not yet, but I'm not sure it'll be worth it regardless." She looked at him, not accusatory, just curious at his reaction. "He wanted you gone."

Kai nodded. That was all. "Then why send Sophia to Irkalla instead of me?"

"I changed his mind." The sadness became bottled anger. "I just…." Helene paused.

"You sent Sophia to Irkalla?" Kai leapt up. "You want to hurt me so much that you'd hurt Sophia, too?"

"I didn't care," Helene said, cold, as biting as the beach near Irkalla—a hellish burning cold. "I just wanted to know."

"What!" Kai said with a fire opposite the ice. "What could you possibly want to know? And why couldn't you have just killed me instead?"

"Because." Helene absorbed heat, ballooning anger and shortening words. "I had to know whether you'd save her." Helene leapt up and pushed him back. "You went after her and not me!"

Kai stumbled back and froze, rooted. "You died. How was I supposed to come after you?"

"Die with me. That was easier than going to Irkalla."

He went quiet. "That night." A revolting, bitter taste filled his mouth. "You didn't have any intention of coming back, did you?"

"No," Helene said simply. "But things weren't supposed to end that way. After the argument, I left, hoping you'd follow. There was a nasty, cold rain to accompany my tears when I realized you hadn't. I was standing on the embankment near our house, wondering why. I considered what to do—go back and make you suffer, or go forward and make you suffer. The mud slipped into the river and made the decision for me. A slight encouragement. I could've fought, I could've swum, even if it was futile. But you know what I did instead? Nothing. I still hoped you followed. That you'd try and save me. Then, we could've died together. And as numbness became slumber, I realized I might not've had total power over you in life, but I might in death." A grin. "I hoped you would love me forever. I hoped you'd love me so much you'd realize your mistake and follow me anyway." The grin faded. "When we were reunited in the afterlife, I was disappointed—I was disappointed that it took as long as it did.

By then, I'd found Victor in much different circumstances than before, and I had no need for you anymore."

"I misunderstood you." Kai paused with sadness, recollecting in a similar, but not the same, way as losing Sophia. "I never thought you needed me."

"I don't know why, but I did. Maybe I felt better with you. And I thought I had you—I thought I had the power to make you do anything for me."

Kai sighed. "You could make me do almost anything, but in return, you couldn't love me. And that was the missing piece—being loved back."

"I loved you. Sometimes, I still do."

"It didn't feel that way."

"I loved you in my own way." Helene was weirdly bright for a terrible memory. "Being broken was neither of our faults. We're both who we are. But what I did to Sophia." She shuddered. "I've never felt so dreadful, so terrible, so horrid."

"You want me to forgive you?" Kai's sadness was too ultimate to be angry. Quietly, he simmered. "I can't forgive you. I could never. Maybe Sophia can. She was better than me—is better. But I need to find Shebu to get her back."

"Shebu escaped." Helene looked through the iron archway. "Cara and Li passed by earlier, headed towards Victor's temple."

Worry for his siblings set Kai into action, leaving the past behind and Helene with it.

"Kai?"

He paused under the archway, looking over his shoulder.

"We may have deserved each other, but Sophia didn't deserve this." Helene smiled at him, trying to be true, but it faltered. "Yet, I can't say that I hope you get her back."

Cara led the way onto the balcony, a sword in hand and Li at her side. Color streamed across the sky like the last time Cara and Li were here, but now, wisps painted across the gradient sunset like rainbows after life-giving clouds retreated. Although the waters went elsewhere, there was no doubt they would return.

Victor was hunched over the railing, an unlit lantern next to him as he watched branches of rain connect heaven and earth beyond the city. His hands clung to the iron banister, contemplative and conflicted, looking quite defeated for a so-called triumphant god. The iron seemed the only place dust had not been washed away. Whereas the rest of the city eliminated any reminder of the torturous plague of heat, a remnant of red lay uncleaned here, a couple initial divots and the rest glued down. A few streaks cleared dust into piles where Victor swept his finger, partially cleaning it away, but since no one else came here, it was only his marks that made any change.

"Have you come to get your revenge?" Victor's waterfall eyes met Cara. He was unshaken by seeing the sword tip. "I wouldn't blame you."

"We came to hear what you have to say for yourself." Cara lowered the point—not wanting to start with violence.

"I finally heard from the gods," Victor said, managing a sardonic laugh. "Late was worse than never. I was right, and oh-so-wrong. For the most part, my diagnosis was correct—to stop the drought, people needed someone to believe in." There was no exuberance or joy. "And although people believe I'm a god, I don't believe in myself. Even if I did, that wouldn't make me a god. It might make the idea of me one.

There are many things that are hard to live with, but I can live with that."

"All those myths and mortals died so you can be a god?" Cara asked.

"I wanted to save the world. I never intended that. Gods can't control people, how was I supposed to?" His shaky hands pulled open the glass panel to the iron lantern, leaving it ajar. "I didn't even get to see a god. From the Fields of Punishment to the heights of Elysium, not one. Helene saw them. She gave me their message. I wish she hadn't."

"Did it say you were a pretender?" Li asked.

"*It's not enough.*" He sighed. "That's all it said. All the lives lost. The stories. The mortals. The myths." Turning towards them, he looked shook. "That wasn't enough. I understand what needs to be done, and I can't even come up with an excuse for what I've done." He nodded. "I'm glad Li is alive. That's one condolence. Last time we were here, I asked you what you saw out there. That's the only question I have for you now."

Taken off guard, Cara considered Victor. Rather than the cheery, confident disposition of usual, he seemed off. There were bags under his eyes like he hadn't slept. There was a hollowness, retreating from the world like Li used to, but with a glassiness of frailty, too. Still, Cara worried it was a front.

"What does it matter?" she asked.

Li appraised the so-called god and softened. "I see the result of what we did in the dark. And I see new light coming."

Pained, Victor returned to his watch over the city. "This time, I agree with Cara—it doesn't matter. I should see colors and life and laughter in this city, all the things that made me love Asphodel in the first place. And it should be wonderful.

I achieved exactly what I set out to do." He leaned and laid his head on crossed arms as if waiting for a guillotine. "Kai and I wanted to be heroes. Our good intentions brought us together. When I withheld the truth, it was for a good reason. When I told the truth, I was for a good reason. Everything was for a good reason. But unlike him, I had no faith in the rulers and gods of this world and the last. For that, I was punished." He shivered. "In the Fields, I was assigned to care for animals, and my punishment was that the same hungry wolf would come for one under my care. The wolf never stayed to fight, and it seemed I was always a moment too late to help. But I always believed I could." He picked his head up, reached inside the lantern for an unlit match, and twiddled it in between his fingers. "Eventually, my herd killed the wolf." An ironic laugh. "From despair to destitution to deity, I believed in myself and those around me. I succeeded—but now that I'm a god, I'm only the god of doubt. Like the animals, I helped the people of this city solve their own problem and now they don't need me. In the process, some were helped, and some were hurt." He turned, looking toward Cara, remorseful. "I hurt you." The waterfall eyes were misty. "When I look out there, all I see is fires and floods and dead myths and dead people. I see the cost of what I've achieved. The means might've been worth the end. But I don't know if I can live with those means."

"You're lying," Cara said, letting the sword waver inches from Victor. "What a convenient story."

He did not flinch at the blade. "Believe what parts you want. I wish it was all a lie. I wish I could be that emotionless. For the most part, it's been genuine. The pain is." Victor took a deep breathe. "For better or worse, people change.

Sometimes, we go back to old ways. But other times, there's no way back."

"I don't think you're evil," Li said with a sympathetic smile. "There may be no way back, but there is always a way forward."

"That doesn't mean there's always a good way forward," Victor said, striking the match against the banister and producing bright flame.

Cara lowered the sword. She wasn't scared of Victor. She didn't love him. She felt sorry for him.

But if he was a monster, she knew what must be done. She glanced at Li, knowing the difference.

Instead of the sword, Cara tried as Rollo suggested and used words. "You can't just sit up here while the people down there believe in you, killing and burning in your name. It's not too late. I'm in no place to judge, but I believe you can be better. I know you can. We have to choose to move on, not dwell on our horrible choices."

"Is that what you need to tell yourself?" Victor held the flame, letting it burn to his fingers before lighting the lantern and illuminating the new night. He blew the match out, tossed remnants into the lantern, and closed the glass. Lit in the halo of light, he outstretched his arms, unthreatening. "Well, will you choose to be good?" A glance at Li. "To get redemption?" A glance at Cara. "And does that require doing something evil?" He smiled at what was Asphodel. "I lit the spark, but what will happen with the light? The last time we were here, I threw the waterskin, thinking that little bit would help. Would it be better, if this time, it was me who took that tumble?"

Victor vaulted back to sit on the railing, wavering between them and thin air. His hands did not hold on, relying on balance alone to keep himself on the thin iron and not the depths below.

"What are you doing?" Cara asked, wondering whether to offer a hand for balance.

"Giving you a choice," Victor said. "Isn't that why you're here? Why you brought a sword?"

"I came here to make sure Kai is safe." One of Cara's hands remained holding the sword while the other still wavered at her side, debating whether to push or pull Victor as he sat on the ledge. "I didn't come here for this."

"What are you willing to do to keep your family safe? Will it be enough?"

"Are you that cruel?" Li snarled. "What are you trying to prove?"

"I have nothing left to prove. It's almost over now." The newly minted god teetered on the railing. "Who wants to end this?"

❖ ❖ ❖

Night had fallen, and when Kai finally found Victor, it was too late.

As Kai had dug in the mines, he did the opposite now, laying dirt. The Root's spire, lit by a solemn lantern like a burning star, watched over him and the world. Victor found slumber near the fallen iron fence that had separated Kai and Sophia, along with Asphodel and Elysium.

Withered spindles of ivy wound around wretched wrought iron rods. Cracking through sun-bleached stems, the remaining dust rained like dew. Kai broke through thickets and found the first few leaves and blue buds, smelling of cool twilight.

Although they were not in bloom, Kai took a few hopeful petals and laid them on the recently disturbed dirt.

Victor finally met a god, and that was too late as well. With a vigil like candlelight, Ahu-Ra asked, "Anything else?"

Kai sat in familiar dirt and memories. "Go and find Shebu."

"I know that. But I feel like there's more you would want to say."

"It's too late," Kai said, standing and dusting himself off. "Sometimes you don't get forgiveness, and sometimes you never get a chance to."

"Meet you at the door?"

Kai looked up. "The spire."

Ahu-Ra nodded and they parted ways. Kai made his way through the temple, up the steps, opening the door to the spire balcony, and found relief with deep, joyous breaths.

"Cara? Li?"

They were standing by the railing together. Cara turned first, and upon seeing Kai, she cleared her eyes as if it was a dream. She ran over to him, and although she did not leap, she still hugged him. Somehow, Kai figured the hug was not quite joy.

When Cara released him, Li hugged Kai, too. Almost not recognizing his own brother, Kai was unsettled by Li's warmth and amiability.

"What happened?" Kai asked.

"Victor's dead," Li said, self-evident and non-elaborative. He glanced at Cara, then back at Kai. "I offered him a hand. He fell."

Kai assumed and nodded, his thoughts on Victor rather than his ending. Kai leaned on the banister, contemplating the city in darkness rather than drought. "Somehow, Victor saved this city where I couldn't. He was a hero—or somehow, a god. After everything, he was right."

"You don't mean that," Cara said, joining him. "He stopped the drought and helped our family back to Elysium, but he hurt so many more."

"He did what he had to." Kai grasped the iron railing, loathing and anger coursing through him. "All the pain he caused for me, I deserved. He wasn't the villain, but he still sent Sophia to Irkalla."

Cara hesitated, but asked anyway. "What happened?"

"I found her. And for one brief moment, we were happy." Kai shook his head. Stubborn, he remained single-minded. "But it's not the end. This world still needs a Victor." For a moment, Kai wanted to revert to who he had been in Elysium before, when he dreamed of being the hero, not fighting myths, but saving it from death and drought. But that desire descended into the depths of his loss, and there was no conflict, only one wish—Sophia. "Although Victor the person is gone, that doesn't mean the god is. With the seed, I can take his place. With the seed, I can bring Sophia back."

"It's good to have you back," Li said.

Kai turned as a leopard prowled out on the balcony like it had the first time Kai had met Shebu, fur waving like wheat, only budding shorter, since Shebu was still a tiny kitten.

The oceanic eyes reflected light in the dark. "Kai, you brought me back to dissolve the fence between Asphodel and Elysium, but I hope you understand that's not why I'm here."

"I know," Kai said.

"Shebu can open the door," Li added. "The drought is over, the myths have left, but us, well, we've got to figure out what's next."

"You can understand Shebu?" Kai asked, as if that was the important part.

"We did what you said and took responsibility for myths and the family." Li laid his arm around his twin. "Good and bad, we did what we thought was right."

Contemplative, Cara glanced towards the railing, where dust was unsettled, finger marks slipping away.

Ahu-Ra arrived deeply out of breath. "You could've waited."

"This is a god," Kai said, introducing Ahu-Ra to the twins.

"Doesn't seem very impressive," Li said.

"Good to see your siblings are alright," Ahu-Ra said. "Shall we open the door?"

"You say that like it's simple." Shebu growled and leapt onto Li's shoulder. "I was given the wisdom to make my own decision when the truce needs to end."

Ahu-Ra smiled. "And here I was, thinking the whole truce ended up as a sham."

Li pet the cat on his shoulder, "I know you might not trust this god, but we can't let the world wither away. I may not believe in heroes, but that doesn't mean we can't aspire to be one."

Shebu nuzzled against him.

Ahu-Ra chuckled. "You do know I made you?"

The leopard glared. "The gods made me and Kai remade me. But that doesn't mean anything. I'm the first defense against gods taking the seed for their own selfish purposes."

"Having you be the judge to prevent gods from taking power from the seed was a brilliant idea." Ahu-Ra grinned. "Remind me to pat myself on the back later. But I don't want power, I want to give it up."

The fur above Shebu's eyes furrowed. "You want things to change? A better world?"

"You can never tell how these things will turn out. As I thought, a mortal brought you back. Fate or not, Kai brought you back for one reason—it wasn't to save the world—it was because of love. That's the strongest belief there is."

"So you say," Shebu said, hopping off Li and onto the god. "Others would say different."

"Maybe. But they don't know mortals like I do." The god glowed like the dawn. "What do gods know of love? Love comes with the possibility of loss. With pain. With death. And yet, no matter what we achieve, it's never enough. Until the end, there's always more to do. So, what do you say? Truce?"

Shebu nodded. "The end of the truce."

"It may not be the first truce, but it might've been the longest," Ahu-Ra said. "I was stuck down there with the mice for ages. Can you imagine that nightmare? Well, maybe that's a good dream for you...."

Li joined his siblings at the railing. "I think Ahu-Ra and Shebu could talk longer than the truce. Unlike the gods, we don't have all the time in the world."

"Will you be alright without us?" Cara asked Kai. "We're going to help the myths. I failed them once, but I'm not scared anymore, I know we'll be better together." A grin raised her from the drought within, budding with new life.

"I'll be alright," Kai said, knowing he wasn't now, but he would be. Despite one agonizing parting, he was relieved to be reunited with his siblings, if only for a moment. This temporary homecoming filled him with love and affection, and caring eyes turned towards them. "You've made me so proud. It's time I did you proud. This world is bigger than me—but I have my part to play. Asphodel and Elysium still need a Victor. They need someone to believe in." An ache of heartbreak left the next words barely whispered. "And although life parted Sophia and I repeatedly, I will not let death do the same. I can do her proud."

Kai smiled into the night, waiting for the sunrise. Despite pain, he thought of the desert night and brief happiness. In the dark's reflection, he only saw Sophia's single-dimpled face smiling back at him. That was heaven, and in this night, he dreamt of that. There was no failure, no sadness, no death— just hope.

And as long as there was hope, there was life.

Darius Ebrahimi is inspired by a love of mythology, storytelling, and different cultures. A graduate of the University of Colorado at Boulder and University of Texas at Austin, with a BA in Economics and MS in Finance respectively, Darius has been writing full-time since 2018. After living in Hong Kong as a child, Darius rediscovered travel as an adult, visiting 20 countries in 20 months until settling in San Francisco with his cat, Ivy.

You can find him on Instagram @dariusebrahimi or on his website, dariusebrahimi.com

Coming in early 2023: *Detective Death*, Book One in The Branches of Yggdrasil, a mystery/fantasy book like Sherlock Holmes, except Watson is a many-millennia old death god.

Coming in late 2023 or in 2024: *Against All Gods*, Book Two of The Seed of Yggdrasil, continuing the story of Kai, Cara, and Li.